MAGNETIC
NORTH

Also by Sue Prideaux

Rude Mechanicals

MAGNETIC NORTH

Sue Prideaux

Little, Brown and Company

A *Little, Brown* Book

First published in Great Britain in 1998
by Little, Brown and Company

Copyright © Sue Prideaux 1998

The moral right of the author has been asserted.

*All characters in this publication are fictitious
and any resemblance to real persons, living or dead,
is purely coincidental.*

A CIP catalogue record for this book
is available from the British Library.

ISBN 0 316 64456 0

Typeset by Solidus (Bristol) Limited
Printed and bound in Great Britain by Creative Print and Design Wales

UK companies, institutions and other organisations wishing to make
bulk purchases of this or any other book published by Little, Brown
should contact their local bookshop or the special sales department
at the address below.
Tel 0171 911 8000. Fax 0171 911 8100

Little, Brown and Company (UK)
Brettenham House
Lancaster Place
London WC2E 7EN

To Laura and John

Remembering with love Kiss, Mossen, Sosse,
and the two Olgas
Deus miseratur

CHAPTER ONE

Katya was Russian. She and Gustav had met in the fashionable but respectable resort of Lake Garda in the spring of 1917, a couple of years later than Oscar's union with Charlotta. How it happened was like this.

War or no war, monied Europe continued to feel the need for winter sunshine. It had become used to spending the fag-end of winter indulging itself in a little irresponsible fun far from home. Sun, palm trees and plenty of ozone were invaluable for health. Doctors, peering deadpan over half-moon eye-glasses, solemnly wrote these things down in hieroglyphics on prescription pads, though only for the better-heeled, of course.

The South of France was obviously out, just for the moment, but the Italian lakes were perfectly safe; and where in the Italian lakes could be safer, more picturesque, warmer, more healthful than Garda? Exciting, too, this winter, buzzy. King Vittore Emmanuele III was even now summoning the Allied Commanders for a conference at Garda, from whose icing-sugar gambling casino these Grand Panjandrums would emerge between the nodding palms to issue a resounding proclamation that the Piave Line would be held. Held to the last man. Tremendous stuff!

This was the place both Gustav Oscarsson and Katya Olovanova migrated to in the February of 1917, two trembling swallows from the frozen North; she from the forests round Moscow, he from a narrow squeak in Oslo. He'd started his journey by sea. Appropriate enough: all Oscarssons sailed the sea, whether to found Dublin, attack Muslim-held Seville, plunder their way down the mighty Russian rivers to Novgorod and Kiev, to take up posts in the Imperial guard at the Byzantine court about the time William was conquering England, or to find Vinland, which might or might not be America. If Oscarsson blood ran sea-blue beneath the skin it was because their veins were capillaries of the sea. Some of Gustav's ancestors had vanquished it. Some had sunk in it and come up again. Yet others had drowned in it and probably (being tough) become pickled with salt, preserved like herring in a barrel, and were spending the subsequent centuries swooping and swerving within the eddying swirls of the deep tides to this day. It gave him no misery, this thought. In fact, he decidedly enjoyed the idea of his kin adding to the rich soup of the sea. It warmed and expanded the feeling of continuity and fellowship. If, one day, he should take a ducking himself and add to the number of stubborn pickled old buggers wafting about in the deeper currents, well, that'd be fine. They'd have a party.

Katya Olovanova had obviously not come by sea. She came from Holy Russia, and such a journey would have been mad, but maybe not much madder than the odyssey by train, an epic in the travel-horror genre, a tale of maggots spiralling from the green meat on the plate, floors of corridors smeared with the overflowings of chamberpots on their way to be emptied in the hands of unsteady babushkas, a case of tuberculosis left unburied for three days, various ladies impregnated by rape or consent, and an engine breakdown in Arctic conditions. The peasant driver taking off his hat, crossing himself and waving his icon in front of the engine while waiting, in hopeful inactivity, several days at minus fifty for God to mend it. For 'He will come. He cannot be everywhere straight away. Too many railway engines have been made for that. But He will come.'

Katya was being sent south for her weak chest. More to the point, she was going through a tiresome *exigeante* stage. The Bolsheviks and the Mensheviks and the utter formless panic of Russia on the brink of revolution was bad enough for her parents to endure without being driven mad every minute of every day by the irrational demands of a hormonally chaotic, beautiful eighteen-year-old.

A stark flat-chested aunt was found to accompany the girl, a financial arrangement was made. The Tëtka, a useless, inquisitive woman with a pinkish-grey hearing-aid, was delighted at the opportunity to avoid her usual dose of winter bronchitis, as well as having her living expenses – such handsome expenses! – paid. A tiresome woman she might be, but Katya's parents recognised the Tëtka's unparalleled qualifications for the job. The deaf old woman's heart beat for two reasons and two reasons alone: notably a strong, almost monomaniacal sense of the family's position, and an unswerving sense of duty to maintain and even elevate that position still further, if further elevation were possible, which the Tëtka gravely doubted.

During the intolerable train journey, the Tëtka proved herself equal to the heroic task of keeping Katya under control. Exceeding her duties, she kept the girl happy, yes, happy, extraordinary word in the circumstances, by means of the contents of a small brown glass bottle. Two drops taken in a glass of water and Katya would droop as beautifully and as languorously as a full-blown poppy too heavy for its fragile stalk. Her young cheeks would blotch scarlet-crimson, the pupils of her great purple-brown grape-bloomed eyes would dilate, unfathomable black dream-pools, and she would sit idle and content for hours on end, watching the ice-light dance on the sparkle inside her lashes.

Katya's parents were people of the world. They foresaw most things, made provisions. Resort hotel life would obviously be bursting with potential entanglements. They knew all about attractive tango dancers with razored cheekbones, swimming instructors with beautiful muscles, parvenu princelings from newly hatched Montenegro, faded south European aristocracy sniffing for money, shoddy spies of irresistible gloom and mystery. The Tëtka's constant watchfulness over the family's priceless reputation could be relied upon to see Katya safely through this sexual and social minefield.

The only thing Katya's parents had not foreseen was their own fate, and that was entirely beyond their control, although they actively believed this was not so. Like most Russian aristocrats at the time they followed the Imperial family's fine example. They kept a tame clairvoyant on the books, along with a palmist. Every Tuesday a fashionable phrenologist dropped in to check on the progress of their cranial bumps.

Passing *tzigoyner* in picturesque dress at the back door gave electrifying readings from the disconcerting Tarot. Nothing was left to chance. In their spare time the womenfolk dabbled in amateur séances, the men taking on the more robust business of the table turning with its ra-ta-ta machine-gun delivery. Strangely, none of these specialists in the occult succeeded in foretelling the disastrous fate waiting to befall the Olovanova household who, along with the rest of the scrying aristocracy, might have done better to have ignored these mystic spheres and kept their eyes fixed firmly on the very real revolution brewing in the undoubtedly corporeal.

As for Gustav Oscarsson, chance was the one thing that couldn't be blamed for his presence in Riva del Garda. Nor did he even pretend to weak health. Like his brother Oscar, he enjoyed a permanent state of vigour; sound in wind, liver and limb. Various things had brought Gustav Oscarsson here. The need for a little fun, a breathing space while the episode of the lady magician blew over, and a fancy for one of the new Alfa motor-cars. There happened to be a convenient Oscarsson ship leaving Oslo for a refit in Livorno. He hopped on board. Once he'd picked up the new automobile it seemed a shame to ship it home without giving it a proper run out first. Back in Oslo the shipping business was pretty much behaving, elder brother Oscar could cope for a few weeks on his own. Besides, Gustav suddenly discovered in himself an urgent longing for a half-way decent casino. The sweet-tuned Alfa turned its nose to the north from Livorno. When he'd been going a goodish stretch, where should he end up but Riva del Garda? Well, well, of all the happy coincidences; quite his favourite place to spend the winter Season.

He'd take a few days – no more – to sit under the lemon trees with a plate of spaghetti at his elbow or a cup of that excellent Italian coffee that went so well with a nice little Havana, savouring the sunshine and mentally grading, out of ten, the lakeside parade. Pearl after pearl, well-bred girl followed well-bred girl. Oh, the loveliness of the girls whose poor, weak, tender chests compelled them to fly south for the winter; a migration of beauty. How agreeable it was to spend warm days in a permanent state of mild erotic arousal, comparing the curves of all those lovely chests. Ailing they might be, but there seemed to be no need to wrap them up unduly. At home in Norway the girls would be swaddled, each one an indecipherable human parcel, an Eskimo horde of bulky shapelessness in thick floor-length furs. Of flesh one saw only a pink nose on top, and at the bottom the thickest, least seductive snow-proof boots. Hardly the stuff of dreams. Here, in sun-drenched Garda, however ailing the chest might be, its outline was always discernible through lightly draped silk, or lace, or velvet. Oh, what chests! Flowing faultlessly into the sublime curve of a waist, the bell of a skirt, the turn of an ankle, the timbre of a laugh.

The few days saturated with a warmth that could be depended on somehow became weeks of soaking up the sunny pleasure of the string of girl-pearls: Lotusland. Time had ceased to be discernible. *Dolce* it was to *far niente*, except in the evening to conduct one's duties at the tables, a little *chemin de fer*, a little roulette ... *dolcissimo* indeed.

Gustav had awarded Katya the title of that year's Most Lustrous Pearl. An acquaintance was not difficult to effect. The two of them spent a few weeks dancing the prim, limited, ritual steps of the holiday-flirt acceptable at that time between good children of good families pan-Europe. Things might have ended there. Nobody would have been too heartbroken. Each would have taken home a warm clutch of fluttering memories, nestling in the sentimental chamber of the heart for life. But it so happened, one fine morning, that Katya's family met that fate that nobody, not even the paid fortune-tellers, had foreseen. They were taken to a forest by the Bolsheviks and butchered, every one of them. A thorough job was done. Not a soul was left.

Katya was now in a strange land entirely without protection. Gustav might have set her up in a dress shop. Instead, he married her. It spoke volumes for her fascinating ways and for his warm impassioned spirit that he did.

Rumour reached Norway via the telegraph of Oscarsson Shipping a/s, now being run by Oscar while young Gustav was in Garda. There was no rivalry between the two. They were happy to work in harness together or turn and turn about. Each was capable, each appreciated the other. Neither felt the need to work himself to death to prove a point of sibling rivalry.

Physically the two brothers were as alike as two blades of grass. The Oscarsson male was a great red-blond blaze of a man with a dangerous temper, a broad-chested lion propelled by bottomless energy whose seat and engine seemed to be in his bull-like shoulders. They barged their way through the world when necessary but they preferred to act like golden, shining corn, and when on form were as hard as the swaying crop to follow with the eye as they danced bewilderingly, dazzlingly in the sun, bending or stiffening according to the world's winds, and always turning more and more golden as their fortunes ripened and prospered. The co-running of the shipping line worked for the simple reason that Oscar, the elder brother, was dyslexic, a condition then quite unknown. It would get neither name nor recognition until much later in the century. During their growing up together the natural dominance of elder brother Oscar had been balanced and mitigated by his lack. Young Gustav had acted as his brother's scribe; and proud he had been too, to act as reading eyes and writing hand. The arrangement undertaken in an entirely matter-of-convenience spirit had never a shadow of crowing or mocking about it. It lasted until the day Oscar was sent to school.

At the dawn of the century it was deemed to matter that the heir-presumptive had some exams to his name. 'I was never clever at my lessons, you see. I don't know what it is with me and books but when I see them the lines dance and fly about like seagulls in a high wind and even the little letters bob about one by one, turning round and moving places when they're in the corner of my eye. They even turn somersaults,' he explained, in reply to Charlotta before they were married. At the start of this conversation she had looked down at his mutilated right-hand writing finger and asked how it had happened, anticipating some seafaring tale, not too terrible, a rope, a hawser; such things happened.

'I cut it off,' he had said in reply, 'with an axe.'

Her eyes had widened like a horse's. He'd thought she'd run.

She had been frightened but he had calmed her. She was laughing now at the comical picture he painted with his words and his fingers jumping about in the air, trilling and somersaulting absurdly as the letters. 'And when I write them they do the same. Hop about the place higgledy-piggledy, though it's a great puzzle to me for they are quite organised when they leave my mind. It's a terrible business,' he said gravely. 'Not to be laughed at. And mathematics. Oh, mathematics, it's worst of all. Those numbers. Treacherous friends! How well they organise themselves in my head, how on the page they dance and jiggle!' His fingers jumped; absurd, frenetic, lunatic.

'So!' She raised a challenging chin. 'You are teasing me. What has this possibly to do with the cutting off of your finger?'

'Not teasing; no, indeed. What I am telling you about was a serious business. Very. Every day I went to school and every day my teacher beat me for being stupid. And every evening when I came home my father beat me, also, for being stupid at my lessons. This took place every day. But however hard they beat me it never got to make the letters stay in place. Maybe they should have beaten my head, that was where the trouble was, not in my arse. My arse, if I could see it, must have been as striped and as pretty as the sandbars at the bottom of the sea. This went on. Then one day when I was fourteen I knew I had had enough of being beaten. That day I went straight from school to the woodshed and there I took the axe, the small one for kindling, and with my left hand I cut off the top of my writing finger. "Now," I said, going down to the house and holding the remains of the writing finger beneath my father's nose, "I have had enough. My teacher beats me every day because I cannot properly make my letters. You, Father, beat me also. Enough of this beating. We are wasting our time. I have made sure that I can no longer write. To write is not important anyway. You know that all I have ever wanted was to go to sea." And with that I went to sea, as I had been determined to do from an early age. I worked my way up in the ranks. My skipper's certificate was won in record time, which was just as well, my father dying so early, before his time. So now I run the business with my brother. As for letter-writing, I have a clerk with a pen that moves like silver mackerel over the paper. The words and the numbers fly straight from my mind on to the page in a miraculous fashion without getting into a tangle. I do them in my head as I have always done, and in my head they behave, as they have always done, and my miraculous clerk, Herr Fulman, makes them behave on paper too, and all is well in the world. Fulman has the longest, ugliest neck in the world, with pimples on it, and a very small but clever head on the top of it. He might be useful to you also when we are married. One never knows when one may need a clerk.'

This was the first Charlotta had heard of any marriage plans. She put her chin up. 'I am very good at writing,' she was saying, 'and I can manage the figures I need. Though,' she considered, 'I do not yet need many.' And she flounced away from the graceless suggestion down towards Oscar's beloved sea, treading the uneven rocks in the same snappy, confident way that a town girl would attack a pavement. He liked that in her.

It was the clerk Fulman, the sobersides of the long neck, now promoted to *sekretær*, who brought Oscar the telegraph from Riva del Garda, clearing his throat as he always did at his employer's elbow and standing patient as a lighthouse until *skipsreder* Oscarsson should finish whatever work absorbed him and signal by the slightest nod and smallest noise in the back of the throat that it was time. Then *sekretær* Fulman would start to read aloud the incoming news, once. He never found the need to repeat even the most complicated documents or contracts, be they ever so full of figures.

'Thank you,' Oscar said, at the end of his brother's telegraph from Riva, exactly as he always did. He waited for a beat of three and then, cocking an eye at Fulman's correctly retreating figure, 'Calls for a dram, I think.'

Fulman stood, awkward in the extreme as the straw-coloured aquavit glugged out of its narrow-waisted decanter, and downed the first drink he had taken in his employer's office with a quick automatic jerk of the elbow as though it were prussic acid.

Oscar sat down at his desk again and forgot all about the domestic issue for the next few hours. Work to be done: ticklish work. The critical question throughout this *fordømmet* expensive war had been this: how might Oscarsson Shipping a/s maintain its lifeblood, the ships that shuttled the seas, when those seas all around swarmed with armed submarines, numerous as cod?

Not only a question for Oscarsson, it was also the question

for the nation. So acute did the national situation become that, in the autumn just gone, Germany was seriously considering declaring war on Norway. It was not until just before Christmas that Foreign Minister Ihlen displayed a degree of subtle diplomatic skill unusual in this whack-first-talk-later race, ensuring that his country weathered this critical moment concerning Norway's export trade and submarine warfare. In commercial terms the Oscarsson brothers had a duty to profit, come war or peace. Boxing clever, profit they did. Oscarsson a/s had plenty of ships now, more than ever. Scaredycats were selling them for nothing because of the submarines. Oscar bought, and he had money to buy. Inflation raged because of the shortage of commodities and the abundance of money available to buy those commodities. Shortly after the outbreak of war Norway had left the gold standard. During the years that followed, the quantity of money was many-doubled. Wages kept slow pace with the rise in prices and wage earners (seamen, for instance) were badly off. With the shortage of commodities came an abundance of money. What all this meant was that the Oscarssons bought cheap ships and manned them with cheap crews to move expensive cargoes about the world. Norwegian ships were hired by the Allied Powers. But the Germans needed tonnage too. Oscarsson Shipping a/s managed to oblige, juggling ships through friend and foe and getting paid by both.

Yes, Oscar had enough to occupy him this afternoon before going up to the house to tell Charlotta the news.

By the time he was locking the office door behind him the cargo of asbestos unloaded this afternoon was stacked in bales. A stiff storm was brewing, its prelude gusts picking up the crystalline fibres and blowing them in vortexes here and there like shiny ghosts.

Oscar Oscarsson in Oslo harbour was like a gun-dog on the scent. The gorges and cliffs and pinnacles, the fabulous toothed indentations snarling dangerously against a storm-dark sky, caused his breath to crisp and his blood to infuse in an excess of vitality. Gundogs pointed ears and tails, lions bared teeth, Oscarsson's cheeks incarnadined. In his nostrils the heavy salt air, warm as blood, smelled of opportunity, deals, good hustling fun. The smell of the place! The racket. The area screamed day and night with the *screak* of capstans, the squabbling hysteria of gulls, the *crak* of ropes as the trackers, helped by sails, struggled along the rocky banks hauling in boats from the deeper stretches. The noise level in the horseshoe harbour was constant and high, an orchestral cocktail necessary as air to both Oscarsson brothers; they only felt alive when their ears were half deafened by the snapping of flags, the slapping of waves, the crunching trundle of cranes and the chants and shanties of the boatmen ringing about the raucous harbour. Everywhere people dashed back and forth, busy as ants in the continuous frenzy that follows when their nest has been disturbed. The buzz of activity was not always immediately comprehensible even to *habitués* such as Oscar, so much was going on, but however apparently random and disorganised, it was, in fact, always organised, never purposeless.

At the dock's limit the large sentry in the little hutch leaned over and spat out his quid of chewing tobacco, which flew in a brownish-yellow arc, as a mark of respect, before raising the barrier to allow *skipsreder* Oscarsson through. Oscar tucked the interesting telegraph into the pocket of his waistcoat. Charlotta would certainly want to read the words for herself in black and white. Listening to him recite, even verbatim, never held the same authority for her. He didn't mind. Didn't understand her paper-need, but didn't grudge it either.

His journey home was a changeable thing. Just now Oslo was hanging in the scales, beginning to stick its neck out of the macabre medieval midden and by a not unnatural metastasis bloom into its own version of a twentieth-century city. Glimpses of the future shape could be caught through isolated examples such as the two houses being put up in competition by the brothers: two brilliant beacons bravely beaming clean, organised, neo-Parisian lines through a shaggy tangle of peasant-muddled present. The two brothers' cream rococo dreams were to spread over the next decades, transforming the bowl surrounding the natural deepwater anchorage beneath the jaggedly fir-clad snow peaks into an enchanted arcadian haze of Northern classicism dressed in cream. Oscarssons' dreams would triumph but, meanwhile, their twin architectural venture flashed and dazzled, intrusive and attention-getting as a glittering comet-tail against an old familiar sky and, like any comet, the two new-built Oscarsson houses shocked. The old guard were offended. They saw nothing but vulgar extravagance, ostentation and shameful humiliation in such modernist fashions.

Not only Oslo's built context was in flux but the great inland routes to north and south were also held in equipoise between smooth grey asphalt and running sewer. The dead-straight treacle-ribbon tarmac road Oscar trod home would take sudden illogical swerves round huge outcrops of grey granite. Wild cream-coloured *nordfjording* ponies with long ash-blond manes roamed wherever they wanted. Chickens marauded the road's insect-harbouring gravel chips as well as its grass verges. Ownerless goats clattered about, causing each brother to sit up at night with a shotgun in the interests of establishing some sort of civilised garden. The new custom of fencing off properties had not yet bitten; boundaries were fluid things providing, on the whole, an object lesson in good manners.

Oscar hadn't progressed a hundred metres down the road before he came to a human clot, a knot gathered round a sailor with a silver earring being accused of theft in shrill tones by Bess, a well-known ancient, wrinkled but popular local tart. Liquor had given the sailor unnatural strength. It took two of his more than able-bodied colleagues to wrestle him to the ground and sit upon his chest while an old man in leather gaskins with a dim face and a white beard was handed a rope that he doubled and passed, with senile deliberation, round the malefactor's ankles before drawing the ends through a loop. Holding the ends over his shoulder, the old man pulled as though hauling a boat. The prostitute's smart curly dog ran out from the gathering crowd and stood barking and snapping at the prostrate body in the dusty road. The man's smell was, no doubt, familiar to the over-excited creature. Bess sauntered out, swatted the dog with an unhurried swipe and stood still as a monument, squirming dog firmly pinned beneath one of the heavy ankle-boots she was never seen without. It was well known locally that Bess kept them on throughout business too, for it hardly seemed worthwhile to take them off, it being such a trouble to bend down and lace them when the whole operation set the black tadpoles in the air swimming abou before her eyes. Much of Bess's preliminary business, her overture so to speak, taking place on the streets, the eventual transaction was often accomplished in a rich reek of cowpat and fresh horse manure and the odd goat pellet sticking to her soles.

Under a crimson frizzed fringe her faded pale blue eyes, made vague by potato alcohol, leaked eye-black that ran like soot down the crêpey cracks in the powdery rouged façade of her face. Impartial as Nemesis, she stood stock still, scrutinising the scene unfolding. One of the sailors pulled the prone man's trousers down and his shirt up, baring brawny buttocks, and pockmarked shoulders, tattooed and hairy. *Thwack, thwack.* Ropes wielded by sinew-knotted arms whistled in the air before falling with a sharp crack quickly one after the other. Street justice. 'En ... to ...' Dead white welts rose on the dirty flesh. The small crowd gawped in a ring around the poor stupid drunken bugger, whose moans droned along like a dreary bagpipe *continuo* beneath the sharp, brisk rhythms of the continuing business of the road: the *clip-clop* of passing horses, the metallic *snip-snap* of harbour flags.

'... *ni*' went the numbers, '... *ti.*'

Only ten strokes. They were feeling generous, then, today.

The sailor was now released to crawl into a corner where a friend poured white of egg on the wounds. No blood had been drawn, which struck Oscar as a curiosity. He must ask Doktor Lund, next time they coincided at the Klub.

'Here.' Tipping his hat, Oscar handed ten kroner to the burly Bess, at which she lunged tipsily towards him, proposing carnal engagement.

'Enough, old friend.' He fended off her fetid slobber good-humouredly. 'Haven't you heard? I'm a married man, a father, even.'

Oscar moved away, Bess following behind him, keeping up an indiscreet litany listing all those in Oslo who found neither marriage nor fatherhood a barrier to a little extra pleasure.

'Enough, enough!' Oscar flung over his shoulder. The old tart had gone on too long, the joke was over. Bending over the prone sailor and holding his breath over the stink of sweat and misery, he tucked exactly the same sum into the moaning man's hand. Then *skipsreder* Oscar Oscarsson continued up the street, whistling cheerfully, for he was on his way to his little wife.

Bounding vigorously up the stairs of his half-built home, that is to say as vigorously as he could, given that the stairs up to the front door were still unfinished and acting as a dry-floored store for the builders' apparatus and *matériel*, Oscar called out loudly, 'News! You'll never guess.'

But there was no reply. Charlotta was not in the house.

There were times when it all became too much for her, when Oscar's break-neck housebuilding programme made the whole place like a whirling kaleidoscope. At such times the only thing to bring her back from the giddy brink was to go outside.

All their marriage Oscar had been building and furnishing. The house was full of so many objects it was astounding. Not only objects of convenience, such as gas lighting and a water closet whereby a handle was turned and the porcelain pool below bore all away before it to God knew where, but also an asparagus bed, an English governess, though the child was not yet three and lisped so prettily in his own tongue. Surely one language was enough? But 'English is the language of business,' Oscar said, 'and if Oscarsson Shipping is to go on to the next generation it can never be too early to get the boy's ear accustomed,' so that was that, although it did seem a shame to introduce these strange, flat, rasping sounds so very early into the darling boy's little ears. There was a grand piano of glassy finish standing ever open like a book imploring to be read, and a staircase of astonishing marmoreal grandeur to which the builders even now were affixing a snakelike banister of some modern metal she didn't recognise.

One would not think a house could take so many new ideas. It grew and grew. Puffs of white cement flew up everywhere. In different places every week workers looked up, wishing her good day, their eyebrows and lashes white with plaster dust. Charlotta in her turn would wish the dusty men a grave 'God dag' wherever she came upon them, for she was polite however extreme the circumstances. The workmen liked to see the young wife as she passed through the house this way and that. Her discreetly corseted figure conveyed a sense of dignity and purpose, as well as dignifying the purpose of their own toil. Charlotta Oscarsson was one of those women whose presence automatically makes people behave better: curb their language, adjust their clothing, take their feet off the table; believe again that somewhere vaguely above their own lives floats a higher order that may be lived up to. Her grey eyes had a slight slant, her light brown hair was massed in the same neat pile by eight every morning; and by eleven o'clock the same naughty strands had escaped to curl disobediently about her pretty ears from which bobbed a pair of good family pearls. Her step was light, her carriage graceful. She was inclined to shyness and to a state of wonderment about the world. So much that was new, so much she did not understand! The workmen had no way of realising that the pretty shyness was, in fact, the smallest visible tip of a massive glassy ice-chasm of fright and isolation that would quite unexpectedly open up before her. The unpredictable panic-stricken stomach swoop would be triggered by the oddest, stupidest, tiny domestic details. To be frightened to death by a new brass coathook being fitted, and a pretty one at that? It was just stupid. Nevertheless it happened, however cross she got with herself. What Charlotta didn't realise was this. All this change, all this flux, all this swirling about of the house disturbed her not only because it meant the limitlessness of possibilities was as infinite as the stars, and included for the first time the possibility of chaos, but also it brought with it the realisation that she was afloat on a sea of time. Time behaved quite differently when things about you were on the constant change. You were ceaselessly conscious of it.

Time did not behave like this at home at the Krigskjold Manor Farm where she had spent all her life till now. You were not conscious of it, because you were not conscious of change. Oh, yes, there was the yearly cycle of duty and routine, the repetition of the seasons and tasks, but change, real change simply did not happen, in big things or small. The place existed, constant and predictable, stable as flocks and herds, a place hermetically sealed against time and fashion as a ship in a bottle. Her childhood home was one of a solid historical type that had existed in Norway since the year eight hundred, practically immutable. There was no need for variety. Manor farms with broad walls enclosing a small community of families who worked in common suited the land of steep-sided defensible valleys with fertile fields. In spring the flocks were driven to high pasture and in autumn they were driven back again.

These days, one needed no armed outriders. That was the only material difference. One didn't expect to be raped and pillaged as a matter of course. Such things happened, of course, but they happened a lot less often, these days, and that was the only significant change over a thousand years (drains and electricity still being a thing of the future in places so far-flung from Oslo's astonishing modernities).

Adrift on this frightening sea of time and change, Charlotta's instinctive sense was against allowing herself to be stupidly spooked by coathooks and such. Chin out, not knowing what she was up to, she developed a palliatory habit effective in relieving this mighty dark uncertainty – for a time at least – until the next time. When her husband's ever-swirling world redistributed reality too fast in its kaleidoscope of change she would take a particular book down from a shelf in the library, go out into the furthest reaches of the garden and make for the place where the English lawn the men were laying (with so little success) turned into Norway again. There, amid the scent of birch and humid moss, with the little yellow umbrellas of *kantareller* mushrooms pushing up through the floor of fallen pine needles, she would sit with her back to the marble mansion, put the heavy *Almanach de Gotha* on her lap and open it to the page that told her exactly who she was in the world.

Her husband's family didn't occupy a place in this august stud-book which details every north European pedigree of note. Superiority is most often the cause for people to look them-selves up in such books, but this was no part of Charlotta's motive. She only knew that the reading of the litany of familiar names set out in the right order on the unvarying page, that the contemplation of the steady pattern of the consequent generations leading with such symmetry down to her inevitable self quieted her heart and settled something indefinable that fluttered inside her stomach and made her feel as she had felt when she had climbed too tall a mountain and looked down. The names never jumped about. Harald

Birch-Leg always gave birth to Waltraute (heavens, what names these early ones had! Thank God and Mama that she had not been called Waltraute). The strange names, the ugly and the beautiful, recurred down the years, sanctified by long use, the opposite of fashion. Once she had finished tracing the long Krigskjold line and come to herself and, beyond her own name, the pencilled-in note she had made of her son Berndt, she would spring up again, tuck the great volume under one arm and pick her way through the green and brown Swiss rolls of turf that ever lay in stacks, waiting to replace their dying brothers. She would walk under the light shade of the lilac tree and enter the house briskly, with an untroubled face. The workmen saw the face she put on the world, and it gave them every reason to go about their business humming.

It was down in the garden among the stacked turf-rolls, thoughtful, chin in hand, that Charlotta was going through the utterly steady sequence of ancestors when Oscar came home with the telegraph neatly folded in his pocket. She thought she caught a waft of his cigar, sensed the timbre of his voice through the bee-like hum of the workmen. She looked up through the shrubs and there he was, throwing away the cigar in a sparkling arc, thrusting his hands nonchalantly into his overcoat pockets. Engaged, even before he entered the house, she saw him make himself comfortable, leaning in a casual comma against a pillar of the half-erected portico and immediately becoming immersed in heated architectural discussion with the plaster-dusted foreman. Both men started waving their arms almost at once, talking fast and stopping now and then to sketch quickly on the ground with sticks. Up she jumped clutching her lineage to her bosom and, happy in hope, headed expectantly back through the indistinct fading light of the garden towards her husband and the chartless house that hung so prettily in nothing, anchored in nothing but intentions for the future, a pale shape solid as shadow against a vast sky meringued with pink-tipped cumulus.

CHAPTER TWO

She must call on her new sister-in-law immediately!

It was a pity the weather was not nice for their first meeting. Charlotta would have liked Katya to know only a sunny Oslo, a blue-and-white wind-tossed flag-flapping regatta town en *fête* but the day she called on her new sister the sun was lost, hidden behind a great heavy stack of brownish cloud streaked with an oppressive magenta. The cloud-wrack hanging low over the sea dulled the town's pretty colours to khaki and sludge. A cargo of cloves recently unloaded from Madagascar scented the air. The lachrymose mewing of gulls flew back and forth on wafts of clove-carnation. The few town-pines on their tall stalks soughed in the wind while the numerous nervous birches quivered and trembled like coy maidens needing more wooing. Even cheerful Charlotta must concede that today the whole world resonated in a minor key.

Oscar would want her to be driven down in the car for the bride visit. Though he himself relished the raw unpolished life on the streets, he felt the environment unsafe and inappropriate for his family.

A child had been kidnapped on the way to school.

This provided Oscar with the excuse to implement the strict regime that had lain for a long time in his heart. From the day of the kidnapping little Berndt, who used to play and tumble about under the watchful eye of Missy, had a Russian body-guard added to his retinue. The Russian was not unpleasant, that was not the point. He was strong and simple, not unlike a dog with bad steel dentistry and the face of a youthful, not over-bright Old Testament prophet. He was a sailor whom Oscar had enticed to jump ship for regular money. Oscar was the only person the Russian could communicate with. Together they spoke unintelligible sailors' polyglot, and had a perfect understanding. At first Missy had complained of having this rough, hirsute creature for company. She had declared him *spooky* (a new word added to Charlotta's growing colloquial English) but very soon the Englishwoman saw her status enhanced by the presence of a dumb giant at her shoulder. It was not long before she started to make use of him in practical ways. The mother was always there to kiss the boy goodbye when the retinue took their morning outing, and day by day she took silent amusement from logging the progress of Missy's gradual empire-building. Missy took to festooning the giant with all the things they might need for a long morning, entrusting him even at last with that most precious emblem, her handbag.

These days when Russo left the house he was hung about with toys and parcels and snacks and musical instruments like a Hallingdal tinker. Such encumbrances would, of course, have rendered him entirely useless for his prime purpose had it come to violence; but these were the terms that suited everybody and, God knew, it was hard enough to keep the balance in this house.

Two tiny lines, no deeper or more substantial than hairs, were just appearing – ghostly pencil dashes – on Charlotta's virgin forehead. One line was called responsibility; the other ingenuity.

'*Adieu.*'

Little Berndt knew it was not masculine to cling. Besides, he also knew that today's expedition to Bygdøy beach would entail a race between hermit crabs, always providing that he and Nanny and Russo were clever enough to find one each, and make a competition. Mama loved hermit crabs. She would be happy if his won.

He planted his bare chubby legs so he stood steadily, frowning up against the radiant sun that made a shadowshape of Mama in front of the brightness of the sky, and said with great determination: 'I shall try to find a fast one, Mama.'

'My darling.'

She buried her face in his shimmering tow-white hair. Love surged so strongly it constricted her throat and she could not speak. Had there ever been a child so grave, so loving, so transparent, so absolutely morally good?

'Adieu.'

The car with its organised interior swept away. She remained standing a moment in the hushed garden before turning to go back inside. There was time yet, but not much time.

Quickly and purposefully Charlotta mounted the stairs. The graded staircase got steeper and narrower as she went higher. On the third floor she opened the door to a place she had no business to go: Oscar's bathroom, a dark close room that smelled of cigars, coal tar soap, the orange flower water he splashed on after the bath and the Trumper's bay rum he put on his hair. The deep enamel bath, which was the whole purpose of this room, was of superb French quality and embedded in a sarcophagus-like construction of deep glimmering mahogany, the whole floating on a gleaming floor under a cylindrical copper water heater like the funnel of a liner. His clothes hung orderly in the cupboards ranked to the right. In the corner stood his shaving stand, a patent American invention of mahogany, much begadgeted, with brackets for gas lights, arms that went in and out to hold things, and a round mirror. The contents of his pockets from last night lay on the dressing table: the leather cigar case, a handful of visiting cards, his battered pistol, his ammunition, gold toothpick, and a new cigar-cutter from Georg Jensen, feminine in taste, enamelled and in the shape of a stork whose beak would do the business. She picked up the new cigar-cutter, made it open and close once or twice, snik-snak snik-snak, an elegant action and a pretty, vapid face.

Serpents came in different shapes in this man-made Eden.

Desolate, she replaced it on exactly the same spot it had been. Her hands fell and she stood quite motionless in her loneliness looking out of the window without seeing how luminously the white sails on the Oslofjord glowed beneath the heavy drama of the great thunder-frown sky.

She looked back intently one more time, searching the bathroom, and then she went to her room to change for the bride-visit to her sister-in-law.

Here in Norway the respectable women of all ages and

stations still wore skirts that swept the ground, and hair that they could sit on, though of course they only sat on it in private. In public it was piled high in baroque convolutions on the top of their heads where it was considered their crowning glory or, rather, their husbands'. A wife's good head of hair was maybe the ultimate hunting trophy, a prize greater even than the well-furnished elk head mounted on the smoking-room wall.

The coiled masses sat absolutely correctly, *comme il faut* above the faultless outfit of palest blue with crystal beading. Charlotta buttoned the prim Paragia boots, slung the silver foxes over her shoulder and, with the elegant feminine shape of the stork-shaped cigar-cutter floating through her mind, she jutted her chin. Through a crack in time showed a sharp edge of the fine-boned autocratrix that circumstances, and the need to win through, would make of her; and then she smiled again, and was young Charlotta once more, dewy, and delighting in a joke.

She had been so clever this morning! Outwitted the car! After Oscar had left the house she had suggested to Missy, it being such an unusually warm morning, that the nursery party might take the air at Bygdøy's healthful beach. Ozone was all the rage. They couldn't possibly walk that far; it was way out of range for darling Berndt with his chubby little angel's legs. That took care of the car and chauffeur, leaving her free to walk. Victory!

She wanted air, and she wanted, above all, time to think. She could not think in the house for all the activities going on, and she could certainly not think in the car because it simply was not a place where you could put two thoughts together. Not when you were high on the hushed cashmere seat, encased behind glass like a circus freak or a museum exhibit, passively swept past the liveliness of the life you lived among, as though you had nothing to do with it.

Passing through the hall on her way to the outside world she paused for a moment to enjoy the rare moment of privacy and quiet in her own house. The leaves of the lilac wove shifting luminous patterns on the hall window. On the table beneath the window stood a Georg Jensen silver salver, ready to receive the day's visiting cards. The Oscarsson family O was skilfully and artistically engraved in the smooth silver; centred within the O was the flag of the Oscarsson shipping line in blue and green enamel. Next to it a matching rose bowl held the great incurved globes of paeonies; it was too early in the year yet for roses.

'God dag, fru Oscarsson.' A man wheeled a barrow, *bump bump*, along the narrow strip of stacking protecting the hall floor.

Flumph! A paeony dropped at his passing.

'God dag.'

Absently she gathered up the handful of spicy-smelling petals, and let them trickle from her fingers as she left the house, making a trail behind her of pink and cream confetti.

The day was warming up. Soon it would be midday. The air in the garden was thick and sticky. The scent of the lilac swam heavy. There would surely be a storm.

Chin high, Charlotta took the road down to the shipping office, the busy road. Here in five minutes you could not help but see businessmen, peasants, town dandies, traders, armies of purposeful workmen in their *blåklær* like a dusty blue shifting sky. Ah! There was old Bess about her usual corner. Oh dear. She didn't look too healthy.

Since Oscar had last passed that way Bess had spent some of his munificence on an unwise breakfast. Just now she was at that low stage before the alcohol began to bite. Soon she would be exalted but for now the drink was exhausting her.

'God dag, Bess.' Charlotta beckoned the woman with her pearl-grey glove, and put two kroner in the red-knuckled mittened hand. 'Buy yourself some good food.' Close to, the woman looked even more ghastly. 'And don't spend it on that dog of yours. He's fat as butter. It's no good for him.'

'Bless you, my lady, bless you.'

This was a golden morning financially for Bess. Following the wife a little way (not a great distance for she could not concentrate on the same thing very far), Bess kept up a stream of gratitude and praise. Charlotta enjoyed the status of Saint and Example for at least ten metres before Bess lost the thread, her mind reverting to its usual track. Graphic and unappetising details followed. Charlotta heard it all as she continued on her way, and didn't even blush. The Krigskjold

farm community had its share of the mad and the indigent,
those poor, lacking souls whose uncontrolled minds so often
run on sex. Besides, she'd grown up amid plain country talk on
farmyard matters.

Oscar would have been profoundly shocked had he known
his wife's unshockability.

If Charlotta had continued to the top of the street she might
have ended up at the yellow and white palace where King
Håkon, the first king of an independent Norway since 1380,
lived with Queen Maud and her endless little dogs, all called
Billy. Because of her birth Charlotta was automatically a
hoffdame with occasional duties at court; a routine that didn't
endear her to her contemporaries. Nor, because of the
dangerous edge to her husband, was she entirely made at
home by the palace set. Neither fish nor fowl, then. The one
person she had high hopes of feeling at home with was this
new fellow-stranger, Katya Oscarsson *née* Olovanova – but
once you had married it was best to put all notion of previous
belonging away. Katya Oscarsson, then.

Katya had not been many minutes in her new home as a
married woman, no less, before she had made up her mind
exactly where she would stand on receiving visitors. With the
dust of the honeymoon journey still on her grey heel-length
karakul coat and all her trunks and hatboxes clustered about
her feet like a small pack of dogs, she took one look and knew.

Golden, voluble Gustav, quite unaware of his wife's
new-taken decision, continued pacing about the tall-ceilinged
hall talking nineteen to the dozen in the polyglot fragments
the two of them used as language. With cavalier flourishes he
was explaining this, pointing out that, taking her hand and
pulling her along to show her how natty was the system of
window-fasteners.

(How iridiscent the glass, thought the grubby, time-dimmed
Tëtka. How sparkly clean the many panes. There are sufficient
servants in this place, the wrinkled old woman calculated.
That is satisfactory.)

The ancient chaperon aunt, who had been given the sacred
trust of looking after the Olovanovas' treasure-daughter on her
travels, had been included in Gustav's generous offer of a new
life. She had not shared the happy couple's meandering

boat-and-Alfa honeymoon journey home: Gustav was not one to confuse generosity with the softness of foolishness. No, the Tëtka had been sent on separately by train, and a very unpopular fellow-passenger she had proved with all her peers. Continent-wide they had given a wide berth to the grey-shawled, muttering, malevolent parcel.

From between the corner pillars in Gustav's splendid hall there poked the old woman's foreshortened black shadow. Her coffee-coloured eyes peered into the brightness: her Katya needed rest. She needed her drops after her journey and here was the jumped-up bridegroom, his arm about her treasure's slender waist, pulling her along to show her this, to show her that. Her treasure peered forward to see, threw back her arms adjusting her veil to see clearer. He squeezed her close, took advantage of the thrust-back veil to press his coarse masculine face against the silky cheek and bullied little Katya like a pasha, though why he was so pleased with himself was difficult to see. He had not even got the place ready for the darling. The dusty beige soil in the garden was strewn with the rubbish and shards of the builders. That cigarette butt too! The scorched remnant of the strong tobacco rolled in newspaper that some clever fellow thought nobody would notice if he poked it down here behind this corner column in whose cold shadow she stood. She had taken note of these things, and more. Why, this great glorious generous bride-groom had not even finished the house he had brought his bride to, and she the beloved girl so grateful, so happy her eyelashes were wet – see how they sparkled – with the kisses of gratitude she gave him.

The Tëtka, like many deaf people, was entirely unaware of her repertoire of incidental noises accompanying thought. A ticking started up in the back of her throat, a sound not unlike the watchful guinea-fowl on sighting the thieving fox. The couple glanced over. Gustav, remembering his Norwegian manners, bade her welcome to his house in the old formula, accompanying the words with an amiable smile.

Memories of how to return a smile lurked somewhere about the old woman's creaking memory. Yes, so. The corners of her thin-lipped tortoise mouth turned up. You were meant to participate with your eyes also, but she had forgotten that.

It was when Katya saw the staircase that she knew exactly
where she would stand. The staircase (marble, grander than
brother Oscar's, fifteen-love to Gustav) was loosely based on
the arch of Constantine with its three openings; two stairways
either side of the main arch led up to celestial heights. The
minor side-arches housed matching alabaster lamps that
burned naphthous gas in their translucent bowls, and this was
amazing not only on account of the artistic tastefulness of the
bowls but also because of the quality of light they cast. Their
steady naphtha glow was fantastic! They were like two full
moons, and this at a time when oil lamps with wicks were the
norm, even in smart Oslo. An incidental side effect, never
discovered and irrelevant after the electrification of the house,
was that the naphthic gas also narcotised the air, giving people
who had to spend long reaches of time in the hall waiting for
Katya (who was always late) a morbid inclination to yawn and
eventually to sleep.

These two splendid lights were the outriders, then. Next
came the twin stairs climbing up each flank of Constantine's
centre. Once you reached the top, the apogee, a sort of
balconied landing affair ran across at right angles with doors
leading off to the upstairs rooms. This was the spot. Here she
would stand. This she knew with the dust of travel still on her
coat and the tears of gratitude to life for tossing her up on
this luxurious shore still on her lashes; here on the high
balustraded balcony at the epicentre, the very zero point
where all the lines of perspective converged.

She would be draped like Duse.

One of the advantages of no longer having a mother was
that she could have entirely her own way with dress. Freedom
to go about in the hot colours she liked, the colours of the
body's organs: liver brown, the bright crimson of the spleen,
the black of bile, the subtle lead colour of the gall bladder and
the petrol blue of veinous blood uncut. The lace and floating
organza and chiffon that softened the look around the ladies'
faces of the time and made such handy background for jabbing
diamonds into would always, Katya decided, be flesh-coloured
rather than the normal white. White she abhorred: a colour for
servants, nursemaids and starched cooks.

It was a long climb for Charlotta up the flanks of

Constantine. Charlotta wore blue, the pale innocent blue of the
sky at six o'clock in the morning when it was promising to be
a brisk uncomplicated day. The frill of starched organza that
framed her neck and bosom was most beautifully and snowily
white. She held out the large white linen tablecloth that she
and her mother had spent years working towards her own
trousseau. Charlotta knew that Katya's trousseau linen had all
been purchased by Gustav in an excess of husbandly love on
the way home through Italy. It was very smart, and every
stitch of it had been worked by strangers. When Charlotta
handed over the tablecloth tied with a white ribbon into
which had been tucked a fresh white flower, she had mimed
the sewing of it, and she had put all the love she was capable
of into the miming, just as she and her mother had put all the
love into the two years' sewing.

She wished she could tell Katya in words. Language was a
further pity as well as the weather. Charlotta had only a little
English (Missy was teaching her when she had time) and a
very, very little French in which to offer the gift. Katya, like all
good Russians, had less French than she thought, more English
than her new sister, and less goodwill than either language.

Receiving the gift standing in the zero spot of Gustav's high
ornate hall she scarcely looked at it but handed it behind her
into space where lurked the stringent Tëtka in her rusty black
with her arms held out like two rigid sticks. The tablecloth
was laid across the rigid sticks. It was borne away, and
Charlotta never saw trace of it again.

There hung about Katya's dark Russian looks a certain
quality of mournfulness, which in the wake of recent history
did her no harm. In Oslo society she stood out. Gustav had
unconsciously chosen for himself a bride not unlike his
brother's, tattle decided. Katya was of fine, that is to say of
ancient, birth. But Gustav was not setting himself up in
competition. It was simply that the need which drove Oscar
drove him too. Both Oscarssons had a passion for possessing
and idealising grandeur. The fine women they chose were a
sanctifying light to them. It was not the brothers' fault they
could not sustain the vision the minute the light itself was
not present to illuminate the path. Fidelity was a tricky
concept; it needed a bit more time – just a bit – to find itself a

fixed place in the Oscarsson post-Viking canon.

'Sisters-in-law,' tattled Norway, 'both strangers,' and went on to discuss the differences within the larger label of strangeness. Katya was the *rara avis*, the tragic heroine never observed without the frisson of a salacious shudder; the massacre in the forest hung about her like a shadowy blood mist. Charlotta was the well-comprehended type: country aristocracy ostensibly admired, brought up to thorough country virtues too well known: duty, charity, the maintenance of routine and social order. Phew! That anyone thought it mattered nowadays. That anyone had the energy! No sooner had she come down to the capital than she had been made *hoffdame* to English-born Queen Maud. Well, that was the Krigskjolds for you, all connections. They wished her joy of such a stuffy appointment.

As for the sisters-in-law's feelings for each other: Katya the mystic, the instinctive one (her Norwegian was not yet that good, nor would it ever be), was made wary by her sister-in-law. The quality in Charlotta that made people careful to sit up straight and behave well aroused only resentment in the tumultuous Russian breast.

Very soon Katya was telling her new Norwegian friends in her own exotic mixture of languages (after she had received them at the top of the stairs, and while they were getting the hang of drinking black tea in tall glasses with long spoons among the curlicues of Oriental rugs from the market at Samarkand), 'My sister-in-law is so clever. So clever! Such a good person. Valorous in the kitchen. A genius of the jam-pots.' Katya yawned like a pretty black cat, just showing the pointed tip of a very pink tongue. Her teeth were small and neat and perfectly graded, and her breath smelt musky with the violet cachous she sucked between cigarettes.

'Aaaah. Mnnn. Where was I? Oh, yes, yes, please. Another Tideman's cigarette ... how I love this blond European tobacco ... Aah, so good, so good ... Pretty little Charlotta, ye-es ... Do you know? I have never met a person so fitted to accomplish all those,' she waved her hand, 'everyday *jam-pot* things ...' her eyes unfocused as her very Being made visible connection with the vague mystic cloud of the infinitely significant that floated so far above the jam-pots and preserving pans of everyday life.

'Living?' she might have quoted from Villiers de L'Isle Adam's Axël, one in the pile of favourite books never far from her elbow, 'The servants will do that for us', except that for the word 'servant' Katya would have substituted the name of her sister-in-law Charlotta.

Charlotta, for her part, began the relationship by a practical summing-up. Her own figure, she decided, was just as slim, but she was not quite so tall, even in the boots with the heels. Above all, she did not have two such fine bosoms. How she envied Katya's bosoms. They were like two separate globes not so big as to be silly but always noticeably there. Otherwise she did not envy her sister-in-law but sometimes was scared of her, as one is of people whose families have been massacred. It is not a normal thing. Sometimes when Katya crept into Charlotta's mind and Charlotta wasn't concentrating she caught herself starting to make the sign of the Cross to protect herself, just in the way that, as a child, she had made the sign on seeing the Siberian tiger chained in the zoo. How everyone had laughed at her that day! So long ago. But the tiger had looked her in the eye and wanted to eat her. It had seemed obvious to her that something greater and more powerful than mere metal was needed to contain such a terrifying, tremendous, bloodthirsty thing.

She tried not to think about this. Thinking of the tiger would not help to grow closer as sisters should.

From time to time Katya would break out of gloom into bouts of frantic gaiety, swirling about in red shawls singing hoarse tzigoyner songs through which howled primeval winds, wolves, wild steppes, weird and dead horizons. Gustav adored these passionate displays and recklessly encouraged them. The Tëtka hated them. She endured them, glowering. It was extraordinary how the start of one of these moods would always bring the Tëtka to Katya's side. The crumpled old woman, touchy and suspicious by nature, inclined at the best of times to see slights where none was offered, now, deafness deepening (and how this aggravated her already jagged mind), was moving from mild neurosis into full-blown domestic paranoia. In Gustav's house she spent her time counting things, vases in the flower room, sheets in the airing cupboard, and screaming at the maids and menservants if she fancied anything was missing. Since the Tëtka had settled in this strange and horrible land she had taken hold of an *idée fixe* not uncommon with people whose material world has been abruptly and violently smashed. Her Katya, her darling, her Only One, was all alone in a spiteful world in which everyone – every man jack of them – was intent on robbing her blind.

When Katya's red swirling moods were upon her it was as though an electric current passed through the house summoning the Tëtka even from the dimmest, most distant domestic recesses. The furthest airing cupboard would spew her up to stand ominously admiring the darling over whom she had no control and hating everybody else. Gustav had a name for the old woman: the hooded crow. He made jokes whose words she did not understand, though she whiffed their import. She would glare, and Gustav would laugh, and Katya would get more and more excited.

These frantic outbursts of Katya's would often lead to a terrible collapse, an endless string of retching coughs. Her racked body could only be stilled, her soul calmed, by her medicinal drops in a glass of sugar-water. The Tëtka's rigid arms were always ready to offer the drops, but Katya would wave away the old woman if Charlotta happened to be in the house. Especially Katya liked Charlotta to administer the remedy.

'*Vite, chérie, vite, vite.*'

Katya's voice, always hoarse, became a rasping husk. Her bony olive-skinned fingers trembled, closing over Charlotta's marzipan-smooth hand, causing jerks in the glass's journey from hand to mouth so that some of the sugary mixture dribbled down her chin. The drops calmed her marvellously. They not only soothed the coughing but lulled her into a slow, beautiful contentment.

Charlotta had never seen an odalisque, but she had read about them in an illustrated copy of *The Rubáiyát* of Omar Khayyám in Oscar's study, which she was not supposed to have seen. The words had stayed in her head ever since. They carried in their sounds the limitless romantic resonances of the half-understood. Seraglio, odalisque, harem, kismet, concubine. Katya conjured this magical procession of words into Charlotta's mind when in her black and red shawls she responded to the drops, her storm-tossed body relaxing in Charlotta's arms, growing heavy, tender, pliant and affectionate with the passing of the tempest and the blooming of dreamy happiness in her eyes.

At such times Charlotta would feel the welling rush of protective maternal love such as she felt for Berndt; love as she had thought it only possible to feel for her beloved son, her darling golden boy. These were the times she felt closest to her new sister and the budding of a tender love between them that was certain to grow. After she had given Katya the drops the two sisters-in-law would sit entwined in the richly coloured pool of light beneath the stained-glass lamp, Charlotta stroking Katya's hair, her face, her hands; feeling the poor, frantic, motherless creature in her arms grow calmer, the spasms turn to flutterings and grow weaker, until at last she was like a still, warm bird at rest, at ... death. The word had almost crept into Charlotta's mind before she dismissed it, distressed that it had even dared to poke its sinister rim above the horizon and into conscious thought.

Charlotta would disentangle herself gently, gently as clouds, from Katya's body reclining on the divan and slide herself away so that the Tëtka, who was lurking there impatient, clucking and ticking in her throat, arms stacked with lace-edged pillows and cashmere shawls, might take over the care of the trusting, unconscious girl.

No matter how delicately Charlotta extricated herself, her small movements would always disturb Katya. She would always emerge momentarily from the trance. Her eyelids would fly up to give her sister-in-law a wild look as though everything around her was unfamiliar, restless, terrifying. Her eyes would roam around, resting on nothing, and then the leaden eyelids would droop and she would sink back insensible, deeper into her dreams, yielding to the Tëtka's wonderfully comforting arrangements of pillows and shawls.

Charlotta would know to tiptoe out of the room, to leave the poor, doomful thing in the loving and familiar hands of the old woman, who was all Katya had left of her own life, her own family. But before she tiptoed out Charlotta, in her pretty well-ordered cloud-coloured clothes, a pastel island in this florid sea, would plant the smallest kiss, light as a butterfly, on

Katya's febrile forehead. Straightening, she would make the sign of the Cross over her sister's tormented soul, and every time she vowed before God that she would find a way to give her sister the love, the everyday bread-and-butter love, the unspectacular family love that was so unready to grow between them.

CHAPTER THREE

After an irreproachably respectable period of time Katya gave birth to a little girl. The dramas and the passions of Katya's *accouchement* were all very interesting to Oslo.

At home in her own valley Katya's people held the superstition that the sharp winds that came off the far mountains must be avoided at all costs during the last month. On those bitter winds flew the souls of those that had died in childbirth.

Oslo being mountain-ringed, avoidance was not simple. Gustav's blue eyes lit at the challenge. All his favourite things were involved: putting up a construction, indulging his tempestuous wife and, above all, just showing the world he could Do It – whatever it was, and however unreasonable.

What he did was this.

He hopped into *Katinka*, his fast new toy, his little one-man sailboat, and skimmed down the Oslofjord. *Katinka's* paper-light hull scarcely dented the trembling ringlets of sunlight on the surface of the sea. The large blond man whistled in delight and sang the old songs, pushing the wooden tiller here and there, trawling a line behind him for lunch while the boat flew into inlets, round headlands, and all the time his far-seeing seaman's eyes scoured the coastline's thousand granite bluffs and islands for a place indubitably out of the influence of any mountain winds.

'Island' is, in fact, rather a grand word for what he found. In truth it was merely some sticking-up tops that were part of a largely submerged grey granite molar poking out of the sea half-way down the Oslofjord. From afar this half-submerged molar had the charming contours of a pair of elephants lolling in the water. More importantly, the two elephants conveniently supplied a deep water anchorage, a snug position in relation to sun, wind (that vital wind) and view. There was also that last important asset on an island: fresh water. From high up in the grey rock a clear, gurgling playful little spring rose up and fell into a well-shaped pool that never dried up, not even when the Oslo heat was at its greatest and the parched northern summer blazed round about St John the Baptist's Day and the northern lights danced like curtains of fire in the night-time sky.

Island located, Gustav wasted no time. He stole away a platoon of Oscarsson workers from the shipyard when his brother was looking in another direction, dynamited a flat, house-sized platform *plouf!* and the minute the dust had settled the best carpenter-shipbuilders from the yard were set to raising a six-bedroomed house.

'Nothing to it,' he told the nervous boatbuilders, who felt overmatched by the project and wasted days shifting from foot to foot. 'A house is just like a clinker-built rowboat upside down with a few windows. Go to it! Noah wasn't afraid.'

A roof of grey-green slate was laid. Next, while the rococo panelling was still being fitted (one could not have a son and heir born in a hovel, after all), a flagpole was run up so that the good news could be broadcast at the first available minute. Now all was ready; Katya installed on the island of auspicious aspect, and blooming. She made his life impossible with her difficult and expensive cravings it was his joy to indulge. The other players were installed in their proper places: doctor, nurse, midwife, grim Tëtka, maid and cook. Gustav, meanwhile, shuttled back and forth to Georg Jensen where he commissioned engraved silver, and to Royal Copenhagen where he commissioned china with the name of the island Fødselsøy, Birth Island, in every conceivable nook and cranny.

He sailed in and out at whim, like a king, thoroughly enjoying himself and planning how later he would throw out a wooden jetty – just here – so that his jolly Yacht Klub cronies could moor up for the odd weekend party. And if he fixed some iron rings – just there – then he could organise bathing steps – just here – a most convenient place. He had noticed that because of the configuration of the rocks the jellyfish were never swept into this cove. It would do very well for bathing, and just here ...

Katya lay passive as a doll on her piled pillows, beautiful in her flesh-coloured lace peignoir, reading a little, but mostly dreaming, and drinking quantities of the raspberry-leaf tea the Tëtka said was vital for an easy delivery from the mortal pangs of childbirth. Every morning the two Russians laid out the cards, the day's one passionate moment of intense ethereal excitement, to read what luck the rest of the slow, unpunctuated day ahead would bring. From time to time Katya would get up, drawn to the window by seagulls' shrieks lacerating the air, and would stand gazing without blinking, as one hypnotised, oblivious of time, studying the unscrupulous games of the cruel-beaked birds as they pursued paths of screaming aggression up and down the smooth, elephant-grey granite or, between squabbles, bobbed up and down on the creamy white mounds of a light-running summer sea. The Tëtka, coming in upon her dear beauty lost in thought at the window, would scold and rumble-grumble at her darling to stop dilly-dallying in the dangerous draught and press on her yet more medicinal decoctions for this new danger.

'They are like us,' Katya teased, snatching at the old woman's reproachful wagging finger and disarming her gaoler with a kiss. 'Can't you see how Russian they are, these birds? Not like Norwegians. They don't bother to hide their real natures behind manners and phrases and smiles. Russians, like you and me: bold and devious and naughty and delightful. I've taken a fancy to these white birds.'

'Stop your fancies now. Be quiet and drink your tea.'

Gustav sailing back to the newly constructed wooden landing-stage loaded down with beautiful things and raspberry-leaf tea (this tea was another inexpressibly difficult errand for him to expend his ingenuity on, and rush about) suddenly realised how a workshop might be fitted in next to the house – just here – why had it never occurred to him before? And because from the Fødselsøy you could see the whole arc of the sky, unlike in Oslo where those fordømmet mountains got in the way, he ordered a telescope from Zeiss in Germany to come on the next Oscarsson boat leaving for Oslo from Kiel, and he was altogether a happy man. Katya was a happy woman. A birthing island of one's very own! This was Romanov. This was Imperial. She doubted even the Tsarina of all the Russias had ever had quite such a pretty and expensive tribute paid.

All this mutual happiness lasted four whole years. Naturally the girl (a small disappointment this) was named Katya and naturally the two Katyas left the island as soon as they possibly could, moving back to Oslo so as to receive all the praise, attention and gifts consequent on a birth. Mother and baby held court in the marvellous Oslo house that Gustav was raising on the opposite side of the Oslo harbour to his brother.

The ostensible reason for building the two houses *vis-à-vis* was for the brothers to have fun signalling from windows. Each had a flagpole in the garden and a vast repertoire of all those shipboard flags that can communicate absolutely anything across the water: 'Cocktails with me tonight', when they felt like a jolly. Or 'Plague on board, keep away at all costs' fluttered the yellow flag when a wife was in a mood. Oh, it was fun, this teasing semaphore between the brothers.

Another reason for building within eyeshot of each other was to monitor each other's extravagances, and not to be outdone. Competition ran neck and neck. Oscar was the more playful. One famous night he raised a complete domed tower ornamented in the Italian manner with urns, balls and snake-twined vases. Some weeks later, when Gustav was well into raising his higher tower in answer, Oscar took the whole thing down in daylight so all the town could see it to be nothing more than a four-sided stage-flat painted on wood with shapes cut out for the window glass. Oslo was entertained to a long-drawn-out dialogue of tit-for-tat architectural vituperation with spy-glasses and stonemasons for pieces.

Katya and Charlotta were not infected by their husbands' spirit of light-hearted rivalry. Young motherhood is not conducive to light-heartedness, being a stage that sits heavy and serious on the heart. As for rivalry, there was, of course, the usual competition as to whose child was more brilliant: pride in the little ones' achievements wrapped in the language of modest disclaimers.

Rivalry beyond that, woman-to-woman rivalry, had no place. They were so very different.

It saddened Charlotta that the mutual bond of children had brought soul-sisterhood no nearer, that her affectionate approaches were as unproductive as wind-eggs. The tender buds of her love shrivelled in the cold frost of Katya's neglect, to be replaced over the years by duller things: routine and *plikt*, that very Norwegian sense of duty that sits so heavy on the national character.

Katya the impulsive used to joke among her cronies how she could set her clock by Charlotta's weekly visits – on the dot! – and while she joked she would feel bitter to be relegated to the position of an item in Charlotta's diary rather than a burning need. If Charlotta really loved Katya she would surely be drawn at other times by irresistible impulse, and that would be real love. That would be need. Perceiving herself relegated to the realms of duty Katya felt herself insulted. She did not return the duty calls.

Duty is not a very developed sense in the Russian race. Had it been better developed, Russia's history might have taken quite a different turn through the nineteenth and twentieth centuries. Katya was, shall we say?, Russian in her sense of duty. It was something she owed herself; doubly now since she was orphaned. Other people owed it to her too, as the Tëtka fondly reminded her.

Not that Katya wasted much time mourning Charlotta's friendship. She had her own coterie of Oslo wives. The coterie had missed Katya's society dreadfully during the time she'd been away giving birth on the Fødselsøy. They clustered round on her return, vying in spoiling and petting the new Katya-madonna who received them lying calmly on the purple brocade of the *chaise-longue* in the half-light of the heavily draped *stue*.

She had changed subtly since the birth: grown in the assurance of belonging, of becoming more physically fixed on this earth. Motherhood had secured her this permanent place in the world. Time to embark on a small voyage of fiction, a little readjustment of her past: a little social uplift, a little romantic Russification here, a little glorification there.

The Romanov double-headed eagle suddenly appeared

emblazoned on all sorts of domestic objects in Gustav's house. Georg Jensen was kept busy engraving. The bird sat oddly with the enamelled Oscarsson flag. She took to referring to her native land as Rus', Tsar Nicholas' favoured nomenclature before events overtook him. Like him she discovered a hatred for the modern word Rossiia. She put up a group photograph taken at a pre-revolutionary costume ball and would point to one of the figures, herself in a Russian headdress. The face in the picture was indistinct, it might well be translated into Katya's face given a sympathetic inclination, but anyone who had a grasp of likely dates (such as the Oscarsson brothers) might be inclined to doubt. The coterie could be counted on to be vague on dates. There was a new costume, too. She'd set the Tëtka to sewing while on the island: the resulting long, majestic caftan of an ancient Muscovite boyar was often worn when publicly 'at home'.

These days it was the Tëtka, the deputy, who stood at the zero point to receive the faintly narcotised guests. The withered woman in the splendid context was the prelude, the suitable preliminary to the holy of holies.

One could not approach Katya on the purple *chaise-longue* without taking in at the same time the Doré engraving hanging on the long wall between the two windows over her reclining form so that the two became inseparable in the mind. Over Katya's head Gustavus Adolfus' cavalry galloped fast over the surface of the frozen sea with baroque swirl and counter-swirl of cloak and mane. Wild-eyed horses and rapturous shimmering demi-gods swept across livid frozen sea, disappearing into evanescent frozen arabesques of snow and icy mist until the last echoes of the baroque masses merged into whirling incorporeality. The picture could be seen only with difficulty in full daylight, a dim grey pool between the dense shimmering window on either side. But there was seldom full daylight in this room. In daytime the light was filtered though filmy rosy draperies and visitors after dark were positively frightened by the energy of Doré's sublime cavalry springing off the wall between the two pairs of tall green brocade curtains drawn tight as a trap in the silence of evening. And Katya beneath, a dreamy smile on her lips. Her strong, hawk-featured face floating limpidly in the aureole cast by the beaded shade of the oil lamp, pointing a most beautifully made olive-skinned hand heavy with rings up at the picture above her head.

'Napoleon's retreat from Moscow.' The tobacco-hoarse voice embarked on the Russification, appropriating Gustavus Adolfus' great piece of history and claiming it for her own. 'He conquered all Europe. But Rus' defeated him, Holy Rus'...' She faltered, dabbed her eyes using a handkerchief embroidered with her initials KO in Cyrillic script, contrary to the Westernised handkerchiefs she and her family had used at home.

From the too-painful subject she would turn to the table at her elbow where the current books were piled in the lamp's circle: Rilke's *Livre d'heures*, Mann's *Death in Venice*, Wilde's *Salome*, Löns' *Wehrwolf*, Freud's *Psychoanalysis*, de Lisle Adams's *Axël*. From behind these fashionable shockers gleamed a soft silver rectangle: her cigarette box, made by Georg Jensen, enamelled with the ubiquitous O and the green and blue flag, and now the double-headed eagle just above the O. Every hour or so her bony, long-fingered hand would move towards the box, her rings sparkling under the light, and then for the next ten minutes or so the cigarette's glowing flame would periodically lend her ivorine face the rosy hue of youthful health. Fragrance from her gold-tipped Balkans curled through the whole house, permeating the atmosphere with a sweetly narcotic and vaguely spiritual scent.

'Like incense in a Romersk church,' the wives who had travelled told the wives who had not. 'The priest's helper in a long gown lights the little navicula, the incense-boat (imagine a kitchen colander hanging up, but more artistic). The smoke escapes through the holes and all the church smells just like here.'

The coterie were not an intelligentsia. God forbid. Apart from Katya's own studiedly negligent dress there was not a loose gown to be seen. No slippers here; no unconsidered hair-dos. Nobody looked as though an owl had nested in her hair and been forgotten, nor behaved as though an owl had nested in her brain and been welcomed. No, it was not an intellectual awakening that she was seeking here, nor indeed a political one. She saw herself more as Scheherazade weaving a mysterious spell, and she was the last to see the irony in the form of spell she'd chosen. This salon/coterie set-up echoed exactly the pre-revolutionary gatherings that had led directly to the Revolution, directly to the execution of her own family; a parallel that passed her by. Irony was never Katya's strong point. Freud and Salome and Aleister Crowley might jostle at her elbow; Katya might see herself in the double role of Rasputin and Tsarina in this little Romanov court, but Katya's little acolytes, her sweet coterie, all came with their hair tucked under this season's hat and their neat necks set off by this season's collar. Predictable as swallows, they pinned identical bunches of sweetly scented violets to their lapels, which were of fur, or flannel, or linen according to the time of year. They came in gloves and boots buttoned up to the hilt by ladies' maids. They came with childish faces. Light caught in their soft hazel eyelashes and rimmed the gentle curves of their peach-downy cheeks. This was the only flesh they displayed, above the throat. Once they had been received they also displayed the flesh below the wrist. They were the wives of merchants and of money-men and the military. Katya had been introduced to all of them in suitable circumstances, a lot of them at the Dronningen Yacht Klub. Suitable women, then; passive, prepared within the context of Oslo's bewilderingly fluid but ruthless ever-forming ever-changing society to step on the rollercoaster of fashion but not of ideas. More than happy to find themselves dewy-eyed at the vaguely stirring revolutionary readings of their rich and influential hostess, the last thing they wanted was to comprehend what they were listening to, or in any way to commit to change. Nearby Russia was boiling in the horrid stews of revolution. Tsars were being murdered in forests. Why, even now Finland, their northern neighbour, was signing treaties with these self-same regicide Russians. The sweet coterie were all of them half in love with Norway's very own darling handsome newly imported king. The last thing they wanted was their handsome King Håkon shot to death in some *skog*. No, they were not an intelligentsia.

The coterie gave Katya the same secure sense she had had at home where she was the *enfant dorée*, beautiful, utterly important, the very heart and centre of an unquestioning worshipping circle from her first appearance in the world until the age of twelve when, for no discernible reason, people had ceased to love her. They had all turned against her. She had done nothing to deserve it. She had not changed in any way. She had stayed exactly the same as she had been as a child and people had loved her then for her pretty looks and her pretty ways. It made no sense.

But then the Good Lord had stretched out His hand and sent her to Riva del Garda. His Holy Hand had scooped her out of that inexplicable and frightening miasma of disapproval at home, saved her as a Chosen One from the massacre, and placed her in this new circle of enchantment.

This circle ... she dropped a scented pastille on the bronze burner ... this circle was even better. Her large-pupilled eyes followed the cobalt-coloured smoke on its serpentine journey. Not only was she Oslo's choice but she was Gustav's choice above all other. This was childhood plus: favouritism enhanced by the beacon of sexuality, with the pliant coterie taking the place of serfs and so forth.

On her return to Oslo she had forgotten all about the Fødselsøy. An island had been purchased for her brief moment of parturition, a house built.

So? A Russian shrug of the olive-toned shoulders. The place could fall into the sea now, so far as she was concerned.

But the snug little island was not falling into the sea. Nor was it forgotten by Gustav who, like nature, abhorred a vacuum and lost no time in putting the place to good use.

It was surprising, really, that it took Katya the best part of four years to discover that, far from standing empty, the island that had been picked for her special moment, the house that had been constructed for that peak of marital experience, had been pressed into service as a busy garçonnière. But, then, Katya made no effort to understand Norwegian, the language of town gossip.

In fact, Gustav's little set-up on the island was such general and unsensational knowledge that it came as a great puzzle to Charlotta when her sister-in-law arrived at her house, throwing herself, with what Charlotta had come to think of as typical ornate excesses, on Charlotta's pale brocade sofa uttering harsh, hoarse imprecations in her fragmented jigsaw of languages, wailing, complaining of betrayal, betrayal.

'My drops, chérie, darling, give me my drops.'

'Hush, darling, hush.'

'C'est fini. Fini. La farce est jouée.'

Charlotta poured the calming drops. Katya had come to visit for once without the Tëtka.

The drops brought Katya no peace but lay like an oily skin on the surface of her terror. For the first time her Olovanova family came to her in her trance. Katya screamed thin screams, she dribbled, had paroxysms. Her sobs were atrocious. Charlotta was terrified. This was not a question of stroking a brow but of holding and restraining a struggling woman.

The sisterly arms were iron bands. Katya's eyes could not even see Charlotta. The restraining arms belonged to the armed peasants who had come to kill her family. She was crouching in the bushes, witness to what she had never seen, the long-drawn-out physical struggles of the destruction of her own flesh and blood: flesh on flesh, metal torn through flesh, badly aimed shotguns in nervous wavering hands, splintering minor limbs, tearing through the unimportant B roads of the flesh to cries at once ghastly and pathetic; the prolonged fruitless struggles as the males of the family tried to take the bullets and the blades into their own flesh so as to shield the weaker women; the prayers, the pleas for pity to spare the babes, for pity before God, spare the babes in the Holy Redeemer's name.

The news had been brought to her that day in Riva del Garda while she and Gustav were by a white balustrade standing in the long-fingered shade of a glossy palm tree. His handsome eyes were screwed up against a scrap of fluctuating sunlight that darted in and out between the fingers of the palm. His eyelashes glistened like gold and copper wire in the fugitive light. He was wearing cream linen, and silk from Paris. His eyes, full of laughter, were holding hers and making love to her while their mouths were being very correct, very bien élevé, making all the correct dialogue about donkey rides, water ices and postcards. Her heart had been rapturous, palpitating. And then the Tëtka had swooped, like the black crow she was, coming up to spoil their fun and Katya had been cross with the deaf old useless woman and shouted at her a little and then the Tëtka had told her about her family and she had fainted. The hazy memory of her quivering return to consciousness was entirely taken up with awareness of Gustav's strong warm arm around her waist. How many weeks had she waited to know the feel of this arm, to smell the masculine delicious scent of his moustache, so close it almost brushed her cheek; to breathe the *eau de Portugal* he put on his hair, the sensuous faintly cigar-scented breath? These things were far more possible, far more real and vivid, than some unbelievable story she was being told of faraway Russia.

On Charlotta's yellow damask sofa, with the door closed against the builders' dust and the haze of paeonies thick in the airless room, Katya wept and moaned and whimpered, and the paroxysms were giving way to coughing and growing less violent. Charlotta wondered if she could let Katya go for a moment to summon help: Missy or Russo.

Paeonies had grown in the neatly kept Russian garden. The heavy romantic waft of the flowers triggered the very first nostalgia for home, the very first real regret Katya had felt since that sunsoaked day under the palm, talking to her lover beside the balustrade.

Over and over she said she would leave Gustav. She would leave Gustav. She must leave Gustav. Betrayed, she must leave.

Charlotta had never encountered anything like this. Her heart went out to her sister-in-law. The pain was real but at the same time she could see how Katya was feeding it. The pain would get better if her sister-in-law would stop behaving like a stoker piling on fuel to see how high the fire would go before the engine exploded.

Charlotta tried and tried to calm her, but she got nowhere with soft words.

'It is your duty to stay,' she said at last, exhausted, exasperated. 'Besides.' Had she really to point out this bald truth? 'Where would you go? There is nowhere.'

Katya's eyes were appalled.

A new look came into them. The stupefied black pools found themselves no longer able to rest on anything but darted to and fro like a lizard and Charlotta was smitten; she had made this.

'I have friends.' Katya clutched Charlotta's arm to the bone, so that it really hurt. '*Des amis partout. Partout.*'

Katya left soon afterwards, walking to the chauffeur-driven car with the stiff tottering steps of a person under an excessive physical load.

The car door closed with a thud.

Charlotta turned to go back inside the house. Her insides felt as though the Siberian tiger had raked them through with his claws. She had a great yearning for the nursery. These days the *Almanach de Gotha* had been replaced by the touch of her boy. Little Berndt would be drowsing, having his nap. She would tiptoe into the dimly lit room, stand close enough to hear his breath in the darkness, to make out the beauty of his neck on the pillow, the delicate line of his ear, and then she would be filled with strength for the next thing, whatever it was.

She turned to go back across the hall.

'*God dag, Fru Oscarsson.*' A passing builder munching on cheese and onions.

'*God dag.*' She squeezed past him on her way towards the stairs.

No.

Duty first.

First she would write Katya a note.

Her hasty loving note arrived almost before her sister-in-law had reached her own doorstep.

No reply came, either that evening or the next day.

Charlotta questioned the chauffeur: 'You're certain she received my note?'

The driver scratched his thinning hair. 'I gave it to the deaf old woman who doesn't bother with manners.'

'She understood who it was for?'

'Oh, she understands everything, that one. What she does about it's another matter.'

CHAPTER FOUR

Charlotta did not know what disturbed her most: Katya's wretched physical fit the previous day or the equally wild mental state. She did not trust Katya's capacity to remain this side of fantasy on either count. What a wicked thought, Charlotta scolded herself, the fit was genuine. That could not have been counterfeit. In that case she should have proper medical treatment not just that awful old woman who hissed like a kettle. Why not ask Doktor Lund, just casually when next she saw him? It happened quite often, he was often at the Klub.

This made her feel a little better; stilled her heart on the physical count but then there was the rest, and this was where it got tricky.

Charlotta took her breakfast roll outside and paced the furthest reaches of the garden dripping honey. Her roll proved a magnet for insects and so she jettisoned it in the lush green knee-high jungle that, later in the day, would fall to the rhythmic semi-circular sweep of Russo's scythe. Odd how insects could smell just the tiniest smear of butter, irritating too. Her hand trailed in the white-flowered syringa bush where the bees would come when the sun was up and the flowers had opened to its warmth. She must make sure to bring Berndt to see the bees busy working the bush. It was a fine sight. She had not told Oscar last night. Nor at breakfast either. How could she? It would be too complicated, stir up the things best left unstirred. The tale would make no sense if she left out the root cause: Gustav's *petites amies*. And if she referred to them, snik-snak. Floodgates. Charlotta's terror never fully seen, but only glimpsed, would have been put on the table between the two of them. Out in the full glare of sunlight. The sun would shine into that certain abyss so well camouflaged. That crack so well filled with pretty flowers would open up at their feet like in a fairy tale, and then there would be no end to their tumbling down down down to be swallowed up at the centre of the earth.

She regained the house quite planless and cross with herself for a fool, but as so often happens when you think it is entirely in your own hands to take control of what happens next, fate intervened. Or in this case the postman.

'Fru Katya Oscarsson requests the pleasure of Fru Charlotta Oscarsson's company to luncheon at Dronningen Yacht Klub, to celebrate the Regatta, etc.,' the polite formula in flowing and unflustered copperplate on thick, gilt-edged pasteboard beautifully engraved with the family O and the irritating eagle.

This, then, was Katya's response.

The Yacht Klub was neither a place to think, nor to have serious conversation. It was a place of dancing, smoking and, above all, gossiping. It hung like a waterfly on the wavery water far out into the harbour, seeming to float because the stilts that underpinned it were invisible, lost in the black reflections cast by the great amassment of Oslo's circling hills.

The Yacht Klub called Dronningen, meaning the queen, was named in honour of the non-sailing English-born Queen Maud and, despite her never coming here, it was very exclusive. It couldn't be reached except by means of a pier for foot passengers or a pontoon capable of holding a few motor-cars and moved across the waters by means of a launch or, in rough weather, the English chain-ferry drag principle. A few people were drowned on a regular basis through cars running straight down from the harbour, missing the pontoon and sinking into the deep, steadily emitting a stately flow of bubbles. It was worth it for the exclusivity. Dronningen was a place of elegant attire and soigné complexions. Once you actually managed to get out there, the octagonal building sticking out into the harbour was like no other place. Over the entrance crouched a bulgy stone Hercules brandishing a rock threateningly. In the course of time the rock dropped from the giant's grasp and Hercules himself fell down into the sea with a magnificent splash, which nobody saw or heard for it happened in the green flash just before dawn, when even the most hardened *ranglefanter* have left off the booze and gone to bed. Meanwhile, for these few years before his fall the giant Hercules enjoyed the status of a landmark, adding greatly to the glamour and importance of the place.

Charlotta proceeded along the wooden pier, taking no shame in her status as pedestrian, all unaware that even in this small thing she was adding to her general unpopularity and mystique. It was considered affected that she could afford a car but didn't use one.

She found no need to unglove her hand through all the three sailor-manned checkpoints. Fru Charlotta Oscarsson was recognised.

The 'Commodore', a nebulous character of tremendous social power with moustaches like antlers and a shark's smile, greeted her effusively: flowery compliments wafted on gin-swept breath. He bent to kiss the air above her hand and she was almost suffocated in the clouds of alcohol, unctuousness, and *eau de vetiver*. At his signal she was piped aboard, and found it more ridiculous than flattering.

Six broad stone steps led up to the entrance of the Klub, adding considerably to the impression of respectability and solidity, as well as to the weight carried by the undersea stanchions. The second step had some persistent insoluble structural problems; it would keep tumbling down again and again. It was the height of bad form to comment on it, or to step over it in an exaggerated fashion. To look down while negotiating the blank was to gaze into society's chasm: a merciless vertical drop into very cold, very deep sea.

Charlotta looked around. It was not possible to miss Katya in any room, not even a big one full of people like this. But then, Katya was always late: she should've known there'd be time to sit and think a little first. A quiet table somewhere. How funny these women were. So many of them wearing the same brooch made of little diamond chips. Fancy wanting to wear a brooch the same as everybody else. Maybe the Commodore was selling them as a sideline. Probably no diamonds at all. Oscar always said he was crooked as a ferret. Darling Oscar. Her beige-gloved hand travelled unconsciously to her heart with the pang of love she always felt when he

husband crept into her mind unexpected. Could she invite
Katya to live with them for a bit? Little Katya would be the
better for Berndt's good influence. The Tëtka would be part of
the package too – hmnn: Missy would be off in five minutes.
They were like two wild cats in each other's presence.

Fru Charlotta Oscarsson's face, which, the usual waiter had
noticed, had been uncharacteristically sombre today, was all of
a sudden lit by a tremendous smile, sun after cloud, as the
thought popped up in her mind wicked as a mushroom, that if
Katya and the dreadful Tëtka had to come to live with them
for a bit she might suppress the Tëtka with a little judicious
food poisoning. Nothing fatal, just constant low-level doses,
enough to keep her out of the way in bed. Such a greedy old
woman! How she remained thin as a rail while eating all the
time so voraciously and disgustingly like one who has escaped
a siege ... Oscar might rebel with all of that in the house. He
might move to the Fødselsøy with brother Gustav. That would
not be a good idea. Not good at all. Clouds moved back to cover
the sun. They were thicker this time.

How was she going to calm Katya?

How pretty it all was here. They would at least be in a
public place, though with Katya you could never preclude a
scene wherever you were. How light and airy, like on a ship,
everything wavery-quavery from the light of the waves
reflected in at the windows from all sides.

She held her hand out for the light to play on the shiny
glacé leather of her beige glove. How did they polish the
furniture so bright? Every one of the little round tables shone
lustrous as a grand piano. The napkins shone too, bright as
bright, tall damask domes with blue shadows in their folds
sitting up perkily on the shiny tables like the heads of so many
decapitated chefs. Maybe Katya might be sent up to her
parents at the Krigskjold Manor Farm. Why had she not
thought of it before? What a good place this was to think –
thank heaven Katya was late. Yes, that might easily be it. From
what she'd said of her homeland, one might assume that the
Russian estate was maybe not so different from the Krigskjold
Manor Farm. The rhythms of the country might soothe her.
Mama would be very good at showing Katya how behaviour is
done in this part of the world, without seeming to be rude or

nasty about it which Charlotta always felt she ended up being herself when she tried to correct her sister-in-law in a helpful way.

'Fru Charlotta Oscarsson! *God dag, god dag.* May I introduce you ...'

Casual visitors were admitted to the Yacht Klub so long as they were foreign and had signed their consulate's or embassy's book. This was a lady from Sweden, very smart, very rouged, a shipping man's wife whose introduction could not be disregarded in the greater scheme of Oscar's business life. Charlotta spent the next half-hour in fatuous compliments, refusing 'Shum-pagne' she did not want, and looking about her anxiously for the sister-in-law who never arrived, so that half an hour stretched to two whole hours of politeness over imported champagne, lobster *majones* served in a green glass bowl on cucumber salad, admittedly delicious, and a ridiculously decorated Napoleon's cake with coffee and cream. Interminable. Charlotta suffered the prolonged irritation of becoming amalgamated with the Swede's excruciating ostentatious lunch party.

Where was Katya? Where could she have got to? She, after all, was the one to have invited Charlotta to meet her and now she was not here.

She was a distracted guest, crumbling her bread, not paying attention properly, contributing further to her already formidable reputation for lofty superiority.

Where was Katya? So unlike her to miss this social parade.

Boum! The mini-cannon was fired.

All the glasses trembled on all the polished tables. Never had she greeted with such relief the moment of the start of the afternoon's regatta. The mass stutter of the glasses was the signal for a great swishing of skirts and scraping of chairs. Everybody jumped to their feet.

The women crowded to the balcony. The boats en *fête* were flying across the horizontal ribbing of the sea. Flags fluttered like flocks of birds. The air was brilliant.

'At last,' Charlotta disengaged her elbow from her new friend, 'the end of this infernal lunch.'

The first thing was to hurry to Gustav's house and see if Katya was there.

The Tëtka stood blocking the doorway with her black umbrella in the crook of her arm. The black bag was clasped with both hands,

'*Ils ne passeront pas*,' said the handbag.

The mistress was out.

'Zhopping.' The gloomy woman was deliberately vague.

Fractured English was the only language the two of them shared. It didn't help. 'Miss Katya buy.'

Was she at *torvet*, the market? Charlotta pointed her voice straight at the pink ear trumpet, and mimed fish.

Was she in Molstad, the glossy department store? Charlotta mimed big house, square windows.

When was she expected to return? Charlotta shook her pocket watch under the lanky dew-tipped nose.

The Tëtka merely stood, an unyielding line of rusty black, mind unbudging, tortoise-tongue cleaving to the wrinkled roof of the shrunken mouth. Then she shrugged, bored, and turned away on her dumpy battered heel.

'You are a bad old woman.' Charlotta let loose her frustration in Norwegian. 'You smell of pee and unwashedness.'

The suspicious old woman swivelled her head like a snake. She fixed Charlotta's eye with her own small dull orb in a bloodshot yellow. A long look passed between them: truth undisguised. The Tëtka was the first to turn away, swivelling her head like a tortoise and Charlotta, because evil thoughts of anyone were unpardonable, was overcome with remorse, a rush of shame and pity for the unattractive old creature. Poor old lady.

The poor old lady the while, entirely without conscience, was happy to leave her visitor ignored, dangling and foolish while she resumed her normal occupation: defending Katya's worldly goods from all comers, inspecting the domestic inventory with the super-critical eye of a general inspecting his troops, treading the domestic reaches of the carpet with all the purposeful intention of the Prussian soldier treading the field of Wissenbourg.

The old lady is like a ghost, thought Charlotta. She has so cut herself off from everyone in this world, except Katya, that she no longer belongs in any real physical space that doesn't hold Katya as well. The Tëtka without Katya is like a shadow without an originator. She shivered. Poor old woman.

The Tëtka's echo-like quality was particularly obvious in this highly coloured rather stuffy room, with its thick, rich, obscure atmosphere that did not need Katya's presence for her to be here. The languorous air was heavy with the fragrant memories: redolent of Balkan tobacco, the burning pastilles and Katya's favourite rather heavy, rather sweet violet scent. Everything was here but Katya, the originator. The shadow flitted about, checking the now-empty purple *chaise-longue* for the tiniest pulled thread, fluffball or wrinkle; picking up the silver ashtray and holding it up close to her gloomy nose to peer at it with her poorly sighted eyes for a trace that a parlourmaid had skimped on cleaning. Charlotta followed the old woman to the wall between the windows where swirled Gustavus Adolfus' gallant cavalry, or Napoleon's.

The pacing reached the baroque liver-coloured porphyry fireplace, and stopped. An amber velvet bellpull hung against the glowing red of the wall. The thick-knuckled arthritic hand grasped its golden tassels and pulled. Somewhere far away a bell gave a cheerful little sparkle of sound that picked up Charlotta's spirits for a moment. A maid appeared. The Tëtka made a rusty buzzing sound, as though a wasp had been caught in the back of her throat. The scared maid hovered by the buzzing aunt who, grim as Nemesis, pointed to a gloomy nook of the Doré engraving's heavily carved gilded frame. A fat summer fly lay dead in a hollow of the intricate frame. Nobody smiled or spoke. The black-uniformed maid disposed of the fly, and disappeared. The room was silent.

Charlotta used the silence to listen.

If Katya was here in the house, as she very much suspected she was, she'd hear her sister-in-law's cough, or her shout, or a staccato rush of footsteps, a slamming door, or a sudden burst of singing about the house. The air was silent but for the crying of a child. Somewhere about the house little Katya was crying unheeded; but otherwise the house was silent as this room. Her sister-in-law was not here, then. Charlotta was certain the old woman was dissembling in some way, but not one more word nor one scrap of attention was to be got out of her. She had triumphantly retreated into Russian incomprehension and was busy on a detailed domestic inspection: the fly might have brothers in the outer reaches. Chair skirts

were lifted, fringes sniffed for dirt; calloused yellow fingers
were run along skirting boards and held up to the close-
sighted eyes. Having apparently seen all she needed, the rigid
old lady turned her back and walked towards the door
without apology or valediction. At the door she cast Charlotta
an odd, flitting glance. The yellow-rimmed coffee-coloured
eyes were much too shiny. This glance disturbed Charlotta
more than anything else. It disturbed her so much that, being a
person whose instinct sometimes got the better of her manners,
she followed the stark black shadow through the door she had
taken rather than the polite door that would lead back to the
outside world. For the second time that day since entering the
Yacht Klub, Charlotta smiled her fresh, natural smile, the
smile that involved her entire being in the pleasure of the
moment. Wickedness! Her eyes sparkled as, silently, her feet
played a game of Grandmother's Footsteps behind the black
intent shape of the Tëtka.

What she would say if she was caught she'd no idea. 'Den tid,
den sorg' was one of Charlotta's pragmatic sayings: 'Sufficient
unto the moment the problems thereof.' The trail led through a
narrow long cold blue Gothic-papered passage, ornamented
with taxidermy and tegumentary relics of things Gustav had
killed here and there about the world: elk heads, furious
red-wattled capercaillie, record-breaking fish, each neatly
labelled in brass with its date and place of death and anything
else that made it interesting: mostly weights and dimensions.
Between the trophies hung greyish-brown photographs of
posed groups of men, all equally neatly captioned and cata-
logued. The men were at various occupations: shooting parties,
drinking clubs, fishing triumphs; men standing by cars, men
crossing ice-hockey sticks, men in plus-twos on mountain
peaks with skis in winter snows, or on the same mountains
with pickaxes and their eyes screwed up in summer glare.
Whatever the men were doing they had one thing in common:
the quality of the faces. They all shared the placid self-
congratulation of achievement.

Charlotta had never walked this passage of her brother-
in-law's house before: gentleman's ground. It did not take much
brainwork to deduce that it would lead to a trophy-infested
downstairs cloakroom with a high wooden water-closet

lavatory and a marble hand basin. Just such a passage and cloakroom had she in her own house. She seldom went there; never for pleasure, sometimes for domestic duty. It was Oscar's domain.

All the time they were walking, the wailing of the child was getting louder, the growing noise masking Charlotta's footsteps from her quarry. Little Katya must be stuck and unable to open the door. Charlotta cast a glance behind her, wondering if she could turn tail. It was very embarrassing to be following the Tëtka like a spy suspecting the worst when, in fact, the old Russian's earlier preoccupation had obviously been motivated by the desire to get rid of Charlotta as soon as possible in order to rescue the child from this small domestic incident.

The door at the end of the passage was of solid German oak. Typical. Nothing was skimped in either Oscarsson house, not even here in the furthest reaches of garçonnière. The child must have quite a voice to penetrate such a thickness of wood. The door furniture was of good brass and, as the Tëtka's knobbled hand grasped the handle, Charlotta caught up with her and snatched at her sleeve with some idea of apologising for her rudeness in playing this game of Grandmother's Footsteps just at the moment the Tëtka was flinging open the door. Charlotta was dragged half into the room along with the Tëtka's arm.

In the narrow wedge-shaped room on the high wooden seat sat little Katya in a most beautiful elaborate frilled and goffered silk checked dress. The beautifully dressed girl was strapped in a wooden superstructure that fitted on to the grown-up seat. Her legs were strapped into stirrups either side of the porcelain bowl and her arms wrapped round her body and strapped to the wooden backrest like a straitjacket. The dark-haired four-year-old was red-faced from bawling. The smell was terrible. She had obviously done her business some time ago and could do nothing but sit above the fetid stink, yowling for attention. Like a savage. Charlotta was profoundly shocked.

Missy would never allow Berndt to stay one minute in this household unsupervised. The practices in this household, Missy always said, were heathen, and Charlotta in her mind always had chuckled a little at the protective rivalry implied, but now she took it seriously. The Tëtka elbowed her away violently, shouting at her loudly. The shouts echoed and bounced about the passage and off the walls of the little room. Charlotta ran up the passage through the fury of noise, taking the quickest route out of the house, too engulfed in her own confused shame to desire anything but the quickest escape.

Once more in the street, Charlotta was surprised it was still daylight. She was exhausted, drained. It had been a lot of day.

A rainstorm she'd had no idea of had come and gone, clearing the heavy atmosphere. She lifted her skirt against the swift rivulets running down the unfinished edges of the road-makers' asphalt. A crowd of grey and white wagtails fluttered and twittered excitedly in and out of the rivulets, making little bobbing dashes to peck suddenly at the ants and insects who'd been surprised by the flood and were being borne down helpless, legs flailing.

How tired she was. The car, she thought wryly, would have been a blessing.

The shouting, she could not get over the shouting. Nobody shouted in Charlotta's house, ever. The savagery glimpsed through that chink in her sister-in-law's home life was ... She clutched her swooping heart.

Her progress along the route from Gustav's house to Oscar's was entirely uncharacteristic. In the low-life bit of Stranden, whose paint-peeling Hanseatic houses had a Siberian bleakness about them, a cripple crabwalked on his way. She was glad she wasn't going to have to encounter him. Then she was shamed at her gladness. This was against her upbringing. What was Oslo doing to her? Eroding her sense of duty? She crossed, gave alms, continued on her way.

What would she tell Oscar about today?

'God dag, Fru Oscarsson.'

Heavens! A workman. Was she home already?

She is the rudest old woman in the world. Charlotta saw herself flush in the mirror over the beautifully clean white porcelain basin where she had been washing her hands for five minutes, for the pleasure of the cool water and the cleanliness and the lovely faint smell of the almond soap washing away all the heavy smells that remained in her nose and her brain from Katya's house. When I find Katya I shall tell her it can't go on.

'God dag,' she replied distractedly, emerging from the downstairs cloakroom.

Only one thing could set her mind at rest: to be with her darling Berndt. She must go upstairs as quietly as a mouse so as not to wake her dearest boy. He would be having his nap now.

His little room was like a misty box. The strong sun had no difficulty penetrating the light summer curtains of spotted muslin. The top of the lilac tree was equal with this window, and the shadow of the leaves trembled against the milky muslin, their fleeting shape projected again on the green-painted floorboards. Berndt loved his bed. Missy said it was exceptional in a child, and a great symptom of goodness. The echo of angels still hung about him, Missy said, from the Place he had come from. He'd a way of smiling when he climbed into bed and falling asleep as soon as his head met his pillow. The room was quiet. Only his rounded arm projected from the motionless covers: pink from the hours on the beach, and dusted with golden down. She bent towards the child, hardly breathing so as not to interfere between him and his peace. A rush of love pierced her heart. In the crease of his neck the fine white hair clung damply behind the delicate curl of the ear. His breath came in shallow sighs through slightly parted lips. The skin on his face was quite white, not burned. Missy could always be relied on for hats and good sense.

She'd been searching for a word ever since she'd left Gustav's house and now it popped into her mind of its own accord: 'victory'. The Tëtka had been celebrating some obscure victory.

So?

This finding of the word neither explained nor helped as she'd expected it to. Nor, any more, did it seem so all-important. Today she'd fallen victim to another of Katya's dramas, another of her stupid brouhahas.

Berndt stirred and shifted into the position that made his face an echo of his father. Charlotta straightened up, made the sign of the Cross over her sleeping son and tiptoed out, but her mind was not as settled as she would have liked. Still she saw the picture of the little girl in her beautiful expensive dress, sitting imprisoned on the awful stinking lavatory contraption. The picture had not been chased out by the happier picture of sweet Berndt in his bed; it would not leave her mind as she went downstairs and, at her passing, the curtains shuddered as if they, too, felt sorry for the girl.

Well, thought the workmen, noting Fru Oscarsson's lack of cheer today, every wife has her time of the month, and carried on with their work.

CHAPTER FIVE

Where was Katya?

After the scene with Charlotta Katya had been unbearably hurt.

'But where can you go? There is nowhere.' Charlotta's blunt words. Nowhere, nothing, nobody. A howling darkness. The quiet car slid up the drive to Gustav's house, stopped. Nobody emerged. The Tëtka, peering through the fogged-up windows, was terrified to see her beautiful, elegant, vibrant darling still as a spectre, slumped in the corner like rags. More unreasonable and bullying than ever in her fright, the furious Tëtka arranged for the precious body to be carried up the marmoreal staircase like a corpse on a bier and now she lay high in the house on flesh-coloured satin pillows in the ivory-painted Empire *lit au bateau*. About her trembling body she clutched theatrically at a huge shawl of violet Chinese silk embroidered with carmine paeonies and viridian parrots. There she lay, a febrile hectically coloured sphinx with enigmatic face turned towards the window caged in by its little balcony. Between the white balustrading Oslo's northern sea was a dull grey wash. There had been balustrading before, a palm tree and water of quite a different colour, promising such brilliance ... ah! But Riva del Garda, that was a world away.

She scarcely moved except to smoke cigarette after cigarette while her whole being assimilated the afternoon's humiliation, narrowing her eyes against the smoke. When she had finished one cigarette she stubbed the golden lipstick-stained end into a silver scallop shell and raised her nervous hand to the velvet bellpull, the shawl falling back from her sharp bare elbows with the motion. The Tëtka must be waiting close at hand, for she appeared almost before the bell stopped pealing, to take away the scallop shell, empty it, and bring it back, shining. The old woman performed this service wordlessly, looking happy for once, and almost normal.

Several hours passed in this way. Twilight fell. Darkness fell. Katya waved away all suggestion of light. The old woman needed no light to see her way round Katya's room, she knew it like her own body.

On the last of the old woman's appearances, Katya interrupted the large-knuckled hand on its journey across the monogrammed satin quilt towards the shell. Putting her own hand out, the slim fingers picked up the ugly tortoise-skinned hand and pressed it to her lips. 'Thank you, darling,' she said in her hoarse voice. 'I shall get up now.'

The Tëtka's blood prickled with tension. What was the dear darling doing, getting up after ten o'clock at night? And so tired. You could see it in the two shadowed crescents in the tender skin beneath her darling's beautiful eyes; like two mussel shells they were, so dark a blue. It would be better for her to stay in bed and calm herself with the drops. Her drops would be better, and then a good long sleep. A compress on those bruised eyes. Cotton pads infused in camomile. There was nothing better to restore the beauty of the skin. Except live cucumber, of course, sliced and applied direct to the flesh beneath the eye. But the lazy cook in this slack Norwegian house never bothered to keep it on hand. Stupid vile cook just pretended not to understand and sliced the cucumber up with dill for salad. Salad! When her darling needed it for her beautiful skin. Tëtka ground her gums.

'Oh, don't look cross,' Katya coaxed. 'We are going to have the most wonderful adventure. Now, straight away! You must dress me, and I shall quickly write a letter while you are preparing our outerwear, and then you must come with me down to the docks for some fun.'

Sitting at the dressing-table and stubbing out a last gold-tipped cigarette she laughed as she wrote that stupendously elegant invitation to her sister-in-law. She'd no intention of keeping the lunch date with the dreary mouse-haired sister-in-law but it'd buy time. Such a clever smokescreen! It would buy the time she needed.

In the triple mirror, three Tëtkas brushed three full heads of rippling blue-black hair.

'Now pile it close up like that and pull the hat right down, so. How ugly I look. All the better. Nobody must imagine who I am. No, not the furs. Come on! Come on! We're going down to the harbour now this instant.'

The usual cosmopolitan crowd milled in the busy harbour. It was well after eleven o'clock by the time they got down there but dock-business didn't watch the clock: day or night was immaterial at the sharp end of Norway. Chains clanked, fenders bumped. A great deal of smoke added to the tumult and confusion: oil smoke from a thousand ships' funnels; charcoal smoke from many oil drums converted by entrepreneurial trawlermen into braziers to cook and sell the day's catch of shrimp; petrol smoke from the high-sided primitive lorries fetching goods from warehouses and dropping them in loading bays. Everywhere, running porters moved goods on long-based trolleys and barrows. Piled bales grew ever higher on the wharves. No sooner had a bale mountain been built than a team of porters fixed hooks from dangling crane chains and the whole thing was whizzed into the air to be deposited in a ship's hold. The sudden swinging of the load into the air would scatter whole sections of crowd in antlike rushes. No sooner had the ants rushed than the porters would run in to build the next mountain in the cleared space. Katya's eyes shone. She'd absorbed enough Oscarsson during her marriage that her heart never failed to give a jump when she saw an ocean-going ship loaded up, swung round by a tug, and the pilot-boat take the lead in beginning its long brave journey across all the blue water in the world.

Flirting with discovery she dawdled deliberately past the modern handsome Oscarsson quay with its blue and green funnels painted with the white eternal O. The Tëtka, who avoided these docks with their message so plain and undisguised that Oscarsson had complete power and control over her own and Katya's world, became deeply disturbed at the familiar symbols and made the sign of the evil eye against the ubiquitous O: 'Thou, Oscarsson, seest me.' She started into the faster ticking, that of the guinea-fowl facing down the rat. Katya, smiling knowingly, responded by drawing up her shawl

into a dramatic incognito; only her elongated eyes showed over
the woollen edge, like a houri or an odalisque. In fact, she need
not have bothered. Anyone with leisure to spare was not going
to be ogling passing talent when there was far more fun to be
had in laying bets on the spirited contest nearby between a
huge ghost-white fighting drunk and the truncheons of the
harbour police.

The two women had to push hard to open the door of the
seedy booking office, a place no less crowded than the quays
outside. In a thick atmosphere a slithering crowd pushed and
thrust forward to bombard the hard-pressed manager and his
staff. The Tëtka's sharp elbow-work brought the two of them
to the head of the queue before their time. Inquiries were
made. Money changed hands.

Head high, humming, Katya led the old woman out of the
mêlée of the booking office and back through the busy port
area, her face naked for all to see. The sickly pallor of her bed
was gone. Two burning spots now blazed on her cheeks, lit by
all this energising disreputable life. She cast regretful glances
at the waterside bars and nightclubs.

Quitting the port the two women passed like shadows
through the thick network of narrow streets where the real
business of the city was done, and out into the spacious no
man's land that led into the residential area, the lower reaches
of Oslo's hills, at this hour an infinite bowl. The pastel houses
made flat, lilac-hued squares between steep black firs whose
tops melted into the inky sky.

The next two days were calm, featureless, an oasis of time-
lessness passed in a meaningless space that Katya in her mind
had already left. She spent the days preparing her material
goods and the evenings much as usual dazzling her coterie of
friends. Finally came the evening before the Yacht Klub lunch
at Dronningen. Katya dressed very carefully in her most
beautiful, most Romanov costume. The bodice was of more
pearls than silk. The red skirt, belling out like a triangle from
her waist, was heavily embroidered in the traditional folk
fashion with animals and flowers snaking round leaves of gold
thread. Tiny circles of mirror were set into the fabric, reflecting the light from the candles and the oil lamps in the house.
When she moved through the dim-lit interior her skirt was

like the shower of a comet's tail. Her purple-shadowed hair mingled with the darkness of the house.

'Katya,' she called in the little loft where her child was sleeping. 'Katya.' She shook the child's thin shoulder.

The daughter was as dark as her mother. Her hair was as naturally curly, but every night before she was put to bed each individual lock was wrapped in curl-rags under the exacting supervision of the Tëtka who, at the same time, made sure that the maid tied a secure double knot in the cotton mittens on the girl's hands: a knot that could only be made tighter if the girl pulled at it with her teeth. Each day two new mittens were impregnated with a mixture of lanolin and lemon juice: when the Russian court was restored the girl would take up her place with the soft white hands of the true-born Rus' aristocrat.

'Katya, darling.' The mother covered the sleeping girl in a shower of kisses. True to fairy tale, the little princess woke.

Oh! The beautifulness of Mama!

One moth-white stump of a mittened hand reached clumsily to touch the tiny sparks of mirror alight in the magic skirt.

'Listen, my darling.' Katya put the bronze candelabra down on the floor. Its golden flame glowed in each embroidered pearl. She sat on the white-painted chair beside the narrow cot, stroking her child's soft cheek. 'Something has happened. I have to leave you for a little while. It will not be for long. But I have to go away and I cannot take you with me.'

The girl started to cry.

'You must not cry. You must listen. This is very important. The most important thing I have ever said to you.'

The girl stopped crying. Katya rewarded her with a kiss and stopped her mouth with a rose cachou.

'Now I am talking to you as a grown-up, so you must listen as a grown-up. Katya darling, you are my love, my life. You are everything, my darling. We must never be parted. We must hold each other tight. But first we must be apart for a little time. Something has happened that means I have to go away now. But I will be back to fetch you. I will come when you least expect me! When you have given up altogether! When the violets bloom again in the spring I will come walking towards you out of the shadows through the fragrant twilight and we will live together for ever. For ever in each other's arms. Whatever happens, they won't keep us apart. You understand? Never, never apart. Oh, we will be so happy together, it is all going to be so lovely, my darling, so very lovely.'

Anticipating this vision of eternal joy she threw her head back. Her long hair tickled the girl's neck above the frill of the nightgown. Little Katya laughed, and in a minute they were both laughing, covering one another in showers of kisses. Not far away the vigilant Tëtka (who was as deaf as it suited her to be) heard the burst of unwonted noise from the girl's room. Her grey plait tightly coiled, her black silk dressing-gown tightly belted, she glided along the passage to the doorway of the girl's room. Unseen, she took up position in an amethyst shadow at the threshold of the glowingly lit room.

'Just you and me together, darling. No Oscarssons. Katya, my life, my heart, you must not trust the Oscarssons. Do you understand? It is very important. They are a shameful, perfidious family. They have no honour. Your poor mama came to them defenceless, all alone. All my own family had been murdered by butchers and I had no one but the Oscarssons to protect me. But they betrayed me. Do you understand? I was shamefully betrayed.'

Tears of self-pity trembled on her eyelashes.

'They smile, these Oscarssons, and seem so good – your *tante* Charlotta, oh, so godly! But there is no good in them, only evil and unhappiness. I would not have the same future for my precious little girl. This is why I must leave you now. To make a new life for us both. How would you like to live in America? Hey, Katya? You'd look so sweet in a little Red Indian costume with a feather in your hair.'

She tweaked at Katya's hair and a curl-rag came out in her hand. The two of them laughed in a wicked conspiracy against authority. Mother and daughter against the world. But the laughter soon turned back to tears in the mother's throat as she returned to her own personal tragedy.

'There is no honour for me in staying here, only shame. While you are waiting for me to rescue you from Oslo and from the Oscarssons you must be true to me, my darling. Only by being true to me you will be true to yourself. Do you understand, my darling?'

The child nodded.

'Will you be true to your mama?'

'True.' The word started strong in the child's mouth, then flickered as Mama, beautiful Mama, was taking her arms away from around her and starting to get up from the bed to leave.

'Mama! Mama!' she screamed.

The black shadow crossed the room and the old dry creaking woman wordlessly replaced the scented, sensuous jewelled beauty, as though this had been prearranged. The girl struggled, a ghost-grey moth in the imprisoning arms of the Tëtka's unyielding blackness. Katya bent gracefully to pick up the candelabra from the floor, her skirt a brilliant shower, a flicker, a dazzle. By the candles' tremulous light she cast a sorrowful glance behind her at the struggling girl. Over the Tëtka's bony shoulder the two stumpy mittens flailed, pleading to be taken up into her mother's arms.

'It is for the best,' Katya said, from the door. The tears still sparkled in the candlelight but her voice was quite different, lighter in tone and unencumbered, as if it had moved ahead into this new, optimistic beginning, and was already existing there. 'Soon. Soon. You'll see.'

Little Katya did not hear her mother's parting words, her own head was so full of splitting and splinters and the world being torn in two. She vomited over the old woman who took no notice but held on fast. Aeons of crying led to paroxysms of hiccups shaking the little body. Her ears were full of the sound of her own fast-chattering teeth. A long time after Mama had passed out of the room, her moth-coloured mittened fists continued to flail, fighting the insubstantial air like the boxer forever fighting shadows; but however much the child cried and shuddered and screamed it made no difference to the pressure of the unyielding black bands round her impetuous jerking body. The bands stayed steadily at the same hardness and strength. This was a contest that might go on for ever.

Downstairs the mother continued her rapid and secretive departure. Gustav was meant to be away but you never knew when he would return. Besides, it would be better if the servants didn't hear her: let them think she'd spent the night in the house. Before she started to cross the marble-floored hall she bent to slip on the thick fluffy felt overshoes to muffle the sharp sound made by the Louis-heeled Ferragamo ankle boots. Even as she covered them up she was admiring the lovely oval pointed toes of her runaway shoes. She'd taken great care. One didn't walk into a new life wearing just any old shoes.

The Tëtka had ordered the cab to wait round the corner at the junction with Oscarsgate. It meant a bit of a walk and she was tired. Oh, how tired she was. Already she missed the Tëtka at her elbow with her cigarettes, her shawl, her drops in their brown-glass bottle.

'The little girl must come and live with us,' Charlotta said decidedly, following her instinct and duty before she had even given it a thought. 'She can be like a little sister to Berndt. And we must say that Katya has gone to visit her family in America. It was an American boat? You're certain of that?'

'I employed a detective,' Oscar said drily.

'America is good. Everybody has family in America now. They will think nothing of it if only your brother can be made to behave.'

Charlotta thought this was a big 'if only'.

'Is it true that Gustav when he heard she had left him played Russian roulette holding his revolver to his head and a naked negress on his lap in the middle of that *nattklub* like they are saying?'

Oscar went as red as turkeycock. His wife was not even supposed to know the word *nattklub* let alone ...

'Hardly naked.'

'Well, that's something. Poor negress. Didn't Gustav stop to think for a minute what would have happened if the bullet had been in the chamber? She would have been covered in gore and so frightened. I have a mind to go down there and apologise to her myself.'

'She's gone. I paid her passage on the next boat straight away. She will be on her way to Havana.'

'And did you say sorry? Did you give her any money to send her on her way?'

'No to the first. You'd hardly expect an Oscarsson to apologise ...'

'That's true.'

'Yes to the second.' He humoured Charlotta. The lissom mulatto would hardly need money from him, with so many males on the passenger list. He'd been generous enough in shelling out on a second-class berth for the girl. A lot of people would have put her in steerage. A lot of people would have put her in the harbour.

'Poor child. What a life.' Charlotta shook her head. 'What an unimaginable life.' The demi-monde held no romantic lure for Charlotta.

The married couple were out walking.

In order to hold an entirely confidential workman-free conversation they had to leave the house and go outside. Charlotta at first had wanted to include Missy and little Berndt on this rare outing with Papa. It would so have gladdened Berndt's little heart to go for a walking expedition with both his parents, but Oscar said, 'You know how the boy darts about. Worse than a damn gnat. He'd be round our legs and back again in no time. Hardly helpful when we've serious things to discuss and decisions to take. Missy's no better. Whirls about after him like an attendant dervish. Not restful. What might whirling Missy overhear, hey? Have you thought of that, Charlotta mine?'

Charlotta yielded to his sense, but a little piece of her walked with regret. A hand trailed empty at her side just as it always had since Berndt had taken his first tottering steps. The hand was always free and available just in case he should materialise suddenly out of thin air, wanting reassurance in this great world.

'We'll go for a walk down to the Akershus castle,' Oscar said.

There was an old castle and a new palace; both built to serve the same purpose, both very different in spirit. The old castle, that had never been taken in siege, signified War. The new pretty yellow rococo palace at the top of the hill (where Charlotta did her duty as hoffdame) signified Peace, stability and civilisation. The new palace was a statement in stone that rape, pillage and berserking were now officially a thing of the past.

Spiritually and mentally Oscar belonged altogether in the old castle, but this wasn't the reason he liked to go there on the rare occasions he felt moved to take a walk. The old castle was sited, logically enough, where it had the very best vantage-point over the harbour. Oscar's ships were in the harbour. Ergo, a walk was not altogether unproductive. It could be combined with keeping an eye. Business was never very far from Oscar's mind.

The old castle was a substantial dilapidation whose more complete sections had the monumental scale and flavour of Windsor Castle. This pleasingly picturesque ruin occupied a large elevated site to the east of the port. Curtain walls the height of hills. Towers and keeps commanding every aspect of the sea approach so that the archers and catapulters could kill in all directions. Fearless seagulls threaded the bastion-lookouts towering over the crashing sea far below.

Within the impressive castle walls was a medieval town, of smaller and neater tower dwellings between which stretched lawns edged with eighteenth-century rustic work and melancholy ivy. It was not easy walking: Charlotta's buttoned boots were continually being stubbed on the illogical stretches of cobbles hidden among the greenery. The cobbles had once all connected in a road, but it had been looted down the centuries for making other things. From time to time in the castle's long history the hefty granite cobbles saw sterling service as catapult-ballast against pirates and invaders foolish enough to come up the Oslofjord. Why, the year before Katya had come into their lives, in the summer of 1916 during Norway's worst crisis of the last war, Norwegian Foreign Minister Ihlen, dining with his German counterpart, had pointed out in jocular fashion how much damage these flying stones might inflict on, say, the modern Zeppelin or, for sake of argument, any submarine mad enough to surface in Oslo's harbour. The politicians had been sharing an excellent dinner laid out in the keep of the old castle, the German legation sitting quite informally with their home-team counterparts at long trestled tables on which white damask, starched to within an inch of its life, blazed against the greensward of the keep. Perfectly synchronised naval ratings in beautiful mess jackets served silvery herring with black peppercorns, fat pink crayfish with feathery springs of dill and lemon, elk in burnt cream and cranberry, and pyramids of glistening raspberries accompanying huge towers of almond ringcake decorated with sparklers,

crackers and numerous Norwegian flags. Despite the tricky
political moment, with Norway's neutrality threatened by
imminent invasion, the dinner had been held in a thoroughly
gemütlich spirit. Over the broken remains of ringcake and
aquavit a bet had arisen, causing Foreign Minister Ihlen to
signal to the corps of buttling naval ratings. To a man the svelte
stewards were transformed into an army of berserkers tearing
up the cobbles and giving a very efficient demonstration
indeed of the ancient catapult. The cobbles flew high and fast
and far. In no time at all an Oscarsson cargo ship, which
happened to be moored within the target area, was smashed
and sunk.

It had been Oscar's idea. He'd doctored the ship and moored
it accordingly. The setpiece had played its part in the German
decision to continue to respect Norway's neutrality. The little
trick had done Oscar no harm, either, in the matter of
government contracts.

Oscar's blue eyes sparkled with pleasure at the memory.
He'd tell young Berndt about it one day. He'd not even dream
of telling Charlotta. Not woman's business. These cobbles
weren't for women's shoes, either. Charlotta kept stumbling. He
grasped her arm more firmly. His own brown pigskin brogues
had been made for him by Lobb in London where his feet lay
in wooden effigy, but his stockings had been knitted for him by
Charlotta from wool of the Krigskjold flock. He wore a
knickerbocker suit of English tweed with a Norfolk jacket for
this almost rural outing. Just as he enjoyed creating a certain
impression with his house, so he enjoyed painting a certain
picture of himself, both as a solo operator, and as the leading
edge of a married couple. He seldom gave any thought to the
gratification his wife afforded him by her uninterrupted maintenance of dignity, good conduct and, yes, that was the word:
suitability. But Katya's recent behaviour brought the point
forcefully to mind. The grey costume suited his little wife
admirably. Katya had certainly never worn grey. He'd go to
Georg Jensen, get her for the first time something in diamonds.
Yes.

He patted her small gloved hand resting so trustingly on his
tweed forearm. Pretty grey gloves, buttoned neatly with pearls.
She was always *comme il faut*. Squeezing her arm he smiled

down and she looked up into his face where the sun was tangled in his golden lashes, just like his boy. Oh, when would they have another child? She'd lie down right here on the grass with him, here, now, she longed for him so.

His return look was altogether more marital, less hectic. His was full of appreciation. He admired and revered. What other woman, wife, mother, had the absolutely clear bluish-white of untarnished virtue to her eye? My God, that Katya. Wild eyes, he'd noticed it straight away; he'd not have bought a horse with those eyes let alone a woman. Not the sort of woman you married. Not that he'd ever asked Gustav why. Not a tactful question in the face of a *fait accompli*. Gustav had told him anyway, in the Klub. Said he simply couldn't resist finding out if she was as volcanic in bed as she had promised to be. Hmmn. If only Oscar had been with him in Garda. There were cheaper ways of finding out than marriage. And now they had to pick up the pieces of this glorious affair; to dress it up in respectable clothes.

'Well, at least she did not run away with a man,' said Charlotta. 'Your detective ascertained so much.'

The Pinkerton's man had been expensive; fair enough, he'd done a good job. Oscar had telegraphed a sizeable *douceur* to the purser shore-to-ship. A flow of information had been the result. Certainly Katya had *boarded* solo, but it was obvious she'd lost no time in gaining admirers. The tango on the first night had seen to that. By the time the ship reached its first stop, Hawaii, it'd be anybody's guess whether she'd be leaving the ship on the arm of the Dominican sugar magnate, the elderly ex-Governor of Madras, or the slim-hipped Argentinian of invisible means and dappled, dubious past career. All bets were on.

That *fordømmet* brown-glass bottle Katya was always taking drops from. He'd always distrusted it. His blood had revolted at seeing it in his pure wife's angel hands. How many times'd he thought of having the contents analysed? Never bothered. No point. What good would it do? Opium? Morphine? What was the point of giving it a name? Well, the harlot was gone and Charlotta none the wiser: that was the important thing; Charlotta's pure innocence had been shielded. His darling Charlotta was right about Gustav, as she was right about so many things. Gustav must be got out of the way until his destructive frenzy passed. Oscar had an idea this would not pass lightly with his brother, or easily, or quickly. Nor without scandal. That had started already (how on earth had Charlotta heard about the negress in the nightclub?); be that as it may, in her sensible way she was not to be distracted from seeing straight to the heart of things. The family position might yet be recovered if Gustav could only be parked out of the way for a time.

A brief mission to the States? Oscar mused. The name of Oscarsson was not without commercial clout in the New York business community. It was a name to add credible mailed-fist support to Nansen's mission now negotiating the agreement for the importation of foodstuffs to blockaded Norway. Foreign Minister Ihlen could be leaned upon; the debt could be called in. Good God! What was he thinking of? The States? With Katya on her way there by boat? The negress too! Though renewal of *that* acquaintance was unlikely. Still, the most unlikely thing was very often the one that happened.

Think again, Oscar, think again.

The Arctic. That was not so stupid. It was certainly well out of the way. When this war stopped, Spitzbergen and Bear Island, both such vital pawns in the international game, would be up for grabs. Yes, the Arctic could certainly be presented to Gustav as a credible theatre for his abilities. In many ways a useful place to build up a shipping presence. Besides – Oscar chuckled deep in his throat – they said the everlasting *fordømmet* cold imposed a degree of moderation in certain departments.

Charlotta's face brightened. Something had turned Oscar to good humour. He laughed. His bright eye gleamed down at her, full of mischief. Her heart rose. She smiled cautiously up at him, hoping. He gave her his arm to help her mount the last steep bank high on the top above the harbour among the salt winds that blew in over the ramparts, and when they gained the top she stumbled in the force of the wind. Her body exaggerated what had begun as a small stumble, taking her further than she needed. She ran up hard against the body of her husband. Would he be shocked if here, now, she should be the one to initiate the delicious uncontrollable flutter, the absolute abandonment of a kiss? Blushing she looked up into his face in apology and appeal. He stepped back quickly and correctly, and raised her hand to within a centimetre of his lips. The very ends of his virile moustache came courteously in controlled contact with her dove-grey glove. Her equilibrium was recovered, and he none the wiser. His upper body straightening, he turned the necessary degrees so as to get his shipping fleet under his eyes.

'The little girl cannot continue in her father's household,' she said, resigned. This, then, this boat inspection, had been the purpose of the walk, after all. Oscar's back was turned. 'It's not a suitable place for our niece now Gustav is...' behaving like a bachelor she wanted to say.

'I know.'

'We will have to take in the Tëtka too.'

'What? The filthy old thing with lichen behind her ears? The servants will resign to a man.'

'It's not lichen, it's a deaf-aid. Missy can teach her to wash it more often.'

'It's lichen, I tell you. Haven't you seen? Her ears are like oak boles, all gnarled and grey. Revolting. We'll take the Tëtka if I never have to see her. Particularly not at breakfast. I say, isn't the *Maud* looking handsome? The refit was worth the money. What do you think? You've long eyes. Is that "Oscarsson" on the stern in the usual size of lettering? It seems to be a trifle smaller. Just five centimetres or so. But five centimetres of gold leaf is a few hundred kroner, I can tell you.'

'It looks perfectly beautiful to me.' Her voice sounded depressed.

'You're certain? I can't afford to be hoodwinked. The minute they think they can get away with it they're off with the spoons before you can say knife.'

'I think it looks just the same size as all the others. Now, Oscar, I need an answer. May I take the little girl into our household to be brought up as a sister to Berndt?'

'Do as you will. Whatever you decide will be right. You know that in domestic matters I rely totally on your judgement.'

She longed to be neither right nor reliable, nor domestic.

'I'll just nip down,' he continued, his eyes with the sea, 'I've ... yes!'

His hand had been roving around the much-pocketed Norfolk jacket, dipping in here and there like a detective looking for clues. Now it emerged with a folding rule. The irritation in his face was replaced by peace.

'I might just go down and measure the size of that lettering. Just to make sure. I'd hate old Kvaerner to think he can get the better of me. Charlotta, darling, why don't you take a cup of coffee?' He gestured with the folding rule to the greensward below them where a refreshment room was salubriously sited among the lawns. Green slatted metal chairs were grouped around circular green-painted tables. Some few respectable bodies could be seen parked on the chairs, taking tea, innocuous ices and harmless drinks.

'I shall send the car up to collect you as soon as I get down to the quay. Don't budge.' And he was gone.

Charlotta descended to the place of green chairs and long-skirted waitresses, to the place that in the next war to come would be the site of execution, where SS troops would march up and down in steel helmets keeping guard on their Norwegian prisoners, among them her golden son, who was to spend two long, tragic years in this place deprived of light so that when he emerged he was blind as a mole and his soul worse damaged than his eyesight. In this place there is now the well-organised museum of the Germans' occupation of Norway in the Second World War, and also a hyper-efficient self-service cafeteria, but this was long before the concept of self-service. A waiter came in a black tail-coat and Charlotta asked for coffee and didn't budge but sat preoccupied in a blur of nonsensical fragmented thoughts, failing to acknowledge the respectful salutations of the odd semi-acquaintance who passed as they always pass if you live in a small town such as Oslo. Was this the only way she would get a daughter? To be a cuckoo-mother, take over Katya's child?

The blunt-nosed car was snailing through the gate.

If only, she rose sighing, one could be as igniting as Katya but not such a fire-raiser as to burn the house down.

CHAPTER SIX

'... there is nothing on the stage but a solitary infant, and its solitary combat with grief – a mighty darkness, and a sorrow without a voice.'

de Quincey. preface to Autobiographical Sketches (1853)

Little Berndt danced at the thought of welcoming a new sister to live with him in the house. 'And shall we always eat together? Always?'

'Yes, yes.' It wasn't so miraculous as all that. 'Stand properly now.' What was this? A little stab of jealousy about his excitement? Already?

'Breakfast too?'

'Yes, yes.'

The boy was thoroughly overwrought. For two nights now he had been subject to dreams that obviously disturbed him and which continued to bear all the semblance of reality even after he had been woken. Missy muttered darkly about the little orphan girl's arrival 'boding no good'. Charlotta felt a strong impulse to shake the uncharitable superstition out of her narrow English soul.

'My niece is not a little orphan girl. Her mother has merely gone away for a short period of time. And as to the arrival of an innocent child boding no good! You should be ashamed to say such words in front of Berndt. You should examine your Christian conscience.'

Missy sulked.

The last day of waiting for Katya to arrive was endless. Berndt was restless as a dog with fleas. How would they pass the time? Charlotta hit upon a notion. 'But we have no flowers for her! Berndt, my darling, we must go picking.'

Charlotta excluded Missy from the expedition as a punishment for all that Norn-like gloom and prophecy.

Russo, the dog-like Russian bodyguard, couldn't be evaded. He put on his fiercest frown to accompany his mistress, and brandished his pistol extravagantly at the slightest shadow, grinning madly the while with his steel teeth.

In fact, Charlotta realised ruefully before she'd even left the house, it'd all have been a great deal easier and more enjoyable with Missy along as well. She always contributed greatly to oiling the wheels. If Missy had been here, the giant's hands would've been full of knitting and whatsits, and Charlotta wouldn't be going in fear of her life from the simple giant's random exuberance.

The walk at least served to calm Berndt. They took the third road, not the busy one leading down to the harbour, nor the majestic one leading up to the yellow place, but the road that wound back on itself and turned, surprisingly quickly, back into rural Norway. Paving soon ran out; asphalt became beige flying dust. They passed a row of log huts, a church with a white spire, kitchen gardens, bath-houses, rickety animal sheds with turfed roofs and big round stones weighting down the chimney slates. Berndt pointed at a goat standing atop a turf-roofed stable, grazing away. They laughed and hugged. Russo gave a belly-laugh of pure joy. The road passed on through burgeoning crops, pastureland. Further on, a girl with a stick was driving a herd to milk: dun-coloured cows ambling up the dusty road, heavy udders swinging from side to side. The boy ran delightedly backwards and forwards between the cows' muddy backsides and Charlotta's skirt in a wild chuckling intoxication of happiness.

At a grassy hillock crested with birch she said, 'This way,' and they turned off into a larch wood she knew because she would pick berries here every autumn since coming to Oslo. The forest floor was thick with fallen fir needles the colour of old hay; a place of rotting tree trunks and moss-covered boulders. Here and there a tangle of bramble and honeysuckle and convolvulus wound round the white stems of the birch.

The bilberries and cranberries wouldn't be ripe for her to pick till August, and then the wood would be busy with Oslodwellers, a lot of mothers and children among them. Charlotta wasn't the only one to have discovered the delightful wood. She came here with Berndt to fill his *spann*. Next berry season she would, she supposed, bring little Katya too. It would be her last time alone with Berndt. Just now there was nobody else. The fruit-bearing bushes showed only their unremarkable greenish white inflorescences. A little pollen dust drifted on the wind.

She pulled up a liquorice fern from a mossy stump, cleaned the long black root on her handkerchief and gave it to the boy to suck. The Russian giant looked longingly; she cleaned a second for him and instructed him by signs to gather up as many fir-cones as he possibly could. He called her Matrushka, little mother. Tears filled his eyes. The liquorice root... he too in the dim depths... His memory dredged out far-distant days of childhood, long days as a child on a country estate where just such woods grew just such flowers and he was the free-range son of two domestic serfs. He did a thing he hadn't done for years. He made the sign of the Cross over Charlotta, knelt for her blessing, and when he had received it, went off hunting, happy as anything. Every now and then she jumped out of her skin at a burst of his roaring chuckle exploding through the woods as he came on an extra fat fine fir-cone, or the revolver's crack as he spied squirrels darting up and down tree trunks like mercury, and as difficult to hit.

Taking advantage of his mother's softer regime, Berndt was eating as much as he was picking: the salt liquorice root, the sour leaves of the *bittekonvall* wood sorrel that made his mouth curl, the sweet drop of honey at the base of the pink clover.

For Katya's bouquet he found wild strawberry flowers, windflowers like white stars against the dusky floor of the wood, and the almost-formed half-flower half-berry of the cranberry. He was just stretching out his hand to pick a fine blue harebell but Charlotta pulled him back: the flower was growing at the base of one of the huge antheaps that occurred here and there in the forest, great mounds of fir needles, taller than Berndt himself and alive with fast sharp black ants whose sting was like fire. He cried a little then, but she consoled him, explaining that the harebell was a field flower gone astray; they'd be able to pick plenty of harebells from the verges as they went home.

Russo took Berndt on his shoulders, trotting home. They reminded her of two puppies, playing.

Wrong of her to dread the new child. She did not believe in fate and nixies. Such things were for mountain people. At home at the Krigskjold Manor Farm (she must stop thinking of it as home) the people would have shaken their heads in astonishment at the foolishness of anybody purposely letting into their home such obvious doom as Katya's child.

But she was not like that. The Christian Church and Charlotta's own soul would consign her own self to everlasting perdition should she fail in this, her obvious duty.

She crossed herself while nobody could see. Berndt and the Russian had gone ahead; Berndt jiggling on the Russian's shoulders and Russo lolloping clumsy as a carthorse.

If there is anything to carry, she crossed herself, let it fall on me, not on the child.

By the time Katya arrived they were almost worn out with waiting. Missy had made tea, laid with the extra place, and removed it again. Berndt had had the quickest bath of his life, followed by an hour of grizzling nothingness shifting from foot to foot. Then he ate the quickest supper of his life so he should not be caught inhospitably eating at table when she arrived. Books and stories were started, toys and games attempted and abandoned, concentration being impossible in the flitter of anticipation.

Would she never come? Charlotta was irrationally reminded of the waiting for the mother at Dronningen Yacht Klub.

Furry little clouds were scudding in the last light of the sky, rippling by reflection on the green-painted floorboards of the day nursery so that the whole floor looked like a mackerel shoal moving in orchestra across a green sea. She had never before been disturbed by the effect. It had till now always seemed pretty.

'They say she's not yet "clean",' Missy was saying perfectly loud enough for Berndt to hear. 'At her age! *Nappies.*'

Such remarks were not helpful. Charlotta looked up to reprimand Missy, the curtains shivered – and there she was, a diminutive figure in the doorway.

The Tëtka had dressed her in an ermine coat and bonnet
tied in a beautiful pale blue satin bow under her chin. Her
hands were tucked into an ermine muff, pale creamy fur with
the little black ermine tails suspended as ornament. They were
penduluming like so many mice suspended by their tails in the
aftermath of the journey up the stairs. Her stockings were of
white silk, as if her little legs had been dipped in cream, and
her shoes were of palest blue leather, and Missy was right:
she was not yet house-trained. A trickle of yellow urine was
staining its way down the beautiful stockings.

Her face was very beautiful, smooth, quite self-possessed.
Only her bladder betrayed her anxiety. Her dark eyes looked
at each in turn and she gave such an impression of dislocation
from anything going on in the room that Charlotta instinctively hurried up to her, kneeling to put her arms around the
child.

'Welcome to your new home, my darling daughter. Think on
me as your extra mother. I will always love you as a mother,
and try to make you happy here.'

Charlotta's kiss landed half on the bonnet, half on the curls.
The little face was averted from her. Katya was taking in all
the new things, she supposed.

'Yes, yes,' Charlotta said encouragingly, following the
direction of Katya's look. 'Your cousin Berndt is your new
brother. See, this afternoon we went into the woods to pick you
flowers.' Charlotta held up the bunch of wildflowers and
started to name them one by one, as she would with her own
child, 'Bittekonvall, skogstjerne, tyttebœrblomst ...'

A little hand emerged out of the muff. It was overheated, too
pink, humid with sweat. It reached out towards the bunch,
grasped it tightly. Katya held the flowers close to her flushed
face for a moment, studying them with all the intensity of the
myopic, then she flung them with all her little might across
the room. Charlotta's ear was so close to Katya's chest, she
could hear the quickening of the child's heart with the action.

Little Katya turned to look her full in the face, defiant,
panting. Charlotta was about to make soothing noises and calm
the child but she got no chance. Not until this minute had she
seen the dark figure of the Tëtka standing in the semi-
obscurity just behind the doorway to the room. Now the old

Russian emerged from the fluidity of the shadows to scoop up the child and, with a practised gesture, flip up the ermine coat. Four vicious flat-palmed blows landed upon Katya's knickers.

Katya was righted, and set to stand on the same spot. The Tëtka retreated to her former position. All was as it had been three minutes ago. Only the yellow trickle had grown.

Silence fell like a bag of feathers.

'How dare you in my house?' Charlotta raged.

Looking Charlotta steadily in the eye, the old woman put her hand up to her hearing-aid. Charlotta was at a loss. It was as if they were all behind bars in a zoo, staring at each other's preordained alien natures.

The old woman closed her decrepit mouth. Her lips puckered like a hen's bottom and now the steady eyes changed, filled with expectation, daring her. The room was silent, except for Katya's breathing. The girl hadn't uttered any cry during or after the punishment. Charlotta's natural impulse was to take the little one in her arms, and cuddle the bundle of hot, furry, pee-smelling child. But to console Katya now would be publicly to acknowledge her humiliation under all these eyes: Berndt, Missy, Charlotta's own eyes, the eyes under which Katya's new life would be led every minute every day to come, and every year. To acknowledge the impossible thing that had just happened would be a drastic diminution of Katya's dignity that would be difficult for Katya to recover from; it would multiply the difficulties of this difficult beginning. Charlotta must join the conspiracy, ignore her own nature, cover over the unbearable moment; carry on through this heaviness that would stretch forward in all their memories as long as they all would live; and now she must find its counterweight, cancel it by cheerfulness, normality; unite this group. What could she find to drop into this vast void? What word or action that wouldn't be trivial and irritating as a fleabite?

In Berndt's corner of the room there was a hurried rustling. Heads turned. The boy was on his knees scrabbling in the bottom of the carved cupboard that held his special treasures. A sunshaft entered Charlotta's brain. She knew the box he was delving for: it was of blue leather and marked in gold letters 'Un foudre de Bière'. Berndt was looking for his most special treasure, the only toy Oscar himself had bought for his son

Oscar had brought it back from a trip to Paris. The occasion was etched on her mind.

She could see Oscar now, flushed, infected with a kind of universal affection on homecoming. He had insisted on waking up the boy then and there. Charlotta, frightened of Missy's disapproval, had protested, 'What are you thinking of at this hour?'

But Missy had proved pliant. Beamed and nodded in encouragement. Any male was to be indulged. The father was only an enlarged little boy.

The starch-fronted Englishwoman had laughed as loudly as any of them in the glowing circle of the bedside lamp when Oscar had undone the box, parking his cigar in his mouth so to do. Narrowing his eyes against the smoke he had jerked the lid off. Oscar had smiled his special smile while bringing out the toy, an oddity in the shape of a carbine-carrying Prussian soldier jointed like a stringless puppet and made of pressed tin. Oscar had held it up in the light for them to marvel at, his whole face infected with the humour of the thing. His smile was altogether disproportionate to the event. A boat-launch smile, Charlotta remembered thinking at the time, too big for a mere toy-giving. But she'd been wrong. This was far more than a toy; and it endured. Berndt and his father loved this toy with an abiding love. Neither of them had ever tired of the enamelled jointed captain in the uniform of the Prussian army. Separately and together they would each play with it on occasion. She would come upon one, or the other, communing with this toy captain and deriving great private pleasure.

The toy had a face of unutterable stupidity, ruddiness and ugliness. His little piggy eyes gazed out at the world from between a vast coal-scuttle helmet and absurd moustaches as long as his gun. Neat jodhpurs clothed his withered calves. His black boots shone with Prussian thorough efficiency. His funny jointed arms held a corkscrew, and a bottle. When wound up he uncorked the bottle, took a swig and gave a mad scissor-jump with his legs. Gales of glee. Every time.

One evening, attracted by gusts of noise and jollity, she'd come upon Oscar and brother Gustav lying on their tummies prone as boys on the carpet laughing their heads off at the stupid thing. The toy was supposed to be funny, but Oscar and

Gustav were laughing their heads off because they knew as well as any that Prussian militarism was no laughing matter. Making the Prussian captain dance was a fine form of underground defiance. He could be read on various levels.

That was in 1917, just before Gustav had gone off to Garda, the very moment when it looked as though Norway might not be quick-witted enough to avoid actual confrontation with the German forces, but have to muster itself against an invasion, the floating moment grabbed so decisively by Foreign Minister Ihlen. The two brothers on the floor had in fact been hatching the plot Charlotta had no idea of to this day, been thumbing their noses through the toy, giving themselves courage through the absurdity of its scissor-jumps. And it wasn't only that year's uncertainties the brothers were mocking. The Prussians had, one way and another, been a thorn in Norway's side since Napoleon gave Sweden to Bernadotte. In this toy there was all of a hundred and ten years' boiling resentment of a subjugated race.

From his first day in the house the Great Captain, as he came to be known, occupied a special place in the private family canon.

'Again! Papa, do it again!'

Papa would do it again, and again, and again. Never were father and son closer. Never was she happier to be on the periphery.

How clever Berndt was, what a wonderful natural instinct. The Great Captain would take all the tension of this moment, all the attention away from little Katya, and turn it into laughter at the crazy mannikin. Across the fractured room her eye caught Missy's. They smiled complicitously; friends again in shared relief. The Tëtka had won the first symbolic battle in the war of nerves being fought out in the darkening nursery. Now they would win the second.

Katya was slowly wandering over towards Berndt, attracted by the toy but prepared to die before she showed it.

Charlotta had a moment to reflect. There was a bad feeling in her heart in the wake of the beating. She had not done well. In the interest of surface harmony she had allowed two wrong things. First, she had allowed the Tëtka to take the upper hand in her own house. Second, she had allowed her own nature to be overruled: at the moment when her instincts had called for a demonstration of love, solidarity and consolation, she had held back. How much was the fact of her holding back the product of the history of the past years? Katya the mother had always scorned her for her natural affectionate impulses and made them seem hopelessly, clod-hoppingly naïve and unwanted. How much of a factor was the fear of meeting the same sophisticated rejection in the child? Somewhere in her heart she was frightened and suspicious of little Katya. How cowardly, she scolded herself, to be afraid to meet the shadow of the mother in the innocent child. Morally, how wrong.

The child might indeed be a curse, but Missy only had part of the story: Katya could be a blessing. It all depended on what was made. The start had been inauspicious. She had not played her part but salvation was being offered. Here was darling Berndt, saving the day.

The white-headed boy had interested the creamy ermine bonnet in the toy; their heads were together, two bent flower stalks. He made the Great Captain do his absurd jump-and-drink trick once, twice. Wordlessly, glance-to-glance, he explained, and the tip of his tongue crept out of the corner of his mouth as it always did when he was concentrating on getting an important thing right. When he'd made certain the girl entirely understood the simple mechanism he held the Great Captain out to her, smiling sunnily. Charlotta was so proud. Missy was almost leaning at forty-five degrees in her encouragement. Charlotta's fine pale features had been set in an assumed serenity, confidence and peace, for she had been made obstinately determined by the earlier defeat, and was conscious of making the example.

Against the shadow the Tëtka, with her glittering eyes, was unreadable. The still expectation in the room was like a roof of lead pressing down on them all.

Katya, the focus, stood with her head bent. Her eyes were invisible but they were not, as the adults thought, looking at the Great Captain. Katya's deep dark eyes looked into the eyes of the donor.

At last, Charlotta lit with cautious hope, considering the two children, at last these two are seeing each other in this room full of so many, too many things: adults, anxieties, burdens. At last there is clarity between them. Charlotta warmed to see those two little ones face to face without a word.

Katya's small, delicate, inquisitive hand took the toy carefully from Berndt's hand. His face so close to hers was full of love and trust. She had the toy entirely now. Raising it above her head with both hands she flung the Great Captain on the floor and with her pale blue leather shoe she stamped and stamped and jumped on him, and jumped and jumped. She only stopped when he was quite destroyed. Then she raised her head and looked at them all. Round the room, one by one. The bonnet had fallen back. Her black eyes sparkled and her hair sprang vivaciously in curls around her flushed face. She blazed.

'Lord have mercy,' Missy gasped.

The Tëtka with ominous courtesy inclined her head to Charlotta, turned to the girl and commanded her, in the language only the two of them understood.

The two of them left the room.

Chapter Seven

Katya Olovanova never came back to collect her little girl. The ship made its first stop in Hawaii, on the south shore of the island of Oahu. She laughed in delight at being able to walk steadily, without holding on to walls, but still despite all this steadiness she might have re-embarked and gone on to New York had it not been for the tropic sunset streaks glimmering through darkened jungles. They decided her. She must stay. Her trunks must be unloaded. Noise. Inconvenience. Fuss.

Two of the three shipboard suitors decided also to stay; to allow the boat to slip away to its next destination without them. The third, the slim-hipped Argentinian, re-embarked reluctantly, with moist eyes and real regret. During the last tango he leaned forward and ravenously kissed her on the clavicle, protesting that if only he had money ... he had never loved anyone so much ... and so on and so on. It was rather a relief when the ship's lights passed away like spectres against the darkness, though she enacted the melancholy goodbye pageant, standing on the gleaming shore all in mothy white waving the handkerchief at the boat growing smaller in the moonstripe. Then she turned, and there was a convenient suitor at each hand to give her his arm and escort her indoors past the hotel's orchestra of old-young men with lacquered hair and lacquered instruments playing the same tunes they'd played in the Hôtel du Lac et du Parc in Riva del Garda; the same tunes they'd played at the Empress Victoria in Madras, Sir Geoffrey noted, breaking into a creaky hum as his step turned sprightly. The same tunes as in the best Dominican brothels, Señor Romero Carvajal shivered, remembering Luisa.

Later that evening, when they'd got to talk about such things, they agreed they might even be the very selfsame brilliantined white-tuxedoed men sawing at their violins; an endless Faustian round.

Not for a minute did one of the three regret having stayed. The boat had been so small, so circumscribed. They discovered with mutual surprise how muffled they each had felt on board, how conscious they had been of limits. Everywhere had loomed bulkheads.

'And when you look beyond the bulkheads,' Katya was animated; behind her mobile features the foliage moved sleepily in the warm air, 'there is nothing but flat grey blank horizon. Intolerable!'

The Dominican had eyes as brown as liquid molasses, and a bony high-crowned head across which a thin wave of inky hair curled. He had made enough money out of sugar to be something of a poet. Leaning back in his rattan chair he observed, in his syrupy voice, 'There is something *too* eternal in blank horizons, rendering them intolerable. There can be nothing more oppressive to the human spirit than to be reminded of its own tiny antishness within the context of all that featureless infinity. Nothing makes one,' he paused to lift a hand to his fine moustaches, 'so horribly conscious of mortality.'

Like looking at the stars, they all agreed. And then they agreed they'd much rather look at the menu instead, and they bent their heads to the question of food, ostensibly giving it their entire attention, but in fact in each of their three minds a corner was saying, 'Ah! We are compatible. We can entertain each other. This will work on dry land.'

The ex-Governor of Madras, correct to a scruple with his grey stubbly head, small moustache, tightly knotted white tie and rigid bearing, was the first to speak. Respectfully he requested permission to invite Madame Oscarsson to dine with him. She accepted graciously and gracefully (and gratefully, thinking of her finances); and he had no choice but to include the bloody Dago. It went against the grain but good form couldn't be ignored, even abroad. The pattern was set for the remainder of their stay.

That first evening had a birthday air about it: everything fresh, seen anew, vivid, delicious. Cocktails came in the prettiest glasses and made excellent foreground to the glorious shore-based sunset.

They stayed on the island of Oahu in this way for three weeks. Or was it four? She lost track. Time passed so delightfully in tourism. The simplicity of their daily entertainments had particular appeal to the worldly trio. There was hula dancing, a spectacle that struck an erotic chord in the suitors, resulting in a handsome pair of South Sea pearl earrings from the elderly ex-Governor, and a less cautious medium-sized diamond clip from Señor Romero Carvajal. Then there was crab-racing on the beach, the three of them enthroned in low wicker armchairs, Katya in the centre of a man-woman-man configuration that had become the habitual pattern. The crabs were released from under a bucket by the same hula girls, with sand grains glittering on their breasts, and boys with sliding muscles. The two men watched the wind tease the ribbon in her hat and play with the tendrils of her carelessly dressed hair while she pretended to be unaware of their glances and totally absorbed in watching the crabs. In fact, her crab-directed glance was sliding from exposed flesh to exposed flesh. Katya was learning anatomy. The beautiful bodies, such a pleasure to watch in the heat and the languor, taught her how it all fitted together. From either side the suitors produced gold cigarette cases, which they offered with gloved hands; and they wished to murder one another.

Katya had long known all about the balance of power. She blew between her suitors now in this direction and now in that, favouring sometimes ancient courtesy, sometimes *arriviste* boldness. The slant of a glance, the offer or withdrawal of an arm, might plunge a suitor into the grim murk of the ocean's inky bottom, or set him high and dreaming on the breast of altogether more honeyed darkness.

If this had gone on for very long it would have bored them all. A drawn-out diet of coquetting is thin fare for the experienced *boulevardier*, even when served up with native entertainment as side dish. But they were saved from boredom by an impulse of Katya's. One morning she saw horses passing by below her balcony. She must ride!

The woman rode like a demon. She was an Amazon. Neither in Dominica nor in Madras had such horsemanship been seen in the fair sex. Never, they shook their heads in brief alliance. They were left far behind, breathing her dust. They fell greedily in love all over again with her flying back view. She laughed over her shoulder at them. 'I was taught by a Cossack,' her hoarse voice floated back through the fine air, 'and a Cossack, my darlings, never lets anyone, male or female, use a saddle for the first six months.'

The suitors squirmed discreetly in their own saddles. The picture was almost too graphic.

But however erotic the resonances, however demonic the skill, it wasn't this new sport of riding that saved the three of them from the boredom of unending leisure: it was where the riding took them. Choreographed Hawaii was left far behind. They penetrated the sickly bloated parts. Here was no shortage of visible death. Pack animals lay where they fell and became subsumed in the brilliantly flowered vegetation almost before they'd time to putrefy. Children played among buzzing flies and black excrement. Bellies ballooned over stick legs. Faces were pitted with smallpox. There was quarrelling and shouting among those who smoked opium every night.

This dark side was what saved the three of them. It added weight, pathos, gravitas. It rounded the shared experience; counterbalanced the lightweight texture of their days. The two men until now had been able to take the wooing of Katya as an agreeable frolic, a rich man's game. The word 'adventuress' had never actually been uttered between them but, well, it had always been floating about the peripheries right from that first moment of the embarkation of the boat from Oslo. The word had been written all over her dramatic unescorted entrance, her manner, her ostrich fans, her frantic cough, her nebulous hints, her mysterious brown bottle, the mysterious unlabelled past. Now the men revised their verdict. An adventuress didn't gallop into villages like a firebrand and turn on them with molten eyes demanding justice, medicines, food for the potbellied children, money for the poor.

Their hotel evenings changed character. Under the dark leaves flickering with yellow blossoms, Katya now resumed some of that prophetic mode that had so enslaved the coterie. She rehearsed theories and philanthropic schemes that would never be more than fine words. Sir Geoffrey was helpless. Señor Romero Carvajal was putty. She had made the transition from Beauty to perfection, from *mondaine* to *spirituelle*. Instead of wanting to bed her, now they wanted to marry her.

Then one day, inexplicably, Katya became urgent to leave. They must leave. They must go. Now. Now. On the next boat. To some civilised place. America, America.

'The ladies will have their little fancies,' the two gallants agreed, over a very decent Havana under a yellow sky blotched pink. The smoke from their cigars hung over their heads in haloes. From behind they looked like twin saints against a stained-glass sky.

'It's been too much for her. All this poverty. It was the same in India, you know, Carvajal. I blame m'self. I should have seen it coming. The little ladies are so much more feeling. It runs deeply.'

In fact, what had triggered her panic was rather more than a little lady's fancy; more, even, than this particular little lady's permanent state of restless need for change.

The trigger was serious, and it was this: the quality of her symptoms had become drastically different.

Changes had been creeping up on her for some time, but they'd had the decency to creep with a circumspection that allowed them to be ignored. The heavy salty Hawaiian climate, suddenly punctuated by the precarious excitement of the whirlwind rides, had the effect of routing circumspection. The symptoms were banging on the door. They could no longer be ignored. At night she lay dry-eyed, coughing, frightened, sometimes sweating, often trembling, her ears tormented by the monotony of the breakers pounding the reefs off Waikiki. She longed to scream at them to stop and then a dim figure would be standing by her bed between her and the window. The figure loomed large. Gustav, in his dinner clothes, a small knot of violets wilting in the buttonhole of his silk lapel, his yachting cap on his head and his mouth working very fast, saying important things very loud, but it was no good however loud he spoke: he was saying them in Norwegian which she had never understood. The stench of decaying violets filled her nostrils and she wanted to tell him it wasn't *comme il faut* to wear his yachting cap with *smoking*, but he would melt away and where he had been would be a million trees: the forest at the massacre of her family. She could never get away, not until they had been killed one by one: Mama, Papa, Semenov, Elizaveta and the baby. Not until they had all been killed and baby, the last of them, had been hacked to pieces could she wake. The moon would be at the window making fearsome shadows like mackerel clouds scudding across the floor towards her, and she would have a deep horror.

'My Tëtka, my darling,' she would call aloud, summoning the baby names, the love names for the only person who had been with her all her life; the only person who knew her entirely and yet still loved her. If only the Tëtka would come and manage the symptoms as she had always managed them before: bring new bottles, new doses, new remedies. But there was no Tëtka, no embroidered bellpull. Terrified of her bed she would gradually overcome her fear of the rapid shadows on the floor and drag herself from the humid linen. Wrapped in her Chinese shawl she'd sit at the window gazing through rough-hewn new-world glazing bars that roused nostalgia – already nostalgia – for the inimitable elegance of remembered balustrades. Cigarette after cigarette lit her night. Eventually the relentless sound of the breakers in the dark would be translated into degrees of coloured lines. A wavering orange rim would break against the turquoise sky, turning the sea to lustrous folds. The very first white birds would swoop and, finding their breakfast fish, celebrate with glorious strident cries.

The brown bottle was failing her. She needed a first-class physician, or a first-class pharmacy, such as could be found on a first-class international ship, or in a large city.

The two men purchased tickets for the first boat. This act infected them with travel fever, action fever. They were on tiptoe. The sniff of focused purpose resurrected all the ramrod gubernatorial impulses that had once controlled Madras and a million pen-busy civil servants. It fired the tyrannical talents that had inflexibly brought forth a vast fortune from sixty thousand acres of swaying sugar. It also resurrected the rivalry between the two men. The truce that had broken out between them during the neutral-territory sojourn on the island of Oahu was over. The entertaining friendship that had sprung up between the unlikely pair was at an end. Now they were to

move on. Things were to change. Progress in love was to be
made. The old antagonism was resurrected.

Oily little Dago, lickspittle of a man, the ex-Governor
thought, forgetting entirely the bar-fly camaraderie of the last
few weeks during which he'd found Carvajal a good sort. A
surpassingly amusing fellow actually – for a Dago.

For his part the sugar man Carvajal was thinking, She cannot
love him. Ex-governor Sir Geoffrey is a prehistoric John Bull. He
has dried-up peanuts for balls and a hanging arse like an old
woman. Carvajal waved the tiny Chinese taxi-girl out of his
bed. Sir Geoffrey's penis must be as withered and thin as a
tobacco leaf. Carvajal, my friend, the Dominican addressed himself, shifting languidly within the mysterious private pyramid
of the mosquito net. The abundant hairs on his dark, cigar-
coloured body lay sleek as a seal from the damp exertions of the
night. Carvajal, my friend, you must have been bewitched. Did
you ever really consider the old man might be a rival?

Putting his hand down reassuringly between his legs, he
stroked his own splendidly rosy plump equipment that was in
such good working order. The girl came back into his room to
summon him to the scented bath and then she oiled his body
with frangipani and he was already raring for the new stage
of the campaign to begin. Now the prize would be his. But
before the little taxi-girl left his hotel bedroom for the last
time backwards, as was her quaint way, making obeisance all
the way to the door, he gave her some folding money and told
her to get herself something pretty from Ruby Jewellers in the
town square. She was a good girl, he told her, and he was a
generous man if the service was good. The sugar man trimmed
his nose hairs thoughtfully. Stage two. He squared his
shoulders in the mirror. Good God, what was this? Was his
splendid equipment standing up again in anticipation already?

Departure day could not dawn soon enough for the impatient
three. By the time the boat arrived the hypercharged suitors had
been on the quay for hours, ready to supervise the stowing of the
luggage with an efficient rapidity hitherto unseen on the island
of Oahu. Then they waited. They paced the deck, annoying each
other, trying to conceal their anxiety from each other. Politeness
broke out. They nodded on crossing, and doffed hats. Each
independently, from time to time, without consulting the other,

paused to distribute huge bribes to keep the boat from departing.

She was almost two hours late.

Sir Geoffrey squared his jaw anew, took the American captain of the boat by the elbow and and launched in for a third time on the anecdote about the occasion he had been invited to dine personally with President Woodrow Wilson, which fascinating reprise was suddenly cut short by a cry from the Dominican's heart: 'There she is, the glorious girl!' Tears swam in his soft brown-sugar eyes.

Katya's violet silk shawl sang against the tropic greens and yellows.

'My dear,' said the ex-Governor, handing her up the gangplank. 'You look upset. Did something happen?'

She was upset.

Plenty had happened.

Once the men had left for the docks to supervise the luggage on to the boat she'd had a scrambled and desperately unsuccessful visit to the pharmacy in the main town. From there she'd gone on to another place in the beach town, a place the chambermaid in the hotel had told her about. It was not far from the pharmacy but the taxi had refused to take her further than the start of the street. She'd had an uncomfortable walk down the dusty track, her nose revolting against the sweet, overpowering smell of the enormous tropical flowers mixed with wafts of excrement, goat curry, peppers and bananas rotting in the heat. Her head swam. She walked under the steady stare of hostile, mocking eyes. The shanty house had a weedy grassy plot with dusty orange and yellow trumpet vines and a few weeds sticking out of a burned-out bonfire circle. A big dog chained to a post growled and hurled himself towards her and there was a loud snap when he hit the end of his chain; but the chain didn't break and there was room for her to squeeze past.

After the visit she walked back to the town square and sat at the café that the three of them had always favoured for their morning coffee. They'd chosen it for the view of the pink church and because it had the best waitress who never got their order wrong, and the most ingeniously woven roof of palm fronds.

Katya sat down at 'their' table. At first the glass of fruit juice rattled against her teeth. Then gradually the strained look went out of her eyes and they became aloof and indifferent, like the eyes of someone looking at something a long way off, across a wide plain. Time passed. A bright bird sang mockingly in a dark tree. She asked the clever waitress if she might bring a postcard. The card, when it came, sat ignored on the table. Almost casually she remembered it, picked it up, examined both sides, and sat for a long time with it in her hands. An impossible little blank space. How could she fill it with words for her daughter? What words? She was overcome by a fit of coughing. Pinhead beads of blood made a tiny glittering comet trail against the white card.

'She was such a beautiful little girl,' she said, almost as if the girl were dead. And then she allowed her heavy eyelids to droop and, against the diamond spectrum glinting through her lashes, gave herself up to imagining the card's journey. Such a vivid picture in her head: the card in the rough, musty mailsack, and the mailsack in the dark, salty hold of the boat and the pitch of the waves and the screams of the gulls and the shouts of the sailors who were carrying her loving words back, back to her little girl. There was something beautifully romantic in the picture of it all. She would find the words, the beautiful words to put on the card. They would be floating about somewhere in her head. They would be so beautiful, so beautiful. She would open her eyes and find the pen in a minute, but see now – a gust of wind had caught the boat and lifted it high on its North Sea wave. The wind caught the brave flag serpentining in the wind. The familiar green and blue. The same flag was enamelled on its funnel. Aach! An Oscarsson boat. Impossible.

The card remained unwritten. It was left on the table when she got up to join the suitors on the other boat, the real boat that flew, thank God, a flag she didn't recognise.

The clever girl from the café ran down behind Katya with the card in her hand. The fine white lady in the spangled silks had paid for the card and nobody wanted to be accused of dishonesty, but when she caught up the fine white lady waved her away, smiling gaily, thanking her and blowing her a kiss, and the clever girl stopped and watched. The dried-up old one in the cream suit gave her his hand up the gangplank and the clever girl thought, What a pity. When she could

have the younger man, the other man with the beautiful brown
moustaches the same colour as his suit and his melting eyes,
and then she looked down at the postcard for the first time
since she'd picked it up. Seeing it speckled with blood she
gave a little cry and, widening her eyes, dropped the card in
the dust as though it carried a curse.

The Panamanian boat went on to America but little Katya
never got a postcard from there, either.

The Tëtka told the little girl that her mother had died in the
San Francisco earthquake soon after she reached the city. This
was partially true and partially untrue, but it was comforting
to believe. Such a huge thing as an earthquake excused the
other huge thing: the broken promise, the never coming back.
In fact, two whole years passed between the time that the boat
carrying Katya and her two *amorosi* made landfall in San
Francisco, and Katya dying. Plenty of time to send postcards.

The Tëtka never received one either, but in some odd,
snakelike fashion the old woman got wind of Katya's location.
The beloved was in San Francisco, that part of the legend was
correct. Maybe the old woman scryed it? She was fey enough
and doting enough and monomaniacal enough for any sort of
necromantic communication to be possible. Maybe to obtain
insight she sacrificed black cocks in some dark corner of her
quarters. Maybe she simply went through Oscar Oscarssons's
drawers and his pockets while she remained those two years in
the house in charge of little Katya and at war with the rest of
the world, specifically Missy.

'But,' Charlotta, ever mindful of duty, reminded Oscar
during some particularly thick salvoes of domestic grapeshot,
'however wearing this domestic war of attrition between Missy
and the Tëtka, we have a responsibility to keep her in charge
of Katya. A link, a language, a mother tongue.' Tears welled in
Charlotta's eyes at the pity of the poor little girl deserted, in
effect, by both living mother and living father. 'Warfare with
Missy is a detail. We can easily put up with it, compared to the
great tragedy of the girl's situation.' It was the thought of
Berndt that made the tender tears well. Imagining her own
darling in little Katya's sad position, motherless, without

herself to love him in the million small ways mother and son loved each other every day. Nothing worse; unimaginable.

Even had Charlotta been less tender-hearted, where in reality could the old woman go? Gustav's town house was shut up, for he was still avoiding Oslo while he licked the humiliating unhealed wounds of the very publicly deserted husband. He travelled endlessly, doomed as the flying Dutchman to sail the ceaseless seas between his useful missions in the Arctic where he was establishing strategic outposts of the Oscarsson empire on blue-iced Spitzbergen and chilly Bear Island and, now and again, when the lure could be no longer resisted, drawn magnetically back up the Oslofjord. Publicity stopped him short of Oslo itself but the Fødselsøy was still there, the stormfast grey island with its house, no longer maternity ward or even *garçonnière* but carapace, home, armour and shell to an impossibly wounded and reclusive hermit crab. He curled up in his house, peered out curmudgeonly dumb and grudgingly through the thick lens of the telescope he had installed, and this provided him with his view of the world, his mental landscape.

No, there was nowhere to send the Tëtka. From pity she must remain but she might not have remained for the rest of her life – or, indeed, two minutes – had Charlotta got wind of the sabotage the old woman was conducting under her own compassionate roof.

An idea is a psychological reality which, in the course of time, may turn into fact. This idea of Katya killed in the earthquake, planted as fact in the little girl's mind by the cynical Tëtka, started as a very conscious deception, a pluperfect propaganda to undermine the Oscarssons and to ensure the canonisation of the mother in the little girl's heart. But it was not long before the legend she had created crept in to take up the status of fact in the old woman's mind. She believed what she told, and her telling became all the more convincing for it. The Tëtka, too, was taking comfort in the fiction that Katya-Mama had never come back because God had claimed her irrefutably in the most dramatic way He knew how. The Tëtka told the girl every night as a bedtime legend, using exactly the same words without variation, in the language that was private to only the two of them in the Oslo house: high Russian.

And maybe this was a more horrible betrayal of Charlotta's hospitality and the little girl's trust because bedtime was the sacred peace of the day, the healing time. Charlotta looked forward to the tranquil hour between six and seven, the last moment of the smaller intimate segment of the whole domestic circle. Oscar would still be at the office, or he might have called in on the Klub on his way home for dinner; or called in to spend a little moment at the end of the day ... snik-snak ... but no, we wouldn't think of that, not at such a happy moment as bedtime with the children, Charlotta sitting alone in the tranquil *stue* with the beautifully draped silk curtains of immense height like folds of snow, closing the dark night out in winter, and in summer framing a dazzle of sun. The mother anticipating a happy moment so comfortable and happy with the children on the pretty silk sofa. On the side table the immense silver bowl made by the great Georg Jensen, enamelled with the clear colours of the blue and green Oscarsson flag and the eternal O, the bowl filled earlier that day and every day with fresh flowers. The children in their pale nightwear brought downstairs, left at the doorway by their keepers to scamper across the room to sit beside Mama-Tante; a jockeying for position to get closer, closest, while the three talked between them of the day's great and valiant doings in the nursery. When they were settled, Charlotta gave them one of the old remembered stories, the sagas and legends she'd heard at her mother's knee in exactly this same moment of her own life, and then she heard their prayers.

This lasted half an hour precisely before Missy and the Tëtka would appear in the doorway: starched white vertical stubbornly profiled quiet and firm against sagging black.

'Time to go up, children. Who wants first kiss?'

Each child wanted first kiss, and last kiss too. Most often they ended up on each side, their lips light as butterflies, breath sweet as milk.

'Walk, don't run, remember!' Across the room each would take the hand of Missy or the Tëtka to be led upstairs.

The Tëtka and Katya always set off to bed first. Missy was a chatty person. She liked to linger longer. It confirmed her status as superior servant, at least in her own mind. She always found something to talk about, some minutiæ of the day gone

by, some critical aspect of the day ahead. Missy would dangle
in the doorway spinning things out; Charlotta entirely aware
of what was happening, chattered on in unspoken complicity,
pretending to be unaware of the passage of time for the
pleasure of Berndt stealthily taking advantage, sneaking back
to Mama for an extra kiss, a fondle of the soft material of her
skirt spread against the silk of the sofa. And Charlotta's arm,
as though an independent entity and nothing to do with
Charlotta at all, would curl about her son, her hand playing
with the soft, newly washed curls while the three of them
kept up the fiction that it certainly wasn't after bedtime, and
that time was not passing. When the French marble mantel
clock with the ormolu swags and *putto* would tell them it was
seven, with its pretty sparkling chimes, Charlotta would
always be astonished: 'Heavens, Missy, how we have been
rattling on! Now give your mama a last kiss, darling. Run
along, run along.'

Sinking back on the sofa she would hear the heart of Oslo
growing quieter and quieter as people stopped travelling and
arrived at their destination for the evening meal. Blackbirds
would sing their last liquid song in the garden against the
sound of Missy and Berndt ascending the stairs, their voices
fading as they rose higher in the house. Their chatter in
English had a brisk sound to it; busier and far sunnier than the
sound of the earlier progress of the Tëtka and Katya up the
same stairs; a fact Charlotta mistakenly put down to the nature
of the Russian language rather than the content of the Tëtka's
speech. She liked to listen to the mysteries of these languages
she didn't understand. She liked the polyglot atmosphere in
her house, the feeling that her very domestic context was
reaching out to touch, however humbly, the hem of the greater
world. This *mélange* of languages and nationalities echoed
Oscar's business tentacles around the world, as a wife's world
ought to echo her husband's. It also put something larger than
one mere house in the place where the Krigskjold Manor Farm
had had a whole village community. She might have been less
content had she understood it all, had she the key to the
Tëtka's web of words.

As the two Russians climbed the stairs and the colours and
light from downstairs receded in their eyes and minds, the old

woman would creak into a higher gear, like a machine gaining velocity. Safely out of earshot her voice would become focused: thinner but stronger, charged with the only real energy she showed all day. The scattered wisps of white hair on her yellow skull would seem to take life, as though she had been plugged in, and the electrical charge of life grew stronger as the old one with the leaden death-mask face progressed through the story of how the Almighty and Merciful Redeemer, in order to capture Katya-Mama's soul, had left half a thousand souls dead, twenty-five miles of city in ruins, twenty-five thousand buildings in ashes and two hundred and twenty-five thousand homeless. The Tëtka did not spare on the detail. Streets split open, horses and carts disappeared into the yawning, flaming crevices to be followed by dozens of screaming people pushed forward to their death by the crowd at their heels. Gas mains broke and blazed. Those doomed to be roasted alive were roasted, trapped beyond hope of release, half crushed under fallen masonry and crying out to be spared; the lucky ones were spared, shot by compassionate policemen to release them from worse, more lingering death agonies. While the infernal flames licked the city, the fire brigade were rendered helpless by the snapped water mains gushing water uselessly from the fractured pipes sticking up like the ends of broken matches.

By the time the Tëtka came to the cruel and tragic end reserved for her mother the child was lying rigid in her bed. Nothing lived in her face but the eyes. Katya's purple-brown grape-bloomed Russian eyes, shining, untouchable. Then the Tëtka would get up and leave the child for the night.

Her work was done. This was her work for now.

Later, in a few years' time when, maybe, this story had grown stale, its terrors too familiar to have such a drastic effect on the girl night after night, the Tëtka planned to tell the child the second story to reinforce the first. She had been saving up the story of the earlier massacre by the Bolsheviks in the forest. She would. When the child was ready. The parallels were there. Then little Katya would know herself for what she was, would understand she was the latest of a line set quite apart. She would know that her own existence was less important than her existence as Katya Olovanova's echo down

the ages: Katya's immortality. When this was accomplished the
Tëtka's work would be done. She was quite certain she would
be spared the time to complete this mission; and she could
die in peace. This was the purpose that had become the
Tëtka's life's work after her other life's work had run away
from Oslo in a boat to meet that superhuman, transcendently
distinguished death.

This bedtime story was little Katya's own brown bottle, the
opium fed into her system night after night. When the story
had finished, when the Tëtka had shuffled her unattractive
way along the top passage to her own room, taking the oil
lamp with her and leaving the little girl in the unrelieved
dark, Berndt would hear Katya's desperate crying through the
wall. Greatly distressed for his cousin-sister, he could not
understand what brought on the paroxysms. How could he
when he did not understand Russian? Nor could he possibly
understand what might cause her to cry at the end of a perfectly happy day passed by the children together in lessons,
in eating, in a romp with Mama and sometimes even Papa,
and maybe an outing to Bygdøy beach, or a wind-wild trip in
Papa's quick sailboat skimming the sea, or an enchanting
walk in the wildflowery country about the town. All these
happy things happened to the children day after day, and
they were together for all of them except, of course, for
bathroom things. So what happened to make his cousin Katya
so sad? What had he missed? What overlooked? It never
occurred to him to tell anybody about her terrible crying in
the night. His parents were all-powerful. What could he tell
them they didn't already know? Flaxen-haired Berndt was
becoming a more thoughtful child than he would otherwise
have been as he lay in his narrow cot feeling great distress
night after night, and failing to understand it. He would ask
God, first in Missy's English words and then in Charlotta's
Norwegian, to take away this terrible sadness that he didn't
understand, from his cousin.

'Our Father ...'

He asked first in English because he knew in some vague
way that his sister-cousin's sorrow came from abroad, from the
foreign words of the Tëtka.

Then he prayed in Norwegian.

'*Kjære Gud i himmelen blå.*'

Maybe if he could pray in Russian. Maybe that was what he was doing wrong. It was his fault, it must be. If he was asking properly God would take her sadness away. It would have to be God who took it, for Berndt couldn't, however much he tried. Every night he prayed and every morning he tried anew to console her. He always considered her first. Throughout the long childhood days and years together he never failed to give her first choice: the best fishing rod, the seat next to Charlotta on the silk sofa in the *stue* at twilight. In the garden he left her the biggest strawberries on the bush. He made sure she won the largest half of the chicken's wishbone. At Christmas when there was the big dish of rice pudding with the one lucky almond for a year's wish, he'd stir the dish around and help himself from the other side as soon as he'd seen the lucky almond. But still she cried. He could only think he wasn't praying hard enough. It was his fault.

The Tëtka on the other hand was never satisfied with the sobs. They were never heartbroken enough for her taste. The fundamental problem with them was this: they ceased. At some moment they always ceased. That was treachery. To the Tëtka the sobs were a feast for her heart. She would only be satisfied by the succulent sobs continuing all night and all day, too, without respite. That would be happiness. That would be faithfulness to her beautiful dead darling. The Tëtka would lie awake waiting, her failing eyes open in the dark and when little Katya's wild sobbing at last subsided into silent sleep the old woman would turn over, sighing into her pillow, assailed by gusts of anxiety, panic. Was she doing enough? Every night on her pillow remembering her dear darling she wondered if she was doing enough.

CHAPTER EIGHT

Coffins in Norway are often painted white. It was not so many years after Katya Olovanova's death that the Tëtka gave up on her own life. The guiding light was extinguished. She could not care with enough passion for the daughter to bother to live.

'Thank the Lord,' said Oscar, mischievously lobbing the pinkish-grey hearing-aid into the open coffin.

'Shh!' said Charlotta, giggling entirely naturally for the first time in two years; the unfamiliar light-hearted feeling of this giggle leading her to wonder how different their lives might have been if her sense of duty had not led her to invite the ill-omened crone to come to live with them.

'We'd better shut the damn thing up now.'

Oscar's strength was not diminished. His hair might be thinning, and grey mixed in with the gold of it, these days; time might have curbed his impulsive entrepreneurial mind of the wildest excesses, but he was still a world away from circumspection. He'd the barrel chest of a navvy and he flung the pine coffin lid as if it weighed no more than a biscuit.

'That's that.'

Neither was sorry to see the last of the Tëtka's lemuroid face.

Charlotta crossed the crepuscular *stue*. They hadn't lit the lights.

She was never still, his Charlotta. Always doing something useful. Now she opened the French windows, to get rid of the awful flower-and-myrrh open-coffin smell and let in the soft welcome hum of Oslo's growing volume of traffic. Blue flashes, manufactured lightning, erratically marked the passing of *trikken,* the streetcar that snaked smoothly along steel rails set into the grey-cobbled streets and sparked through its antennae. These days, it carried her from Drammensveien up to her palace duties door to door. She'd finally won the battle against the pompous limousine and thoroughly enjoyed her democratic journeys.

Oscar stood in the shadow, for once doing nothing, just looking at his wife across the expanse of white coffin that sailed like an ice floe through the dim air between them. She was slim as a mermaid against the bright window embrasure and he was struck by her all over again as she smiled at him over her shoulder, telling him some domestic detail that wasn't important.

She was a spring morning. God, what a woman he'd married. What a good bargain he'd struck. He took a step towards joining her, and stubbed his toe on a coffin trestle. These *fordømmet* Russian women. Nothing but trouble even after they were dead.

They'd hardly ever spoken between them of Katya Olovanova since the day she had disappeared but right now she was almost visible, she was so much in the room with them. Tropical vines with poppy-red flowers reached octopus tentacles from the walls. Hula girls undulated in the shadows. San Francisco's melancholy Chinatown blinked at the northern Oslo-light from the dazed gloom of the opium den.

Oscar and Gustav had been keeping an eye during Katya's Hawaiian interlude. The Pinkerton's man had been retained: an ordinary presence, unremarkable and unremarked by the glittering trio as they whirled their days away in pursuit of themselves, each other and the tourist round. Poor Pinkerton! Tailing the three of them wasn't cheap. When Katya and the suitors decided suddenly to leave the island he'd cabled frantically for funds. The Oscarsson office had cabled the fare just in time and Pinkerton managed to board the boat by the skin of his teeth. Those two hours Katya kept it waiting had made all the difference, if she had only known it.

The voyage from Hawaii to San Francisco was not entirely uneventful. One night in his narrow bunk the ex-Governor's heart gave out; over-exercised maybe by love and longing. He was found in the morning by his steward bringing the customary breakfast tray of prunes, bran, strong native *chai* and a kipper. The steward was used to random deaths, but he was still quite shocked. He had expected on opening the cabin door to find the old sport in his cotton combinations performing energetically on the Indian clubs as per usual, but there instead was the wide-eyed cadaver, rigid and yellow, with bony bits sticking up from beneath the sheet.

This changed the game drastically for Katya.

During the remainder of the voyage she gave up ice in her cocktails as a mark of respect (where else could Sir Geoffrey be stored?). But lukewarm cocktails were not the only change. Rapidly she recruited a second suitor. A ratio of two to one kept these flirtations *blanche*. A second suitor was a permanent excuse to prevaricate. Without him there would be no escaping the Dominican's bed, and that was a place she refused to go until the ring was on her finger.

The replacement was not a success. She had chosen too quickly. The absence of Sir Geoffrey shrank the whole situation. What had been serious (overtures to a marriage, though God knew which) dwindled unaccountably into formulaic froth: shipboard ping-pong of the heart. When the boat made landfall at San Francisco, Pinkerton reported, the three *amorosi* walked down the gangplank and went their separate ways.

Three days after this rather *triste* disembarkation Oscar received the cable telling him about it. Landfall in San Francisco, eh? He was luxuriating at home in a good, deep, soapy bath, remembering the place, the feeling on his own first sailing into that stupendous harbour to beat all harbours, the steep taper of the rocky promontories, the booming blue of the sky and sea smeared with stripes from an egg-yolk sun. He was remembering the incredible readings of the fathom line, the sailors' gleeful faces, and then he was trying to recollect something else about the bar they went into that night, all of them under a kind of collective intoxication from that harbour, but all he could remember about the girl was how her shaved pubic mound resembled a sea urchin. He tried to put a name to her, or a face, or even a race, but he was drawing a blank and chuckling at the thought, Well, at least I remember the essentials, when Charlotta, surprising woman, broke the etiquette of a lifetime by walking into his bathroom. Her primrose silk teagown floating against her stockinged calf was incongruous but not unpleasing against all that male mahogany.

'Well, well.' He swished his flannel, a little self-conscious to be caught among the warm bubbles, unarmed and defenceless as a baby.

'Do you know,' she said briskly, 'that forty-three per cent of the prostituert in San Francisco are White Russian ladies fallen on hard times?'

Where on earth did she get such news?

Her pretty eyes had given him a strafing look while she reported the extraordinary statistic.

Whoops, Oscar old boy. He'd put his head back against the tub. Steady under fire.

'I was always going to send her an allowance you know,' he invented. 'As soon as she stopped jumping about the world like a flea on heat and settled down somewhere with a bank handy. A bit difficult to organise while she was whirling about the oceans like that fordømmet Flying Dutchman.'

Charlotta raised an eyebrow.

Oscar hummed a few bars of the overture from the opera, seeming quite self-absorbed, happy to have recovered the situation, but if she didn't leave the room soon he'd have to repeat those first few bars again and again, they were the only ones he knew. The dignity of the situation would be entirely ruined. What more did she want? He turned his head theatrically as if to say, What? You still here? and met her eyes smiling down at him with just the humorous indulgent expression with which she'd smiled down at little Berndt as a baby in his soapy bath.

'Well,' he grunted, 'one can't have a Fru Oscarsson loose on the streets of San Francisco without a decent hat on her head.'

'A decent allowance, then?'

'Of course.'

Charlotta had smiled, told him dinner would be ready when he was clean and, magnanimous in victory, left him feeling like a schoolboy.

True to his word Oscar organised the allowance and caused it to be sent from the Oscarsson Shipping offices to Katya's bank. It appeared quite openly as a monthly sum in the firm's books. Gustav must know all about it but it was never mentioned. Oscar had taken over responsibility for the wife as well as the daughter.

Pinkerton's monthly reports also lay quite open on Oscar's desk in the shipping office for Gustav to read. Or not. Tact had made very good friends of the brothers over the years. Pinkerton's San Francisco bulletins proved amusing. Californian social life under Prohibition was rich and imaginative. It was a scene both brothers recognised from every big city they'd visited in their bachelor days, and every dockside too. Both saw that Katya was dipping into the danger zone, the seamless flow of underlife that went on in every city in every age. Only the names of the drinks were different according to the fashion of the hour, and the names of the places, tunes. These days Katya was taking whatever she took from the little brown bottle, with hooch, illegally brewed wood alcohol, and she was taking it in speakeasies dark with something more than night, and round her humanity swarmed up and down the greasy pole, mostly down, to the sound of black jazz. The monthly update caused Oscar some wry amusement and woke some memories, too, but twenty-four months had not passed before his amusement came to an abrupt end.

Katya did indeed die in San Francisco. That part of the Tëtka's story was true. The absolute fabrication was the earthquake. Not an absolute fabrication in historical terms, of course. It happened. But it didn't happen to Katya. If Oscar or Charlotta had ever got wind of the legend the Tëtka was building in little Katya's head, they should have been able to explode it in a minute by putting hard dates before the child. Who knows? They might have been in time to salvage something, had they a notion of the faceless abyss being created. With no idea of the elusive sorceress's magic potion, the smooth, insistent monotony of her unvarying tale designed to poison the future as well as the present, how could they know they should have taken little Katya on a fond knee, stroked her soft hair, looked into her deep eyes and told her lovingly, 'The San Francisco earthquake happened in 1906. Your mother's meeting with Gustav in Riva del Garda took place in 1917. Later in that same year Katya came to Norway as a bride. And later still you were born. You see? It's impossible for your mother to have died in the San Francisco earthquake. It happened in 1906'?

Little Katya would not necessarily have believed them. The mother's parting words, each word the sharp point of a star, were embedded for ever in her heart: 'They are perfidious, these Oscarssons. I trusted them and they betrayed me. Never, never trust an Oscarsson.'

Little Katya would rather believe the impossible than believe the word of an Oscarsson, particularly if it contradicted the Tëtka, her mother's representative on earth. However clearly little Katya's caretaker parents might have gone through the dates she'd probably never have believed them anyway. In the circumstances it maybe didn't matter that Oscar and Charlotta didn't know the legend being perpetrated in their own house by the malefic woman now in the coffin. But it might have been fairer if they'd been given a chance.

Katya Olovanova did not die in the earthquake. No. She died of drink and drugs, as far as Oscar was concerned, of bootleg hooch, the speakeasies, the wailing saxophones, above all she died of the drops containing the ever-increasing strength of opium in the brown-glass bottle.

Charlotta had a different explanation, though her information came from the same source as Oscar's. She kept herself fully informed of events via *sekretœtr* Fulman in the Oscarsson Shipping office.

That day, so many years ago now, that curious windblown day at thirty degrees of latitude when Oscar had deliberately gained Charlotta's sympathy with the story of chopping off his finger on account of the dyslexia, and then gone on to surprise himself by proposing marriage, he'd rightly said how much she would enjoy *sekretœr* Fulman, who read and wrote for him. This was indeed true. Over the years the wife and the secretary had become friends, as far as the corset of social structure allowed. That is to say: they trusted each other.

Pinkerton's cables arrived at the office. *Sekretœer* Fulman, he of the unfortunate neck and tiny head stuffed so full of sense, was loyal to his master first, last, entirely. But. These Pinkerton's cables were Oscarsson family business, and if Fru Oscarsson, who was a *hoffdame* attending on King Håkon and

Queen Maud, was not too proud to ask, then it was sekretœr
Fulman's plain duty to let her know.

In the Oscarsson office of pale, silvery wood and metal, not
unlike Oscar's shiplike bathroom except that above the wood
ran a frieze all the way round the room painted by that tiresome Edvard Munch, a painter Charlotta didn't understand
nor ever could find sympathetic, though Oscar and Gustav had
always supported him through thick and thin – mostly thin,
drink and nerves and disreputable shootings – she read
Pinkerton's last cable.

IT IS MY DUTY TO INFORM YOU, SIR, THAT MRS KATYA OSCARSSON
DIED YESTERDAY AT HER LODGINGS. HER SYSTEM WORN DOWN BY
UNWISE LIVING, SHE BROKE DOWN UNUSUALLY RAPIDLY. THE CAUSE
OF DEATH ON THE CERTIFICATE IS A FATAL CARDIAC ARRHYTHMIA.
ACCORDING TO THE POLICE SURGEON AND OFF THE RECORD, THIS
METHOD OF DEATH IS OFTEN ASSOCIATED WITH THE INTEMPERATE
INGESTION OF CERTAIN NARCOTIC DRUGS; OPIUM, FOR EXAMPLE,
COCAINE. THE RACE, HE SAYS, WAS BETWEEN MRS OSCARSSON'S
HEART AND LIVER. THE EVENTUAL FAILURE WAS UNDOUBTEDLY
ACCELERATED BY A PERSISTENT TUBERCULOSIS.

Pinkerton had added over the telephone on a more personal
informal note to his employer that, as well as the narcotics
specifically mentioned above, the new capsules of amyl nitrate
were very popular in certain sets just then. Mr Oscarsson
would probably be familiar with the effect the drug had on
the heart as well as other parts of the body. Oscar raised his
eyebrows and had the honesty to say, yes, he was.

Charlotta fastened on the last word in the telegram. Tuberculosis. As she walked out into the street, picking her way
between inky puddles reflecting the same image again and
again, tears filled her eyes. Katya had died. The pity of it.
There was no one to cry with: Oscar would think she was mad
to cry, the Tëtka – well, what an ally. Little Katya, yes, there
would be crying there. The child must be told but not yet, not
until Charlotta had got over the knives of sadness turning in
her heart. Poor Katya Olovanova. There would be no possibility of redemption now. The door had closed.

Charlotta blotted out the other words, the words she didn't
want to believe in Pinkerton's report. She red-pencilled all the

doubtful implications. Only the word 'tuberculosis' remained. From that moment she believed fervently in that tuberculosis.

It rang round her head. Louder than Oslo's traffic noise, louder than the cat-screech of the gulls as she made her way up from the harbour. *Tuberculose*. The viscous grey word slithered about the folds of her brain, making a terrible heavy porridge of imperviousness to ooze between her and the world all around her, causing a grey, infected lung-membrane misery to dim the sunny world of broad Eidsvolls Plass that had to be crossed, its greyness cresting this high kerb that had to be mounted, this asphalt that must be trodden, and during the journey she revisited the past, regretting that she had never before appreciated the gravity of her sister-in-law's condition. The cough, the hectic poppies blooming and fading on the parchment-pale cheeks, the wild moods. She'd never fully understood the bottle. Now she was full of remorse at her lack of understanding, even to the Tëtka. If this was what the old woman was concealing and protecting it mitigated the fierce undermining, the protective hostility. By the time Charlotta reached her beautiful house and her boots were ringing on the marble floor of the hall, she was full of resolutions. However difficult it was to love Katya's dark, illogical, tempestuous daughter – and she did find it difficult – she would make up for the *tuberculose* by loving the child and doing right by her whatever the cost. Nothing was to be grudged the cuckoo-child. From now on there would be no trace of reservation. She would do absolutely right by the girl as, in retrospect, she had absolutely wronged the mortally sick mother.

Curious, how one piece of paper can provoke diametrically opposed reactions. Curious, how Pinkerton's report had produced an entirely different effect on Oscar to the pathetic effect it produced on Charlotta. When *sekretœr* Fulman in his stiff-collared grey arrived at his master's desk with the words, 'Ahem, *skipsreder* Oscarsson.'

'What is it?'

'A ... communication from America.'

The secretary held up the blue featherweight report so that Oscar should be pre-warned by the paper as to exactly who it was from.

'Read it, then,' instructed dyslexic Oscar, quite without self-consciousness. 'Read it to me.'

The confidential secretary had a habit of adjusting his pince-nez over difficult documents. He read it out in his dry machine voice, as he read all incoming mail aloud to his dyslexic master. Fulman used the same expressionless voice he used to read from the Bible in church, that other place where one's voice was merely the channel, the machine for conveying the greater meaning.

Oscar's chin sank on to the navy blue silk Charvet tie as he listened. He reached for a cigarette from the Georg Jensen silver box, twin of the one at home, flourished with green and blue and boasting, as usual, the all-encompassing O, and omitted to light it. One would never suspect from the secretary's desiccated demeanour that the speedy glance he gave Oscar was freighted with pity and anxiety. But the secretary underestimated the master if he expected the news of a sister-in-law's death to make any perceptible difference to the ship-owner's controlled façade. Oscar looked exactly as normal to the secretary's sympathetic but unperceptive eye. He grunted, raised an eyebrow, though not in surprise, and from that moment Oscar believed as fervently that Katya had died exclusively from drink and narcotic drugs, as Charlotta believed exclusively in the *tuberculose* as the cause of death.

The truth was somewhere between the two. Compromise-land. Without the drink and the brown bottle there'd have been no TB. Without the TB there'd have been no death.

Chapter Nine

The child was a highwire artist, a spangled figure on a trapeze. She was always moving, always dancing on the edge of danger. Oscar's mind categorised people in terms of water. Katya was a snowmelt, a glassy sheet of water hurtling icicle-thin over a granite crevasse a mile deep. No one was more surprised than Oscar himself that he should come to love the child. To think of her as his own. That he should become attached to Katya's daughter, of all people. No one was more surprised, or more aware of the irony. But there it was. She had such courage. She adored the sea and was always running into it to escape Missy's warnings and cautions. She'd run in fully clothed, dive like a porpoise and swim far out, waving and laughing at the anxious figures back on the silver shore.

In regatta week she would beg to go with Oscar, nagging at his hand, his arm, his coat-tail till he relented. In the boat she would stand on the very tip of the pointed prow of *Bollinger*, the skittery little sailboat, keeping her balance like a ballet dancer however tall the glassy waves towered and toppled on either hand, however hard the wind was blowing in its personal contest to claim her as its victim. Her satiny cheeks, pale as jasmine flowers indoors, would bloom on the boat and her black eyes would sparkle, her long wavy hair would escape its plait to blow about her face in seaweed strands till Oscar could spare a moment from the tiller to come for'ard and jam his own yachting cap down on her head and hastily tuck up the fluttering curls before stretching back to resume control of the rudder.

She was beautiful. She had courage. She was a source of pride. Oscar tried to kindle similar feelings in the girl's natural father.

'Gustav, you should have seen your little girl at the helm today. Took the Wolf's Teeth rock straight as a die, only swerved to avoid it at Hel's Gate. Later than we used to at her age, all those years ago. Remember?'

Gustav was not to be caught by this. The girl's mother, he pointed out in an even voice, had also been endowed with more than enough beauty and daring and love of danger. Then he turned his broad back on his brother and stomped angrily away from the conversation.

These were the years when the brothers, whose rivalry till Katya's flight had made them almost comically alike, diverged so sharply they were never again taken for each other. Oscar maintained the tradition they'd both shared: he remained smart young(ish) man-about-Europe. Starched shirts and navy suits of superfine material clothed his shapely if stoutening figure. He still went to London once a year for the motor show and to replenish his supplies of incomparable attire from Savile Row. He was a clean, bright, well-built, handsome man smelling of cigars and bay rum with blond, carefully parted hair from which the wild red glints of youth had faded. Instead of pacing up and down the office crackling new directives like electric sparks and flustering the three secretaries who had difficulty keeping up, he'd taken on a new habit of sinking his chin on the knot of his Charvet silk tie and resting his eyelids at half-mast. The thoughts, no less Machiavellian, no less effective, came out in a softer voice and far better edited.

Many there were, reading his outward appearance, who mistook Oscar for the solid sofa-like burgher of his *Akademi portrett* on the stairs and, indeed, the exterior he showed to the world painted the complete picture, even to the discreet gold watch chain that Katya so loved to play with while looking up at his face to wheedle a boat ride or some other treat. But for all this polished civic veneer Oscar was not above frequent expeditions, carrying the battered revolver round Oslo's badlands when occasion merited, the faithful giant Russo grinning his vulpine steel grin at Oscar's heels. Though it must be said that, compared to the early days, Oslo's streets were largely free of banditry and extortion, and Oslo's business life, too, these days (the two activities, cleaned up and institutionalised, had moved off the streets and into banks and balance sheets as the country had settled into the between-wars world boom). But shipping was shipping, and always would be. It would never cease to be primitive about the edges and there would always be occasions for rough-housing, which was exactly how Oscar liked it. The revolver was no longer in his pocket for everyday wear but handily taped to the bottom of the table in his dressing room where it could be reached at any time.

Women were women, too, a habit, a post-prandial pleasure almost exactly on the same moderate pleasure-parallel as a good brandy or a good cigar. He no longer fell in love with shrimp girls on street corners, no longer walked miles in dreaming pursuit of an ankle, or a waist. In fact, he felt few really strong emotions these days. Life was under control. Yes, it was a precipice. Of course. It was always a precipice with a slavering wolf waiting at the bottom to devour you. But Oscar knew he was through the dangerous days. He had achieved. He'd have to be extremely stupid at this moment in his life to fall down and be gobbled up by the dripping maw. He sighed. Life now was really just a question of making more money, making the edifice more solid, dipping into the same bucket. Better pictures on the walls of the house, better pearls round Charlotta's neck, a better pile of money in the world.

And here, in the middle of this calm, successful picture of progress and achievement, fate had placed a neck-or-nothing *hulder* of a child, a hurricane of desperately felt enthusiasms so that sitting with the child in *Bollinger*, a walnut-shell of a boat that didn't cost a millionth of one of his great liners and tankers, a piffling nonsense of a craft, he felt a thrill as in no other boat. Not even his status-prize *Stiarna*, the nine-metre sloop built in England by Charles Nicholson himself. No, cranky, absurd little *Bollinger* was damn' badly built, to tell the truth, but in her rickety-rackety riding of the waves he felt again the danger and excitement at life's edge as they flew over the skin of the water chasing the glory of winning a rubbishy machine-made silver-plated *pokal* no bigger thanan egg-cup that he wouldn't give house-room, even in the servants' quarters.

If only brother Gustav could get interested in the child he might discover life's zest for himself. Certainly he needed it. Since Katya Olovanova left him Gustav had been turning into

some damned gnarled sea-troll on his island. He looked like a
piece of bog oak mouldering away. Never came to Oslo, never
came to the Klub. A night out with the boys'd do him the
world of good. He wasn't the first chap to be deserted by a
crazy tart of a wife. Gustav was really taking this business too
hard.

But Gustav was sick with a sickness of the soul. Katya
Olovanova herself was his tuberculosis, his ulcerous, lupous,
invisible disease eating into his substance and leaving deep,
infected scars. She had deprived the younger brother of that
fundamental Oscarsson characteristic, the chief family credo
from which all others sprang: he had ceased to believe he was
a god.

As soon as Katya Olovanova fled, Gustav had also flown Oslo
with its darting eyes and double-sided tongues pretending
sympathy. He'd taken an instinctive line to the isolated sea-girt
rock in the middle of the Oslofjord, Katya's birth island, the
Fødselsøy. The island wrapped its primeval granite rocks round
him like the ancient barnacled carapace of a hermit crab. From
out of the rocks' slits and narrow grey ravines Gustav gazed
truculently at the world with a round, fierce, bloodshot eye.
Unlike his brother, whose chin sank further on his chest with
every further degree of circumspection, Gustav wore his chin
contemptuously jutted at the heavens, daring a second helping
from the gods who had dealt him this grinding doom. From the
day of Katya Olovanova's abrupt desertion and flight Gustav
had refused point-blank to see his daughter Katya. Oscar was
the only person who occasionally dared, in Gustav's presence, to
pronounce the name he hated so much that in a fit of Oscarsson
spleen he banned from his island everything that began with
the letter K. When Oscar brought him a bottle of Krug to share
he snatched it up in a fit of violence and hurled it at the rocks
where it exploded cataclysmically. The yellow champagne
spume ran down the steep rockline to join the lapping froth of
ocean's edge. The flying green shrapnel shards flew so fast and
so straight through the air that each brother threw his arms
above his head and flung himself down as if under strafe from
a Gatling gun.

'You might have waited till we'd enjoyed the contents,' Oscar
said good-humouredly, straightening up from the rock, picking

at the seaweed and gull's mess adhering to his front as a result of the sudden dive.

'You might as well go back to Oslo now. I've nothing to say to any fordømmet tweedy townie.'

Gustav turned on his heel, and Charlotta, when she asked how the peace-meeting had gone, was told, 'No progress.'

Gustav had remained as frugal with his emotions as with his words.

It was difficult these days to see how the two brothers could previously have seemed so alike. Gustav let his hair and his nails grow. He put a pudding basin on his head the first day of every month and gave himself a haircut, laughing hugely the while and oiling the process with straw-coloured aquavit straight from the bottle. He could not wear the boiler suit which would have suited his life best, because kjeledress began with the hated K. Instead he wore blåklær, the hardy blue cotton jacket and wide trousers of the working man. He became scrawny. No business lunches for him: no trawling of the long Lucullan table at the Grand Hotel picking out plump crayfish, summer raspberries, succulent mayonnaise. Gustav trawled the rough seas; he caught his dinner bleeding on the hook. He scraped the storm-blue mussels from the salt-scoured margins of his treeless island. His soul twisted like an old wrecked hull, rust-crusted with sea-salt. His emotions were razor-painful as barnacles. But he was still half-owner of Oscarsson Shipping a/s. There were no barnacles on his mind. Oh, no. Daily he would scan the airwaves and the information sheets from round the world. He'd go to the radio in the corner to open up the high-frequency channel many times a day, and when the AC hum had died down he'd shout fortissimo at the machine's horn to a whole business-intelligence network of hams, and then he'd shout to the clerks in the shipping office and to his brother; and when this system broke down, as it did whenever the weather was not entirely docile, he'd swell up, a turkeycock in fury, and hurl things about like Odin hurling thunderbolts. And if this hurling didn't mend the radio he'd take to the boiling seas in Hel, his fine motor-boat, clinker-built of the best white oak, maintained as impeccably as he used to maintain himself in the old days, and named after the blood-soaked goddess of death. An hour later he'd lurch pugnaciously into the office, oilskins sluicing on to the soft beige carpet, deliver his shrewd advice, turn tail abruptly and leave without more small-talk than a stone.

Meanwhile, his Oslo house stood empty and gleaming, daily dusted by servants and entirely bereft of point. The Tëtka and the girl were specifically forbidden entry. The last family footfall to have crossed that splendid marble hall was Katya Olovanova's tiny elegant foot in its double skin of woollen slippers over the Ferragamo running-away boots in order to muffle the noise.

Oscar missed his brother's presence in town. The twin house was a blind eye on the opposite hillside. There was no one to send mischievous signals to, no leg to pull, no equal to share the joke of the Snakes-and-Ladders journey through the switchback highs and hollows of commerce. Gustav was no fun to bait, these days. You couldn't bait a barnacled bog-oak hermit with moss coming out of his ears. You couldn't bait a fuzzy voice roaring through the air on a radiowave, a voice shouting from an island that on a lunatic whim was bereft of kayaks, Krug, coffee, file indexes, spinning tackle and caviare, all of which in Norwegian begin with K. No, Oscar must make his own reality now. He must spar against himself. He must find it in him to spur himself on. He no longer had an *alter ego*, though he still had a brother.

And Charlotta. How did she deal with this new stage? Dutifully, methodically, as was her wont. Gustav was shamed into receiving his daughter once a year on the girl's birthday, painful occasions looked forward to for months by Katya so that when the day finally came round the child was hollow-eyed with sleeplessness, her nerves wrought up to a pitch of anticipation and her imagination in the wildest fits of self-dramatisation. Worst of all for Gustav, the child in overwrought mood became an exact echo of her volatile mother in *tzigoyner* mood, Katya Olovanova at her most *exigeante*. On the dawn of the birthday Charlotta and the pathetically excited child would make the journey down to the Fødselsøy – there was no question of Gustav coming up to Oslo – and it would break her heart to see the child churning in a wild maelstrom of hope, love and worship. The day would always have started with a fight about breakfast, Charlotta being convinced the

child would be calmer, and thus more lovable, with a lining of
porridge in her stomach or at least a few steadying draughts of
good farm milk, but Katya would be so excited that her
oesophagus could not even open to admit liquid, let alone
slippery food.

The girl would embark on the annual visit hollow-
stomached and red-faced with rebellious fury, having been sick
more often than not. Charlotta would take the tiller of the boat.
Knowing the outcome of the voyage every year to be doomed,
she refused all assistance, steering the boat herself through the
terrifying waters of the long Oslofjord whose submerged rocks
like teeth waited to eat up the unwary, but Charlotta preferred
to run the risk and keep the shame and the pain of the emotion-
ally overcharged birthday outing to herself and the little girl.
She would point the prow southward and proceed, concentrating fully on the matter in hand. She would have spent
some days the week before making a sensible plan for the day in
her head: neutral topics of conversation at which the girl might
shine. In her basket there would be cakes the girl had made
with her own hand (well, more or less) for Gustav to marvel at,
and packs of cards for jolly games, Snap! and Old Maid, to fill
the spare moments. And even as she packed them she knew full
well in her heart there would be no spare moments and
certainly no jollity. No jollity whatsoever.

Katya would scramble into the prow of the boat where she
would sit, her small tense face white as paper, her legs astride
the very apex of the prow, almost in the water, such was her
impatient desire to reach her destination. She would have
dressed in the most garish colours available to her: purple
shawls and scarlet ribbons and even black – this one day of the
year it was allowed. But where she got such things God alone
knew. The Tëtka hoard? Missy denied all knowledge.

The actual visit was too painful to be described. Her heart
bled for both father and child at these meetings in that bitter,
comfortless hermit's house, that place now so barren in which
little Katya had been brought into the world among all the
expectation, material comforts, and high spirits of Gustav as a
father-to-be. Katya would leap off the boat in an arc of hope
and hurtle to embrace her father whose body could not help
but stiffen and contract in the revulsion propelled by memory

of the first Katya and reinforced by this second. Gustav found his daughter more difficult to deal with for being the fruit of his loins. Fifty per cent of her was him. And she was – this! Charlotta would observe the struggle within him to cope with this blood-fact. Her brother-in-law was enough echo of her husband for her to be able exactly to evaluate his reactions and emotions. Charlotta tried to flow through these meetings like an emollient. There was no proper place for a third person in this precarious space where father and daughter were trying to find each other. She tried to extinguish herself, to become a purpose rather than a person. But it was hard. The father and daughter left to themselves would have striven in bloody combat and whichever was stronger would have killed the other.

Though Charlotta tried to extinguish herself she found herself all too often becoming the vital intervention, the substitute for the shedding of blood.

Sometimes the meeting would not last ten minutes before Gustav put down his pipe in a certain ashtray, and left. Katya's stricken eyes would meet Charlotta's on hearing the sound of *Hel*'s engine starting up and her father chugging out from the small wooden jetty. Charlotta would move to enfold the child whereupon Katya, unable to speak, knew the only way to keep from screaming was to hurl herself into the sea fully clothed, and swim and swim and swim, dissolving herself in those saline waters until she herself chose to come back to a Charlotta mad with worry. Or she would fling herself down on the rocks writhing and slamming her head and her body again and again on the cruel granite seeking, and achieving, some sort of oblivion. Once, she had hurtled wildly at Charlotta like a Valkyrie looking for a body to eviscerate and she had kicked and bitten and clawed, drawing blood, grazing and bruising her aunt-mother. Charlotta had to pretend to Oscar that a fall accounted for such injuries.

'From a great height I should think.' He had the kindness to pretend to believe her, confining his comment to the nuance of an eyebrow.

Oscar had the tact to leave her birthday visits to the Fødselsøy alone; and she was grateful. It was impossible for Charlotta to admit to anyone, even to her beloved Oscar, that on these terrible birthdays the complicity between herself and the child overrode every other loyalty. How could she betray the child's shame? Even to Oscar she could not talk about the waiting, every year, for the fiction of Gustav's 'fishing expedition' to come to an end. Five o'clock, fearing to navigate home by dark, Charlotta insisted they re-embark for the journey back to Oslo. Chugging back northward on that blank grey sea, the pain of passing the figure of Gustav in *Hel*, anchored and waiting only for their departure to dart back to his hermit crab's shell home. How slipshod his evasion! In his boat he would not even pretend by mimicry to be decently fishing. The little girl would hail the sight of him and fling her whole body into an excitable state, waving her hands and arms with all the vehemence of one drowning to catch his attention across the water between the two boats so that Charlotta and boat would rock dangerously with the momentum of her efforts.

And Gustav? He would never even raise a hand to wave back, but turn his head away without even miming a manufactured reason. How once their voyage northward had been accompanied by his curses on the wind, the dark words pouring over the blinding silver of the water between them; he had ranted and shouted, his booming voice disembodied, cadences carried on the air all around them as if emanating from the denizens of the deep. He had cursed his daughter. He had begun by cursing his child's cunt, and then he cursed whatever barnyard cocks might thrust their way into its slippery darkness. Finally he cursed whatever fruit might emerge from the accursed place that was her womb. The words wakened a primeval fear and horror in Charlotta, who sprang from the tiller and rushed the length of the swaying boat to cover the child's ears, moving foolishly as a drunkard in treacle, and too slowly to keep the words away from the girl. And with Charlotta's guiding hand away from the rudder the boat began to swing round and round on itself, till it was buzzing in tight circles like a hornet, madder and madder in the waves of the rock-strewn treacherous coastal sea and she must leave the girl to go back to the rudder or the boat would be matchwood and they both swimming for their lives.

Charlotta spent the rest of that darkening voyage home praying to the sweet Lord Jesus and fervently negotiating with Him, hope against hope. 'Please, Lord, may she not have heard.

Please, dear sweet Lord, if she heard may she not have understood the disgusting words.'

Cursed by her father. Deserted by her mother. Misled by the Tëtka into thinking her mother was a saint so special that God had covered half the world in smoke and hellfires, had opened blazing chasms and poured roiling ambers rivers of lava, that He in short had re-created hell on earth in order to mark her apotheosis. That night the child had found it impossible to sleep. More impossible than usual after the birthday outings. The only thing that would have comforted the child was gone: the Tëtka with her ritual story of Katya Olovanova's death told in the sacred mother-language. Katya lay in her bed stare-eyed, her forehead filmed with sweat, her body quivering, and Charlotta found herself entertaining the extraordinary and subversive wish that she would never have expected to cross her mind in this world: Charlotta found herself wishing for a narcotic, a soothing opiate, a little brown bottle to bring some rest to the glistening eyes.

'Oh, my darling little girl.' She bent over the fevered forehead in pity to embrace the child and kiss her tenderly.

Katya's body stiffened. Her eyes narrowed to silvery mistrustful slits.

'You can go now.'

There would be another paroxysm if Charlotta did not do as the child wanted. She left the girl's bedroom, walking through the violet evening in the house whose silence whispered around her, in the spaces overhead, and within the secret selves of every person under its roof.

Charlotta stood looking out of the window in the nursery passage so as to be within earshot should Katya's cries resume, escalate, and turn into one of her dangerous choking fits. Beyond the night-time garden the cars blazed by. A limousine with a dummy-like chauffeur swept a party in evening dress down to the Yacht Klub gala. 'If only I could find it in my heart to love the little girl. Truly to love her. Not to force myself into mimicking affection.'

Did Charlotta love the little girl? If she could not love her certainly she made it appear as if she did. She looked after her beautifully; much better than Katya's own mother would have done. Charlotta did her duty, and more. Because of the *tuberculose* Charlotta made it her duty to take extra care of the girl. Bland food was judged safest in such cases. There was always milk and fruit and eggs of the freshest. Pepper and spices were not served in the nursery quarters. Herr Doktor Lund, now promoted to Professor in Oslo's Akademi, heartily recommended cloudberries. Katya hated the feel of the pips in her teeth. At pudding time in the children's quarters she'd sit neat as a pin at the scrubbed pine nursery table, managing somehow to confer an aura of elegance to her white cotton meal-time pinafore, straight-backed, head gracefully inclined, delicate fingers stirring the silver spoon investigatively to see what lay beneath the good farm cream in her porcelain bowl. However thick the cream, her sharp eye would always manage to penetrate it. She'd never miss the tiniest piece of healthful cloudberry, however disguised. It was as if the orange fruit signalled sonically to her from under whatever camouflage blanket it lay: cake, cream or custard. Her body would go stiff as a board, she'd clamp her jaw tight shut and even a beating wouldn't prise it open. If Charlotta happened to be present at the children's meal she'd overlook Berndt's spoon sneaking out towards his cousin's plate to save Katya from a beating, and Missy would afterwards berate Madam on the impossibility of keeping discipline if rules were not to be enforced, and Charlotta would bite her lip, feeling flushed and shamed as a child under the justice of Missy's complaint. Wherever Charlotta was having lunch – even those duty days lunching with the King and Queen up at the yellow palace – she always knew when there were cloudberries on the menu in the clean simple room on the first floor where the children ate. On those days, till everybody's lunch-time was well over, shoals of orange cloudberry-cumulus would overcast her mind, oppressing her, and the people she saw during the course of those mornings would say Charlotta was on bad form.

As far as the nursery regimen went, Missy had right on her side and iron in her soul. She who had thrived in a state of permanent claws-out jealousy during her co-existence with the Tëtka remained wildly resentful of the niminy-piminy spoiled little heathen who hadn't the sense she was born with, and the back of a hairbrush was the only thing to beat it into her. Missy retained this healthy unprejudiced outlook even after the sinister shadowy woman had died, and by her death involuntarily conferred on Missy what she'd always wanted: sole charge in the nursery.

Katya was taken to Herr Professor Doktor Lund every six months for an examination. She was a perfectly healthy child to all appearances but Charlotta would never forgive herself if the disease developed on account of any neglect on her behalf. These routine visits to the doctor roused peaks of jealousy in the flatlands of Missy's starched breast. Little Berndt, Missy pointed out, Madam's own son, did not receive such cotton-wool treatment, and anyone could see that he was the delicate one.

'It's the boy as is peaky. Anyone can see with half an eye. In England he would be given Radio Malt,' Missy said, with unassailable aplomb.

It was true about the peakiness. Berndt's blond hair was like ashes in the pale light. His skin was so thin you could trace the blue map of his blood. Charlotta would catch sight of the vein at his pale temple beating, beating, pumping the necessary blood to keep him alive, and her heart would feel pure terror. But when Missy complained she would say, 'Missy, you must calm yourself. My son is strong enough. He is an Oscarsson and he is doing what Oscarssons do. They grow pale and thin and straight as white birch saplings for the first fifteen years and then you blink, and suddenly they have turned into great roaring Vikings. That is how they are.'

'But why take the girl to the doctor? That young woman's fit as a fiddle and twice as cheeky.'

'Missy dear,' Charlotta put a gentle hand on the nurse's stout gaberdine sleeve to stem the flow of righteous complaint, 'she is not my own. She is only in my care. I have a duty towards her dead mother, you see. It is for that reason I must make checks and take every care.'

Missy was miffed, and unconvinced. The only way to mollify her would be for Charlotta to tell her the shameful fact of the mother's TB, and then the secret would be out to all the world and it would be a stigma on the girl for life. Young men of blood and fortune did not marry girls with *tuberculose* in the family. Charlotta had told nobody, and Oscar, well, it was not the sort of thing a man talked about. The dreadful disease was secret and safe between the two of them. Missy would just have to continue to be cross. That was that.

They were on their way to Doktor Lund's smart, warm, consulting rooms panelled in lime wood. Charlotta was taking both children and a basket of newly baked petal-thin Goro biscuits under a white cloth. It was the routine visit following the girl's tenth birthday, mid-July: waiting for the children to be ready.

Charlotta subsided on to a yellow silk sofa on the top landing. There was no air anywhere. The windows were open and the gauzy muslin summer-curtains hung stiff and straight as shut-up winter. What were they doing here in town? They should be up in the good mountain air of the Krigskjold Manor Farm. Charlotta should be with her mother; anyone could see she would not last many more summers on this earth. But Oscar was preoccupied with *business*, the untranslatable English word. If left to himself in Oslo in this mood he was likely to take up residence at the Klub, along with all the other summer-bachelors whose wives were taking air, and we all knew what that meant *snik-snak*. Instead the family would stay here in this oven and find air sailing on the crowded Oslofjord, rubbing elbows with every other Jan and Peter. And all because there was some treaty of arbitration being made between the Scandinavian countries which couldn't mean more than a snap of the fingers. Everywhere countries were signing so-called treaties of friendship. It was just the fashion this year of 1929 with Germany lurching from crisis to crisis and these stupid *Nazister* making speeches. Oscar said there was money trouble coming in America too. He said he must stay in Oslo to call in his payments and turn his stocks and bills into gold. Well, he could just as well do that in September as in July, surely?

A racket was set up in the nursery landing above her head. Katya was coming.

'Are you pelting rocks up there, children? Is it Thor the thunder-god practising? Or is it a clog-dancing party?'

It was Katya of course. Katya the chaotic. She hadn't changed in the six years she had been here. Her dress was less rich than on arrival, that was true. Charlotta still shuddered to remember that urine-stained ermine. It had been put away wrapped in *silkepapir* and stored in the Tëtka's dragon horde cupboard, which Charlotta had discovered after her death. A spine-shuddering experience, opening the door on the Tëtka's holy relics: the landslide of empty brown medicine bottles, the clothes discarded but still carrying the faintest ghost of Katya's sweet violet perfume under the fustiness of time. The notes signed with the squirly affected K, the silver-plated keepsakes presented on the old woman's name day engraved with the pretentious Romanov eagle. And in that horde of sentiment not a trace of the younger Katya: no milk teeth, no first shoe, only in the rustling grey *silkepapir* the outfit her mother had chosen for her daughter to embark on her new life. Charlotta felt quite sick and cold thinking of it. A goose walked over her grave.

Uff da, she jumped up out of the heavy shadow, though she'd never been in any shadow, the sun streamed along the length of this upper corridor without interruption. And here in the sun-stream came the children, clattering. The girl looked well today, her hair in a neat dark plait down to her waist, neat at least for the next five minutes. Her pale oval face, which on occasion could out-scowl Lucifer, today was serene over a ruff of pale lace and a tunic of rose linen, pleated and falling in a column down the straight body to the thin white-stockinged ankles in their almond-toed shoes. Berndt was a little behind, in Katya's shadow as usual. He was in linen the colour of straw fields at harvest. His hair was so white with the sun that when he passed the window his head shone with exactly the same luminosity as the muslin curtain. His skin had bloomed hazel with all this summer boating, and the colour made his eyes blaze blue. Mother's eyes met son's in a quick, quiet exchange of love.

'Katya dear, do try,' Charlotta said at the top of the stairs. The girl was too old still to be behaving as she did. So much noise and clatter. She never travelled in a straight line. Like a butterfly she always took a meandrous route. The simple journey down the stairs was a flittering voyage of small incidents and surprises, always new. Each time they passed a chair or curtain she shied like a pony seeing a ghost. Then, on the next half-landing with the truly terrible *akademi portrett* that made Oscar look like an overstuffed pugnacious munic-ipal sofa with cheeks like slabs of roast beef in a pompous gilt

frame Katya would wave gaily at him and blow him a kiss.
Then she'd take three tripping steps up to the picture and
stretch on tiptoe to try to stroke his moustaches, and however
she jumped and stretched it was always a surprise to her that
her small rosy fingers could only as yet reach up to his
waistcoated stomach though this had happened many times a
day for the last six years.

'Will I be tall enough next birthday?' she asked, as if her life
depended on it. 'Will I?'

As soon as the bottom of the stairs had been gained there
was a new adventure for Katya, whose journey across the
aqueous light of the high-ceilinged hall was a series of oblique
dashes from landmark to landmark. Today her long scatty legs
took her first across a segment of green and white marble to
see what flowers occupied the Georg Jensen silver bowl.

Always such beautiful flowers! Creamy roses or sugar-pink
tulips or today – the child looked back over her shoulder,
beaming thanks at Charlotta – Oh, today! Wonder! Wonders!
Wonderful round flowers clashing as if a rainbow had crashed
into the smooth silver bowl. 'What are they called?' Katya
flushed hectically.

'Anemone,' Charlotta told the girl, who had already turned
back to bend over the electric explosion: red, purple, royal
blue, shocking pink. At the base of each cupped rainbow
bloom a perfectly round black eye ringed with black-pollened
stamens stared back at her own dark elongated eye.

'They have eyelashes in the middle,' she screamed with
excitement, 'dusty eyelashes.'

'Katya,' Charlotta called to the bending girl, 'husk, du skal
bare lukte på blomstrene.' Always she called the same warning
and always she called too late. The girl could never be content
with merely looking and sniffing but must bury her head to
bathe in the glory of the flowers.

Katya straightened. Her face was blotched with the dusty
black pollen and the collar frill of her white muslin blouse
was stained and powdered black.

'How many times must I tell you? You will have to wash
and change now and we will be late for Herr Professor Doktor
Lund, which is very rude when he is a busy man with lives to
save, and poor Missy will have more washing to do.'

The girl burst into tears. 'Oh, Missy. Oh, my beautiful blouse. It's not that I'm naughty. It's not. I can't help it. I'm sorry, oh, I'm sorry.'

While Missy was repairing the damage upstairs, Berndt took a book out of his pocket and went quietly through the front door to sit on the broad stone stairs leading down into the garden. The filtered shade of the linden tree was no shade at all from the pewter glimmer of this scorching day. His head bent, he was immediately absorbed in the world that ...

... that Katya had driven him to. These thoughts found Charlotta standing in her dove-grey linen summer dress, restoring order among the crushed petals of the violently coloured anemones.

If Katya the cuckoo, Katya the usurper, was not in this nest then Berndt would not be bent lonely over a book. Charlotta would be playing games with her son, or they would be talking together, or taking out the little rowboat, just the two of them on a nonsense fishing expedition for tiddlers and crabs. His father would like him better, too. Oscar would find him manlier. Oscar would have preferred a rowdier, less bookish son. If Katya was not here and if her boy had no one else to consider he would be less quiet. He would put himself first rather than always considering his cousin, always thinking ahead for her, shielding her from the hurt she seemed incapable of anticipating, from the consequences of her own wild excesses. Charlotta's heart was wrung by her boy's quiet and patience, there on the steps today and every day, his unquestioning calm at being put in second place behind the cuckoo-child's wildnesses. Cuckoo-children always took up more room and made more fuss. Gratitude was foreign to them. A little modest shame might not be out of order.

She sighed. The girl affected her so. She could not feel for Katya the type of love that suited her heart: that gentle river of uninterrupted love she felt for her son. No, when it came to the girl she must be always overwhelmed by strong emotions, loving or hating, or feeling aggravated to the point of murder, or heartbroken with pity. The cuckoo-child took a toll on her host birds it was true, but it must be remembered that the alien nest was not the natural place for the poor cuckoo-child to find herself either. There! The girl was clean and downstairs again and marching like a soldier in a straight line, one two one two, ostentatiously turning only her big black eyes towards the flowers.

'See, Tante Charlotta, I can do it!'

'Well done.' Charlotta bent to give the top of Katya's head a kiss. 'Now, come along, children.'

She handed Berndt the basket and put out her hands one on each side for the children to hold. They were on the road to Herr Professor Doktor Lund at last.

The days of bodyguards were over. Russo, he of the elaborate dentistry and wild disarming impulses, had settled into a less military capacity as factotum among Oscar's horses, among the Alfa Romeos that were the fruits of the annual trip to the English motor show, and the English lawn-mowers that Oscar always hoped would procure him an English lawn. In all these departments, each one – horse, car, mower supremo – Russo won medals for incompetence. The big square-shouldered Russian had stopped gangling now. He'd grown imposing, matured in the way that Tartar peasants do, his appearance leaping in one bound from shambling, gangling ploughboy to forceful, slant-eyed, craggy-browed Old Testament prophet. He lived happily in the tiny quarters above the horses, mowers and cars, and had achieved a pretty little wife, though how he'd done this was a mystery and a source of private giggling between Charlotta and Oscar for Russo spoke no more Norwegian than the pretty little wife spoke Russian. Wordless communication obviously sufficed. The medals for incompetence came from the fact that he still, despite his venerable appearance, was child enough not to have gauged the measure of his own enormous strength. Things came to pieces in his hands. Mild steel bent like thread. For some reason (Charlotta could only marvel and be grateful), Russo's cack-handed accidents did not unleash the famous Oscarsson temper in Oscar. They only made him laugh, even when terrible things happened to his beloved motor-cars.

As far as Oscar was concerned the trail of breakages was a small price to pay for such a mountain of willing muscle. The continual trickle of the repair bill was of no account when set against Russo's usefulness on the revolver expeditions to the shadowy docklands, the secret sharp edges of Oscar's life that

Charlotta thought had stopped a long time ago but that never stopped if you were to maintain your place in the forefront of the rough, tough, profitable world of shipping.

Russo was happy – if he stopped to think about it, which he didn't. All he had ever expected of the world – food, warmth, a woman – he had. But he had more too: the unexpected bonus of spiritual bliss. Above all things in the world Russo was devoted to Katya. The wee girlie encapsulated the dark drift of his homeland. She was the holy corner in his heart where the icons were hung. She was Holy Mother Russia in Norway. She was the thaw of the spring, the April ploughing, the summer cherry blossom stretching from hill to hill. Katya was the smell of the Kizyl-Kum desert carried on the wind off the icy Pamir mountains. She was the fertile Fergana valley groaning with melons and grapes, dusty roadsides festooned with cotton and silk and tobacco leaves like giant bat's wings stretched out to dry in the sun. Katya was the opium fields of Chaktal, scarlet and black swaying to the horizon. She was the bazaar. She was glistening sheep's guts, beaten bronzes and silk carpets, betal, hallucinogens and Chinese bargains, she was pyramids of almonds and pistachios so large and lavish you could kennel your dog inside. She was the gold onion dome powdered by the first snows of early November, she was the frozen lake turned bronze in the sunrise of a winter's day. He'd no idea that this Russia of his, this Holy Mother Russia, child of Genghis Khan, Tamurlane and the Khanate of Kokand whose history was written in flowing Arab calligraphy, had almost nothing at all in common with Katya's own Holy Mother Russia. How odd it was that the Olovanovas' Mother Russia wore an entirely different face while sharing a name. An altogether Europeanised old lady, interchangeable with Oslo in many ways: Christian, neo-classical to look at, neo-Mediterranean in terms of literature. She was a world away from Russo's Samarkand skullcaps and silk sashes. Why, even when Russo thought of the very bread, tea and meat of his own good homeland he was not thinking of the same commodities as Katya, the Tëtka and little Katya: unleavened *lepeshka* to brick-shaped Russian loaves, green tea to brown, mutton *shashlyk* to beef Stroganoff.

He'd do anything for the little Russian girl. It mattered not a jot that the two of them could not exchange a word. His thick khanate Uzbek croak was harsh and incomprehensible as a raven in her ear; while in his ear the high Russian she had learned from her mother and continued to speak with the Tëtka after the mother had left was as pretty and incomprehensible as the song thrush. He recognised the notes but not the words. Who needed words when he could bring her a fieldmouse's nest cupped in the bowl of his great hand and watch the wonder bloom in her flower-face?

As Katya was the holy child in his iconostasis, Charlotta was, of course, the pure and holy Mother of God and he, Russo himself, had been chosen by the Almighty as St Christopher, the carrier of the precious child. She'd too much fire, the little one. She burned out too quick. She ran and jumped and skipped through life on those thin little legs and then the life force was cut off sudden quick, like the life force of the master's car was cut off when the motor was stopped. Used up, she'd plump down wherever she happened to be. She'd sit on the ground comical as a newborn foal collapsed, and pretty as a flower on a stalk new-broken. And then it was Russo's pride to scoop her up and carry her home to safety with her arms twined round his neck like a rose in a tree.

There she was, the little maid, coming out of the house now, skipping down the stone staircase curved like the moon and her aunt and the boy following more slowly down the silver stone path that cut through the master's cherished lawn. A fine picture they made but no coats. The gentry hadn't the sense they were born with. He shook his head. The storm would break before the hour was out and then it would be hard rain. Hard as all the horses in heaven pissing at once. They would be wet through, the three of them, and no Russo to protect them. His brow creased as if he'd all the woes in the world on his shoulders, but there was nothing he could do about it so he turned back to spuddling the weeds out of the lawn and soon he'd forgotten his troubles and become entirely absorbed in the excellent and skilful game of decapitating daisies with a single stroke. His peasant face creased into brown parchment folds, rounding his russet cheeks and narrowing his eyes as the sharp blade of his hoe pursued a mutinous daisy.

The route to the smart consulting rooms took them down
Stranden, the rough road that had been Bess the tart's old
hunting round, though Bess hadn't been the roughest of it by
any means, as Charlotta well remembered. The six years since
she had first come to live here had wrought a remarkable
change. The gap-toothed town had grown smart new white
house-teeth, almost a full set to fill the gaps. Trees and shrubs,
glimpses of curved lawns and ornamental iron railings curled
down in a continuous margin either side of the pearl-smooth
tarmac, a graceful funnel leading neatly down to the high old
Hanseatic buildings fronting the sea. And along the road the
peasant huts had all vanished now. One could wear one's best
shoes on any outing without fear, these days there were no
spots where the pavement abruptly turned into a midden.
Wherever she went between the Oscarsson house and the sea
Charlotta no more needed to watch like a hawk where she
trod. The peasants had moved further out, and with them had
gone the milky-smelling moss-roofed log houses where the
straw-strewn sleeping area was shared with goats, foals and
calves bedded down on the floor alongside the humans; where
the axe was always to hand for the woodshed or for animal-
slaughter, or for settling a quarrel, and the fishing nets drying
in the wind. Instead of primitive hodge-podge Charlotta and
the children passed a succession of intricately-patterned
highly competitive flower-beds. Oslo's residents were now
taking up much of their time vying in the ways they could
torture carpet-like patterns out of foreign bedding plants
whose strange smells hung on the air, the odour of interlopers.
Look at these Italian geraniums, a foreign red, like her sister-
in-law Katya's poppies.

She had always made sure little Katya was dressed in pastel
colours, as though the coolness could work its way in from the
clothes to infuse and calm down the hot foreign-blooded girl
from without, though Katya did her unconscious best against
this imposed restraint, tucking brightly coloured flowers in
her bodice and persuading Missy to tie her plaits with
explosions of red or purple ribbon.

As for Katya, she loved this journey down to Doktor Lund:
her eyes ate the strident foreign flower-beds with their scarlet
Italian geraniums, their Mexican marigolds reeking of the pee

of cats, purple Peruvian cherry pie, cheap-smelling as tart's hair oil, and stiff, scentless English hybrid tea roses.

How differently Oslo smelt these days. Charlotta was far from certain that she preferred the smell or the look of these colourful badges of civilisation to what had been here before: the moist warmth of the animals, the muck heaps at the back of the houses, the goatish smell of the peasants themselves and the stench of the filthy black tobacco they used to get at the docks and smoke rolled up in newspaper.

Not that these things had gone altogether from the greater Oslo district, far from it, but they were moving further and further from the centre as the town shook itself out of becoming and into being. Oscar had had no idea of creating a residential zone when he had first started building his big white neo-Parisian adventure of a house, but this was the effect that it had had in a decade. For better or worse and entirely unplanned, Oscar's blazing white beacon, conceived as a joke and a brother-tease, had turned into a controlling force, influencing the development of the town around and burning out the earlier peasant way of life. The young man's exuberant stone fancy, light-hearted in conception, had achieved a stonelike weight in the greater context of the public perception. These days, it was a tablet of stone. In the remains of the century to come it would be transformed from present fashion icon to sacred immutable heritage. And the story of Oscar's house was the story of the whole of Oslo in microcosm. During the decade the same had been going on throughout the town, Oslo transformed from piratical Wild West to classical beaux-arts baroque in wood and stucco and stone, so that now it seemed to Charlotta in her daily round that the Norwegian race had moved from short, thick people with sallow lardy fat and warts to flaxen-polled smiling willow-wands with slim figures and cheerful children in pressed clothes. Was Oscar responsible for all this too? Was he responsible for Norwegians becoming calmer, quieter, richer; for the marked diminution of brutality, prostitution and drunkenness on the streets? But this was merely an illusion. In reality, plenty of slatternly houses and poverty were left, but they'd gone from here, just as the white plaster dust had gone from Drammensveien. The Oscarsson house was finished. The endless workmen were only a memory, and a hazy one at that, but round about Charlotta's journey through the neighbouring houses to the doctor plenty of clouds of plaster dust were puffing up in little explosions. White-floured workmen were rushing about labouring busily in other places where great hopes were springing up for a good life. Hopes that would – or would not – be fulfilled; and, if they were not immediately fulfilled, then the next occupant would be luckier, or the next. Such was the time.

And which was the reality, which truth absolutely belonged in this place? Plaster dust or cow-dunged hovel? God only knew. The thing that seemed to belong completely to this time was that people could not construct their lives without deconstructing others, too. And that was the difference about this time. Charlotta felt sure it had not always been like this in Oslo. It was still not like this today at her childhood home, the farm up in the northern mountains, but this was how it was here and now at this forefront not only of fashion but of the country's historic development.

Charlotta was one of the few to perceive, stop and ponder the town's growing out of angular teenage into full townhood, with a place for everything, everything in its place – and that included a new device of wooden poles at regular intervals along the streets with arc-lights that hissed and flickered especially in wet and windy conditions and that spoiled the view of the moon and stars at night, and that was a pity. One could not say that the coming of light had converted the Drammen road's one-time vice into virtue, but vice had deserted the Drammen road. Beggars were even a rare sight, rare enough for Charlotta's attention to be caught by the slow, shuddering walk of an old beggar woman the size of a barn door wrapped in rags, hobbling on huge legs ballooned with elephantiasis. Berndt walked closer in to his mother's legs. Katya skipped naughtily away to the other side of the road. The beggar's rags were all the more pathetic for the oppressive heat of the July day. The beggar gave the family a rheumy unsteady glance and put out a mittened hand, none too clean, for alms. How terrible to be entirely subject to the vagaries of passers-by and weather. The air was leaden, full of muted thunder. The first drop of rain caught in a curled leaf.

Charlotta judged they would make the surgery before the pent-up rain burst out of the sky. When the consultation was over she would ask Doktor Lund if she might use his telephone for the car to collect them. But how would it be for this poor old beggar woman? There would be no car to collect her, nor any dry clothes at the end of the shower. Charlotta slowed up to say a polite 'God dag', and to give something to the sad old specimen of humanity.

A mittened hand was stretched forth. The smell was something abominable. The face was something familiar. 'Bess?' Charlotta asked tentatively.

The frizzed fringe was no longer crimson but there were the faded baby-blue eyes, the wood-alcohol breath, the cracked façade that make-up used to gutter down like candlewax. It was indeed the old prostitute, circumstances reduced even further. Charlotta was shocked. When Bess had disappeared from the street she'd hardly given it any thought but some vague corner of her mind had, she supposed, imagined the old street trader retired from her practice in profitable love and married to some nice regular client. Happily ever after.

'Murdered, more like,' said Oscar, and Charlotta told him to hush, it was bad luck even to say it.

Apart from the tree-trunk legs and huge frame, she'd grown a goitre the size of a golf ball under her jaw. It pendulumed, wobbling like a turkey's wattle with every painful shuddering step.

'Bess, my old friend. What has become of you?' Charlotta felt it a sad thing to see the old institution in such a state.

The upshot of this meeting was that when Charlotta came back from the visit to the eminent professor (Katya declared blooming as always, her lungs unshadowed, and the health-giving properties of the hated cloudberry once more warmly talked up) Charlotta set to work effectively, the result being a bath-chair that procured Bess a certain amount of independence. Every month thereafter the grateful Bess arrived in her chair, like Freya in her chariot pulled by rams, to pay a visit of thanks and, quite incidentally, to receive the blankets, food and women's clothing found surplus to the Oscarsson household. Lucky, how they had women's clothes in such great big sizes when none of the women in the house was fatter than a fairy.

Katya and Berndt hated Bess's visits. They were always made to say hello properly, to shake hands. *Uff!* The *ekkel* feel of that puffy fat humid hand that they must shake. Where had it been? But Katya must *neie* and Berndt must *bukke* just as they would curtsy and bow to any visitor who came to the house. Charlotta was most strict on this. Berndt on these occasions was hesitant and over-polite, he was considerably frightened by the gummy unpredictable old lady, who looked so exactly like the witch in the woodcuts of Grimm's fairy tales. Between visits she obviously lived in a cottage made of gingerbread where she gorged herself to her great size on imprisoned children.

For her part the old prostitute scorned the boy. He would grow up to be a man. And we all know what *that* means, spoke the voice in her rheumy old head, where the thoughts ran crooked and strange. Once she played a game. Berndt had that scent about him she'd smelt so often on the street, an unmistakable smell never forgotten, however addled, slow and shuddering the progress of thought through the long skein on skein of cortex, hemisphere and medulla. The boy smelt of easy victim. Bess made herself hexy, volunteering to initiate him with a wheeze of her old filthy gums but she had forgotten the time, forgotten her place. She was not on the streets but in Charlotta's beautiful drawing room when she put her hand out towards the young boy's buttoned fly, telling him to get his little jewel out so she could fasten her bald shiny gums around –

'Enough.' Charlotta's voice. 'Or you go. Now.'

Katya, on the other hand, Bess adored. Katya was the most beautiful girl she had ever seen. The girl was cheeky, mischievous as all Satan's imps, and she was stuffed full of the qualities Bess recognised. In a few years she'd be running rings around all the men who would be falling over each other to climb into her knickers. Bess had known many a Katya on the street. They'd none of them made a late grave but by *pokkern* they'd had a good time getting there.

The combustible Katya was not frightened of Bess. She was simply furious, resentful, felt it below her dignity that this woman should bowl up to the house like anybody else, and she was rude. On one memorably explosive visit she poked the

goitre with a sharp finger that made Bess cry out and tears
flow down the the slopes of her cheeks but it made no difference to her love for Katya the tease. Bess knitted the girl a
scarf, a scratchy barbed-wire masterpiece of love and dropped
stitches. The girl refused to wear it, even for the five minutes it
took to get Bess into the house. Charlotta sighed, threw up her
hands and eventually consulted higher authority.

'What am I to do?' she asked Oscar, the higher authority in
question.

He roared with laughter. 'Trouble in the hen-house, hey?'

Well, he couldn't be expected to meddle in women's business.
That way lay trouble for a mere man, besides Charlotta could
sort it out perfectly well for herself, but his opinion, for what it
was worth, was that if Katya was forced to curtsy to a half-
mad old sailor's tart it was hardly surprising she mutinied.

This left Charlotta with no ally except her own sense of
duty. Even Missy broke the habit of a lifetime by siding with
Katya against Charlotta. Missy's realignment ought to have
given Charlotta cause for rejoicing, considering the state of
permanent submerged combat existing between Missy and
Katya. For peace to break out between them must make for a
calmer household overall. But it was plain as the nose on her
face that the new Missy/Katya alliance had nothing creditable
about it at all. A blind bat could see that the alliance was
founded entirely on snobbism. Missy was far too respectable a
lady to associate with an ex- ... ahem ... The English nanny's
respectable pendulous lower lip wobbled in refusal to utter
even the most delicate euphemism for the oldest profession.
She knew her objections were less forceful for ending in
strangled ladylike evasions, but so be it: such a word had never
passed her lips and now she was expected to remain under the
same roof. Missy sought permission to take the children out on
these occasions. Charlotta refused her.

There was, then, a considerable degree of pandemonium
caused on every single occasion of a visit by Bess. The
household found no neutral pattern to fall into. The approach
of the bath-chair crunching on the gravel spoke warfare as
surely as banners, heralds and trumpets. On Bess days the
children spied through windows in horrid anticipation at the
elephantine mass of grey shawls overflowing the basketwork

chair heaving and hauling up the stone path between the arcs of pluperfect lawn till, coming to a stop, the untidy bundle rested becalmed, waiting for Russo's strongly muscled arms to extract her from her chariot and help her up the beautiful serpentine stairs into the house where Charlotta would kiss the bloated cheek without any sign of disgust, without even feeling disgust. The children having reluctantly discharged their duty were then sent out to play: Charlotta was not one to prolong torture. Children dismissed, the two women crossed the hall slowly, and in Bess's case painfully, to gain the morning room where tea was laid out and the windows open (lots of fresh air was always a wise precaution in Bess's proximity). Then the two women would sit down with their backs to the *chaise-longue* on which, so long ago it seemed, Katya Olovanova had flailed in the prolonged violent spasms of dramatic melancholia, and Charlotta had maybe said the wrong things to her, having no idea at the time that this violent self-indulgent melodramatic scene was the very last in which she would see her sister-in-law in this world. Charlotta still was capable of being ambushed by spine-freezing moments when she wondered how much of a difference it would have made had she been more sympathetic and less matter-of-fact. At such times she looked at little Katya and thought, I am your mother's murderer, and then she would redouble her efforts towards the little girl. But still she could not help seeing her ward Katya's most innocent action without the hovering possibility of sin.

Bess's slow and shuddering walk across the green and cream hall on her blown-up legs took forever.

'Such a beautiful carpet.'

When they reached the *stue* door she made the same remark every time, in all humility, her gigantic ankles visibly relaxing into the thick wool pile. 'It gives me pleasure just to walk on this carpet.'

This appallingly sincerely felt remark reminded Charlotta exactly why it was worth the household fights to give this poor old thing some comfort, discreet alms and, above all, a feeling of her own worth.

'Well, my dear, I have baked your favourite *Napoleonskake* and while we eat it will you tell me all about how you are and what you have been doing since I last saw you? And after we have eaten I will massage your legs and feet.'

Bess had a certain dignity in acceptance that made it easy. The two women sipped watery coffee. Gone were the days when Bess would take it hot as hell, black as night and sweet as sin. Her heart condition forbade. Charlotta didn't mind the watery coffee but one thing she did find difficult was eating opposite Bess. Nobody had ever told Bess to shut her mouth when she chewed. She marauded through whatever was put before her like a locust on short commons, snatching at her food as though it would be taken away at any moment, talking, coughing, drinking through her food-filled mouth like a horse, and never doing just one thing with her mouth when she could be doing three. Charlotta's solution was to sit at right angles to her visitor, and look out of the window as often as was polite. There was darling Berndt in the string hammock between the branches of the lilac tree. Around and above him the leaves of the lilac were dry as beetle's wings, their mauve pyramid flowers turning to crackly brown husks. He lay supine with a book in his hand. One brown leg dangled down, its boot laced to the knee, and swung from time to time to make the hammock move a little in the hot air. The sailor cap with ribbons was slanted to shade his eyes. He wore everyday blue shorts and the sleeves of his white shirt were rolled up to the elbows. One thin brown arm supported the book, the other was bent, hand up to mouth in characteristic concentration, sucking the pencil. The studious boy was working towards the examinations in navigation, far before his time.

'Every map is an invitation. I have only to see a map to make a journey.'

He loved maps of the oceans and maps of the stars. His interest in these invisible roads that ran round the heavens and the waterways of the earth was quieter than his father's, though Charlotta knew it was just as intense. Oscar saw only the lack of sailor robustness in his son, and was irritated. Charlotta saw the cerebral passion for voyaging and was content that Oscarsson Shipping a/s would find strong and capable hands in the next generation. Oscar would see, eventually. Behind the boy and the lilac, in the beds around the sun-dial stood yellow and blue lupins that had stuck up brave as candle flames in the first morning sun but now were drooping with the prolonged thundery heat and going crooked in their tops. Russo in his leather apron was poking among them with his misguided hoe. Even as she looked a lupin spire was felled *clask!* Charlotta frowned.

Bess thought she had offended her hostess in some way but Charlotta was thinking that any more poking and Russo would have them all down like a row of ninepins. He'd never make a gardener. She longed to spring out to tell him to water them instead of hoeing them down so disastrously but she must sit still and look interested in the important things Bess had to say about her granddaughter and her emphysema. Charlotta didn't know which she hated more. The emphysema affected the poor woman appallingly but was at least impersonal and involuntary. The granddaughter was a monster of selfishness and ingratitude. She'd political ambitions in the embryonic Arbeidsparti, the Workers Party, which promised a welfare state to take care of such people as Bess and look after them all their days at the state's expense. What a dream! As if the Norwegian country – any country – would ever be able to afford such a thing. Charlotta would have thought more of the idea, at least given the granddaughter credit for altruism, if she ever lifted a finger to look after her old grandmother but the girl, Gro, lived an entirely selfish life theorising and sponging. A *flâneuse*, as Oscar would say, a political *flâneuse*. From the stories Bess dotingly told of her, Charlotta gathered that granddaughter Gro had a capacity to be even ruder to her granny than Katya, and was commensurately adored.

Through the open window the scene in the garden became more active as Katya decided to take Bess's bath-chair off for a roll around. Often the children would give each other rides in the chair, pushing each other round the garden, and Charlotta loved to see their innocent play through the window. This morning Katya, restless child, prone to games where she was queen and needed a lot of servants, was today, sweet child, playing contentedly alone; a quiet game, a game that needed nobody at her beck and call. Maybe the calming influences were taking their turn. Certainly she seemed to leave Berndt in peace while she rolled the empty chair down the path singing to herself and disappearing round the shrubbery, a last

glimpse of unravelled plaits against primrose cotton dress.
Charlotta turned to the task in hand. After food, succour. The
poor old legs were covered with senile excrescences, the nails
on the toes were thick and yellow as reindeer horn. She
sprinkled aromatic oil and rubbed carefully so that the scaly
flesh, powdery and distended to its limit with the disease,
should not be bruised or torn. Neither the sight nor the smell
made her squeamish.

'You are an angel sent from God.' The old woman leaned
back, closing her eyes.

'Merely a friend, dear Bess, merely an old friend.'

The afternoon drowsed. Bess dozed. Charlotta continued,
but more gently, to aid the sluggish circulation, raising her
head from time to time to take pleasure in quiet glimpses of
the family through the window. Berndt was still in his
hammock, little bookworm! He hadn't moved all afternoon.
Katya came up the garden path now, returning the bath-chair
and then skipping off to avoid saying goodbye to Bess, little
scamp! How fortunate Charlotta was, how much more fortunate than poor Bess. Hard to believe this flesh had once been
a vessel of pleasure, snik-snak. Ah, well, time now to wake her
and send her home.

Berndt was extracted from his hammock to say goodbye with
his eyes hazily full of latitude and longitude and his mind in
some other corner of the globe entirely. He bowed just as
beautifully as he had bowed to the Queen, and remained by
Charlotta's side at the gate till Bess should be out on the
pavement and rolling down out of sight, but the bath-chair had
not gone twenty metres when the whole top-heavy contraption
lurched to one side and collapsed as suddenly as matchsticks
into splinters of wood. The piles of grey shawls billowed like a
shroud in the wind before settling into their separate scattered
rags and scraps. One wheel stuck up at an angle from the kerb
and was revolving endlessly stroboscopically, clicking with
each revolution in the air while the other rolled down the street
a little way before falling over on its side and coming to a stop
on the grey asphalt. Under the mountain of rags nothing moved.
Blood was seeping slowly into the gutter. Bess, always so
vehement in her movements, who had been so noisy in her
goodbyes not five minutes ago, lay utterly silent and still.

Charlotta and Berndt, who had been waving so courteously, stopped short with a shocked tremor. Berndt ran a palm across his mouth with a frightened glance at his mother who, with uncharacteristic haste, ran down towards the accident. The old woman was lying on her side with her eyes closed and her skin as cold and yellow as death. Blood made a slow black trickle down the forehead of her motionless face. Her thick spongy tongue lolled slackly out of her mouth. Among the wreckage of the chair and garments the body was twisted, one of her bloated legs sticking out painfully, and now with this rude impact the skin that Charlotta had so carefully tended was broken in many places and there was much blood.

The suddenness had so flustered Charlotta she merely stood, incapable.

'Allow me,' a voice said firmly but courteously: a passer-by, a respectable-looking military-looking fellow. Smoothing his moustache he set down a little leather case he was carrying, opened it immediately and produced a bottle of ammonia and a roll of cotton wool, which he soaked and applied under Bess's nose. Straightaway there was twitching movement to her eyelids and a snuffling choking breath.

'It was a great blessing he was there,' Charlotta told Oscar later that evening, when she was trying to distract him for he was very furious to hear that the military-looking fellow, after he had organised a wagon to take Bess to the hospital, had bent to examine the wreckage remaining in the road and, when eventually he straightened from his peering and poking, he turned slowly, with a serious face towards Charlotta who still stood, stunned and immobilised, Berndt at her skirts trying his childish best to soothe her. The passer-by had attentively been examining a useless piece of split wood in his hand.

'The wheel sheared off. It had been sawn away,' he said with a sigh. 'Ah, the tricks people play on the helpless poor. Some mischievous boy, in fun, I daresay.'

'What are you saying? What do you see down there in that wood?'

'See here. The wheelshaft is not splintered. It is very neatly sawn almost through so that just a little bit remained to break by itself. God knows when it was done. Today? Yesterday? Last week? It would hold just so long until the chair came upon its first obstacle. The first high kerb. The first big stone in the road. Thank God she was not killed.'

Oh, God. Charlotta's mind filled with the picture of Katya in her primrose dress singing as she wheeled the empty chair through the hot sleepy garden, disappearing behind the shrubbery. The tool shed lay beyond.

Whatever happens to me in life, she had thought, standing on that pavement, I will always remember this picture of the military man who has ammonia in his bag, these pieces of wood in his hands, and those words in his mouth.

'Yes. Thank God,' she had said. 'Thank God she was not killed. Come, Berndt,' and she took the scared boy's trembling fingers firmly in hers and led him back home by the hand.

An hour or so later Berndt had come to her in her little study. By the oval table of glossy golden wood he had said, 'Mama, I did it.'

'What's that, my darling?' she asked sleepily, for she had been dozing in the aftermath of shock. 'What did you do? Something clever for Mama?'

'I cut the wood.'

'But, darling ...'

'I took Russo's handsaw and lay on my back and cut upwards till it was almost cut through but not quite.'

'But you were in the hammock all along. I saw you.'

'I slipped out.'

'You were in the hammock during her visit. I saw you there all the time.'

'You were not watching every single minute.'

'Don't be silly. I would have seen.'

'I did it, I say.'

'It's very simple,' Oscar had said when he came home. 'Berndt says he did it, he gets the hiding. And good for him. I think the better of him for it. Manly to take the punishment for his sister.'

'But ...'

'The sooner it's over, the sooner forgotten.'

At supper-time the atmosphere in the household had been heavy.

Charlotta had been embarrassed when Katya had come down dressed for the meal in extra-fine finery. The conclusion of the evening stretched before them, oppressive, repulsive, unjust, inevitable, and it was made worse by Katya's bright frock, glistening shoes, exaggerated pleases and thank-yous, dainty chewing, meticulous unfolding of the starched napkin and the stream of vivacious polite conversation she kept up. To the last minute Charlotta was waiting for the girl to own up.

While father and son were shut up in the study, Charlotta was pale and cold with anger. Standing on the other side of the study door in the green and ivory hallway, she looked up at the bitter stars. The silence stretched. She turned her head. Down in the yacht harbour there were many lights. Out in the water Dronningen glittered en fête. Strands of music drifted faintly across the water. He must be biting his lip, his father would not spare him.

The heavy nostalgic waft from the lilac tree scented the still expectation in the soundless house. There was movement in the air and Charlotta turned, expecting Missy's comforting presence in silent support, but the figure at the foot of the serpentine stairwell was hardly as tall as the beautifully wrought metal banister. Katya had sneaked out of bed and downstairs in her mothy-pale nightgown. Charlotta's breath came hot and confused.

The child's hair was in white curl-rags, ringleted for the night. She wore her slippers for once, for she was being the model child in contrast to her brother.

'I couldn't sleep, Mama-Tante.'

Now for the confession. It was still not too late. Charlotta could go into the study and stop this stupidity. She smiled sweetly at the penitent child, encouraging her to approach. At the smile Katya rushed forward, both hands held out for an embrace, fingers stretched, pink and slim. These days, when she went to bed she retained the full freedom of her hands. The lanolin-impregnated night-mittens had been the first thing to pass from her life with the Tëtka's passing.

'Why do you look so worried, Mama-Tante?' Katya twined the pretty unfettered hands about Charlotta's waist and played with her belt, smoothing its silk pleats. Her pretty face smiled light-heartedly up into Charlotta's. Her ringlets trembled in their curl-rags as she placed a kiss on the silk. 'There's a kiss for you.'

A cry came from the study, only one.

'Will I go to the beach tomorrow with Missy?' The girl was still playing with Charlotta's clothing, twisting her body close and standing with one leg twined about the other. The tip of her small tongue protruded between the rose-petal lips as she concentrated on some private and absorbing arrangement of the silken pleats. The smell of her newly-bathed body wafted up: clean, and lightly scented with almond soap. Charlotta listened for further cries.

'Oh, please say yes, Mama-Tante,' she said gaily. 'Please. I was so hot and uncomfortable today. I prickled. I couldn't bear another boring day cooped up in the boiling garden. I was so bored.'

'Go to bed, Katya.'

The following day Berndt went about his daily occupations a little stiff but quite cheerful and untroubled. And all the day long Katya's eyes were like drawn curtains.

CHAPTER TEN

In 1935 Katya was seventeen. Old enough to be sent away somewhere, ostensibly to be 'finished', in fact to give Charlotta a rest.
Charlotta cast about her. The years had been wearying to both of
them. Luckily there had been no repeat of the attempted
homicide. Bess continued vitally intact; living and thriving and
paying her calls to Drammensveien once a fortnight, which calls
largely accounted for her tremendous living and thriving. But
though the old prostitute was not again a direct target there had
been plenty of high-spirited incidents verging on the violent, the
thoughtless or unkind, depending on interpretation. Above all,
there had been the drip drip drip of the girl's reserve in the face
of all that Charlotta was willing to offer without condition. After
thirteen years of love, yes, love, offered by dutiful Charlotta,
sometimes against all her natural instincts and through gritted
teeth, the mother-aunt must concede defeat. Katya at seventeen
did not love Charlotta an iota more than she had loved her the
first day of coming to live in the house in Drammensveien.

Oscar was another matter. Katya was maddened to find she
loved Oscar absolutely and instinctively, in the same way he
loved her, but just when she was relaxing into the comfort of
his love she would be reminded. She might be sitting at the
sunny dressing-table with its view through the upper branches
of the lilac tree whose heart-shaped leaves made rippling
shadows on the silvered mirror she brushed her hair in, using
the silver-backed hairbrush with her mother's initials KO
floridly inscribed under the profiled Romanov eagle.

'Oscarsson?' The bird regarded her squintingly with its
single eye. 'You are friends with an Oscarsson? Your mother
also loved one of them. Not such a good idea, *ikke sant*?'

Then Katya's love for Oscar would make her maraud about the house doing riotous things, snapping her knicker elastic unkindly at the gaunt, red-haired simpleton who delivered the bread, burying pieces of Georg Jensen silver in the garden and saying Russo had done it for his running-away fund, hurling the big glass inkwell against the marble floor so the stain is there to this day and saying Berndt did it, which was impossible, as the gouts of blue-black ink streaking her legs and pinafore attested. Berndt would always bear out the impossible stories, much to his mother's irritation. But, then, Charlotta knew nothing of the duty he had vowed to the Almighty that night in his narrow cot that he would bear whatever pain he possibly could if it would spare his cousin-sister her nightly paroxysms of heartbroken weeping. Even as he took the punishments, deflecting the blame from Russo to himself, bearing out Katya's inventions that nobody believed in the first place, saving her flesh the small hurts of blame and beating, he was aware, young as he was, that for Katya to own up and take her own punishments would have made her more happy inside herself as well as more loved in the house by Oscar and particularly by Charlotta who, Berndt knew, could forgive anything but deliberate deception.

What should he do for the best? Who could he ask without giving away Katya's crimes? The boy had had no one to ask but God. The pages of the ivory-bound Bible brought him back to the clarity of the original vow: the first duty was to God, whatever the consequences: 'I shall not violate my covenant, nor alter what I have promised. I have sworn by my holiness once and for all, I shall not break my word.' He continued to shield his cousin-sister against immediate pain, to be painfully aware of the resentment against the girl growing in his mother, and to worry for the complicated, possibly evil, consequences of what had seemed such a straightforward and utterly innocent promise to God.

And Katya. What did she feel for Berndt, the last significant member of the household?

'Who?' Katya tossed her hair.

'Your cousin-brother,' croaked the knowing old Romanov eagle from the back of the well-polished hairbrush, 'Berndt.'

'*Pluff!* Useful, but hardly a player.' Katya continued to brush, counting the strokes. 'Fifty to the left side, fifty to the right, makes a hundred altogether. The old Tëtka with the mouth like a chicken's bottom brushed Mama's hair like this, with this very same brush, and then she brushed mine with it counting in Russian, like this. Om, plom ...' But Katya hadn't ever been listening in the first place. And now with the Tëtka dead the words were fading and so she made up the Russian numbers out of a rag-bag of nursery chants, bits of Norwegian, much of Missy's English, and variations on Russo's abrupt garden imprecations, and because a hundred was an awful long fag of a way to go she was only at forty when she crowed the last made-up number, 'Cento!' and jumped up jubilantly to sneak out of the house to take out *Bollinger* alone, strictly against all instructions. Managing the tight white sail through the needle rocks and complicated billowing currents of the Oslofjord she sailed towards an enormous water-colour sunset with the wind-up gramophone she had stolen out of Oscar's study, hurling forth her step-father's latest scratchy Grieg; but still it didn't make her feel free, or stop her wanting to scream, or make her glad to be alive.

Where could the volatile girl be sent to be finished? Charlotta felt strongly and instinctively that here was an opportunity to quiet the girl's soul. Further, the unquiet soul could only be calmed if some sort of belonging was established, some sort of connection made with the girl's very own heritage and roots; as cuckoo-in-residence, not usurper.

A year with Gustav on the Fødselsøy? The mind boggled.

A year in Russia, then? Hardly feasible. Not exactly a place for tourism and gentle imbibing of mother-culture with a volatile Stalin in the saddle.

'It looks,' Oscar said lightly, 'as though Stalin's gunning to outdo the French Revolution. Make 'em look amateurish in terms of arrest, trial, arbitrary execution, play top trumps in universal terror. Possibly not the place for Katya just now.' He ruffled his wife's hair. 'The Riviera,' he suggested disingenuously. 'Riva del Garda's still there, if you're really looking for a link.'

This was not altogether a stupid idea. The Riviera was a pretty ambiguous place to be sure, but, like Oslo, vice and virtue were well zoned. The ankle-braceleted poodle-clutchers co-existed in a tactful bubble, transparently close yet invisible to the *bon ton* finishing schools for Europe's nice girls, both having the good sense to run the same course in blinkers.

Charlotta knew she could have every faith in finding Katya a strict establishment hedged about with high walls and chaperonage, where Katya might be one of a bevy of misses *de bonne famille* by day absorbing the lessons of becoming useful and ornamental wives, by night tucked up in chin-to-ground nightdresses; the treat of the week a Sunday ice-cream in the café of the *parc municipal* and it was a wonder the treat didn't melt under the molten piercing glances of love-at-a-distance hurled between the girls and whatever men below dotage happened to be passing. Even though she knew all this, Charlotta in the end could not bring herself to support Oscar's really very sensible idea.

When it came to the nub of this issue Charlotta found herself overwhelmed by superstition.

To send Katya to any part of the Riviera at all would, her instincts said, be condemning the girl to only one fate: to live out her life as a luckless replica of her fatal mother, to court the duplication Charlotta so feared, dreaded, felt was utterly inevitable but would not have a hand in conniving at. The Riviera would be connivance.

Oscar was gravelled. He'd shot his one bolt.

Charlotta was stupefied with inertia and most uncharacteristically low and depressed. The yellow palace, affectionately concerned, came up with the answer. Charlotta had been *hoffdame* for fifteen years now; they were as fond of her as any, and worried to see her so low. What more educational for the girl, suggested the royal voice, than to be sent to England, the seat of one of the world's great monarchies? The court network came up with a countess in London who took in paying guests. The countess came highly recommended. Katya was sent over by the next Oscarsson boat, first class in the state cabin to show she was now grown-up and to assuage the guilt of Charlotta's relief at sending her away.

The countess was named Lulu, and the title was genuine so far as it went: the remnant of a brief *mariage blanc* swiftly annulled, and she was a reckless thirty-year-old with a line in *Debrett*, a vertiginous slice of a house in Chelsea and a bottomless need for money. Her unsteady income came from what she

liked to think of as 'profitable romance' and she'd have done a
lot better if she'd been more disciplined about it. An ebullient
woman, Lulu was prone to non-profitable falling in love with
brilliant young men of Utopian expensive ideas that always
seemed to need financing. Lulu had platinumed hair and a
myopic bravura about her that was often mistaken for great-
heartedness but, in fact, was just a huge incapacity for fore-
thought.

Katya arrived off the boat one smoky tea-time when the
October fog hung in milky swathes about the iron railings of
Carlyle Square. An actor friend of Lulu's pretended to be the
butler at the door and made a point of not widening his eyes
at the resplendent quality (if unfashionable cut) of the
Norwegian furs. Katya followed him past the chipped gilding.
A foxtrot filtered through the floorboards. The actor led her
up a stair-carpet threadbare as a gambler's elbows, into the
drawing room whose subdued lighting did nothing to conceal
its afternoon squalor. Various hermaphrodites were dotted
about the *chiaroscuro*. The foxtrot, louder now, was coming
from the radio in the corner. A couple danced without great
conviction. The room dripped *longueurs*; it had the air of a
place where people who knew each other very well were
marking time till something more exciting happened. A strange
naphthalic smell from some broken capsules hung in the air.

'It's the girl ...' Katya's appearance jolted Lulu. Temporarily
stumped, she jammed another cigarette into the amber filter
(nicotine stimulated the memory cells) and embarked on
remembering, '... the Nor – Scandi – wegian – navian!'

Lulu had a swampy notion of what was required of her in
relation to this dark streak of beauty who was to be her steady
income for six months. She'd had paying guests before, but
never one to 'finish'. A deep puzzle this, but Lulu being a
woman of ingenuity soon lighted on the main essential: Katya's
English. Drammensveien nursery vocab had been learned at
Missy's knee and it betrayed Missy's class origins.

'Toilet?' she shrieked. 'Brutish word. Lavvy, darling. I'll do a
word list for by your bed. Remember: goff not golf, and what,
not pardon. Looking-glass, not mirror. Writing-paper not note-.
And, for god's sake, sweetie, table napkin, not serviette.'

'But that is the word in Norwegian.'

'All the more reason, all the more.' Lulu adjusted her furs and took a nip from her gold pocket flask. 'Why don't you just trot down to Harrods?' Her hand described a vague arc that ran out from sheer inertia. 'They always have everything. They probably have a list of words that aren't brutish, or a dictionary or something.'

Harrods was fine. Just like Molstad's, only even finer. The book department certainly had far more books. She chose them by the covers. The dictionary had a boring cover but there was a beautiful one that the assistant said was the latest thing from America and everybody was reading it so she bought that too. The man on the cover had eyes sharp and dangerous as flints under a fedora hat and looked quite like the handsome first officer on the Oscarsson boat, except for the smoking revolver under his chin. The blonde was called Miss Wonderly and her eyes were huge like sapphires but hardboiled (a new word) and behind Miss Wonderly was a most modernistic sports car beaming headlights into eternal mystery.

Lulu pronounced the cover 'glam' when Katya brought it back and showed it to her, as Katya had always shown books to Charlotta for approval, so that was all right. The book was called The Maltese Falcon and she had to read it under the bedclothes at night by a torch because Lulu was hot as hell on electricity bills. A bulb burning after twelve was an evictable offence. When Katya had finished The Maltese Falcon she went back to Harrods and bought a more powerful torch and the nice assistant on the fourth floor directed her towards more Dashiell Hammett, Raymond Chandler and Mickey Spillane, hot off the press. The three crime-writers taught Katya English. It gave her conversation a distinctive quality, purging her vocabulary entirely of brutishness and replacing it with a knacky idiosyncrasy. Cars were heaps, even the Bentleys that sometimes called at Lulu's door. Policemen were the prowlies, and when the notoriously slothful head waiter at the Caprice was particularly sluggish Katya's voice rang clear through the restaurant's cleverly-mirrored, elaborately-chromed interior. 'Get them fleas outa your pants. Ser-vice!'

London enjoyed Katya's English.

Lulu enjoyed her paying guest. Katya was an utterly painless way to get cash, even though by some mysterious process the monthly cheque for Katya's board paid for in advance and drawn on Hambro's Bank, barely covered the cocktails, let alone the Utopian boys. The one or two profitable protectors weren't necessarily cash-cows, being better for furs and things you couldn't eat or pay bills with. This left Lulu always looking for ways to make money. Her latest wheeze was decorating. She copied Sybil Colefax for half the price. Lulu turned out expensive modern black-and-white interiors with silver paper on the walls and patent leather on the banisters, abstruse modern canvases on easels, and not entirely success-ful experimental floors. Floors, it must be said, were Lulu's Achilles' heel. They were always having to be taken up again and relaid. For some reason, floors had a habit of making whole jobs run over budget and everybody got very cross.

When Katya arrived Lulu was working for Oliver Hill on the two big white houses he'd just completed in the west corner of Chelsea Square, now numbers 40 and 41. It was all very exhausting. Real work. Grimbo. And then, one magical afternoon, things changed. Lulu had got in from shopping as usual. She was dying for a drink as usual. After the drink she'd give ready money to spend the rest of the day drinking Gibsons in the heavenly subterranean gloom of the Silver Slipper in Regent Street instead of earning her crust making Oliver's interiors spring off the drawing board and into three dimensions.

'Oh, the brutish life of a working girl.' Lulu collapsed on the rather unyielding brushed-steel sofa, letting her parcels sink to the ground. 'Hell! This thing's uncomfortable. We must get some cushions. Zebra might look glam. What d'you think, Katya? I'm so utterly miz. This brutish work. Why doesn't money just *come* to the deserving? Could you bear to run round to Poland Street and pick up those silver satin swatches for Oliver's sofas and run them round to Chelsea Square? I simply haven't the energy. Could you just?'

A habit was formed. 'Darling, could you just?' rang round the house in refrain.

Lulu had a slave.

Katya had good fun, and a purpose.

'Could-you-just' became about the best era of her life, dash-ing about London on top-urgent missions. She wrote the very first letter she had ever written to Charlotta saying she had found a job, which was overstating the case a little, but the letter conveyed so much genuine, undisguised *joie de vivre* that Charlotta believed what she most wanted to believe, that Katya was enjoying a period of good, innocent fun and sorting herself out in the process. Charlotta sighed with relief, and relaxed.

Katya wasn't telling her everything, of course. Her letter didn't say she'd dropped the surname Oscarsson and had started to call herself Katya O, initially because it was easier in sweatshops and factories. In society it gave her a certain *cachet*. In her mind it stood for Olovanova, the surname she did not quite dare openly adopt but hugged to her heart. The change didn't even register with Lulu, past whose emerald-bedecked ears foreign names simply flowed in an indistinguishable stream unless they were Rothschild, Gulbenkian or Croesus.

Katya O changed her colour to black and her style to hodge-podge *nostalgie de la Russie*. She wore what she imagined Russian anarchists wore. The mean streets of Moscow might have been surprised at the cut of her black, and even more so at her berets. She'd a neat line in entire raven's wings garnished with inky-spotted veiling and worn tiltingly over the eye. She took to interjecting her speech with one or two of the abrupt imprecations she'd heard Russo utter when a fan-belt had just broken on the Alfa, say, or a brown molehill sullied the perfect green of Oscar's English lawn. She discovered the shop in Burlington Arcade that sold black Sobranie cigarettes with elegant gold tips that came in a packet embossed with her mother's old friend the Romanov eagle. Black gaspers made her one up even on the Chandler dames.

Despite the gaspers Katya's cheeks achieved the bloom Charlotta had never managed to instil via healthy cow's milk in pastoral Oslo. The vigorous pulse of the capital city was responsible. Katya found London wildly exciting. Its rhythm pumped fast in her veins. Maybe this was happiness.

'It's the champagne darling,' Lulu told her. 'We pee out so much every night it fills the drains and then there's nowhere for it to go so it simply 'vaporates into the air,' vaguely waving, 'and rises and rises all around. A scientist told me at a party. If ever I'm short of a bob, darling, I just open my pores and breathe. If it's raining I stand and lick the rain off my upper lip. I swear to you it fizzes on the tongue. And it's a lot cheaper than Krug in those brutishly tiny thimbles those meanster robbers sell you at the Ritz.'

Katya was never still long enough to stand and lick, nor was she ever low enough to want to. She streaked across London, a quick black nervy leggy sham-anarchist, a crayon-dash trailing smoke like a forest fire from her black cigarette.

Katya learned London in the way she had never been allowed to learn Oslo's comparable dimensions and diversions. She went from lockups in Limehouse to sweatshops in Soho picking up a ribbon here, upholstery there, soi-disant genuine Lalique at suspiciously low prices from drossy outlets where nobody had a face, let alone a name. Screwing up her eyes against her Sobranie's smoke she'd lean up against shabby door-jambs demanding in her extraordinary English whatever Lulu was wanting from the surprised man who answered the doorbell to this vision in black telling him: 'Lulu needs her samples. Ankle it.'

Then she'd take the goods to 40 Chelsea Square where Oliver Hill's chef des travaux intérieurs with his silky moustache, marcelled hair and gold-plated workbook was trying to complete the job as specified in the teeth of a stupefying budget already dead, buried and now on its way down to hell, thanks to Lulu's floors.

'I've brought today's samples, Chef. Want to check the parcel?'

'Flooring?' The polite simper would turn to hollow despair without a muscle moving.

'Yup. Flooring's what I said. Chin up, it's your lucky day.'

Lulu's flooring samples always affected people in the trade. Either they'd turn oddly lifeless and quiet, or they'd start to laugh in an odd, shrill way just the far side of hysteria.

One day she suggested to Lulu that she dump flooring altogether. 'Why not quit floors? Can the comedy and take air. Face it, you're on a loser so why not close your eyes to the possibilities? Sub-contract to a little man in pale ash parquet. It won't lift or stain or melt or,' she touched on a nerve, 'erupt like Mount Etna in the middle of a party for the Archbishop of Canterbury. It won't ruin your career.'

The two of them were in the first-floor drawing room in the Carlyle Square house, keeping warm under Katya's sumptuous royal-grade (but dowdy) Norwegian full-length silver-fox coat, due to be remodelled by a little woman Lulu knew, and meanwhile doing sterling stuff against the frost flowers that bloomed on the window glass and London's freezing fog that infiltrated everything solid, bricks, bones, but never touched Lulu's optimism or Katya's eternal sense of adventure. They were sitting on the floor, leaning their backs against the icy brushed-steel sofa. None of Lulu's protectors had yet stumped up with the zebra cushions.

'Darling you're very young.' Lulu squinted at the ash on the end of her cigarette.

'Just a little girl, I know.'

'Can it. I'm about to offer a secret of life.'

'Need an ashtray while you're offering?'

'Always so helpful. I don't know where you've been all your life and I didn't get a full specification from your parents about finishing but I'll take a risk. Somebody's got to tell you about fetishes. It's probably part of finishing you off. I dream about them: floors, floors, floors. Reaching for miles into the far blue yonder. Stone, metal, putty, glass, pink marzipan, black ink. Some people have fetishes about shoes, or they're blubber fiends or rubber fiends. Or they can only do it with turbans of wax fruit on their head. Fancy. With me it's floorings. A world full of pale ash floorboards simply wouldn't be the same.'

'Brutish?'

'Brutissimo.'

'Tough.'

'I'll say.'

In the evenings, when the lockups and ribbon factories closed and life under the railway arches came to a standstill, even for trade, Katya must stop running round London on her missions; instead she and Lulu ran around to parties. Sometimes together, sometimes separately. There were a lot of parties. Lulu's were unfettered affairs freely populated by opportunistic good-looking young men: mashers, polo players, sailors, butlers on their nights off dressed as executioners, suicidal poets, Jesuits from Farm Street dressed as sailors, decorators got up as soutaned priests. Somebody always did an exotic dance. Everybody was looking for everybody else's money and when the drink ran out they were none of them too proud to rummage about in the housemaids' cupboards for *eau de Cologne*, methylated spirits, naphthalic-smelling varnishes, metal-polish and floor-polish. Often the entire party went on to the delicious frantic subterranean cavern of the heavenly Silver Slipper where everything was on offer, and often it finished the night in the cells of the Gerald Row police station.

For Katya there were other parties as well, thanks to Charlotta.

Impeccably correct pasteboard would suddenly arrive in the post announcing out of a clear blue sky that somebody she'd never heard of would be At Home on a certain date at a very grand address. Lulu explained to her what this meant. In essence it meant Charlotta in Norway had pulled her lady-in-waiting strings so Katya could dance. Queen Maud the English-born had been flung into the equation. Town houses by Adam and William Kent opened their carved mahogany doors to Katya. She was welcomed warmly by hostesses in musty ancestral dresses of heavy curtain fabric saggingly draped to reveal a long depressing clavicle or a sharp shoulder-blade. It was a world of flushed débutantes. Nobody had scarlet lips or platinum hair or long shiny dresses that looked like milk poured over them to form a glistening pool round their feet. They danced the waltz and the quickstep in these houses, not the foxtrot and certainly not the creep. They talked bloodlines, human, horse and royal, and when they'd exhausted genealogy they analysed the coming Coronation in obsessive detail.

The air did not taste of champagne at these parties, but stale wine cup. It hit the palate without fizz.

One night as she was coming home from one of these dull dances and the February rain was swarming like gnats in the haloes of Carlyle Square's yellow street-lamps, Katya realised a crisis. She had now spent five months in London. Five down, one to go. To go back to Oslo.

She opened Lulu's chrome-plated front door. Faint strains of radio music hung on the dusty air of the house. A waft of the current Utopian's eau-de-Portugal hung miasmic in the hall.

'Raided early?' she shouted up the stairs, in case Lulu had company and needed to do up buttons.

'Come in, darling.'

Lulu was sitting on the floor alone, bereft, the sentimental turbid fog of the Utopian's hair oil only emphasising her lack of companion.

The curtains hadn't been drawn. The yellow light glowing high in the rain above the street didn't flatter Lulu's tawdry drawing room, which looked as though it had been strained through pea soup. Ella Fitzgerald was singing the year's hit from the radio in the corner '... a-tisket a-tasket'. Lulu was on a striped cushion on the floor, her back against the sofa. She'd kicked off her shoes and was bebopping her toes in time to Ella. A bottle of Benedictine sat within easy reach of her hand, whose nails were varnished the colour of arterial blood.

'He's gone,' she said, and Katya understood.

Another dream had crashed.

'Drinkie?'

Too gloomed even to answer, Lulu flicked her cigarette ash on to the tired Aubusson; depths of despair.

'One more month,' Katya said, joining her landlady on the floor, 'and it's home to the snowbound hutch in Norway.'

'Five months already? Must you? I do so adore having you here. And the lovely money that comes with you. Always on the dot. A standing order is such a bright golden thing.'

'It's the lovely money that's the problem. If I'd money I'd stay for ever but I've got none except the allowance the shipping office sends each month and it goes through my purse quicker than water. London's a greedy monster. It eats money worse than Ymir. He was the father of the giants, you know, and he ate all sorts of things, mostly bits of his relatives.'

In fact, it wasn't Ymir that was the culprit but all the taxis: Lulu's could-you-just taxis ate money and Lulu couldn't possibly offer to pay her back. How could she, when she'd just taught Katya it was brutish form to talk about money?

'Katya, don't cry, you'll start me off. Don't you want to go home to the big house and all those lovely servants cleaning things all day?' Lulu hitched the skirt dipping between her thin-as-a-racehorse knees, caught sight of the carpet which, puzzlingly, had crossed the line from Bohemian to dirty when she wasn't looking. She rubbed at it a little. 'And the snow sounds rather sweet, even if there is rather a lot. Tell me about the snowbound hutch. What's it like?'

Katya rubbed her eyes with a handkerchief that could have been cleaner. They owed the laundry maid. 'Big and grand and out of style.' Her voice sounded flat and discouraged. 'Its time has run out but it doesn't know it. The house is so solid it'll last another thousand years. They built it twenty years ago. Built and new-furnished throughout. *Style Norvégienne* 1917. Biedermeier. Furniture on tiptoe. High Horror Potential. Everything's just gone out of fashion. Goody-goody primrose, not elegant beige.'

'Floors?'

Katya frowned. 'I never noticed.'

'Good God.' Lulu frowned, profoundly shocked. 'Limewood, I expect. Northern climes. Limewood for show, and deal behind the green-baize door.'

'Floors didn't mean anything to me then.'

'We were all children once, I suppose. But what's it like, apart from *passé*? You haven't told me very much so far, apart from brutish Biedermeier. Bobbles? Fringes? Mashed-potato brocade?'

'How odd.' Katya ate a second-hand olive out of the vanished Utopian's abandoned glass. Her mouth had suddenly remembered the powdery custard taste of the deb party's trifle. 'It's ... dead. Wholesome dairy-fed, no pepper, no olives, certainly no absinthe. Clean. Organised.'

'Servants?' Lulu envied.

'Battalions. Domestic clockwork. The sofas go into summer covers on the seventeenth of May, winter covers the seventeenth of September. At ten a.m. on the dot. Every year. Exactly the same man does it one year older. Spotted muslin curtains blow in the good, wholesome, ozone-laden air and the window panes are so bright both sides it looks as though there's just air, no glass at all. And, boy, it's quiet. The house is so quiet you can hear a mouse combing its whiskers. It makes you want to scream, it's so quiet and polite. I did scream once, just before I came to PG with you. I screamed as loud as I could just to make a noise, and screamed and screamed. I pretended I was being murdered. A whole wagonful of police came. Charlotta told them she was the one who'd screamed because she'd seen a rat and this becalmed them and they became calmer and calmer. Charlotta's strong on coffee and home-made cake and conversation. When they arrived they were hopping mad. When they went away they had stomachs big as anthills. She told me that a young girl could never be too careful of her reputation and that up in the mountains was the place to go if one wanted to test one's lungs. She didn't even smack me, or lock me up, or shout. The Tëtka would have beaten me till I bled. She loved me so. It's a long time ago but I remember. It's like that always. Charlotta is so sensible, so correct, always so correct. She's like ... what's she like? I don't know the name of the type of flooring she'd be, which is what you'd really understand, but if she was a piece of furniture she'd be one of those upright gilt chairs on tiptoes with crowns on the velvet seat that *hoffdamer* sit on in royal palaces. She's a human piece of court furniture that just moves about from place to place from time to time very quietly indeed, never crashing into anything on the way. She never has dirty fingernails. There's nothing you can do to make her cross or raise her voice or to hurt her except if you hurt Berndt. And I managed that once or twice, I can tell you.'

'Berndt? What an odd name. I suppose they can't help it in Norway. Tell me about Berndt? Should I marry him?'

'He'd be impervious to your charms. Don't get me wrong. He's no pansy. But he's got God. Brother Berndt's about as much fun as a stiff in a morgue. I threw him into an anthill once. They have huge ones in Norway. It's the Manhattan of ants. And I threw a honeycomb on top, all drippy. It's a Red Indian torture, I read about it in Fenimore Cooper. Except the Red Indians tie them down, of course. They worship Berndt but not now so much as they did. He's refused to go into the army because violence is against his convictions and he's being a missionary instead.'

'A missionary?' The word was strange to Lulu's lips.

'He's gone to Lapland to minister to the heathen.'

'Goodness.' Arterial blood moved towards Benedictine.

'My real father hated my mother and so he can't bear to see

me except when Charlotta puts the blacks on him because it's
my birthday or Christmas. And then I get taken to his house to
see him except he doesn't see me because he looks at a spot
above my head where the wall meets the ceiling. They say I
look like my mother, She's very, very beautiful.' Katya used the
present tense because a bit of her mind didn't believe Katya
had died at all.

Since coming to London and assuming the identity of Katya
O, a lot had changed in her memory's theatre. The emotions
and the versions of stories were muddled. In Oslo, fact and
fantasy stayed in their boxes. An odd thing happened here that
never happened in Oslo. Here on the streets she'd started to be
certain she saw her mother; just a glimpse or a feeling and a
waft of scent; the rim of her mother so to speak. The ethereal
intimation was at its strongest when she passed the flower-
seller at the corner of Belgrave Square where the air was
infused by violets. She'd linger, talking to the poor fat old man
with the badly shaved dewlaps and misshapen body lumpy as
porridge swathed in grey cardigan, for Katya, too, could be
compassionate if the hardship case was her very own
discovery and Charlotta wasn't there to oversee. The flower-
seller dealt in violets over a long season, a popular flower in
all its forms. Parma violets, purple-black in big opulent
bunches the size of a good bunch of hothouse grapes, for
pinning on mink and silver fox, shy laneside Devon violets in
thin farthing bunches for housemaids' followers to buy. Standing in that aura of violets she sometimes felt as though she'd
dissolved the boundaries between herself and her mother. As
though the two of them were enveloped inside the pool of
flickering scent, as if the anarchist's black contained both their
bodies. Then she'd give the old man a coin, pin the bunch to
her lapel and leave on a rush of the brilliant air that sparkled
between Belgrave Square's dazzling high white houses.

'Tell me,' Lulu said, eyes narrowing, 'about Oscar Oscarsson.'
Lulu harboured secret hopes of the unseen sender of big
standing orders. 'Does he ever come to London? What's he like?'

'I know he thinks I'm a moocher, trash, just like he thought
my mother was trash. The thing is, they own me. It's a life
sentence, for ever. A one-way street.'

'Bit early to declare defeat, darling. The campaign's hardly begun. Why don't you just borrow? I'm sure you can find some lovely rich man at one of your grand parties. You've got the *entrée*. London's awash with rich men. Running with lucre. Find one and bend him to your will.'

'Bending's not on. Oscar and Charlotte would kick and scream at bending. It's marriage or bust.' Half-moon wisps of fog floated by the window. 'If I'm to stay here I'll have to hang myself on a hook in the meat market. Husband-hunt. Everyone thinks Norwegian shippers drip gold. It shouldn't take long.'

Lulu put her carmine lips together and whistled. Then she applied the gold hip flask to them for the shock.

Katya reached over and used the surface of Lulu's shiny flask to peruse her teeth. 'At the next party I might play Russian roulette with men for bullets.'

Russian roulette appealed, and not just because of its nationality. It gave a certain piquancy to the next pre-dance dinner party. Katya took her seat, and a deep breath. Custom demanded she turn first to the man on her right, who would engage her in conversation during the first course until after the fish course when the whole party would turn synchronously to the left, whatever point the curve of their conversation had reached with their right-hand neighbour. Sticklers had been known to turn mid-word. Katya's first port of call was an accomplished flirt rather past his best; he read her card and the cupidity was too evident, the charm too familiar from Lulu's opportunists and Utopians. He had dark skin and a handsome head of iron-grey hair, rather too perfect. By the end of the soup she had an urge to test its veracity.

'Tug the rug,' Raymond Chandler whispered subversively at her elbow. By the fish course she had realised a fatal resemblance to Oliver Hill's marcelled *chef de travaux* and she recalled a conversation they had conducted on the merits of Pond's Vanishing Creme for the complexion. Macabre and fascinating as this all was, it was certainly unalluring. When the turtle soup had come and gone, also the curled white fish, and the entrée was about to arrive, every head at the table behaved like a flock of weathercocks caught in a simultaneous capricious wind. They all turned exactly one hundred and eighty degrees.

The face to her left was set in exhaustion, it was dark and drawn and spiritless and it belonged to Sholto Fortescue, who was also in a crisis; but neither he nor she had an inkling he existed in a giant teardrop of inertia and melancholy. He certainly seemed a very jolly fellow, saying 'attagirl' and 'whizzo' in vigorous tones where others would have used the word 'yes'. He laughed obligingly at all her best stories about flooring and bishops, was modest and sardonic in his banter and, from what she could see of him sitting down, was energetic and lean. Neither of them had any idea he'd lost his way in the utter fog of pessimism pervading this period before the coming war.

He spoke of learning to fly and 'fiddling around with navigation'. Had already qualified as a pilot because 'Obviously it's all coming to a head quite soon and the RAF'd be most laughs,' and he didn't tell her that in the teeth of a family who all went into the Greenjackets in order to keep the generations in every-increasing honour, penury and mourning widows, he had taken himself off to Harvard where he read engineering, while paying (brutish word) his way by taking jobs. Unlike his forebears, the best moments in Sholto's youth were not spent in the school corps squarebashing the parade ground shoulder-to-shoulder, but in the school's maintenance man's workshop where, as a mechanically minded schoolboy, he built cameras that worked, wirelesses that sent and received, and deliciously complex alarm systems, whose results were not wholly predictable. By the age of sixteen he had registered his first scientific discovery, a radio component later taken up by the manufacturer Bush, and written a paper on the likely path of development towards a high-definition electron microscope. He was now building a business in an engineering workshop developing aero engines by day and studying navigation by night for the aerial war that would so obviously be wide-ranging and critical. Sholto combined hoeing this individual, and indeed nationally vital, row with a huge load of shame and guilt that he wasn't doing the proper thing expected of him by tradition and antecedent: he'd robbed the immemorial regiment of this generation of Fortescues. He was shaming history.

As well as doing all these things Sholto was also flogging the party circuit because glamour was as much part of the nascent RAF ethos as bravery: you were no one unless you danced a smooth foxtrot. Lounge lizards only need apply, so chocks away, chin chin, and happy landings. No wonder Katya thought he looked exhausted. She'd no idea her dinner-neighbour had so much in common with Oscar who, coming to the same conclusion about present days and the likelihood of war, was even then putting out contracts helter-skelter to shipyards all round the world, building as many ships as he possibly could and leasing or buying others. Troop carriers would be needed, and cargo ships, and it was bad luck that his *fordømmet* commercial contracts precluded him from tendering for submarine contracts as well.

At dinner she looked marvellous. Her black eyes sparkled, her funny accent enchanted him and her language made him giddy, like leaves spiralling down and veering wildly at the last minute just when they seemed within reach. He asked her to dance.

She inspected him thoroughly when they stood up from the table, the usual top-to-toe, making certain he was clean, free of bow-legs, flat feet, insect life. Hazel English eyes, hazel English hair, parted to the side, fair for an Englishman; a long, bony nose that cast a shadow, and sallow-skinned, but maybe that was partying and tiredness. He was, at least, not one of those Englishmen so fair they looked like plump pink pigs. He looked lonely and stifled in his black tail-coat and white tie, and there was something absolutely transitory and sad about his rational fatalism, his acceptance that war was inevitably to come, together with the correct way he wore this evening uniform, as though white tie was just a prelude to blue combat uniform, and that a prelude to the uniform white shroud; all interchangeable, inevitable sequence. His acceptance of the skull beneath his own skin touched her; but this wouldn't have been enough if there hadn't been part of him in rebellion against the set order of things.

'It's just so bloody dim. In the age of the aeroplane the top brass in the war ministry are still making plans to send cavalry regiments into battle.'

She explained that she, too, was a modernist and an iconoclast. That her and Lulu's interiors were the exact interior equivalent of the RAF planes being sent in to do warfare in

the drawing rooms left behind fashion, the lagging cavalry in
an aeroplane age, and this pleased her very much and made
her think they had a great deal in common.

When they left the party, the air touched their faces with a
finger of ice. It made her shiver, as though a goose had walked
over her grave, and she was ready to be convinced that fate
had had a hand in suggesting roulette before that very party
and it wasn't much of a step to transmute fate into Katya-
Mama, here in the town where the street corners smelt of
violets in the twilight.

He rumpled his fair hair under his pushed-back hat, as
though happier to get the air into it. They walked close, as if
the cold was the reason, and he invited her to spend the next
Friday-to-Monday at his family house in the country.

Lulu, sitting up agog, said golly, how glam, and Katya had
all the luck and if she, Lulu, had decided to play roulette she'd
have found herself between a pansy and a penniless chaser.
Fortescue was obviously neither and sounded as though he'd
probably do very well for a husband; he was unlikely to be a
complete brute because he'd said Friday-to-Monday rather
than 'weekend'.

'Where would I be without you, Lulu, in this jungle of
brutishness?'

'Gobbled up by the mashers of Mayfair.'

The family house was far out in some unpronounceable bit of
the country that had great age, no mountains, and was as far
from the sea as it could possibly be. The house itself had sat so
long in the same place it had sunk down in a dip and never got
the sun's rays at all. It was as if the earth had slid in stealthy
erosion from the rounded hills, piling up about it in a gradual
extinguishing mound, an impression only reinforced by the
green and sluggish moat lapping its toes, a primeval soup from
which some primitive sea monster might any time emerge,
blurring all distinction between prehistory and now, just as
Fortescue consciousness blurred all small distinctions within
the long Fortescue continuum, between today and the last few
hundred years they had lived here.

Sholto became silent but far more genuinely cheerful when
the tops of Michaelmas Hall's tall diamond-knapped barley-

twist chimneys showed, looking to Katya merely like two or three bricks scattered on the turf horizon. He flipped back the lid from the motorbike's sidecar, gesturing and mouthing things she couldn't hear, nor particularly wanted to, so blissfully isolated had she been, transported through space in her transparent capsule.

Passing slowly towards the timeless house over the swamp-moat she expected giant palaeolithic life forms to rise up from the brown water and devour them, machine and all, in one gollop, an image bringing to mind the Tëtka's apocalyptic account of the huge cracks that appeared in the San Francisco earth and spouted fire. (The Tëtka had made it her duty to accumulate a grotesque collection of illustrated periodicals of the time and show them to the little girl. Both had believed the ruptured gas and service pipes rippling under stress to be giant animal tentacles waving up from a submerged under-crust world such as Hitler and his scientists believed in, and Hieronymus Bosch painted. No wonder they neither of them thought it worth even trying to win a place in heaven with the pit so near, so real.)

Sholto's heart saw quite the opposite to any under-crust world. The swampy moat always had the effect of lifting his spirits into a realm of positive glee never matched the far side of the ancestral water. Pushing his goggles up on his forehead (he was always pushing constraints away from his face and neck), he looked like a white-eyed penguin, as she tried to tell him over the engine noise of the motorbike while he, simultaneously, was trying to tell her the history of the house and indistinct garden, taking one hand off the handlebars to gesture towards the things he was speaking about. Neither had a clue what the other was saying; shrugging, they motored on.

The sunken walls of the house were of mellow Tudor-sized bricks, oblong biscuits sandwiched with lime mortar so decayed they stayed together by habit, like an old marriage, rather than by cause.

She was surprised at the malnourished English lawns, scalped, balding and rabbit-scuffed. Oscar would have frothed and thrown things, had Russo's grass ever reached such dismal depths. A few carefully shaped sparse beds had been carved out of acid clay. Greenfly, leatherjackets and thrips throve on the singleton bushes of hopefully-named roses, 'Orangeade', 'Super Star', 'Salmon Sensation', that Sholto's mother had introduced in a desperate play for her generation's craving 'a bit of colour'. Lulu would have clutched her forehead and Sybil Colefax would undoubtedly have fainted.

'Mother'll be in the kitchen.'

When chopping onions Mrs Fortescue always kept a glass of sherry to hand as an antidote, and sang rousing hymns at the top of her voice to keep her spirits up in the damp dungeony kitchen.

She was a tall, capable, bony, rather masculine horsy woman, whose brindled hair came corrugated on Mondays but thereafter gradually untwiddled until the Lord's Day. Widowed in the First World War, any efforts towards beauty had long seemed pointless in the face of the endless grinding needing to cope, with no money and a position in the world to keep up. She was in the kitchen, as her son had predicted, at the preparation of their supper. When they came in, her back was turned. Katya's first impression was of the hair hanging abruptly short of a brown neck criss-crossed with thin cracks like an outdoor servant's.

Katya thought she was a cook.

'Thine be the glory ...' (loudly, to the tune of Macabees) *chop*. Moisture ran down the walls that Katya was later to describe to Lulu as abattoir red. 'Ri-sen conqu'ring Son ...' *chop*.

Katya thought she was a drunken cook.

Sholto leaned over the lachrymatory fumes to kiss the cheek whose broken blue-red veins told an outdoor story covered in unevenly-applied face powder.

'Mother, this is Katya.'

Mother extended a right forearm, still holding the short sharp chopping knife and bending the wrist back in upon itself so that Katya should put her fingers round the wrist to shake hands. Katya, not understanding the purpose of the gesture, reverted to childhood and upbringing. She bent her knee and gave the bobbing curtsy Charlotta had taught her to give any elders and betters that happened to come her way: Queen Maud, old Bess, her father Gustav, whoever. Mrs Fortescue thought she was being mocked in her own kitchen. The misunderstanding begun between them was never to be remedied.

'And?'

Back in London, Monday night, and Lulu wanted to know.

She charged the syllable with a world of expectation. 'And?' meant 'Please describe the furnishings down to the smallest detail, not forgetting the flooring.'

'Morgue. Museum. Formaldehyde house,' Katya waved an arm, Schiaparelli chiffon billowed, 'pickled ancestors. Things only there because the people before had them. And don't ask me what because I don't know your English periods and things.' Head cocked, she considered. 'A few pretty things. Chinese pots. Things like that. Most big, and broken. Yes, a lot of broken things. Mahogany whatnots actually with whatnot in.'

'Whatnots?' Lulu repeated the word in joyous contempt.

'Stuffed birds, wax flowers inside domes and things people have shot all mixed up with the first tennis racquets in history, baby carriages and cricket sets and hats with mildew. They've never thrown a stick away but they've sold everything that could raise a penny, which is the reason for it all being so big. Sholto says nobody wants to buy big things. They've got no money, you see. It's all gone but he's going to make it back.'

'It all sounds like the height of respectability. Deeply drear. You won't blush for your in-laws. When you've your feet under the table we can have a wonderful time making the house all pretty with your lovely money that your daddy will have given you on such a suitable marriage. What fun!' Lulu's eyes lit with Oscarsson-fuelled budgets and decorative schemes.

A few weekends later, Katya lay alone in the ancestral woods between grey-limbed beech, contemplating his question, while above her head some remnants of dry brown foliage clung on against the dying falls of winter. They had been riding and she was still in her tweed hacking jacket, yellow high-necked jumper, jodhpurs and string-backed pigskin riding gloves. Riding might take the place of sailing? It wasn't unlike flying over the face of the water in funny little *Bollinger*. Her fingers searched through the tired beige-bleached end-of-year grass tufts, looking for the dark heart-shaped leaves of the ground-hugging violets that would tell her something. She didn't find them, which was maybe a good thing and better than an uninterpretable signal. She found instead the close flat dark rosettes of next year's cow parsley, sturdily pushing up through the brown-tinged ivy and a thin trickle of late ants, brown and shiny and almost exactly the same colour as her eyes, mountaineering laboriously through the hills and valleys of the greenery. Yellowhammers flickered nervously in the dry rattling of last year's left-behind leaves overhead; pale primrose cocked heads watched the ants covetously but dared not dart down with Katya in situ on the wood's floor.

At home the fieldfares would just be arriving. Great flocks of the tiny birds landing in pine forests, weighing down the branches and twittering. Charlotta always loved the arrival, saved bread-heels in the basket weeks ahead, and funny old Russo staggered about the garden in his wolfskin coat on snowshoes like tennis racquets so he wouldn't sink in and spoil the prettiness of the snowy garden while spreading the food evenly for the little birds. Year after year it was a heart-stopping moment, the noise of the flock landing and teeming in the garden, and the gleam of the sea beyond. That was something to look at. Here, there was no water at all. Nothing that moved or shone. Only the amphibious amorphous wreath in which the house was mired, and Daphne Fortescue's appalling fishpond with a simpering concrete cupid rising from dirty, tangled weed like an unfastidious mermaid's hair.

If she was missing home-birds and water, what on earth was she doing here? Katya kicked moodily at the earth, picked a stiff stalk of dried grass and started poking it between her teeth: gum health was all the rage. There was a far stronger imperative to end what had gone before than to start anything. And yet. It was a way out. Obviously she was loved. Nothing new or particularly important in that. She was touched by her effect on him, by the curious lyricism she seemed to unleash in him. She liked that, and she liked what it was aligned to: toughness of character, independence, sense of purpose.

In this old, tired, frightened world tottering on the brink of war, Sholto was part of the most purposeful intellectual and practical expansion plans of the time. Katya sensed this and, while not being particularly interested in the details, the mechanics, she'd picked up on his involvement at the cutting edge. Power oozed a special seduction. Oscar Oscarsson had the same quality (not that the parallel occurred to her). Oscar Oscarsson and Sholto Fortescue both were world pirates prepared to look fate in the eye and have a go at hijacking it.

Such people at this moment had an extraordinarily urgent, purposeful quality, distinguishing them from the rest of the world, which was feeling flabby, desperate and inadequate, relying on hope rather than action, and preferring to bury its head rather than confront the need for what Sholto was working towards: the defence of the realm, the effective defence. In nitty-gritty terms: to put an armed cordon of barbed wire in the skies about the British Isles. In terms of shopping lists, Sholto's concern was to establish an eventual bombing force equipped with twin- and four-engined truly heavy bombers, a metropolitan fighter defence of modern eight-gun monoplane designs, along with a coastal command force to protect the UK's vital import shipping supply lines.

Sholto was, then, at the height of things and the depth of things. At the top end he knew exactly what was what and what was wanted. In personal terms blank, zero, zero minus. Even in the pre-war moment he was learning exactly the things his mother had learned in the previous war: that war might be presented as glamour but in fact it was about separation from hearth, kith and kin, deprivation, often barely civilised living and working conditions. Perceived as drama, it could only be conquered by routine drudgery in combination with hazard, boredom and frustration.

This society by no means perfect: was it worth fighting for? He'd been asking himself the question over the last three years. Worth losing his life and a whole generation again, as his father and his father's generation had been lost? Before Katya came he had been foundering in an odd dualism, on the one hand sick of a present glitter-society, seeing no reason to give his life to perpetuate its pointless structure; on the other hand throwing himself into the sharp end of things well before he needed to. Preparing early for various reasons.

Reason One: he might as well do well what needed to be done.

Reason Two: if he ducked out of this he was ducking out of

the latest chapter in the continuing cause for which his father had given his life.

Reason Three: his life and society being worthless was all the more reason for doing this thing well; why not blaze like a comet in the pastel sky of indecision and mediocrity?

Reason Four: aha! This was the turning-point; this turned the other three on their heads. Reason Four: Katya, Katya and again Katya, cancelling out all thoughts that the world might be mediocre, not worth saving. His period of limbo was broken, his desire for life surged as strong as the day he'd elbowed his way into the world through Daphne Fortescue's spread legs and howled for air. All the introspective questions were forgotten. The soul-searching over the last three long, pointless, dragging years flown out of the window. Katya, Katya.

Katya put her hand in her jodhpur pocket, dug out a match, relit her cigarette. The winds teased the match's little flame and gave a death-rattle to the dry leaves above her head. Shall I, shan't I?

He had a certain style both raw and elegant. That appealed to her. His uniform was devastatingly chic. He told her he'd had it made in Savile Row out of non-regulation cloth, a mixture of cashmere and gaberdine: 'If I survive it'll be comfortable. If it's curtains, well, I might as well have an elegant shroud.'

Resting on one elbow, her head bowed intent over the marching column, she yes-no-yes-noed the passing column of ants but kept losing count so she stubbed the cigarette out in the busy brown stream, which hesitated not a moment over its smouldering brothers. She threw the butt away, picked one flailing individual ant in her gloved hand and started taking it apart like an amateur vivisector.

'Shall I, shan't I?' she questioned the dry crackling sections of the shiny brown broken-down body.

'Nei! For noe tull!' she shouted abruptly. It was too silly. What had she been thinking of? To live among this dullness of the English country classes whose national pastime seemed to be the stifling of life?

She would go home when time was up and she would wheedle Oscar for a ticket to San Francisco and have huge adventures.

Of course!

She beamed at the poor ant who'd given his life for this insight. Had he not been quite so squashed-raisin juicily messy she might have kissed him for the clear decision he'd brought her. A life not given in vain.

CHAPTER ELEVEN

The proposal had come at night, under swarms of stars.

Over the white balustraded balcony a section of Green Park, a hinted sheen of water under a black and navy blur of foliage against sky, was framed by live torches with leaping blue-yellow flames on the two gateposts of the In and Out club. He had only to glance to his left to see the cool lines of her profile in oyster satin with a high Byronic collar, her arms misty in long gloves that gave her the charming air of coming fresh from a dairy where she'd dipped them in cream. She shivered; he took off his jacket to put it round her shoulders, the usual dance-time sacrifice of the anxious and expectant lover.

'Milkmaids used to herd cows in the park,' he said. His throat was swelling convulsively. Tonight was to be the night. He'd made up his mind to pop the question, and here he was talking about milkmaids and choking up. His hand went up to his white tie, his throat. Take a pull, Sholto. The hand ended up giving his jaw an irresolute rub.

'I cannot imagine cows in London,' Katya said, in the decided voice of one who spends all day chasing bullion fringe and Indian chintz in the cat's-pee-smelling hinterland of fuggy sweatshops smeared along the Thames's muddy reaches towards Limehouse and the Isle of Dogs. 'No cows is one of the prime reasons for living in London. Oslo is full of health and cows. Here they are simply incredible, thank God. Give me London and a cow-free future.'

'I will, if you like.'

'What, both?'

'Till death do us part, if you like.' (He might have said for richer for poorer or one of the other marriage phrases. His lighting on this one showed he had not entirely shrugged off death and the heavy clouds of despair.)

When the party had finished he drove her back to Lulu's round Belgrave Square. She started to speak about her deepest secret in the plainest possible language, giving him the idea she was for once translating a childhood story word for word from Norwegian into English, putting nothing of herself into the received story: no Chandlerese colour, no Lulu slang. In fact, he was wrong about the language. What she was translating was the Tëtka's never-forgotten Russian bedtime story, the every-night-identical word-for-word litany the Tëtka had concocted to make this second Katya's own mental brown bottle of dependence.

' "I will come back to fetch you." That's what Mama said.' Katya's voice was thin and flat as a child's. ' "Look for me at that uncertain hour of twilight. Look for me when the violets are in bloom. When you least expect me, there I shall be!" That's what she said, you see.'

'Poor kid. She never came?'

'It was not her fault. She could not. This earthquake came instead, you see.'

His heart, already lost, sank into a further loving pity unlike anything yet known.

While she was speaking of her mother it wasn't only her voice that changed. Reality reconfigured. He asked himself if the whole of her life had been spent in trying not to seem unhappy? If she, too, had as constant companion the dark seductive pull of the brink of eternity, the pull towards oblivion, the lure of the abyss where lurked the tender lover Death who, until Katya so recently had routed him from Sholto's heart, had been Sholto's own melancholy lover.

She took one of her endless cigarettes out of her silver evening bag, put it between her lips, waited for him to light it. His unsteady hand zigzagged the Zippo's flame towards the target and he was ashamed at the lack of control. He wanted to tell her about his own loss, the death of his father. He, too, understood the brutal ways of adults when they think they are sparing children pain. He'd been not much older than her, as it happened.

His mouth opened to start telling her. His eyes flickered to the warm silk of her knees. Almost he put out his hand to touch, to feel close but his hand retracted before it had even started. It'd be taking advantage. He frowned through the windscreen's broad span. If he told her now she might think he was jockeying for position in the tragedy stakes. It would be the work of a sympathy-hunter, a Brylcreem Brian, to slime into the moment and say, 'My pa died too. I know how it feels.' What Katya needed now – and for ever – was a strong shoulder, not a sob-sister. It took an act of will, but he fixed his eyes on the calm silhouette of a high town-house cornice slicing the sky, shut his mouth, jutted his chin, and kept quiet.

Katya was surprising herself. You didn't tell anyone about Mama. That was part of the pact. The pact with the old Tëtka, with the old one-eyed Romanov eagle on Mama's hairbrush, with the Mama who'd promised to come back and who would. Somehow. She'd always known that if she spoke it would be like shining a strong light into twilight, dissolving all mysteries behind the mauve shadows where magic Mama lurked. Bright light would dissolve her into the deep darkness for good, never to be conjured up again. Mama unlocked, shared, would be Mama dissolved. But by the same mysterious and occult rules this Sholto, this husband-to-be, this instrument, had been chosen in some obscure way by her mother to be the one to cross dimensions, he had been conjured up from the flower-fragrant ether of Belgrave Square. He was a fragment of Katya Olovanova's great plan. He must be told.

It was not intimacy, this telling, but obligation; and while she told she was entirely unaware of her arms describing that white-gloved mothy beating against the dark air. She had no idea, no idea at all, that her hands were remembering of their own accord the protesting arcs they had described that night pummelling against the iron bands of the Tëtka's encircling arms and against every minute of her subsequent fate.

To his shame he found himself unable to say anything in response to her tale. Nothing, not one word; a silence, which at the time he knew to be inadequate and in retrospect horrified him. His lack of sympathetic word of comfort must, he thought, have made him seem a monster of insensitivity in her eyes.

He knew enough to realise this, but not enough to remedy it.

Sholto had not been trained to words. He had been a school-boy in a knickerbocker suit of hairy tweed the afternoon of the

First World War when his mother received the news of his father's death. The telegram had come at the same time as the late post, the yellow envelope one of half a dozen. She had read out the official words to her son, paused again, then carefully slit open the day's two remaining envelopes, with him still standing there in his school shorts. There had been a ghastly deep-drawn howl in his soul and complete silence in the room while she read the last two letters meticulously each to its end. Then she had folded them exactly as usual, looked up as if to say, 'What, you still here?', consulted her watch and told him it was time for her afternoon walk now.

'Please fetch my Jaeger scarf. The wind seems to be getting up. You will find it in its accustomed place.'

Her only deviation from the norm was to push the telegram roughly into her pocket while putting the rest of the post on the 'unanswered' pile on her desk. The walk had taken exactly the same time it always took her. In precisely forty minutes she had reappeared to take up her place at the tea table precisely as usual and to eat her customary piece of thin bread-and-butter folded over and her single piece of home-made shortbread just exactly as she always did. She poured him tea as if nothing had happened, said nothing of the news received earlier in the day. By way of conversation she passed the one or two remarks she usually passed after her walk, commenting as usual on the weather, the state of trees and crops observed, the likelihood of rain. There had been silences over the tea table but there were always silences, and these were no more or less deep or jagged than any. She was not, nor had ever been, a woman of flowing conversation. She had seemed calm, entirely normal, unaware of hell's very visible gaping abyss. But her eyes were not behaving. Sad and unfocused, restless, her eyes were never still while her hands again and again repeated an insistent stirring of her tea, again and again, long after the sugar had dissolved. Sholto, usually as hearty a trencherman as any schoolboy at the tea table, had eaten nothing.

'Eat up,' she had said sharply. 'He is not the only one, you know.'

No, Sholto had not been trained to words. After Katya told him in the car he had not reached out, not said a word, paralysed by a wretched inadequacy and a reluctance to intrude at any level other than the highest, which he knew himself unable to reach. They sat a while completely quiet and then he started the motor and drove her back to Lulu's door. She hadn't given an answer to his proposal.

Since that night in the car Katya had never mentioned anybody: mother, living father, or Mama-Tante or Papa-Oscar, the couple who had taken her so unhappily in. She spoke and behaved as she had always spoken and behaved before: purposely as though she'd sprung up of her own volition; owing nothing, beholden to no one, not even for language, zigzagging through life on a brilliant butterfly path self-invented.

And still he waited for his answer.

'Katya, mind the ants!'

Just at that blue hour when day leaches out of the sky, before night puts in its different blue, he found her lying in the grass still in her riding things, busy poking about the undergrowth at some task demanding great concentration, her face close to her hands, and he thought she looked like a child at that age-old innocent game of chance, 'He loves me, he loves me not', pulling the petals from a daisy. He used to do the same at idle moments in cricket whites as an outfielder on the wildflowery boundaries of school pitches.

The ride had brought a blush bloom to her cheeks. Her hair gleamed like mahogany and there were sharp lights in her eyes.

'Katya, look out. There's an army of ants on the move. They'll bite you if you don't move.'

'Not me. They know I'd bite back harder.'

She'd tell him now. Michaelmas Hall made a dark silhouette against the sky's neat rows of silvery herringbone. Behind his handsome head an even stripe of cloud shone orange, caught by a sun below the horizon. Yup, he was a looker. But there were plenty of lookers roaming the streets, plenty with the old glint in the eye. Analytically she scanned her suitor's figure against the sky. The hands bagging out the pockets of the ancestral tweed jacket; Oscar would kill for that jacket. Might one say, 'No, I won't marry you but what about giving me your jacket?' Christ, the hands were trembling. What a bore. She'd tell him quickly and cleanly now. She'd say she'd just decided against marriage. Not against him. She wouldn't be unkind unless he yelped and squealed, she couldn't stand a yelper. If he did that she'd give it to him straight from the shoulder. Tell him he must be cracked to think she'd want a future among the embalmed and mummified Fortescue ancestrals. Could he really see her dressed in woollies and flat shoes re-creating his mother (and how Daphne Fortescue brought to mind Chandler's grand old war-horse with a heart of gold, and the gold buried good and deep) padding about the dark formaldehyde house circumnavigating the ragged, venerated velvet, mottled mirrors, embalmed objects and embalmed attitudes. Just a weekend here was making her crave a lifetime of Silver Slipper shiny thrills and dark, delicious, dangerous places. She'd just say lightly, 'Sholto, truth's dawned. Splicing's not for me. Now spare me the scene. Dangle. Ankle it.'

Maybe he could see what was in her mind because he took the initiative in a straightforward way that strictly speaking was too forceful to be gentlemanly.

'Wait,' he said, almost rudely, not looking at her. 'If you say no, and I've a feeling you will, I won't have the courage to tell you the one thing I have to tell you. So let me tell you this one thing. Please.'

She wouldn't listen. These sorts of things didn't amuse her. She would put herself somewhere else, as she used to put herself somewhere else in Herr Professor Doktor Lund's room – on his dreary panelled wooden wall, actually – oh, the woodgrain of that wall! – when the nurse was to give her the injections of mysterious things that were to strengthen her. Charlotta torturing her with injections. Typical. Where could she put herself now? In the sky? Big empty sky. No. Something swirled in her mind like a big fish in water. How lovely. She'd put herself into the North Sea. Oh, how she'd longed, how she'd missed it, she hadn't realised. She couldn't shut out Sholto altogether, as she couldn't shut out the nurse, but he was hardly there now with just his voice coming into a little bit of ear and brain while the rest of her was on her father's island, the Fødselsøy, and she was immediately entranced by the progress of a middle-sized mauve starfish, mounding and flattening as it climbed up the steep granite rockface reaching for the water-line where the slick olive seaweed fringe rimmed the rocks. How the seaweed bobbed and danced on the lapping water, with its air bladders breaking the surface like bubbles and the funny clumsy *paltosk* crabs peeping through the forked brown fingers of the warty bladderwrack thinking they were very clever and invisible like children under a table. And above the water-line the darling grey wagtail *linerle*, the same colour as the rocks, rushing busily up-down up-down between the quick dashing of the waves to peck at the creamy pyramids of barnacles throbbing delicately as they syphoned water in and out in imitation of breath. However mushy it was, what Sholto had to say, it wouldn't really matter to either of them because she was in that cold, delicious sea and if she didn't keep a lookout and really pay attention to what was round about her in the indistinct undersea garden she'd get herself stung by the candyfloss shreds of the jellyfish and be left with long red threads of blister-weals on her skin that burned for days and days on end. They congregated, sociable creatures, in huge pink soupy masses. Once she'd pushed Berndt into a whole mass ...

'Katya, your mother can't be dead. I've been thinking about it ever since you told me. Not in the San Francisco earthquake, anyway. The dates don't fit. The quake happened long, long before she left Oslo. Before you were born.'

She shut her eyes tightly, feeling the burning heat of tears. Shimmering bliss. Nothing in the sky or on the earth was as warm or bright as she.

'Not dead?' She had promised she would come. 'Not dead?'

'No. Not in the earthquake at any rate. That's historically impossible.'

'Not dead! Impossible. I knew. I knew.'

The visions by the violet-seller in Belgrave Square had been little premonitions, little cracks into the world behind the horizon, hints to persevere. She had been right to heed them, to play Russian roulette, because only if she had the courage to plunge in at that left-and-right dinner party would she be sent not only Katya's messenger but Katya-Mama alive. Alive! Nothing was won without blind trail and test. She'd passed the test. Sholto was the link, the messenger. Marriage to Sholto the act of faith. After that Katya-Mama would come. Of course she

would marry him. Of course, of course. Grasping him, she
showered him with an inexplicable frenzy of kisses from
which her very self seemed absent.

'Mine,' sang Sholto's dizzy heart, opening itself at last to all
the risks and perils of the world like the tight petals of a rose
uncurling from the safe green shell in response to the warmth
of Katya's radiant sun. The lowering cloud of futility he had so
long lived with, telling him he would soon be either pointlessly dead, or pointlessly alive in an utterly pointless world,
was now finally lifted.

'Look!' His amazing bride pointed at a far window pane
where a beadwork of raindrops beamed dazzling refracted
light from a hidden sun. 'Your house is shining.'

'Yes,' he said, without a clue because he could see nothing
through eyes brimming with tears.

His mother, seeing the approach of the two of them through
the diamond-paned kitchen window, fortified herself with gin
and, sealing the brisket of beef in dripping, hoped against hope
that Sholto hadn't done anything silly. There were various
things Daphne Fortescue's unvarnished long-sighted eyes
knew about human nature. One thing she knew was the
shining hopeless truth that if a mother said a bride-to-be was
not a good idea she only sounded shrewish, jealous and
impossible. Why, oh why, had that wretched bullet found
Sholto's father? There weren't many things Daphne Fortescue
couldn't manage since being widowed but this was one. 'Just
now,' she chopped carrots, 'I could damn well do with you, old
helpmeet.'

Later that evening Daphne Fortescue donned musty velvet
of an indeterminate colour not unlike the curtains. They ate in
the dining room for the first time.

Meanness and pride must be the spur of this dour room,
Katya decided. There couldn't be any other reason for keeping
a table that kneecapped you every time you tried to move a
leg, nor for such big ugly ancestors. But Katya beamed,
radiantly happy, and coquetted with the sad Puritan with a
wart on the wall opposite. Had she been alone she'd've jumped
up to tickle him under the chin and make him smile. She
beamed despite the ungrateful shin of beef, which had stoutly
resisted Mrs Fortescue's best efforts to transform it into

anything markedly delicious. The meat, like the atmosphere, was tepid, flaccid and grey. Nothing was noticeably festive about this engagement party: a heavy silence punctuated by the crescendo and diminuendo ring of the char's hollow footfalls to and from the kitchen fetching and carrying the nasty food along the cold stone-flagged floors between courses. They ate off crested silverware so tarnished it was as black as they always keep silver in Russia where it is considered beautiful unlike in England where it simply spells not enough servants.

Daphne Fortescue was hardly vivacious, her mind running on sabotaging this marriage plan at all costs. No effort too huge, no sacrifice too great. Even good manners. That night at her own table she broke two golden rules at once: she spoke at the table about food, and about money: 'You must forgive the brisket, but I am too poor to be able to celebrate with a better cut.'

There, that should deter this fortune-hunting foreigner.

Daphne Fortescue smiled, triumphant at her own cunning, before falling asleep over pudding, drooping suddenly in half over the table like an exhausted hollyhock until woken by the char's next journey with home-grown celery, water biscuits and a sweaty odoriferous nubble of very old Stilton.

Later, over the coffee, there was a conversational variation on the earlier theme of brisket. A small crimson-leather jewel case not much larger than a matchbox reposed beside the three ancient cracked Coalport pheasant-pattern coffee cups. One thing Katya had imbibed from Charlotta was the Scandinavian fastidious attitude towards dirt and germs; she was trying to drink without her lips or the coffee coming into contact with the grey, dirt-harbouring chips and cracks. Mrs Fortescue handed Katya the leather jewel box. 'I am not rich enough to give you any better jewels but these are of great historical value, having long family connections. Heirlooms better worth prizing than the bluest of diamonds.'

Katya saw a pair of rather grubby earrings. She must wash them in disinfectant before she put them on, which she wasn't in a hurry to do. The earrings in the shape of flowers were made of garnets, each stone not much larger than a pin head.

Prompted earlier by her son in a stone-passage aside – 'Mother, do try and say something' – Daphne Fortescue shook herself into friendliness like a dog emerging from water.

'You must call me Mother,' she said.

Katya stopped beaming.

Why were the old women in her life, women like Charlotta and now this horsy one, always wanting her to call them Mother? There was only one person she ever had, or ever would, call Mama, and she'd see that person quite soon now.

On her return to London Katya put the morocco jewel box on the mantelpiece among the ashtrays and party invitations. Dammit, where was Lulu when she needed her? The invitations? Aha! Here we are. This one was for tonight and was emphatically ticked in green ink.

She made her way to the address in Pimlico. Lulu-party noises were rising from the paint-peeling basement: screeches, hoots and jazzy crescendos. She couldn't see through the window for a lot of smoke billowing from cigarettes of various kinds. The basement took some reaching down rickety metal-fatigued suicide stairs. As she tottered down, a thin grey cat shot up. Once she got into the room it wasn't as big as a cabin trunk but there were certainly a lot of people in it. At about three in the morning the room was slowly rotating as its inhabitants receded against walls and carpets. In the even smaller bathroom Katya gave her virginity to one of the opportunists who took it cursorily and indifferently, pressing her hard up against a mirrored medicine cupboard. She never did find out the opportunist's name.

'Well,' she shrugged, lit a gasper, 'that's done.'

CHAPTER TWELVE

The strangest thing of all was that in all the crazy mania before the Second War Katya O, the decorator's pavement-trotting gofer, did actually fulfil her plan and get herself spliced to the hero, the Britisher with Wings: Sholto the Flying Ace, smooth as ice in Air Force blue and as unmoved by Lulu's self-advertising charms as was Oscar when Lulu went over for the wedding.

'Ah ha.' Oscar stood at the broad wooden door of the white-spired church whose graveyard, a sea of pink-tinged hydrangeas at that late-summer season, gave its occupants the best panoramic view over the city of Oslo. Lulu had just swished through the grave-dotted sward, wearing a black-and-white chequered dress. She had bluish shadows under her eyes, a black ribbon at the white nape of her neck, and from under her veiled hat she gave Oscar a glance that broke off and isolated a dry little section of time. On she swept through real sequential time, entering the church and taking her seat, leaning composedly forward to pick up her printed service sheet with a small social smile. At the church door Oscar remained exactly as he had been, to all appearances imperturbable. He put up a hand to his already perfectly tied white tie and turned his eyes towards the fine view where, beyond the graves, the pretty yellow-and-white rococo palace stood artlessly framed between two tremulous white-stemmed birches. Beyond the enchanting palace rose the wild rocks of Oslo's harbour. For a few years Dronningen's stone giant had added his muscular presence to the middle distance but by now he had long tumbled into the sea in whose dark, sunless deeps he was growing a mighty bush of slimy brownish eel grass, which waved gracefully with the currents. Healthy clusters of pearly mussels, blue as thunderclouds, nestled in colonies under each gigantic armpit. Beyond Dronningen's long wooden pier stretched the picturesque moods of the Oslofjord, ever changing. And in that moody haze one of the constant points, no bigger than a speck of dust from here, was the Fødselsøy where Gustav was engaged in doggedly gutting glittering fish between shouting at the radio on this, the day of his daughter's wedding.

'Ah,' Oscar would have said to Gustav if Charlotta had managed to persuade him to attend – and she tried, oh, how she tried! In the absence of Gustav, Oscar had to say to himself (which wasn't nearly so much fun when he could be nudging his brother in masculine conspiracy): 'That hungry English Lulu is pretty. But she's not as pretty as she thinks. She's showing wear and tear. Word has it she knows the Chinese clutch, which is always an amusing trick. She'd do well for an afternoon in the Grand, a whole night, even. But more? *Er du gal*? She's common-sense-deficient to harbour such ambitions.'

And that was the moment he realised he was getting middle-aged. Judging the girl's degree of common sense would not have played a part in the equation when he was truly young. Ruefully he cast a glance from directly above down to the convex curve in his own white waistcoat. Things in that area were not, these days, as absolutely flat as they had once been; but Oscar didn't flatter the moment by sucking in his stomach muscles. Time ignored no man; a little convexity was just one of those things.

At the arrival of Katya in white satin with numerous Oscarsson diamonds pinned here and there and three perfect lilies in her small white hand, he pocketed these thoughts unsaid, feeling just a stab of loneliness, of mortality, while offering his niece-daughter the steadying prop of his English-tailored arm.

Oscar went on directly, the world agreed, to make an excellently substantial, elegant yet humorous job of giving her in marriage to her chosen one, and before we leave this scene it might be recorded that Lulu did indeed know the Chinese clutch but even so Oscar decided she didn't *vaut le détour*

sufficiently to prolong the event to a whole night in the Grand;
and not for reasons of economy either.

Katya's first child, the boy Robert, was born during the war,
a time she spent with staggering lack of success at Michaelmas
Hall. The first time she came back to Norway after the war
was for the christening of her second child, a daughter. The
christening happened in the church she had been married in;
that same white church in the forest where many years earlier
Charlotta had taken Berndt to pick wild flowers for Katya's
arrival as a permanent resident in the Oscarsson household;
that day that Russo, off the leash, had roamed about shooting
so exuberantly and inaccurately at squirrels. Oslo remembered
this christening. Not for the reasons people usually remember
such occasions. The baby wasn't drowned, or dropped. The
devil didn't whiz down to the font to make a personal
appearance. Fairy godmothers didn't hex.

The famous thing was this: Katya's daughter had been
flown over from England, and under the cot mattress Katya
had hidden four bottles of champagne. They were the very
first bottles of the real stuff to enter Norway via the free world
since the start of the German occupation in 1940. The bottles
symbolised restoration. Good times could be had. Throughout
the children's early years, whenever they were in Norway the
little girl would be greeted by people putting their fingers into
their cheeks to make popping noises like champagne corks.
The little girl saw nothing unusual in this. It seemed a perfectly normal greeting from complete strangers as far as she
was concerned, but for the elder brother it was wormwood
and gall. He was five years older than the girl, he had been
born during the war and had lately outgrown the dimply
sweet stage. For Robert these pop-pop fusillades of pleasure
directed at his little sister did nothing to foster brotherly love
or to help his self-confidence, but Katya thought them a hoot.

She didn't christen the baby Katya, which was surprising.
Charlotta would have done perfectly well as a name. It
would've been a nice compliment, but Katya's emotions in that
direction still didn't run to compliments, indeed had the thought
crossed her mind she'd have been more inclined towards
calling the baby Not-Charlotta, but she didn't do that because
the morning of the birth, when people were badgering her for

a decision, the name Anita was in *The Times'* birth column. It belonged to nobody in the Oscarsson family. She said it in English. She said it in Norwegian. It did not set her alight, she decided, looking down the length of the bed where the remaining hummock of her stomach mounded the bedclothes so tiresomely. Katya put a match to another appetite-suppressing Player's Navy Cut in preference to the nursing home's semolina-and-jam lunch. Two children. Fat tummy. A semolina-and-jam future stretched. Anita. The smoke meandered prettily, lazily, without taking wing, like the name; curling up against the dreary soup-coloured curtaining where bizarrely enough the name did take wing: Anitra! the girl with the troll's tail in *Peer Gynt*! She cheered. It might even be amusing to have a daughter, providing the daughter had enough wickedness in her to grow a troll girl's tail.

Actually the name didn't matter. The little girl was never known by it anyway. Katya's daughter was always known as the Shrimp because:

'She's so thin you can see right through her like a shrimp in the sea.'

'She has to run around in the rain at top speed to get wet, I can tell you.'

'She's so thin you could shave with her.'

The razor thinness might have been due to the ragingly fashionable doctor Katya consulted during her pregnancy. Lulu had found him during one of her abortions and he was absolutely the latest thing. Dr Viridian had a scientifically proven theory that babies didn't actually need to spend the last month in their mother's womb, they were perfectly developed at eight. He found a place in Brighton prepared to bring them into the world a month ahead of schedule for those discerning mothers who put their figure first. This was extremely popular with the mothers in Lulu's set, though less so with their in-laws. Indignant Daphne Fortescues and their ilk lost the first hundred or so particular battles over particular babies before eventually winning the war and making even Brighton too hot to hold the fashionable Dr Viridian. He skipped to Switzerland with a little gold and high hopes, which first were dashed by the country's strict childbirth laws but, with his dauntless attitude, it was only a matter of time before he discovered there wasn't a word in that accommodating country's constitution concerning monkey glands. Seamlessly transmuting from baby-guru to anti-ageing guru, Viridian became the big monkey-gland pioneer in the 1940s and 1950s by which time all his lovely flat-tummied Lulu-mothers were in need of their first youth injections, and flocking to his charmingly appointed Alpine clinic, niftily decorated by Lulu on a no-cash *quid pro quo* basis. Monkey glands in Switzerland proved even more profitable than early Brighton babies. Fewer died; that was a help. Almost he wished he'd skipped the baby stage and plunged straight into monkey glands, but then of course it would have been more difficult to get started because he wouldn't have had his ready-made nucleus clientele of happy mothers. So all was to a purpose, even a bumpy eviction from Brighton.

And before we leave Brighton and meditations on purpose, it is worth noting that the only ill-effect of Anita the Shrimp's curtailed stay in the womb appeared to be a lifelong under-development of the capacity to store fat, and a lifelong scepticism when it came to star signs, astrology, horoscopes or fatalism in any form. All her life she would balk at the notion of invisible tracks written in the sky unavoidably connected with birth dates. She would balk at any type of formed, or formless, superstition. This scepticism, logically leading on to a sturdy chin-out determinism, and an absolute belief that fate is there to be controlled rather than to do the controlling, proved a most useful thing, enabling her to break the Katya-cycle, the phantom of nostalgia that otherwise might have stretched God knew how many generations, daughter duplicating mother like those maddening endless mirror-in-mirror reflections. And so it happened that Dr Viridian the monkey-gland doctor turned out far from entirely disastrous in this case, though obviously his elastic approach wouldn't have done for everybody.

'Ankle it, Shrimp. Snap it up or you'll miss the flying hutch.'

After her marriage Katya had retained the Raymond Chandler turn of phrase.

Shrimp was doing her seven-year-old best to ankle it at speed over the tarmac at Northolt airport in her mother's perfumed wake, but Katya did walk very fast, particularly in public. Pace-walking got the right swing to the way the lean thighs moved under the rippling dress. Katya's hair was black with plum lights, and just as fascinatingly wavy as her mother's had been. One wayward lock had a helpless way of falling over one browbone so she had to look up at you with the brownish greenish eyes from under the mascara-ed lashes. Katya looked wonderful in anything, but was at her best in endangered species tightly belted. Today's ocelot coat practically purred on its way towards the plane that was to take them all to Norway once more.

The children took Katya at entirely her own value, and worshipped her. The family settled in the airliner's row of seats, whose musty rubbery smell induced a throat-panic in the Shrimp. The blade-thin seven-year-old was motion-sick to the point of parody, up-chucking the minute anything moved: rocking horses, aeroplanes, the garden swing, anything. Possibly this was a contributory factor to her enduring shrimpish skinniness. Katya, accordingly, always sat with Robert beside her, placing the girl at the farthest possible perimeter.

'Steward.' Katya's voice was not high but it carried. The gulf between the English she'd read and the English social class she mixed with clothed the Chicago gangsterese in a faultless *Debrett* accent.

'Hmn,' she mused, on the debonair but effeminate whitecoat that appeared. His gloved hands hung limp. She gave him the usual up and down inspection to see if he was clean and free of insect life. 'Well, you can't win 'em all.' Then, in a different tone for public consumption: 'Sick bags, steward. Three or four. The little one anti-peristalses before the end of the runway every time. Oh, and hang the big cat on a decent hanger somewhere out of the way.'

The time Shrimp had sicked all over her mink was never forgotten.

Out of the egg-shaped window the distant row of Northolt's corrugated-iron Nissen huts receded. Shrimp's tummy was slowly rotating. Katya's cigarette didn't help. On marriage she had given up the black Sobranie cigarettes for Player's Navy Cut, unconsciously taking another road Katya Olovanova had taken. Not even the Tëtka had told her of Katya Olovanova's tendency to convey political message through brand of cigarette, so it wasn't emulation: she did it instinctively. The packet of Player's had a man on it, a virile sailor with an unstoppable beard.

'Light me a gasper,' she'd say languorously at intervals, during a hot afternoon's sun-worshipping in Daphne Fortescue's defeated garden at Michaelmas Hall. She would be holding up the packet with the make-believe man. Sholto would lean forward to do his duty, his chest a golden slab under the central triangle of hair that trailed away into the woolly line down into his trunks that was embarrassing, extremely embarrassing, to both children. Why couldn't parents just wear clothes?

Click, said the worn Zippo lighter.

Katya wanted him to get a gold Dunhill but he wouldn't. It was his good-luck piece from the war.

The war was over, she pointed out.

He still wouldn't.

Katya detected *Freya*, Sholto's wartime aeroplane, Katya's unbeatable rival.

On her first long exhale she might say, 'Thank you,' and then life would be fine; or she might say in the voice of a happily satisfied feline, 'Aaa ... the Senior Service.' In which case the tips of Sholto's ears would turn the colour of geraniums and Shrimp could never understand how her father's face could change so, without changing. It was like a cloud formation: the same clouds were there but the rearrangements within them spelled out a completely different message in the space of a heartbeat.

'Ah ... the Senior Service.' Thunderclouds. Lowering still-ness, hard sunshine; spaces opening into chasms between the family of four and stretching big and empty as days on the yellowing lawn leading down to the moat.

'Ah ... the Senior Service.' The blood in Shrimp's thin body turning to iced water despite the sun. Sholto might spring to his feet then. Just as he would spring to his feet when Katya said in that voice, 'Take air, Manny,' or 'Dangle.'

If they were in the garden when these things happened he would challenge his son to cricket, which was always a disaster, Sholto being so much older and stronger and having something very specific to prove under Katya's intent gaze behind her fashionable white-framed sunglasses. Or she might uncoil her evenly-tanned body, remove the foil sun-reflector she wore under her chin so it shouldn't be a pale patch in that sea of the desired colour, get up, ruffle her husband's hair and tell the children to start making a record daisy-chain now this minute and she wanted it as long as a Norwegian mile (which is eight times longer) by the time she and Sholto came outdoors again.

'No slacking, ankle-nippers,' she'd cry gaily.

'Half a crown if it's over ten foot, kids.' He backed her up.

Katya was already running back to the house and giggling back over her shoulder, 'You'll have to run to catch me!'

He'd just be catching her by the time they were getting indoors and she'd be shrieking and they'd both be laughing but it wasn't really nice laughs, Shrimp thought, not like the laughs they laughed at the clowns at Bertram Mills' circus at Christmas-time.

Then Robert and Shrimp would set about their daisy-chain to earn the huge sum that meant Mars Bars practically for life. The Shrimp worked hard on these occasions in her cotton dress with puffed sleeves and short gathered skirt fluttering in the breeze, a thin pale-skinned child with Sholto's fair colouring bending over the green lawn to pick the short-stalked flowers. 'Oh, do help, Robert.'

It was annoying that Robert was always surly and lazy on these occasions and didn't help. It didn't make sense. Robert liked Mars Bars better than her but he'd sit like a lazy lump, or hang about first on one leg then the other like the flamingoes in *Alice* looking up at Mama and Daddy's bedroom window. Shrimp supposed he was waiting for them to switch on the wireless or play a gramophone record. They did that some-times but not always. Robert was very good at music, he had a big piano accordion so heavy the Shrimp couldn't lift it at all, even if he would let her touch it, which he didn't. But even when Mama and Daddy played the music and it drifted out of the bedroom window on the air it didn't stop him being bad-tempered and lazy about picking daisies so Shrimp had to do it all by herself and the worst thing was that by the time Mama and Daddy came out again they most often had forgotten the half-crown bribe and this left Shrimp and Robert in a terrible bind because to remind them would only earn a reprimand because it was the most brutish thing possible to talk about money.

Take-off.

Past her brother's face the wing was shivering and shuddering against the rushing tarmac, parting the air between the juddering wing and the green-tinged rim of the sky. Shrimp felt nasty qualms in her stomach. Behind Katya's back her brother made a death's head face at her. Whenever they were in motion the balance was definitely in his favour, Shrimp being hampered by this inconvenient, repulsive and inevitable tendency to be so appallingly sick. She was the only person anybody knew who was sick through her nose and mouth both at once, which was some distinction at least, but very painful to the nasal passages.

'We-ell, hello, there. You look as if you need rescuing.' A man with a hotel face and a neat moustache held out a red and white packet of cigarettes towards Katya. 'Craven A to your taste?'

His voice had a sugary lilt. They went through all the cigarette business: the offering and accepting, the flashing of the gold-plated lighter, the cupping of hand within hand. With the sugary voice went a well-cherished head of chestnut brown hair, a deep tan, yellow sports shirt with matching cravat, slacks, and a blue gaberdine blazer with vaguely regimental implications on the buttons. The flashy lighter was flourished by a left hand that boasted a signet-ring on its hairy little finger.

'There's a wonderful spot just a row or so back. And, do you know, the steward's even produced syphonated soda? I did not think such a thing was possible at this altitude.'

Katya got up from her seat and went the few rows back to this nirvana of soda syphons in the sky. She had passed into a new world and the children, belonging to the old one, had senses raw-tuned as if they'd been sandpapered to pick up what signals were coming from the few rows behind.

'Is he an "uncle"?' Shrimp asked softly.

'Not one I've met.' Robert considered. 'I don't think.'

He couldn't be quite sure.

'Dishy.'

'Yes.'

Uncles tended to come dishy, which was why the children couldn't be quite sure if this was a new one or an old one reappearing. Similar in libidinous type, uncles were like piled jumpers from the same drawer; you had to be a specialist to recognise the minor differences in detail: colour, collar shape, length of arm, hairiness or smoothness, circumcised, uncircumcised.

'Read to me, Shrimp.'

The awkward boy wriggled in his seat to get the book out from his suit pocket, his clothes were as tight as a sausage skin, he had a flitting glance that never rested and discontented mouth. Too many uncles and too much competitive cricket against his father intensified in him a perpetual under-layer of sullen timidity and resentment. The boy was dyslexic and it was starting to matter very much indeed. Prep school was about to give way to public school: the Fortescue school, sixth generation. The world would end if Robert was not successful in the family tradition. He was expected to win the King's medal his last year in the corps, bat for the second eleven if not the first, and get a decent pass into wherever he wanted to go, which really meant Oxford, but Cambridge if he must. The perpetual claims of sport and ancestry were on the line.

With his dyslexia it was doubtful he would even get into the school.

If the girl was shrimplike, Robert was fatly rounded as a well-nourished pink crab. He ate and ate whatever came his way in the fashion of all war babies. His grandmother Fortescue (Katya and the children spent the war years entirely in England, in the formaldehyde house, Norway being occupied by the Germans) stuffed him at every opportunity like all wartime grandmothers. As a result the word most used for Robert during his early years on earth was 'bonny'; a high compliment, they came no higher. This well-covered toddler inspired nothing but admiration from family and strangers alike. He attracted crowds of lean, ration-book fans, who adored him unconditionally for his pink plumpness, the many bracelets of marzipan fat on his arms, and his admirably dimpled anklets. He might have served Rubens for a *putto*. He won first prize after first prize at wartime baby shows. Inevitably, cruelly, the dimpled babe

was turning into an obese teenager. The thighs paralleling
the skinny Shrimp's on the aeroplane seat might have
contained six of the girl's tied into a bundle. His vast
prep-school thighs were mottled blue-mauve and chapped
from the regime of shorts, winter and summer. Shrimp had
no idea that any changes were taking place in the public
perception of her adored brother, but to him it must have
been very puzzling why the universal admiration excited by
his appearance suddenly changed at the switch of a button to
universal scorn. All this at almost exactly the same time his
balls dropped and the embarrassing stuff started. His Russian
grandmother's intellectual beacon Herr Doktor Freud might
have had something to say.

At the age of twelve, nearly thirteen, continually confronted by his own mountainous flesh, tortured by self-
consciousness, he was in fact no longer admired by anybody
except his little sister, but she believed utterly in him. Robert
might not be able to read but *anyone* could read: it was the
easiest thing in the world. Anyone could read. Nobody else
Shrimp knew could name every bird singing, or always know
north even in the dark, or could pick out any tune on the
heavy piano accordion just like that, or remember exactly
which road number led where and the number of every car
that Sholto had ever owned. Those were the really clever
things and Shrimp admired him for them greatly. He could do
nothing wrong whatsoever, in any department. His bulk made
her long to be a chubby endomorph instead of an etiolated
shrimp people could see bones through.

In England Robert's dyslexia was unrecognised, unacknowl-
edged; he was just plain stupid. In Norway it was just starting
to be recognised and given a name: 'word blindness'. Charlotta
took a great interest in it for family reasons. She gave money to
the institute looking into such things and instructed Herr
Professor Doktor Lund to keep her abreast of the latest
thinking, which she sent in the shape of clippings from
Norwegian journals, pithy passages underlined, to Katya in the
English formaldehyde house where Katya wasn't particularly
convinced or even interested, except to use this information in
the continual war of attrition against Sholto. To him and to his
horsy mother, clippings on word-blindness read out in free

translation over breakfast did not forward the progress of the mixed marriage.

'Word blindness.' Daphne Fortescue snorted like a horse, shifting her hoofs at the stone double sink in the scullery where running hot hadn't yet been laid on. Her raw-boned hands, gnarled as oak roots with a lifetime's capable dealing with icy cold and with pulling at reins, paddled in what looked like a basin of gore, water incarnadined with the bleedings of cut beetroots. Beetroots didn't scrub themselves. It seemed there were other people to do such things in the grand house in Norway she never stopped hearing about. At any rate her posh foreign daughter-in-law was always mysteriously busy at something else when this task was to hand. And what would Sunday supper be, month in month out, with no pickled beetroot to cheer up the leftovers?

'Word blindness,' Mrs Fortescue echoed. 'Goodness, how handy! How very conveniently they arrange things in Norway, Sholto dear. I expect they have property blindness for thieves in Norway, and bed blindness for adulterers.'

This last thrust drew a short, sharp reaction. Sholto drew in his breath, squared his shoulders, tightened his face into a look which to those who didn't know him made him look even more marmoreally handsome. His mother remembered the very same look when he had first been sent to board at prep school aged seven. Later that look had resurfaced when Teddy had been killed, and again when he'd not been chosen for the football team and at other moments throughout her son's life's progress; most recently at various points in the war. The look caused his mother's tough old calloused heart to bleed the only way it knew how: stoically, sarcastically, grudgingly into the thin water of life drop by beetroot drop.

How typically Norwegian, how soft, how left-wing was this word-blindness that Katya had come up with for her son's stupidity. Katya's blood had certainly been a bad bargain.

'Read, Shrimp,' Robert said, shifting his bulk on the aeroplane's narrow seat.

In his life his sister fulfilled the same role that first Gustav, then *sekretaer* Fulman had filled in Oscar's. She was ungrudging reader and scribe.

'Frederick the Great was born on 24 January 1712, the year of
Denain, Louis XIV's final and victorious battle in the war of
the Spanish Succession.'

She deciphered the page precociously. She made the jumping, jiggling letters into sounds that made sense and that could
be memorised. He had no trouble at all with the memorising. It
was taking the words off the page and putting them back on
that was the trouble. If only he could take Shrimp to school
with him there would be no problem, she could be his channel
on and off the page. But he couldn't do that. So nothing worked.
He could memorise phenomenally but that was no good in
isolation without the capacity either to take in primary
information unaided, or the ability to give it back clear and
unscrambled.

'Read, Shrimp.'

All unplanned, her brother was giving the girl a great gift.
Via the assorted fruit salad of the prep-school curriculum she
was introduced to a far greater variety of subject than a mere
girl would have been taught. More important still, this reading
started in her the life-long dialogue with the written word, the
livelong dialogue with the dead that is so much more rational,
and fascinating, than the living.

Katya returned to the children only after the plane had
come to a stop on the runway. They'd done quite a lot of
Frederick the Great by then and the girl had even forgotten to
feel sick because it was so interesting about Frederick William
collecting giants over six foot for his army, sending out secret
emissaries throughout Europe to kidnap any giants they saw
and to bring them back to him, which made Shrimp think that
Russo would have been kidnapped by the King but it wouldn't
have mattered probably because of the King loving his giants
so much that when he was poorly in bed he had them
marched through his sick room in single file to cheer him up.

'Hi, tiny treasures!' Katya was back.

Feigning casual abstraction badly, Robert looked up. Behind
Katya the neat moustache was carrying the ocelot over his arm
and baring his pearly teeth in a smile that was all helpfulness.
And then a strange thing happened that only the Shrimp saw
and puzzled over. Robert was busy being Katya's 'little man',
organising the bits of things from off the shelf and under the

seats, bullying their possessions as irritatingly and self-importantly as an inefficient hectoring sheepdog: to every sheep-possession marshalled in the pen, two ran away, rolled or spilled or fell. Katya was sitting down again now in her original seat giving her lips a last fluent Cupid's bow, powdering her nose and things like that, and Shrimp had nothing much to do but look at the things she could see over the top of the seat-back. The top half of the uncle was doing a strange thing. He was burying his face in Mama's coat, closing his eyes, and his skin had gone very pale and oddly shiny and his eyelids were having spasms and he was looking quite ill and Shrimp thought he might be going to faint or be airsick like her. His face looked so funny. But she was glad to see he was doing the right thing: breathing deeply. His diaphragm was moving and his breath was coming in fast fluttering gasps, like somebody running a race. He was probably burying his nose in Mama's coat because he was embarrassed for the panting breathing to show but if she had not been so shy Shrimp would have told him to take his nose out of the ocelot coat and breathe some good clean air instead. Mama's coat would be smelling strongly of fur and of Mama and of Arpège. Mama always wore Arpège, a dab at her wrists, a dab behind each ear. It was a very special smell. Papa called it 'Katya's cocktail' and said how it was fatal and more potent than a gin sling. The uncle was breathing even faster now and the colour was coming into his cheeks very fast and he was shuddering. He must be very ill.

Oblivious to all this, Katya was getting her vanity case organised, her hair arranged and her lip rouge entirely to her liking, and by the time all this was accomplished the uncle's hectic blush had faded as if it had never been. He had resumed his normal colour, had straightened up, taken his hand out of his trouser pocket and was holding out the coat for Katya, who smiled. She did like a man with manners.

'Cheerio, kids,' he said, his voice full of the fake chumminess it is always such a mistake to use to children.

The children scowled and pretended not to hear.

'Brutish little man.' Katya yawned, and stretched like a cat.

The passengers were leaving the plane. They were the very last to leave. It was brutish common to rush. The whitecoat steward was maybe trying to hasten them on their way by taking in hand the little girl's velvet-collared coat, Robert's school cap, Katya's gold-initialled vanity case and the travelling rug too; the nuts and bolts of their departure that somehow had evaded sheepdog Robert. The steward gave the little girl a barley sugar, maybe for consolation for the greater thing. Shrimp knew from experience it would just be something to be sick on. She could never eat or drink anything for half a day after a journey of any sort, but she took it anyway to be polite, unwrapped it, pretended to put it in her mouth while secretly dropping it on the aeroplane floor, and then she suffered terribly in her mind about the steward finding it on the carpet and feeling hurt but it would be too noticeable to bend and pick it up.

Oh, oh, oh, thought Shrimp, suffused with embarrassment. If only (descending the metal steps with care for she always felt disorientated and light-headed after a bout of sickness), if only I had a pocket, or at least had thought to keep the sweet melting in my hand. I know he will find it and he will know I threw it down.

She began to cry.

'Don't blub, Shrimp,' Robert said, 'keep up.'

CHAPTER THIRTEEN

Fornebu airport was airy, not busy. Adequate concrete runways sprouted spires of purple loosestrife in the cracks. Dandelions' glistening heads reflected the bright sun, their gauzy clocks breaking into tiny gossamer parachutes caught in the tail winds of taxiing planes. Real parachutes had been tossed through the same space not so long ago: Germans, Britishers dangling on their slow trapeze, like leaves descending.

Shrimp, green-faced, bare-kneed and so very much smaller than the rest, trotted behind, keeping up. Fornebu was smaller than Northolt, but its surrounding sea and vast grey granite rocks were more than compensation for its younger-sister air. The human life seemed much the same in the two places: semi-military, semi-civilian. Army trucks were parked about and soldiers in khaki doing things with jacks and wheels and vaguely mechanical things. People this side of the North Sea were skinny as the rationbook English but less pale, and different in other ways too. In retrospect the differences were obvious. The English shellshocked from the grim disciplinarian task of subduing the individual to the vast humanitarian idea of protecting liberty and freedom of conscience throughout the civilised world; the Norwegians liberated after a stern and humiliating occupation of their nation, were busy demonstrating further those guerrilla characteristics of buoyancy and individualism that had been their way of coping with five years' cruel oppression at home. The Norwegian soldiers, customs officers, service policemen, and even the pingpong-bat men guiding the planes, all were going about their jobs with grace and humour, abundant

energy and age-long inextinguishable Viking individuality.
Some of them whistled as they worked. Nobody reprimanded
them. One or two chewed gum, and all of them looked more
pliant, more independent and cheerful than the ramrod auto-
mata soldiers and working men the Fortescues were used to
seeing in England. The contrast brought out the Fortescue in
Robert. Generations of army spoke through his recently-
broken voice. 'A pretty poor show, I'd say.' His puzzled, unloved
eyes glinted, giving back malice to a world that disliked him.
'The discipline in this country is a disgrace.'

Katya put on her white-framed dark glasses against the
glare of the sunny tarmac. Her gold charm bracelet jangled as
she pointed authoritatively with a kid-gloved hand: 'Shr-imp,
thataway!'

Shrimp trotted off to the indicated ladies' and irritated her
family by lingering far longer to clean up because after
she had carefully washed off the sick she found the ladies'
so fascinating. The porcelain bowl was not called 'The
Thunderer' in black writing and the water in the bowl was not
cloudy with acrid-smelling Jeyes fluid, but clear peaty brown
water that smelt like a river. On top of the cistern somebody
had put a jam jar of wild flowers. She had to put the lid down
and climb up to look, and there were harebells, two white
ox-eye daisies that Mama had told her in Norway were called
priests' collars on account of their white ruff, which was
interesting and must be examined, and three pink clover
flowers, and Shrimp hesitated for a long time wanting to pull
out a pink tube – just one – from the clover to suck it and see
if it tasted of honey nectar the same as in England or if it was
different in another country, like the language was different
though it did the same thing. In the end she did not try the
nectar. People were always warning you about the dirtiness of
lavvys, though this one was so nice she had sat on the seat, not
stood above to pee. She jumped down. Nobody knew that she
had sat down on the seat, and she had washed and dried her
hands, but they were still very cross when she came out
because she had taken such a long time.

Outside the customs shed taxis waited, a crawling line of
cheap, pastel-coloured American sedans. Katya looked round,
drawing her thin, arched eyebrows into a frown. No car had

been sent. She beckoned a taxi. 'Drammensveien, driver, and make it snappy.'

The in-flight uncle had made it out of the customs shed ahead of the family party. He stuck his head out of the window as his taxi swung out from the loading zone ahead.

'Toodle-oo, Katya. Return match soon, Hotel Bristol.'

'Soonest.'

'Don't forget.'

Katya took the cigarette out of her mouth. 'Remember, just bruise the gin.'

Robert scowled and hunched his shoulders so Katya should notice. They were in the back seat of the taxi. Shrimp occupied the front. This was how they customarily travelled in cars; that way the vomit zone was limited to Shrimp and the hapless driver.

The uncle's hand was still sticking out waving to Katya's taxi. Because the Shrimp knew herself inexperienced and young, she immediately had doubts about her dislike and revulsion for this uncle – all the uncles, come to that. She and Robert agreed uncles were smarmy; gaudy sometimes, too, but always smarmy. But how could she think such things without being wrong against Mama? Obscurely, in a way she didn't understand, her anti-uncle thoughts betrayed Mama. Mama wrong? Impossible. It was herself. She was the one getting things wrong. Children misunderstood what adults saw clearly. Children were not yet wise. That was why they must be seen and not heard. Because they were at the learning time.

A wave of definite conviction hit the Shrimp. She had done wrong by the uncle. Poor uncle, him feeling so sick and hiding his face in Mama's coat when they were getting off the airliner so that nobody should see how queer he looked and felt. She had done him a great injustice.

The Shrimp sat up straight away, looked out of the taxi window. The uncle's taxi tail was still in front. Hurray! She waved vigorously, maniacally, pumping her arm like a lunatic conductor in crescendo mode, and making herself more motion-sick but it was worth it. The signet ring glinted as his hairy hand waved back. Shrimp basked in the warm righteousness of one who has acted with moral rectitude.

'Do stop jiggling, Shrimplet,' Katya said, into the mirrored lid of her compact, 'I can't get my lip rouge straight with you dancing up and down like a Mexican jumping bean.'

'Yes, do stop,' Robert echoed sullenly.

It was just the three of them. Sholto wasn't with them on this trip, being *non grata* with Gustav. Gustav had taken a huge Oscarsson antipathy to Sholto and would not knowingly have him in the same country, let alone the same house or, heaven forbid, room. This antipathy wasn't a personal thing. It was not to do with Sholto as a son-in-law, but as a representative of his country and more particularly as an RAF pilot. Gustav was taking a stand on a point of principle about an incident that had happened during the war, an idiosyncratic stand in the circumstances. To the rest of the Norwegian nation, Sholto was a bit of a hero. His name was known. He had played a significant part in two key moments of Norway's war. Unfortunately the first key moment had included, as a minor incident, the destruction of three Oscarsson-owned ships. Sinking his in-laws' boats had never been Sholto's first object, it just happened, a casualty of the bigger picture, but Gustav didn't see it that way.

In 1939, the year Russia invaded Poland and Finland, Norway quaked in its sealskin shoes. The perspicacious German C-in-C memorably observed that 'the military organisation that has the best photographic intelligence will win the next war', a truism it took Britain a little longer to realise. When they did, Sholto was tailor-made: pilot's licence, photographic and technical skills, almost-completed course in navigation. He was called in at the formation of the highly secret Photo Reconnaissance Unit before it even had a name. In domestic terms this meant dissembling a little.

'Desk job, sweetie. Mere humble plumber. They also serve who only man the NAAFI.'

But he was obviously more cockered-up than if he was merely bashing tea. Katya's extra-sensitive antennae for such things divined his excitement and the existence of a woman called Freya in his life. She who had never tidied a drawer in her life tidied every one of his, and taught herself to steam things open.

Freya was a 'cleaned-up' Spitfire, gutted of all armaments to reduce her weight, modified to accept fixed cameras and fitted with special fuel tanks to increase her range. Her range had been extended from the standard four hundred miles to a distance of about seventeen hundred with a tail wind behind her. The question of range was so important that *Freya* had even been painted with a newly-invented high-speed paint finish. Sholto adored her, despite the strains and lies she imposed on the start of married life. As a compliment to his wife he had called her after the goddess in the Norwegian pantheon who could see a hundred miles day and night. Useful in spy photography.

Like all goddesses, *Freya* was demanding. Because of having no guns, he had to keep his darling machine as high as possible so the enemy's guns shouldn't spot them. On the other hand he mustn't allow *Freya* so high that she wrote a giveaway vapour trail in the sky. Sholto and *Freya* danced about Europe, keeping themselves a whisker below twenty-five thousand feet and photographing the German airfields and fortifications and the vast build-up in the Ruhr. By the time the phoney war came to an end and the real one had started he had already contributed materially to the photo-picture of Germany.

With real war his job changed. Still he was based at Benson in Oxfordshire, where Photo Reconnaissance had begun. It wasn't too far from the formaldehyde house. Snatched moments of leave revealed tiny wedge-shaped intimations of the progress of the war between Daphne and Katya as they moved from armed neutrality to outright confrontation. Hmn. Catfights would be solved the moment Katya started breeding, which surely wouldn't be long; a son, a son. Meanwhile the job in hand: buzzing all over the place in the wake of the bombers, Sholto and *Freya*, the fleas on the backs of the angels of death. When the smoke had cleared from the night's bombing targets *Freya's* tiny whining note was added to the next dawn chorus: high, invisible against the morning light, their glass fish-eye lens saw and recorded the detailed truths of the actual damage achieved to bricks, mortar, flesh, blood. These impersonal photos dictated what follow-up destruction was needed, if any.

He couldn't liken it to his favourite game of cricket for it wasn't a team game, but every time Sholto climbed into *Freya's* cockpit it was like swinging open the wire door into a perfectly kept lawn-tennis court anticipating a good game. The lines on the map were the freshly-drawn lines in liquid chalk on perfect green grass. The film within the camera was the amber catgut tautly drawn within the beautifully functional wooden frame. Sholto and Freya were a pair of athletes in a game of doubles in which every stroke of the racquet, every linear flight of the ball, every pass over the target, gave a profound sense of physical fulfilment. Between sorties he put in hours and hours on the ground, refining the photo technology and honing his flying machine. Sholto had never been so happy. Body and mind had never been so balanced. Life had never been so completely purposefully focused.

After a year or two he might have been sent with his fellow pioneers to set up the same thing in some other theatre of war, North Africa, the Middle East, Malta, perhaps, or Italy. He was certainly good enough. But then in 1942 the Tirpitz crisis arose; Sholto's Norwegian–Russian connections were remembered and the incident took place that put him outside Gustav Oscarsson's pale.

The powerful battleship Tirpitz roamed the northern waters like one of the slavering many-headed sea-monsters in the ancient hair-raising sagas Katya had been brought up on, marauding the seas around the north of Norway and Russia seeking what she could devour. The monster ate well. Her haematic fangs reddened the northern seas with the blood of the British convoys carrying war matériel for the Red Army to Archangel and to Murmansk. The deepest undercurrents of the Barents ran with her victims' sea-bleached bones between transparent fishes. Already the mere rumour of the Tirpitz had been enough to scatter the PQ17 convoy, with terrible results. To pinpoint the lair of this omnivorous Leviathan would be a prize. It was known she stabled in northern Norway, but where among that toothed coastline of a million fjords? The waters this far north were out of range of the English and Scottish airfields. Even the lovely Freya couldn't reach. The nearest semi-friendly base was the Vaenga airfield in Russia, near Murmansk. It was here that Sholto must make his base for reconnaissance flights.

He must fly from Britain to Russia in one hop.

'I'll get you there.' Sholto fixed his Mae West over his flying suit, stroked *Freya's* freshened-up paint job, and hopped in. 'Piece of cake, you'll see.'

Vaenga, his destination, was at the outer edge of the Spitfire's fuel capacity. It would depend on wind, and on his judgement: there would be a moment on the journey when he'd have to weigh the risk of running out of fuel against the shorter route over the enemy guns. Flying alone you could at least break the rules: Sholto smoked a cigarette every twenty minutes. Every fourth cigarette he topped up with benzedrine. The drug would make his heart race and his hands go clammy but he wouldn't go to sleep. The problem was with the mind, but that had been kept under control before. There was a technique. He knew to keep his mind on the physical, nuts and bolts, nitty-gritty; to focus on detail. He worried for the maintenance facilities for *Freya's* upkeep once they got to Vaenga. To anchor his mind he devilled the detail on a routine of supervision to be kept on the Red Erks, the Russian ground tradesmen who'd be working on *Freya*. He must be sure to be there daily at the weighing of the oxygen tanks. They'd scrimp and sell him short. His brow creased. *Freya* seemed to buck at the thought. The weather patterns in this part of the world were not something he had experienced. It could be relied upon to be unreliable for sure: zero visibility and high winds over the Norwegian mountains. He went over the details of received wisdom.

The nicotine and benzedrine cocktail combined, as he knew they would, to make his mind seem progressively detached from his body. His mind floated. *Freya* was joined in the air by a flock of Madame Blavatsky's well-nourished theosophist ladies on an out-of-body trip. Fat as seals with pearls round their necks and artistically loopy hairdos, the spiritualist ladies, who had taken off with all the ponderous heaviness of Bomber Command from the ouija boards of Belgrave Square, performed graceful elephantine aerial ballets round *Freya's* wing.

'Look into what the crazy ladies put in their tea,' he said abruptly, in a loud voice, then surprised himself with a disjointed burst of laughter. 'Steady, the blues.'

Sholto gripped the joystick, read the altimeter. He'd been at this, the intermediate stage, before. Introspective but not unreal; it wouldn't be hallucinatory. Reality would be transfigured, but it wouldn't deceive unless he wanted it to.

Judgement would be reliable, sense of time reasonable, ability to judge distance unimpaired. This was knowledge to cling to through the empty night of smudge-mirror murk, crack and quiver, electric uncertainties. Trust to good all-seeing *Freya* as she sped into gleam-distances, which themselves sped away – towards? The world was a cool, spinning opal. Cloudtracks pursued their own lines, real and as invisible as sheep tracks through the greater spin. His cockpit was a cosy fug, nicotine-sharp, smoke-wreathed, his dials accurate. *Freya* was skittish but fun; vivacious, airy and impetuous under his hand. Like Katya used to be in the first days. Not to be bullied or she'd break. There was a rapt exultation of coaxing her through the strains while imposing his will.

The light-headed flight through the down-flecked air above the enamelled toy-like seas gave way to the silver-frosted mountains of Norway. The country's cosmic draughts billowed up at him. Norway held the chill of fairy tale, exuding wan gleams. *Freya's* all-seeing eyes were going to make the world safe for the Oscarsson house in Drammensveien, purge it of the occupying Boche for Katya's family to resume their proper place in the world in whatever history was waiting. The things she remembered would have a future. Poor kid. Her life was bare as despair without that mother she idolised. Ma did her best at home but Ma was so up to her neck in keeping the whole thing going and the war effort. It wasn't her fault she couldn't see that Katya needed special love and care.

'Take care of my baby for me, Ma, while I'm away,' he'd said, and Daphne had replied, 'It'll do her a power of good to stand on her own two feet. She will grow up while you are away. I shall keep her busy and happy,' and he knew his mother's busy and happy consisted of the sock-knitting and other noble community deeds that had been Daphne Fortescue's own solution to making her own widowhood initially tolerable, a solution which had, with the passage of time, bled into happiness. He couldn't see Katya finding equal fulfilment in the endless fruitful round of needle-plying, garden-fork wielding, de-fleaing of dogs and sweat-browed tasks in the steamy kitchen, but they would work things out.

Katya had neither real family nor social context, poor kid. How could she be expected to have a sense of social duty?

Ma's formula wasn't going to provide a solution. Any idiot could see that. Ma couldn't see it. Funny that, when it was plain as a vapour trail on a blue sky.

How could you expect a dispossessed kid, a girl with two families, two countries and none of them hers, to get excited by village activities around Michaelmas Hall? He slipped into wish and dream. Into the mystic relationship between what his journey was doing for his country and what his journey was doing for Katya: his St George trip killing the dragon so the three countries might be free; then and only then would Katya the maiden be liberated from her chains of unbelonging. If a free Norway could be achieved with life going on as it had before ... If a free Russia could be achieved with life picking up where it had left off before the Revolution ...

The steel-chilled countries below his wing were forum for the hypothetical.

Down in Oslo the Hun was in her very house. In Russia, her other home, one could only presume the Communists were living in her family's ancestral farm, and had been these thirty years. To rout the Hun. To win a victory for Russia too, aligned now with the Western powers. Surely, then, when this was all over Russia would join the world again; he and Katya would find her origins. Taking her to the place, treading the soil together; this, surely, would give her the peace so lacking.

When he got home he would do some work on exactly where the Olovanovas came from. After the war the two of them would repeat this journey he was making. He and Katya would fly to her Russian home in Freya. 'Game for it, Freya, old girl? Carry my lovely baby as well as me? You wouldn't be jealous, now, would you? No. You'll be nuts about her. Everyone's nuts about her. She'll be nuts about you, too. She likes clever things, gadgets and gizmos. She's beautiful. We'll do this trip again, flying over Russia. But we'll do it in daylight. We'll fly over as friends. Over a warm and welcoming land-scape with cows and flowers in place of these guns below. Sun on your wings; you'll like that. And I'll know where her family place was and we'll home straight in. Straight as swallows, we'll fly. And when we get there she will know where she belongs in this world. We'll present her with her Russian family – well, not family, they've all bought it, every one, poor

sods, but her family home and the fields and the trees and the
fences and the garden where her mother played as a child. Her
mother,' tears occluded the clouded swirling sky, 'how that kid
loves her mother.' He must have another cigarette. 'We can't
give her the mother back but we can give her what is left of
her past, whatever is left of where she belongs. How about
that, *Freya*? How about that for a plan? Wait till you see her
face when she comes home to Russia, and sees it all and knows
where she belongs in this world, eh? And with the feeling of
belonging in the world will come peace; and with Katya at
peace all will be different. Easy. Piece of cake.

'I've always had Michaelmas Hall, you see. Solid as the
proverbial Rock of Gibraltar. Unchanging. Through centuries.
Thick and thin, kith and kin. It's easy for us Fortescues. We
know exactly where we belong in this world. Same bricks and
mortar, same cattle tracks in the fields, same trees taking their
time to grow over the centuries, same bloody bunnies to keep
off the crops. She has no idea how it feels to know exactly
where you belong in time and space, in a world you can rely
on not to change. But we'll show her, hey, you and me?'

Earlier in the war when he had been trying to tell Katya
this, what his home meant to him, 'Stuffy house,' she had said,
her adorable nose wrinkling, 'formaldehyde house,' and had
gone on to talk about how she was going to get Lulu in after
the war and set about redecoration. To tease him, of course,
funny kid.

Over the edges of Russia, morning was coming, a red
periphery. He flew north up the river Lotta. He wondered
what unknown family connections of hers he might be flying
over even now. He looked down at the vast Russiascape, a
muskier presence, more masculine than Norway, wolfish,
snow-glittery in the day's new sun, seductive and heavy with
the unresolved problems of his marriage. Maybe if this mission
succeeded Katya would forgive him for, in the first place,
raising her hopes by putting her straight on the date of the
earthquake (but surely this had never amounted to the deception she'd taken it for? He'd never actually said her mother
was alive, for heaven's sake). Then later, when her hopes were
still up, Sholto had been the one to break the real story of her
mother's death.

Oscar had shown him Pinkerton's telegram. The two of them had been alone in the little sailboat, a nice, homey kind of atmosphere between them. Sholto was basking in the benevolence of fate in sending this extremely sympathetic surrogate father-in-law. He was allowing himself to speculate, unprecedented occurrence, on what his relationship with his own father might have been if ...

'Now you are her husband you must know all the truth.'

Looking back on it, Sholto saw the care Oscar had taken over the planning of the moment. Putting the aged yellowing flimsy in Sholto's hand he'd cannily headed off towards a cleat needing his urgent and prolonged attention. Sholto was given time enough to digest, and to re-emerge as if all was still exactly the same as it had always been. Later that day, standing by the discreet wallpaper in the spacious bedroom Charlotta had allocated the married couple, Sholto had told Katya straight, thinking truth the only remedy to close the door of hope for ever and get on with life. He'd broken it as gently as he could. But she had held it against him personally, and that was hard, but harder still was the Katya that emerged from the news. There had, till then, been an inchoate spirituality about her: rays of optimism and hope that couldn't help shining out from the dark centre of her eclipsed sun. In removing all hope of her mother he'd murdered at one blow her faith, her hope and her god.

But if he'd murdered her optimism, he'd revivified his own. Firmly he believed that when this mission succeeded all would be clear and well again. When he'd found the dragon *Tirpitz* in its lair and set Bomber Command to kill it, freeing the maiden and both her countries at one stroke. She, the maiden tied to the rock like Theseus's ... what was she called? An– Ann– the pretty girl in the painting – didn't matter, the girl was Katya. Katya, the lovely Katya, was chained to the rock. She would be his prize. Easy. Piece of cake.

Below him a scaly silver and black sea crawled, wrinkled and shivered like a dragon on the move, winking occasional jewels. Details unreadable from this height. A great plume of heavy soiled black smoke coiled up from off the coast: something had been destroyed here by one side or another.

Sholto ran out of fuel just before Vaenga and was forced to come down in a strip in the forest. His navigational skills told him, correctly, that he'd reached the Russian side of the battle-front: no need to destroy *Freya* the beloved. He sat for a time propped on his elbows attentively examining the plane, the moon, the trees, the strip. The troops who surrounded him were surprised and mistrustful, inclined to shoot nuisances and explain later, but Sholto's hour had not come.

Sholto, son of Empire, set about conciliating the natives. Long weekends of house-party after-dinner charades came into play.

'Churchill.' He mimed bulldog, paunch and big cigar. Drew the line at two fingers. You never knew. 'Churchill *prosit*. Stalin,' moustache, oily grin, '*prosit*.' A fair degree of incom-prehension on the flat Slav faces of the reception committee. The tinkle of coin. Smiles and hand-clasps, vodka and singing. The long night yielded to a long day of glass-smashing, lachrymose bonding and incomprehensible promises of eternal brotherhood.

The hunting down and killing of the dragon *Tirpitz* proved a long job, too long for Katya. Sholto stuck to it from the spring of 1944 until November. Daphne Fortescue, meanwhile, stuck boldly and unfalteringly to the task of training her daughter-in-law in the skills of supporting the lifetime of church fêtes and WI meetings that stretched before her. Katya, despairing, found a different kind of occupation in the stimulus of a fiery OC undergoing educational vocational training. The OC was killed in July but he had plenty of colleagues to take his place. It was about this time that Katya, who so offended her mother-in-law by referring to Michaelmas Hall as the formaldehyde house, started to refer to Sholto as 'my sleeping pill'. Daphne didn't find this any funnier than the other. Meanwhile, *Tirpitz* was taking some killing. Wounded once or twice, it was not until November she was damaged so severely that she had to put into Tromsö for repairs. At last the dragon was motionless, licking her wounds for long enough in her lair for the *coup de grâce* to be administered. The trouble was the *coup* must be such a tremendous one to make sure. Lancasters of squadrons 9 and 617 operated thoroughly, over-efficiently, with no intention of risking the rebirth of the hydra-headed monster. She was smashed utterly. So were three good Oscarsson ships in the Tromsö area – and insurance impossible in war, of course. Oscar Oscarsson in the Oslo office heard the news, sank his chin, lowered his eyelids, weighed the fact. *Fordømmet* waste of good tonnage. But such was war.

The crackly ether brought the news to the Fødselsøy where Gustav was repairing the balance on a slightly warped oar in the metallic light of a thundery evening. He flung the long-bladed chisel in an arc. It landed quivering in the floorboards, embedded quite some centimetres.

Gustav's fury and persecution mania was at meridian.

Woeful Britishers, false friends. They'd done it on purpose of course. To lessen Norway's tonnage after the war could only be in their own interests. The British were a seafaring nation; damn' bad they were at it, too. And now, cunning foxes, they were obviously planning to bomb out all Norway's shipping so they could take over after the war had ended. Well, we'd see about that.

Picking the chisel out of the floor he put it to work immediately on the beginnings of a big tube gun that would point from Fødselsøy at the sky. He aimed it up at God, at impartial fate, at Nazi aircraft cosying over the airspace of the subdued country, at English so-called allies who destroyed good, profitable Oscarsson tonnage out of sheer spite and incompetence. *Fordømmet* son-in-law.

Sholto *non grata*. Outer circle of the damned.

When Sholto got home to England in time for Christmas he found the present as difficult as he expected, but it came as a hard blow, and unexpected, that the future – that slippery thing, the future – was going to be so much more complicated to settle than he had imagined.

CHAPTER FOURTEEN

Oscar was dead. In four hours' time Charlotta would un-characteristically forget to send the car to meet Katya and her children at Fornebu airport. They would have to take the taxi and enter the city in the wake of the new uncle. And while they were taking this journey Charlotta would still be sitting in the garden as she was now, entirely unconscious of Katya and her family in the cheap Packard with its lousy springs, lurching and rolling through Oslo's winding, unevenly surfaced streets like a drunken sailor on a spree.

The sun had just risen when she first went out into the garden in her everyday navy print dress. If she did not wear black it might not have happened. Death might even be magically reversed if she carried on as usual. Oscar might come bursting out of the garden door, vital as a gust of wind, laughing and exhorting her to join him for lunch or for some harebrained spree, and with this in mind she sat precisely as she always sat: no sagging, no trembling. Behind her, the pale house shimmered as it always shimmered in the fine morning air, profoundly indifferent to whether its creator continued to live or die. Fresh blue shadows were long on the June grass. She sat so still and so long that the family of fledgling song thrushes paid her no more mind than if she was a statue parked on the white-painted bench. The song thrushes darted about the segment of English lawn in little rushes, rehearsing for life, showing off. Mama thrush foraged in the midges that spiralled in the whispering birches at the edge of the garden. Soon she would come back to stuff her children's beaks. Charlotta had watched this same spectacle every year she had lived here. She felt a detached tenderness for the doomed comedy of their short lives. How did souls ascend? When? Did vortexes of midges part for souls? Did the diaphanous insect cloud shiver and hesitate, or did the souls part for midges?

The birches at the margins of the garden flickered above a glistening sheet of bright yellow fried egg flowers, and there was Berndt, little Berndt of twenty years ago, rolling his sunny limbs in the golden flowers, laughing while Oscar in crumpled summer linen bent over and tickled his chubby son with the long powdery wand of a flowering grass. Missy hovered near father and son, blinding in starched white, her front curving like a spinnaker, waiting as she always waited for the imminent accident, but Oscar shouted something up to her in a playful voice and she forgot her care. The rigid English back unbent on the discovery that the yellow flowers had the same common name in England as in Norway.

'Speilegg?' exclaimed Missy, to whom the existence of any language other than English was *au fond* incredible. 'Fried egg! *Speilegg!*' she cried, making such a spectacular muddle of the syllables that even she realised and hooted with laughter.

Beyond the trunks of the birch gleamed a mother-of-pearl sea. One minute it dazzle-danced, the next dulled with the fast sweep of cloud-shadow. Then out came the sun again to rekindle the dizzy wavelets brighter than ever.

Oscar would invariably look straight to the sea the minute he came out of the garden door. He would screw up his long-sighted seaman's eyes against the weather as if he was on deck and survey his fleet at anchor in the distance; an automatic checking of stock. Today's collection of flags at half-mast would have made him blink once or twice in puzzlement. Who was the latest old devil to kick the bucket?

'Charlotta?' he'd roar. 'Who're we planting today?' It was women's work keeping tabs on the business of hatch, match and despatch. Shrugging dismissal at the grim implication, he'd breathe in the sparkling wind, turn to his wife with the sun in his face.

'A *Bollinger* day,' Oscar would have said, eyes dancing at the prospect of a bracing sail. 'Come with me! I have a proposal. A picnic! You steal a white loaf from the kitchen when cook's back is turned and I'll go down to the quay and buy a paper of shrimps from old Axel.'

There was nothing he liked better than a handful of fresh-caught shrimps straight from Axel's petrol-fumy rolling old tub of a trawler.

'Broader than she's long!' he'd marvel, watching the sprightly eighty-year-old trawlerman cast a wiggling handful of the transparent glassy grey catch into the perilous cooking arrangement he had on deck. It involved boiling up seawater in an old oil drum balanced over a propane gas cylinder. The two of them would chat solemnly of sea business while the seawater turned to a roiling seethe and the unpromising greyness of the shrimps turned miraculously to pink opaque delicious mouthfuls.

'Let's run away from the world. It's ages since we had a bread-and-shrimp picnic. What do you say, Charlotta?'

And she would have said no; laughingly, gracefully, but nevertheless always no. Because there was always some duty to be done, at home in the house, or among her good works in the town, or some Palace obligation to be put first.

Why had she never neglected her duties? Just once or twice? But it was never once or twice, was it, once you started to break the rules? That was why.

Never since he died had she dreamed of him. Once of a chill blue-green sea and the boat in which his bronze legs had been stretched out. No more, only his legs, and she so wanted to see his face.

He had come back from the undertaker's waxy and puffed up, all the wrinkles taken out, and powdered white as a geisha girl. Every piece of flesh on display, even his hands, had been powdered to a velvety vileness. The right-hand index finger that he had cut off in his hot-headed way had been concealed beneath the other hand, and that had made her cross and want to put them the other way up to show his courage, his absurd courage. But she had been afraid the powder would puff up from his skin and dust the suit, the incomparable navy suit from Savile Row, just as the puffs of plaster dust had flown up round about her from all directions when she had first come here as a bride to the building of Oscar's house. White dust would spoil the superfine navy worsted; mar the beautifully laundered shirt from Jermyn Street; dull the watch chain stretched from pocket to pocket. They'd put rouged circles on his cheeks like a tart on Karl Johan Street. His hair was carefully parted. That, at least, was as it had been in real life, but it no longer smelt of cigars and bay rum. His eyebrows had been tidied, edged like a lawn, shaped in a stupid way like a vain girl's. Somebody had subdued those three hairs that sprang out like an overhanging rock. Oh, how she hoped they had cut them with scissors. She flinched to think of them plucking at his dead flesh with tweezers for the sake of tidiness.

On his feet they had fastened one of his many pairs of English shoes, made for him by Mr Lobb of St James's who kept Oscar's feet in wooden effigy on a shelf awaiting Oscar's written instructions for the colour and style of the next pair to be made and shipped to Norway. These brown pigskin brogues that had been chosen by somebody – who? – to tread the path to heaven had been polished by Russo day after day until they rivalled the deep glassy gloss on the grand piano. They had such heavy soles, so much too heavy for his poor dead feet.

Stealthily, slyly, she looked about. Nobody. She bent over, started to pick at the knotted laces. With the solid substance of the biting leather in her fingernails a gleam of glee entered her mind and she experienced her first sense of real purpose since he had died. And then she stopped. His poor feet would be so cold without them. The hot blinking started behind her eyes, and the suffocation in her throat. If she did not write to the bootmaker in London and tell them of Oscar's death, then his dear feet would live on side by side among the other clients on Mr Lobb's shelf! This felt like a little victory.

All this glitter in the garden was tiring. She closed her eyes but still the light flooded orange through the thin eggshell membrane. Katya was coming today. How ghastly.

Could she keep up the remorseless forgiveness that was her pact with the girl's dead mother? Could she manage to sustain her duty of compassion? It would be more difficult than ever today. With Oscar in his coffin in the house, Charlotta herself was feeling that same terror of absolute abandonment that she had seen in four-year-old Katya's flickering eyes; a terror that, Charlotta now knew, nothing had ever been able to extirpate.

Oscar was waxy, puffed up, less Oscar than the insubstantial and fugitive memories that danced in and out of her mind. Dead, and Charlotta must think of Katya. Why could the selfish girl not stay at home and leave her to nurse her darling man, to put him to bed quietly, peacefully, in her own way?

It wasn't him at all. For hours on end she couldn't think what he looked like. What had Katya thought when she tried to see her mother?

I at least have the thing in the coffin, Charlotta thought. I can go back and memorise the reality for all eternity. I am adult. I can do that. But the poor child, the poor lost child, Given no warning by her mother. Nothing real to memorise.

Real?

She stopped for a moment. What did she mean by real? The gluey glistening of the hair and skin shot her through the heart and she was brought up against the appalling falsity of memory, any memory: present, past. Little Katya could have no concrete memories. The child had clutched instead at an identity she found in the Romanov hairbrush (ridiculous affectation), and the made-up 'Russian' gibberish, and the self-dramatising on every occasion that so reminded Charlotta of the other Katya.

And now Charlotta fully understood the terror and loss lain coiled in Katya all her life. Katya's rages and spites, her extremely calculating duplicity, her manoeuvrings to hurt the mothered child, her brother Berndt, to put the odium and blame on him whenever and however she could. Now Oscar was dead and Charlotta was at the end of the line, she understood.

Only if Oscar had died earlier (which sweet Jesus forbid) might she have understood Katya and in that understanding have found the real way to help her.

Clear-eyed, seeing beyond the skittering song thrushes in the garden, she saw her own failure. All those long years Charlotta had seen it as her duty to overcome the duality of the orphan. She had tried to make a wholesome healthy unity of the girl's world, to cancel out the instability of the mother's influence by year after drip-drip year of unvarying duty. And all those years she'd never till now understood what she now knew: exactly how much Katya needed to hate her and to resist, how it was vital to the girl to feel that she belonged to the other world of memories, the world in the coffin. Just as Charlotta's world would always be a diminished place now that Oscar was dead, a partial place where re-created memories ran parallel, so with Katya. Both of them from now on would lead the dual life. Memories of the loved one were the only consolation; deathless, superior, romantic, exciting even, the very own private parallel realm.

It was time: eleven o'clock. Russo, bent with arthritis, was the only person in the house who dared approach her through the speckled shade of the shrubbery. He wore his best Russian outfit, too hot and heavy for the day: wide black trousers tucked into black Cossack boots. These days the high-collared tunic gaped at the corded neck like the beak of a hungry bird; a good thing the padded collar stood up of its own accord, unsupported. The outfit came out at Epiphany, St Nicholas, at the children's name days and since the war (which had been difficult for him, a Russian, in German-occupied territory) this symbolic outfit was also dusted off each seventeenth of May, Norway's national day.

The minute the Germans had marched (or, to be more accurate, boated and parachuted) into Norway, Charlotta had hurried down to the office where *sekretœr* Fulman had, as usual, not disappointed, but provided her with what she required, the Russian words for, 'You, Russo, are a Norwegian. You are deaf and dumb. Say not a word until the Germans have left Norwegian soil, and you will be safe.'

Russo had nodded and surprised everyone by having the intelligence to obey to the letter. He'd even forborne to sing his usual lawn-mowing song until the German capitulation of Norway on the tenth of May five years later when a Catalina and a Sunderland came out of the grey-red mist hanging over the Oslofjord. This was Sholto's second moment of the war connecting him with Norway, though he didn't travel in *Freya* this time. The two planes contained a party of sixteen Allied commanders, one of whom was Sholto representing the British Air Force. He'd been chosen for his powerful Norwegian connections, and on the incorrect assumption that he spoke the language. In Sholto's pocket was a sealed note from Håkon, Norway's exiled king in London to his late wife's lady-in-waiting. The letter was a form of touching base, a piece of paper containing polite formulas, words and phrases entirely insignificant in themselves, but embodying both to sender and receiver the hope that all might soon be restored to exactly the state it had been before the war; and then it would all have been worth it.

The two planes swooped and swerved and thrilled their passengers half to death; the citizens, crowded to suffocation below them in Drammensveien and Karl Johan, ducked like a swaying cornfield. Even Russo, tall as he was, could hardly see the planes in the sky for Norwegian flags that continued to wave, and the thunder of applause that continued to roll long after the two planes had landed on the slip at Fornebu and the rigid black-uniformed German *oberst* was shouting his long speech at the liberators of Norway while his men lined up, formal, rigid and self-disciplined even in the act of capitulation. That day Russo had uttered his first word for five years: his first and last Norwegian word, ever. God knew where he'd picked it up from.

'Hevn,' he had said, his voice creaking at the resurrection, 'revenge,' and though he'd never apparently achieved anything so concrete, from now on he considered himself no longer a Russian but a Norwegian, and took to donning his formal tunic on the Norwegian national day, an act of great symbolism to himself but perfectly unremarkable to those around him, who all naturally assumed that anybody would automatically wear their best on such an important day.

Thin as a rail, bent as a hairpin, bearded as Father Time himself, Russo's measured passage across the sun-shadowed English lawn spooked the entire family of song thrushes, who scuttled into the shadows under the nearest leafage where they waited, heads cocked, to see if the danger was worth hiding from.

The old serf broke courtesies. The taxi from Fornebu airport had arrived with Miss Katya and her children. Muttering unintelligible words, his enormous hand reached out to take Charlotta's and raise her from the bench.

'Yes,' she said, smiling shyly up at him till his heart would break with pity. She squared her shoulders. 'Thank you.'

CHAPTER FIFTEEN

Charlotta came in from the garden, stepping through the canted bay window.

Katya had come up the steps and was at the open front door. Her back was turned. In silhouette against the bright light she looked so very like her mother that gooseflesh tides swarmed chill over Charlotta's skin despite the greenhouse heat of the day. Katya, briskly in her hoarse voice, was telling the children to stick in the garden on pain of death till the Shrimp was back on form. It wasn't going to improve the shining hour any if the little one sicked up all over the place.

Charlotta frowned. This informality might well do for Katya but was a great danger to herself. Any informality, any impulse or instinct obeyed, would collapse the paper barrier kept in place by ritual and discipline; then terror and delirium would gain complete control. Only formality could oil the long day ahead. She walked deliberately towards Katya, making her footsteps very loud on the marble floor. She would at least attempt to impose the proper rituals of communication.

'Katya darling, how was your journey? I hope you are not too exhausted. And the little ones. So good of you to come,' she said, in a tight *salon* voice. 'How lucky we are with the weather.'

Hardly into the green and cream marble hall the women were embracing.

'Brutish flowers!' Katya exclaimed, at the view over Charlotta's shoulder. 'You've jumbled the colours all anyhow, like tinned fruit salad. Norwegians have no idea. Look,' she was already disengaging. 'I'll show you how. Goodness, Charlotta, pretty dress in the circs. Are we wearing colours?'

'No. I shall change. How are the children? I had not realised you were bringing them.'

'Mother-in-law trouble. You won't mind them, will you?'

'And Sholto?'

Katya made an avoiding dodge towards the fruit-salad flowers. 'Lulu would die if she could see these colours!'

They had been placed hierarchically one on each step of the curling staircase in descending order. Each bunch sat on the curved edge nearest the curving cream stone wall. Beside each bunch was propped its accompanying card. At the very top step were the personal flowers from the King; step number two the formal bouquet from the court, and so on. Down the flight they marched in strict order of protocol through church, state, judiciary, family, business colleagues, acquaintances, known tradesmen and suppliers. Lastly, right at the bottom, stood the self-interested hopefuls touting for business: the speculative begonias and gladioli in Cellophane from those who dealt in widows' investments, probate valuation, headstones, house sales and clearances, even coffin-makers, belatedly.

Katya's long, swaying stride had taken her across the glittering marble, she'd flung her ocelot coat and long brown leather gloves over the serpentine metal handrail and was on her knees crawling about the staircase rearranging the chaotic harlequinade of colours; snatching up pink carnation to put with harmonising pink rose, and separating fizzing orange alstromeria from velvet-textured purple violets with little cries of horror. 'God, why can't people just send cream, or white? It's far the chic-est. You really should have specified colour in the paper. The house would have looked wonderful with a froth of cream-coloured flowers flowing down the stairs like seafoam. Hey!' Katya cried in a commanding tone to the two uncertain shadows hovering in the doorway. 'Ankle-nippers! Eyeball this!' and held up a miniature cruise liner sculpted from a million chrysanthemum heads in the gold and red colours of a rival shipping line.

'With deepest sympathy,' she read from the card pinned to the funnel, 'my arse.'

'Katya!' Charlotta felt faint and had to hold on to the edge of the hall table where the Georg Jensen silver bowl with the green and blue enamel flag stood symbolically empty of flowers now and for ever more. Before the empty bowl the first pages of the book of condolence were already inscribed with a satisfactory number of signatures. By this evening it would be entirely filled, and closed.

'Please leave the flowers, Katya. Even the abominable cruise liner. They are arranged in order.' Charlotta explained the hierarchy, adding, 'These are Oslo's tributes to Oscar, not interior decoration.'

'Just this lot, then I'm through.'

Katya had already hastily moved more than half the flowers, parting the bunches from the cards that belonged to them. There would be no possibility of putting them back in the right order. After the funeral those who came back to the house would be confronted by muddle, they would be socially insulted. Charlotta would have to pretend to her guests that grief lay at the bottom of such disorder. Start again. Put her arm round Katya.

'Darling. Shall we go up and change?'

'Oh. So you really are climbing into black? It's never suited you. Tell me – tiny treasures upstairs, one two one two – what's the "in" colour here this season? In London it's French navy. Skirts have gone up, but only a little bit. About half an inch.'

Oslo had obviously not heard about French navy. Its skirts hadn't gone up much either. Oslo was in black, the streets clotted with a black crowd thick as treacle; thick it seemed, as on the day of capitulation. The large crowd turning out for Oscar had, inevitably, something to do with bread and circuses. It had something to do with Oscar being a big and popular man in Oslo; something to do with the scandalous rumours surrounding his death; something to do with expressing civil liberty in the face of a new and unreasonable law; and something to do with the crowd (wrongly) expecting the King to join the procession, a thing he couldn't possibly do because the monarch never went to private funerals for anyone. Anyone. It was protocol. Just one of those things.

Heat rose from the asphalt streets. Doves cried, 'Orukucoo orukucoo,' through silvery quivers of heat haze, the birds protesting at being disturbed. People were usurping their trees, climbing into forked branches for a better view, and flapping like outsize black crows, funerary birds ousting the peaceful pastel doves and shouting down to those below on the progress of the procession. The doves got no peace at all.

For once the Norwegians had left their national flags behind: no red-white-and-blue relieved the black that stood out stark from its context in the shivering glare that dissolved geographical boundaries, paling sea and sky and pastel-painted buildings in an uncertainty of firmaments. At the dot of two the quivering air was given form in sound. The bells in the city's churches sang, 'Tong tong,' in chorus. Their last resonance had not died on the air before the funeral procession issued from the house with metronomic precision. The *Biskop* walked ahead of the coffin, inky cassock rippling like dark waves with each slow step. Gaunt, tall, reddish-haired, he wielded his crucifix pugnaciously; a man more used to wielding a boathook; not inappropriate, not unimpressive.

Oscar's white coffin was draped in the blue and green of the family flag. It shone, an enamelled rhomboid widest at the shoulders, floating on the slow rhythm of the six tall men who carried him high on their shoulders. Russo, being the tallest, was placed at the head end, tilting it up. Charlotta could not bear for Oscar's head to be banged against the coffin during the journey. Russo's *placement* was suitable in protocol terms, too. Russo had before him the Court Chamberlain, a fusspot quite five centimetres too short to offer any material support, and about a hundred years too old. The old Russian retainer's Cossack cheeks had high colour. He emitted a fragrance of vodka and herbs, and when he exposed his teeth in the grimace expressing his mental pain, his steel dentistry was green-flecked for he had picked great pawfuls of feverfew from the garden, stuffed them in his mouth and was chomping on the leaves against the sorrow that ached in his head. Between Russo and the Court Chamberlain came one very young ship-owner thinking it would never happen to him. The other side was borne at the front by one of the younger government ministers, tall, overweight and cheerful; at the back almost matching Russo for height a senior *kaptein* from Oscar's own fleet, fond of his old boss. Lastly brother Gustav, the melancholy brigand, wild-eyed, elf-locked, drunk and terrible, tears streaming down the creases of his leathery cheeks. He had been strategically put in the middle so that an end should not be dropped if unreliable Gustav suddenly did a berserker and decided to bolt.

High they bore him through the streets, and behind them walked the various official mourners in long black overcoats, marching with measured steps and burdened with the appropriate symbols: wreaths, flags, velvet cushion with his orders and medals.

Protocol might forbid the monarch but it couldn't legislate for his curiosity. Håkon looked out from under the sharp neo-classical mouldings of the palace window at the toy-like miniature procession, the long, thick, black articulated dragon snaking its way up the hill to the white church.

'Wonder if I'll get as good a send-off?' He chuckled. 'Maybe I'll get Charlotta to organise it. Looks as if she was taking notes two years ago when we went over to Sweden to plant Gustav the Fifth. Well, she's always known how to do things properly.'

Thump thump. The slow march of the merchant seamen's band.

'Curious way to die.' The King stroked his fine black moustache. The pane of glass conferred a separateness. He couldn't hear the music through the window, nor the rhythm of the slow march, only the light buzz of the habitual silence in the palace. 'But then the Oscarsson temper has always been something a little out of the ordinary. To explode in such a temper tantrum up a ladder that you have a fatal fall and break your neck is hardly normal.'

The King was remembering the day he had been to see the painted frieze that had, by all accounts, been the direct cause of Oscar's rather scandalous death, a scandal that Charlotta (trust Charlotta) was doing her best to suppress with this heroic funeral.

How had it come about all those years ago? How had the King found himself in Oscar Oscarsson's office? He supposed he'd just asked to take a look at the Munch frieze. One of the handy things about being a monarch. You could just ask. People didn't often refuse.

He had asked to see the painted frieze, and Oscar had given him the conducted tour. Afterwards they'd shared the conducted tour of the aquavit bottle. Very necessary after Munch, possibly the only reaction. The frieze had been very arresting, very striking. Norway's foremost artist had been in one of his morally questionable nadirs that always produced his highest art. And why had the Oscarsson brothers given him the commission to paint their shipping office? An odd thing to do in itself.

Why? The King had speculated. Social rebel supporting fellow social rebel? The bottle expressing solidarity with the bottle? How had Oscarsson come across Munch? Unlikely alliance. The brothel? The docks? There were limits to the questions royalty could ask, for fear of the answer. The long, grave, royal face lit with an ironic smile. As though it were yesterday the Oscarsson offices floated before the deep-set, hooded royal eyes.

Oscarsson Shipping a/s. A modernistic place in the style the King thought of as American. The walls were flat-panelled in some pale fashionable wood. The carpets were thick, silver and soundless. The clerks behind the uncluttered desks were austere and all of them, to a man, had worn eye-glasses. He remembered being struck by that, and by the fact that the tall long offices were lit with white light from invisible sources, light that emanated in pools from the ceiling and the panelled walls. Not a bulb or shade in sight. He'd wondered if the two facts were connected, the pools and the eye-glasses.

In the space between the top of the plain panelling and the ceiling came the surprise. Here rioted Munch's libido in a horizontal band as though squeezed out of the toothpaste tube of his bloodshot unconscious: maidens, murderers, top-hatted madmen with jealous eyes, floating embryos, crazy moons, sinister sea beds and wide white seas.

No wonder the clerks looked austere.

This was his first visit to Oscarsson Shipping a/s and he'd expected something quite different: ostentation, decoration, money shouting about money. He'd expected boastful models of shiny ships in shiny glass cases on the walls. The only thing on the wall was Oscar's *skipsreder* certificate, writing faded with the passage of time, framed in a thin band of plain wood; modest to the extent of self-effacement. And then this ravening art, this masterpiece.

'Why?' the King had asked Oscar, when eventually he had found words. Gesturing with his aquavit glass (suitable, this).

'It can hardly promote the flow of "business"?' The King used the English word.

'Poor bugger was on his uppers,' Oscar had answered. 'You should have seen him, sir. Ill, mad with drugs, drink, starvation, God knows what. I couldn't actually press coin into the man's hand like a street beggar, so I paid him to paint. You know how it is, sir.'

Now, fifteen years and a determined Labour government later, Oscar's act of charity had fallen foul of the new wealth and possessions tax. Billed for a million kroner against possession of the frieze, Oscar had crumpled the demand in a fist of iron. He'd rather destroy the work than submit to such a draconian and illogical tax. He'd balled up the impertinent tax demand and hurled it high through the window of his study into the garden where Russo found it a day or so later, picked it up from under the lilac tree and brought it to Charlotta, who smoothed it out, smiled in love and complete understanding, and shook her head to clear the tears from her eyes. After hurling the note, Oscar had stormed down the garden stopping only at Russo's shed to gather up his instruments of revenge, and stomped towards his target with his face scarlet as a turkeycock, engorged with indignation and reflecting the blood-red fury in his mind. What was this *fordømmet* country coming to if a man couldn't do an artist a good turn without being billed a million kroner for it? Had anyone said freedom? What was that word? The Nazis might as well be back if this was how it was going to be in Norway nowadays. Oscar carried the ladder on his shoulder as if it weighed no more than a matchstick, and the rusty old blowtorch picked up in Russo's workshop swinging in his free hand.

The journey through Oslo's most respectable residential streets had been well-documented. Remarked and remarkable. The last voyage of *skipsreder* Oscarsson, pillar of the Chamber of Commerce, trustee of charities too numerous to mention, Honorary Chief Scout, et cetera, et cetera. If only Edvard Munch was still alive. Here was a subject to paint. Here was raw emotion.

'Madman.' The King shook his head at the bright blue and green rectangle shimmering out of sight on the sea of black. Herr Professor Doktor Lund, whose duties included the royal body as well as checking Katya's little body year after year in case her mother's TB was brewing deep inside, had reassured his monarch: told the King that at least Oscar had been killed by the ladder, not by the blowtorch. Well, that was something. A suffusion of blood inside the head, Lund explained, fury made manifest in a seizure, a momentary loss of consciousness, the fall from the ladder, the broken neck. Death instantaneous, so Lund had first told Charlotta, and then the enquiring King. But, then, the King suspected, they always said that. They'd hardly say the other, would they?

She had been entirely self-possessed, as Håkon would expect. He had hurried down to Drammensveien as soon as he had heard. There had been a brisk breeze up from the harbour. Hunch-shouldered seagulls had mocked his progress through the sunny greenery of her garden. Her court curtsy had not varied one iota from the norm. Only the moist streak of a recent tear betrayed her composure.

The procession wound out of sight of the palace window, a toy parade you could hold in your royal hand. The tall gaunt King turned away. Duty called.

Further along the route out of sight of the palace and just outside the palings of the white church on the hill, old Bess was stationed in her bath-chair. It had been a bit of a business getting here. Her arms were sore from wheeling half the night but it was worth it. Gro had said she shouldn't go. She'd said it would reflect badly on her own future career if her grand-mother was to be seen paying respects to a capitalist enemy of the new people's tax. Gro was getting such ideas it was hard to keep up with her. A shame Gro wouldn't let her have a little dog. Bess missed her little dogs. Something to cuddle now there weren't any clients. No, Gro had refused to wheel her to their benefactor's funeral, though she had been a very good girl about wheeling during the time of the pensions rights rally – none kinder. Gro had wielded the bath-chair with the best of them on that occasion, but once the pensions had been achieved there had been a falling off. Bess's head dropped on her chest. A little snooze now would be a good investment; she'd be all the more alert and bright-eyed when the coffin came and she wanted to see exactly who was here. A shame, this hazy day. It warmed the bones but hazed the eyes and today she wanted the eyes. Her jaw dropped open. She slept. Granddaughter Gro, whose loose, imprecise philanthropic ambitions had been characterised by Charlotta as 'love for the masses but not for her grandma whose scandalous profits, augmented by Oscar's charity and wisely invested by Oscar in *aksjer* and annuities, produce the roof over the stupid prim girl's ninny-head', would have been mortified to hear her own name mumbled in the jaws of her grandmother's sleep.

On waking Bess fixed her immediate neighbours in the crowd with her rheumy eye.

'I knew him well.' The smelly half-mad old woman embarked on the odyssey of her rambling tales, some true, some not; and she, the author, was the first to have forgotten which. Soon there was a wide space around her. In all Oslo that day she was the only one worrying that the funeral was not well-enough attended.

Katya got through it all on the calming pills Lulu had given her in London. They made you torpid (but that was just a side-effect) and a little quarrelsome too.

'Why can't I sleep in my old room?'

'Your old room and Berndt's, the children's rooms, are made up for your two children.'

'Then I'll sleep in Oscar's dressing room.'

Only Oscar had ever slept in his dressing room.

'You would be much more comfortable in the best spare room.'

'No, Mama-Tante, I'd sleep best in the dressing room. I expect it still smells of his cigars and his bay rum hair lotion.'

'The bed is unmade. If you must, I suppose you can sleep in your old room, and one of the little ones could go into the best spare. But it would be most irregular.'

In her old bedroom Katya smiled her cat-smile. 'I wanted this one all along,' she said, running her fingers down the lines of the old familiar wallpaper. 'Thank God for old shoes. Never change it, will you, Charlotta? Never never.'

Charlotta wondered if Katya was drunk. She was certainly under the influence of something. Katya didn't drink at all, as far as she knew. Not that she knew very much nowadays.

'You will go home now, Katya?'

'No, I thought I'd go down to the island, to Fødselsøy. We've nothing to do till Robert gets his common-entrance results, and it's about time Gustav got to know his grandchildren. And you, Charlotta?'

'Oh, I shall stay here.'

'Good. I like to think of you in this house. Everything exactly as it always was. Old shoes. Can we take *Bollinger*?'

'Too small, surely for you and the children and the luggage?'

'*Stiarna*, then?'

Oscar's pride and joy. His nine-metre sloop, greyhound of the sea. A cigar end in an ashtray. The legs stretched out in the dream. Charlotta turned away, taking the cream-coloured counterpane off the narrow bed, folding it and laying it on the rose-and-white *toile de Jouy* sofa, gaining time. So now Katya wanted his boat. First the girl had turned the carefully-arranged protocol of the day topsy-turvy with the flowers, then she had wanted to sleep in his dressing room, now she wanted his boat.

'Why do you push so? Why say these things, do these things?' Charlotta wanted to ask. 'Everything you say is designed to upset the balance of my world, and when you have pushed me off balance and I am swaying like a Russian doll you try to push me over into behaving as badly as you. Where did you get this behaviour from?'

Instead she patted the counterpane into a perfectly level square, aligning its corners and saying, quite colourlessly, 'If you really are going to the Fødselsøy I will telephone in the morning for the company to lend you a sensible launch, big enough for the children and the luggage and a pilot to guide you. During your years in England you will have forgotten how complicated the waters of the Oslofjord are to negotiate.'

Katya was under the white cotton covers, a child again.

'Pretty mouldy of brother Berndt not to show up for his own father's funeral. But, then, he's always too busy doing his Christian duty to take care of his own family.'

'Katya! That's grossly unfair.'

'I expect that's why Oscar loved me best.' Her eyes were luminous, dreamy; they saw her words go through Charlotta like a spear. 'What sail trips we had together, just the two of us.'

She was silent a while, watching; Charlotta had stopped tidying her possessions and was standing at the window. Over her shoulder was a delicate white moon.

'You were always answering the call of duty, poor you, while me and Papa-Oscar were in darling little *Bollinger* having fun. God preserve me from the call of duty! It's my lifetime's ambition to avoid answering it. I'd rather be flying over the waves. That's best. And best of all was with Papa-Oscar.' She shifted on the pillow and said in a more energetic voice, as though passing comment on an astounding fact, 'There's no sea near the formaldehyde house. No water at all.'

'I wish you wouldn't call it that. It's horrible.'

'If the sea was nearby I could stand it.'

Charlotta was not convinced.

Katya turned her head towards the window.

'Will you keep the curtains drawn back? I want to listen to the bees working the linden flowers in the morning. I want to wake to the linden tree full of bees like it used to be. Will you bring me a cup of warm milk with cinnamon and sugar now, the way you used to? Please, Charlotta darling. I won't sleep without it.'

'In a minute, my darling. Now will you listen to me seriously for a moment?' Sitting on the bed, she took Katya's hand. 'Have you ever thought that Sholto fought the war for stability? That lack of change is like precious balm to him after war. Give him time. It's too soon yet. What he is needing at the moment is the same as you wanting to sleep tonight in your same room and have me bring you the milk with sugar and cinnamon you had as a child.'

'That's different.'

'Silly noddle! Of course it's not different. When Sholto is settled and the war is truly behind him you will be able to change all the wallpaper you like and paint the house your Lulu's perfect shade of beige from top to toe!' Charlotta dropped a kiss on the beautiful unlined forehead.

'You don't know Daphne Fortescue.'

It had long been war to the knife in that marriage.

Katya and Daphne Fortescue shut up together throughout the war – what a recipe! Katya of all people living with the horse-woman, that woman deep-eyed in the vat of routine and

generational respect, who adored the dullness of the English
spirit and was afraid of nothing so much as originality. The
husband returning from war, joining the two women, too kind,
or too unimaginative or simply too English-gentleman to grasp
the nettle. Sholto sinking, as so many sank after their great war
effort, into despair as the dreamed-of war's end merely turned
into two great overwhelming facts: squabbling in the hen-
house and the existence of the Bomb. Where was world peace?
Neither in his house nor the greater world where the
deepening hatred between East and West spelled, it seemed,
inevitable global atomic annihilation. It was only a question of
which side would drop the Bomb and when. And Katya
wanted to go dancing.

Charlotta had been well aware of the exact progress of the
marriage through armed neutrality to outright war. She'd
lived a little at the edge of their trenches, she'd ducked the
futile missiles of marital bombardments. Even here in Norway
she was not out of range of the thundering warlords and the
top A shrieks.

Throughout the fourteen years of Katya's marriage, Charlotta
had never abandoned hope that, with wifehood and motherhood, would come that proper sense of belonging in the world
along with the duties and responsibilities, but even after all
these years in another country she still seemed to have no
desire for a social context so she'd never developed the sense of
duty that should go with it. Katya, like her mother, appeared to
enjoy only a sense of duty to herself, and this she took very
seriously indeed. Charlotta had heard Katya call Sholto 'my
sleeping pill' and her lovers 'just a few sideswipes'. She'd seen
the children impaled on the mercy of the marriage. Her sickly
granddaughter's refuge lay in words and books, her backward
grandson's in music and Meccano. How they would end God
alone knew.

The dark head fell sideways on the pillow. Through the
window, other windows were lighting up and down the town.
With relief Charlotta imagined Katya had gone to sleep.
Already she was forgiving Katya. What had begun as self-
discipline in Charlotta had become habit, second nature. She
was making kind reasons for Katya's behaviour: funerals were
exhausting, it had been a difficult day. Quietly she started to

tidy the room, to hang up the ocelot in the cupboard that used to house quieter clothes when Katya was a child and Charlotta still had the authority to edit out scarlet and the wilder shores of fashion.

'Will you talk to me about my mother?'

She asked from the pillow like an orphan. Her face was soft. It was not often during the years she had mentioned her mother.

The pain in Charlotta's head stabbed acutely. This was too much to ask tonight. 'Another time. Not tonight.'

'God, you're always tidying, Charlotta. Can't you stand still for a minute? Where's old Berndt?' Katya sat up sharply, her voice loud and scratchy. 'Sainted brother Berndt. Up in Lapland saving the Lapps? No, he's done that, hasn't he. I forgot. Has he leaped the ice-floes in his seven-league boots to save the Eskimos? North Pole next stop? Father Christmas converted to Christianity? Oh, no, Father Christmas is one already, I s'pose. I wonder if brother Berndt gets tired of saving things? No wonder Oscar loved me best. What with busy old Berndt saving things all over the place and you rushing around doing your duty and tidying.'

Charlotta straightened. 'I wonder, Katya, if you remember the Great Captain? A long time ago. The first day you came into this house.' Charlotta had tears in her eyes. 'Since first you came into this house, Katya Oscarsson, you have taken your greatest delight in smashing things.'

Sharply she shut the door behind her. Tears were scalding her cheeks. Her mouth tasted of bile. She stood still for a moment, steadying herself on the striped wallpaper of the passage. She regretted giving in to that undisciplined chink of words. Down the broad flight of stairs to lock up. The beautiful serpentine staircase was clear of obstacles now. It had been cleaned and swept after the flowers had gone away with the cortège. Passing through the house, everything was frightening: the clean empty silence, the stillness, the bookcases so stiff and straight, the empty bowl, the closed books.

Russo, in his high window above the garage, keeping watch, peering through the leafy veils at the man-less house, saw the glimmer of her figure in a pale shawl passing noiselessly through the garden towards the white-painted seat. Above and about his beloved mistress the bats flittered through the warm dark, tumbling after insects, scolding and flicking their wings. Up at the edges of Miss Katya's open window indistinct folds of ghostly curtain moved on the breath of the breeze.

No, Charlotta sat down on the bench, unsteadily aware of her own heartbeat, Berndt had not come to his own father's funeral. How could he when people could not look at him without the superstitious veneration of people who devoutly hoped not to have their own bones crushed or fingernails pulled out for the sake of truth, or integrity or call it whatever you will? And the fact he'd had them pulled out on their behalf as well, so to speak, did not prevent them from finding the sight disgusting and wishing he wore gloves. How much more difficult it was to love a hero whose face was pale as the bones of a fish, floury with psoriasis, whose skin flaked constantly in a dandruff of the whole body since the trauma of torture had triggered the unattractive disease. Stigma or stigmata, the sight was disgusting, his presence was embarrassing to the society he had suffered for. Small-talk didn't readily spring to the lips when you were talking to a man of such spiritual force that he looked not only into but behind your eyes, a man who'd spent two years locked up in solitary confinement, months at a time in complete darkness, other months more actively tortured in the bowels of Akershus, the ancient castle on the ramparts overlooking the port.

At the start of the war Berndt had come back home from his missionary work. As a Christian and a strict pacifist consciously he had made the symbolic journey home to his occupied homeland, a reverse journey few others made; misunderstood by the Germans for only a few minutes until he reached the end of his manifesto, recited on arrival. Once home he started immediately to fight the Germans, using weapons perfectly acceptable to his strict pacifist principles. Satire, humour and irony were his weapons. Berndt was among the founding band of the secret resistance radio station and press, and great strength he gave by his moral leadership. Charlotta had no idea of his other line of work hidden deeper beneath the first secret. He was working actively in the organisation getting Jews out of occupied territory into neutral Sweden. Charlotta didn't find out till much later about the

Jews. Enough for her that the Nazis soon found they had had enough of resistance jibes and wit. In 1942 they issued a sinister ordinance, condemning possession of anti-German propaganda to death, resistance to be broken by firing squad. The walls of every building in town became inhabited by howling megaphones shrieking contra-propaganda as though possessed by banshees. One Saturday shortly after the ordinance an unusually large police detachment had been patrolling the streets with steel helmets, clubs and machine-guns undertaking a rash of house-searches, executing one here for not carrying a passport, one there for some other crime, and they had taken a boy of nine for having a cartoon cut out of Berndt's news-sheet, and executed him at the official place outside Akershus castle. A boy of nine.

Charlotta remembered with insufferable shame – her breath came constricted in her throat all these years later (a whisper of wind stirred Katya's gauzy curtain). Russo, content that all was quiet, had gone to bed exhausted by the day. The old retainer did not see Charlotta doubled over on the elegant white bench in the agony of remembering that long, tear-blinded night on a chair in the prison where Berndt was being held. Many questions, seemingly innocuous, being asked of her and answered. The feeling of suffocating, drowning in her lack of knowledge. When you were asked exactly what day and time your hall floor had last been washed, what on earth was the right answer? Was it right to assume the question had some significance, conferring on a truthful answer the weight of a hangman's noose? Or was the opposite the case? Did they know the true answer already, so that the innocuous question was merely a litmus test of her truth-telling for later important questions? What did you answer when they asked who had the key to your house? When they poised pencils over paper to know the names of every friend and stranger who had passed through your door every hour of every day of the last three months? What exactly had become of the potato ration of last month? Who exactly had eaten what proportion of the niggardly blight-scabbed half-kilo? Cooked in what way? How much blank paper did your house contain? What size sheets?

'What?' she had asked back in disbelief. 'Every potato? Every sheet of paper in the house? Every single person?'

Yes, under this regime it was her duty to know every sheet of paper, whence it came and where it went. She could explain, but could not make the blank-faced men understand, that through her life greater concerns had flowed so that even during this war of shortages and near-starvation rations it had been a link to sanity never to descend to the pettiness of considering either the provenance or the fate of any single sheet of paper or last potato, as well as a point of pride to extend unquestioning hospitality to whoever required it.

And at the end of the pointless (or too pointful) questions which, in the end, she had decided she must answer with truth. (Had she understood the point of the questions she would have lied and lied to achieve specific ends, to save her darling Berndt, but the ends of these questions, if they existed, and their connection to Berndt, if it existed, were so obscure as to be invisible altogether.) At the end she was conducted out of the basement through one grey corridor after another, an endless succession of doors being unlocked in front of her, and locked behind her as she ascended towards the level of the ground, helplessly leaving her beloved golden Berndt, abandoning him to the terrible darkness under the ground below old Akershus fortress castle. With sore frightened eyes she had blinked at the light of the world outside, astonished at the sun in the sky. During her own short immurement she had lost realistic connection to the passage of time. How much more Berndt? Two years. And Katya had the temerity to mock. But, of course, Katya hadn't the glimmer of a beginning of understanding. Just as Charlotta had not the beginning of a glimmer of knowing how her own answers had affected the outcome, Berndt's doom. She could only guess with mounting horror at her own culpability, at the irresponsible naïvety of her own answers, as his captivity stretched and stretched.

Charlotta straightened her back. The air was cold. Surely she should have needed sleep but she was wide awake, not even tired. Maybe this was the real penalty of widowhood. Maybe like the bats who lived in the well, one never slept again. Morning was coming, lemon creeping into the sky. Bats had given way to flittering pearl-grey flycatchers. Down in the fjord below single rowing boats made wide-spaced specks on the mirror-sea: dawn fishermen. It was the mackerel season.

Stiffly she got up from her seat. Time for bed. She must at least lie down; rest her muscles if not her mind. Her work was not over. Tomorrow would be another big day. There was Katya to get off to the Fødselsøy. If she really was determined to persist in this mad idea of taking the children down there to visit Gustav.

'And she will persist.' Charlotta walked back to the house through the soft dreamy echo of the garden in the cool blue night. 'When has Katya ever been deflected from something she wanted to do?'

CHAPTER SIXTEEN

'So you've come.' Gustav's voice creaked like an unoiled door. He didn't use it much. 'Charlotta radio-telephoned and said you would.'

These first transports spent, Katya and her father stood on the smooth grey rock. Katya looked the complete nightclub aristocrat in beige slacks, a navy and white striped fisherman's jumper, red lipstick and her hair tied up in a bandanna against the salt wind. As a concession to night she'd abandoned the dark glasses with the spangled rims; that apart, she might have strayed here off any riviera *boîte* or *plage*. Gustav wore his broad-brimmed lion-hunter's hat, it being dangerous for the pate to be exposed to the light of the moon. His large, spare frame was undefined in the faded and much washed *blåklær*, the blue uniform of the working house-painter, electrician or plumber. He'd never grown brother Oscar's prosperous burgher curves; the cotton folds hung concave as a windless sail. Under the deep moon-shadow of the hat jutted the thin eagle-beaked face of the Norseman, two deep creases incised from nose to jaw. In this family context he'd set his face in what he thought was a smile of welcome but in fact looked like a grimace of protracted strain so that Katya wondered if he had some secret internal illness he was telling nobody about, in which case she could stay here in angelic capacity as a nurse and maybe win a father.

From father and daughter's feet the bright moonlight cast elongated linear shadows wavering along the uneven rocks towards the wooden bathing steps. Screwed into the steep rocky shoreline by iron stanchions, the steps disappeared into the slaty smoothness of a sea cut in two by a blinding moonstripe, which lay flat as foxfire on the water. Gustav had insisted the children swim, though they'd not arrived till after eleven.

'They'll want to wash that filthy Oslo-stink away,' he said, because he always did. Couldn't imagine anyone not.

The little girl swam like a mayfly, hardly dimpling the smooth skin of the sea.

The boy, on the other hand, blustered like a grampus. Gustav couldn't believe this was an Oscarsson making such heavy weather of his native element, the sea. He flinched at his grandson's antics blowing, spouting, displacing water, making waves and jellywobbles in every direction, disturbing the natural order of things with his clumsy heaving to stay afloat. Wherever the children moved, the water kindled with millions of atoms of the sparkling silver phosphorescent plankton *morild*, so that they left comet tails glistering in their wake and their bodies were rimmed with tinsel eddies and flaming trails of fire.

'The boy's ugly as a catfish.'

'I thought it might do him some good to stay here until he goes back to school. Exercise. Ozone. Do us all some good. I could cook for you and look after you, Papa.'

'Marvellous how I've managed to feed myself so far. Besides, your cooking might get me as fat as the boy.'

They went inside to get warm.

Shrimp had swum in a Fair Isle bathing costume knitted by her English grandmother. She hated it. Not because she hated her English grandmother. Shrimp aged seven was at the age of unquestioning acceptance; judgement was not yet an option apprehended, let alone realised. She hated the costume because it itched when she got wet, and harboured great saggy globes around her bottom that dribbled out gradually on dry land, like warm pee down her legs, which was embarrassing. Head down she scuttled upstairs as quickly as she could in the funny light of the oil lamp and this was a shame because the interesting surroundings downstairs would have absorbed her mind.

These days, the house that Gustav had specially put up thirty odd years ago to be well out of the way of evil spirits for Katya's birth resembled nothing so much as a rococo *cottage ornée* after the army have marched through.

Thirty-four years of Gustav was the army.

Nails bomb-splintered the pretty white-and-gold panelling where Gustav hung his vital kit: his top-quality thermometer, barometer, binoculars, brass sextant and large blueprint navigational charts. He'd knocked the top out of a window so his telescope-on-legs could see the upper quadrant of the sky. The elegant pitchpine table where Katya hoped for a cosy family supper was entirely full of writhing split cane and dark odoriferous tarred rope that Gustav was weaving into a new ingenious sort of lobster pot to his own design. On no account was it to be disturbed.

The muddle in the place was illogical but not entirely uncomfortable; a succession of girlfriends over the years had seen to that. One by one Gustav's floozies had held high hopes, installed whatever indispensable domestic object symbolised a claim staked, and waited for the proposal of marriage that never came. As a result there were enough actual beds and proper sheets for Katya and the children to sleep in, as well as a waffle iron, a spider-garlanded loom and festering sacks of Jacob's fleece in the sail loft, a lifetime and more's supply of Roger et Gallet scented soap, triple-milled in Paris, and other marvels and irrelevancies piled up here and there decaying gently in various degrees of salt-corrosion and mildewing. When the current floozy produced the blancmange-shaper, or the cut-glass vase or whatever it was that in her mind spelled territorial expansion, a certain bland look would steal over Gustav's face.

'She's cocking her leg on my lamp-post,' he'd say to himself, behind blue innocent eyes, and as soon as it was convenient he'd get up from his easy chair, leave his pipe alight in a certain ashtray (always the same ashtray), and leave. If the leg were cocked in the waterlily season he would go as far as Oslo, change his method of transport, hopping smoothly from boat to motor-car and take a little run down to Monsieur Latour-Marliac's aquatic nursery garden at Temple-sur-Lot in France.

The formation of islands was so shaped as to enclose a tiny freshwater inland lake at a higher level than the ocean surrounding. The lake was fed by a spring that mysteriously dribbled, rain or shine, at a constant dependable rate from a cleft in the high rocks. Gustav would not hurry the long drive down through Denmark, Germany and North France, to Monsieur Marliac, king of waterlily growers. Nor would he rush the day or so spent choosing the new hybrid to add to his collection. He might pause a further day, or week, or month, aiding his old French friend with the cross-pollination programme and making new hybrids. And then the two middle-aged men, dressed so like scarecrows you'd never guess either was a millionaire, king of his chosen trade, would be entirely absorbed dawn to dusk wading knee-deep in the spreading water-beds flooding the landscape like Oriental paddy fields but clotted with huge starry blooms and mirroring a gentler European sky. Gustav Oscarsson and Marliac would spend all the livelong day in rubber waders held up at the waist by knotted belts of shabby binder twine, and bent double over the red and pink, yellow, cream and white *nymphaea*. Mildly intoxicated by blood-flooded brains with all this day-long upside-downery and by prolonged inhalation of the sweet narcotic perfume, they would squint with intense concentration at the rounded boss of honeyed stamens, dewdrop nectar, pollen-dusted pistil, and concentrate hard on playing God with genetics by grace of a squirrel-hair paintbrush and plastic bags. The miraculous thing (one of the miraculous things, apart from the resulting hybrid blooms) was that – lo and behold – by the time he'd motored back to Norway he'd find the Fødselsøy a floozy-free zone once more.

During the closed season for waterlilies there was always a motor show to visit in some part of the globe or other.

By the time Katya brought her children to visit, Gustav's island had the finest collection of waterlilies in Norway, and a mighty archive of domestic necessaries, but there was neither reliable light nor plumbing. The WC was in a sentrybox, a round hole in a wooden seat over a drop to a bucket. Three large photographs were pinned to the wooden walls: King Håkon in full uniform with hat and sword, Queen Elizabeth of England erect and glittering beside her doughty Prince on their wedding day, and foxy squint-eyed Josef Stalin looking even less trustworthy than usual. King Jo, Gustav called him, and sometimes used him for dart practice, but only when his late wife Katya Olovanova had been preying unusually on his mind. On the fourth wall hung an embroidered text in bright wool Berlinwork: 'Thou, God, seest me.' The place was permeated with the pungent odour of slaked lime and disinfectant. Every three days Gustav took the lidded bucket out to sea and disposed of it overboard, having first ascertained the direction of the wind.

Candles and oil lamps constituted the lighting on Fødselsøy. He might have had a generator but he revelled in the notion that his house was archaic, primeval, essence of Norway, Viking lair. The floozies hadn't made much of an impression, for all their bazaar goods.

Katya and Gustav were sitting in the stue, either side of the driftwood fire. The lion-hunter's hat was off his head and on its due nail. From under the fly-spotted lace-covered shades the oil lamps spread a turbid yellow light. Katya could see that the lion-gold Oscarsson hair was still crisp and vigorous, except at the temples which were snow white.

Her father was sixty.

The children had taken a candle up to bed. Katya had made a great production of hot cocoa, not that the hasty drink had done much towards warming bodies chilled to the core and marrow and soul by the long emotional week: the journey from England, the funeral that nobody had told them was the purpose of the journey until it happened, the choppy and extremely nauseating boat ride culminating in the meeting with the odd, rough, storm-tormented, barnacled sea-god of a grandfather. No, cocoa had not been sufficient to warm the children, in the circumstances.

Downstairs the young mother was opening her heart, which had to share her father's attention with the wireless set switched on in the corner at the open channel on the airwaves where he could be found. Out of the ether came a constant background crackle with abrupt crescendos when the atmosphere was rent with odd swoops and whines like a commentary from a chorus of invisible witches.

Katya was smoking nervously: Player's Navy Cut, the packet adorned by her bearded friend, her friend in the Senior Service. The only ashtray was serving her father's pipe and so she had to lean forward from time to time, flicking the ash into the fire.

'I stick out in that English society like spats at a picnic. I couldn't tell Charlotta but you'll understand,' she was saying confidentially to Gustav, misunderstanding the sympathies of her audience to a degree. 'Sholto's no good for my inferiority complex. He just brims with perfect husbandly qualities. He's so damn decent. Stable? He's on gimbals. Nothing I can do upsets him. The worse I behave the slower he speaks, weighing every word on the scales of the most exact and exasperating common sense so as to calm me. I know precisely what he's up to and it makes me want to climb walls. Except that, frankly, I'd rather climb quicksand than the walls in that for-maldehyde house. Lulu took one look and needed reviving with brandy. Nice-girl sprigged wallpaper handcrafted by Jane Austen fighting a losing battle with the fruiting bodies of dry rot. You should see the fruiting bodies in my bedroom. I'm thinking of holding conducted tours. It's just not a possible place to pass your life. Your mortal span. Lulu told me once there was a Pope in Rome ...'

'Ah, Lulu.' Not the most obvious source of ecclesiastical information. Gustav recalled his brother's report on the Chinese clutch. Six out of ten, Oscar had reported, and the brothers agreed it was a respectable score for an amateur. Ah, brother Oscar, brother Oscar. Was it possible he was dead? Gustav's eyes slid towards the bottles gleaming on the table, his hand went out, withdrew as if scorched and then, in a new gesture that would be with him now all the rest of his life, he put his left hand up to the right shoulder that had supported the appalling lightness of the white coffin.

'... who exiled modernity. Pope Nicholas something. Fortescue we decided. They won't let me change a thing. Change is the blackest sin. And you know why? Because I'm not me. It took me some time to realise it. But in fact I'm not me. I'm a link. They're all links and it's far more important to be a Fortescue link than to be a person. In fact it's the greatest thing you can possibly be. It's a great privilege to live your whole life as a link in a dripping jungle of fruiting dry rot and walls painted operating-theatre green under the gaze of the pickled ancestors.'

Katya took an unlit cigarette out of her bandanna, put it into her mouth, bent forward to strike the match on the stone floor, inhaled.

'Living with Sholto and his mother is like ... like driving in a car forwards but only looking in the rear-view mirror. They're always looking backwards at the pre-war Never-never Land rushing away from them. And the past is like a lover's face. You know how you can never see your lover's face when he's gone? And you try and try. And they want so much to see their past alive that their imagination turns it into something else, a screwball made-up land that never was. A land of fictitious nostalgia. And however hard I jump up and down there's no room for me in their mirror. It's sad. Take tea.'

Gustav shrank back into his chair alarmed. More to eat and drink? Was she trying to kill him? He was bursting already.

'Every tea-time four-thirty pip-emma on the dot, she pours tea from a teapot of incredible brutishness. It's ugly as a baby and it dribbles like one. It drove me mad to see it every day so I went to Georg Jensen's and purchased his finest. Cost the earth, beautiful modern design. Didn't dribble, perfectly continent. I wrapped it all in ribbon, did the thing properly. You know what the old coot said? "My husband didn't die and my son risk his life for his country so you could fill it with new-fangled foreign teapots." She has whiskers on her chin, did I tell you that?'

'Most mothers-in-law have,' said Gustav, with all the Olympian detachment of one whose mother-in-law's timely murder in a forest had precluded whiskers or any other sort of irritating singularities.

'Let me tell you about every Saturday of my married life.'

Gustav put up a hand to halt her, but she was into a head-long rush. Flashing red lights and sirens wouldn't stop her now.

'There's a disgusting dish of meat they always have on Saturdays called steak and kidney pudding. Have you ever met it, Papa? It's awful, I can tell you. Beef pulverised to mud under a heavy wet hat of yellow slimy suet and it sits on your stomach like whalemeat for six hours after. And if it isn't served every Saturday of the year between the months of October and February, life ends. Michaelmas Hall wiped out. Every Saturday my mother-in-law brings in the triumphal sludge and Sholto on first sighting says, "Ah, steak and kidney!" in great wonder and amaze, and I think, My goodness me, what a surprise, and the third circle of hell is reserved for people like me who don't like steak and kidney pudding. The Shrimp loathes it too. Shrimp and me smuggle it down to the dogs under the table and by the time the brutish perennial cheese is wheeled in to make its sixth sweaty appearance of the week (the cheese is another story by the way) the dogs are making terrible farts and Daphne Fortescue is lighting a Swan Vesta match under the table for the sulphur to absorb the smell of the terrible farts and she roars with laughter like a jackass at the huge joke of the dogs' wildly amusing digestions. If they didn't have steak and kidney I wouldn't feed it to the dogs and if I didn't feed it to the dogs they wouldn't fart. And lunch would be civilised and it's not such a big deal. The world wouldn't stop if they changed just one little menu to make me happy.

'I'm getting fat with inactivity. Every night I go to bed I feel the suet creeping round my hips and the fruiting bodies creeping down the walls towards my pillow to get me. Before I know where I am I'll be operating-theatre green all over and I'll not have done anything with my life and then Daphne and Sholto will be happy with me at last, because I'll have turned into a link while I wasn't looking, and when I've finished being a link I'll be a pickled ancestor. But, Papa, I don't want to be dead without making a mark. I don't want to be a link. I want the new. I need the new. The try-out. I want change. I want bustle. I want at least one new thing every morning. It's the unknown that excites me. I can't see the point of life as a museum curator, treading in dead men's paths. I want to make my own way. Anyone can preserve. I want to create.'

'Create what, precisely?' Gustav interrupted, allowing himself a touch of pedantry in order to stem the babble and focus on what, if anything, lay beyond these passionate issues of menus, teapots and embalming fluids. 'What is this creative urge, Katya? Is this a focused urge you are referring to? Do I have an artist for a daughter or merely a revolutionary? Are you driven in a specific way to create? Is this creative drive specifically hindered by diet? Can you only fulfil your true potential on locusts and honey, for example? Or are you, in fact, making a catalogue for me of your directionless reaction in the face of their conservativism? In the face of the Fortescue edifice that you chose to join?' By *pokkern*, this was a long speech. But it was right to let her have it between the eyes. *Soren* knew, he'd pussyfooted around her mother long enough, and that hadn't got anybody very far.

'Are you,' Gustav continued, 'translating your somewhat incoherent emotional turmoil into the non-specific grudge that I believe St Paul with his inimitable turn of phrase calls "kicking against the pricks"?' Gustav asked the question disingenuously, raising for a moment his heavily creased sunbrowned lids.

She might surprise him. A daughter might be different – even Katya's daughter. His reading of her so far might be wrong. But, judging from his experience with the original Katya and with the subsequent procession of floozies, he'd say this daughter of his was pretty much like all the others. Sex was the true north on her compass; and if sex was below expectation (and when wasn't it?) any excuse would do. People only got snippy about meals and the colour of walls if their sex life was wrong. Teapots, of all things! Stupid girl to pick a fight over teapots. There was probably no more burning local issue in the entire Fortescue household. After all, this was England we were speaking about here.

She was still a pretty girl, his daughter. The fruiting bodies hadn't got there yet. She remained deceptively fresh-looking; the image of her mother. Katya Olovanova, Gustav reflected, had no sticking power either; that aligned with a state of permanent concupiscence which had, let's be honest, been a large part of the original attraction. If only he'd known that a permanently concupiscent wife was a non-starter. You couldn't be rogering them all the time. Business life had to go on, and then if they didn't take open lovers they'd be mesmerising clatches of equally febrile maidens and leading them into the murky realms of intellectual exploration. It all came flooding back. The novelty-mania. No sticking power. Katya Olovanova adopting whatever new toy came along: Freud, eurythmic dancing, red walls (red the colour of Life), Puvis de Chavannes, sunbathing, Gurdjieff, vitamins, Ouspensky, Blavatsky, all the -iskys and -isms, the keys to life she passionately espoused *pour épater les bourgeois* and to prove she was absolutely in the forefront of modern creative thought.

When he came to think about it, Charlotta was the only woman he'd ever known not ruled by this permanent pre-orgasmic febrility, the only woman he'd known who was capable of reasoned response, objectivity and sticking power. Far above style wars, she had settled serenely into the physical world shaped by Oscar, giving her surroundings no more thought than the air about her, and got on with the important business of living in the world. Gustav had never known her confuse wall coverings with moral statements, or fashionable bandwagons with moral thought. Charlotta was the only woman in the world. My God, how she had stuck. My God, how Oscar had chosen well.

Charlotta had always been telling him what great faith she had in his daughter Katya's marriage to Sholto. Michaelmas Hall was just exactly what Katya needed, Charlotta had told him, he remembered as if it were yesterday.

'The strain of wild recklessness must have been purged from her soul for her to take such a step,' Charlotta had told him, with the air of someone who had always known it would turn out happily ever after. 'Now she has from choice grafted herself to some stability; she wants to belong.' Charlotta had been bright-eyed, believing for that moment that her inculcation of steady, unexciting values had not been in vain. The Fortescue family represented Katya's hope of salvation through permanence, but even as Charlotta had been saying it Gustav was, through kindness to his sister-in-law, reserving the thought that Katya's attitude towards permanence and family structures had, to date, resembled nothing so closely as the demolition contractor's swingball and chain.

Why should it be any different in England? She'd never shown any inclinations towards an ordered life.

And then, throughout the long years of the war, with all the family but Katya at home in Norway, embattled, silent, separate, only the poorest slivers of personal news had slipped through chinks in the barbed-wire lines. And Charlotta's faith in the marriage had grown and grown.

'With Sholto such a hero it must all be going well between them. How could Katya fail to worship such a husband?' Charlotta confided with satisfaction.

'Idealisation might lead to disillusionment,' Gustav had hinted gently, knowing it inevitably did.

'But without idealisation,' Charlotta had sunnily countered, 'there is no striving.'

Wheeeee. Banshees wailed in sudden loud chorus on the saturated air. Up on the landing Shrimp flinched unseen, unheeded. Atmospheric conditions were disturbing the radio airwaves. Through the unnaturally elongated window, an army of cumulonimbus were massing heavily, dark over the moon. Prospects looked poor.

'Unsettled over the next few days,' the forecast had said, '*stiv kuling.*'

Looked like it was coming earlier than expected. Had he set the net too high this evening? Fish went deep in these conditions.

... St Paul. St Paul. Kicking against the pricks ...

Gustav had, as he said, time to read. Along with a lot of other big books the Bible was at his fingertips. Not through religious zealotry. His intellectual curiosity had been ignited by nephew Berndt's remarkable endurance and tenacity under test. Well, maybe it wasn't such a great marvel. Gustav liked to think any Oscarsson would do the same under pressure, though two years, two whole years in solitary, that was something, even for an Oscarsson. But the real oddity, the real interest lay in Berndt's expanding and enduring faith while being treated with such abominable and pointless cruelty. This was what fascinated his uncle Gustav, raised an envious curiosity in him, led him on those really bad storm-scoured soul-stretch nights to underscore the lines in the Bible with his broad black fingernail, punching the book gently from time to time as one playpunches a delicious chubby baby, as if to bully the thick book into revealing the gift of – whatever it was it gave Berndt. The gift had not been punched out. Gustav at sixty was not certain of conviction in any direction. Before Katya Olovanova he used to believe in Oscarsson luck. Since what he thought of as the San Francisco fiasco he hadn't found anything to replace it much, with the honourable exception of the weather signs observable in the sky and their resultant symptoms legible in the waters of the sea and further confirmed by the clinical signs and social behaviour of the inhabitants of the aqueous element. Remarkable what you could tell from fish.

Tonight, almost unconsciously, he had taken his seat in the chair angled across from the floozy chair. When women were about he sat here in this different place, a place where his face was bound to fall into deep shadow. With your face in shadow you could simply say nothing when women paused in their endless stream of words because they were waiting for a response. The only pause women ever took was when they wanted a response. And he'd be damned. Words of response meant taking sides, saying things, things invariably held against you later. Wise fellows kept mum; fell into blameless slumber without being spotted. Women would talk so. It was written in Berndt's sacred scripture that the serpent had offered an apple. Actually Gustav knew better. It was an apple-shaped ball made of all the words in the world compressed that the serpent had offered. Eve had eaten it that day and she'd never stopped regurgitating since. Words, words, words.

Katya, happily unaware of this hypothesis, was feeling more and more comfortable in the floozy chair as her recital went on. She inhabited her chair like a cat; impressed her shape on the cushions, struck attitudes in the firelight, kicked off a pretty shoe, curled and uncurled her varnished toes. The Fødselsøy gave her a feeling of everlasting girlhood, of safety within range of the warm rays of her father's golden, shining corona.

'I never loved Oscar as much as I loved you,' she said, in her small melting voice, the special voice she kept for uncle-snaring and for seducing dogs. In the oil lamp's light her eyes had melted and softened like butter, 'Even though I hardly saw you.'

His spleen rose in peevish indignation on his newly dead brother's behalf. The bitch must think I'm a rare idiot. 'I hope,' he said drily, 'you never told Oscar of this great love for me all the time you were living in his house.'

"Oh, no. I never let him know.'

'How many years were you living with Oscar and Charlotta? Twelve years? Or was it fourteen? How old are you now?' he asked, with a sly glint. Glamourpusses always hated this direct question.

Upstairs in the dark the children, in whom cocoa had done nothing to extinguish goggle-eyed wakefulness engendered by their first encounter with this astonishing place, this strange grandfather and the night swim in the cold North Sea, had crept out to the tiny dark flat platform at the top of the stairs. Here they crouched mousy-still in shadow, listening to words not designed for them. Blade-thin Shrimp was shivering. She'd never warmed up from the bathe. She had been spooked by the strange fire she'd swum through in the sea, and now she was doubly frightened by the eldritch shrieks from the radio witch. She shrank in on herself, queasy with fear, but it would be worse to go back to the dark bedroom and lie rigid in the damp, mildewy bed hearing the disembodied noises coming up through the floor. There were spirits in Norway. Nobody had told her in case it frightened her, but she knew they were there because she had read about them in England. High in Michaelmas Hall's immemorial nursery she had taken the few books her mama had contributed to the shelves and learned of these spirits from the two thick-spined volumes bound in green cloth, *Grimm's Eventyr*, the grisly German tales in translation. Nobody had taught her to read in Norwegian but Shrimp had her own particular gift. She was young enough yet not to have been taught that the different languages had hedges and spiked palisades around each, separating one from the other, making each language impenetrable from the other side of the hedge. And as she didn't know that what she was doing was impossible, she found no difficulty in working out the written words to fit the spoken. The brothers Grimm told her that here in Norway there were giants who saw for seven miles and they walked with seven-league boots so there was no use at all in trying to get away from them if they were after you, however fast you grew up and learned to run. Under bridges lived the ogres waiting to drink your blood and grind your bones into bread. In the clefts in the rocks (and the Fødselsøy was all grey rock, rolling, falling, humped and cracked) trolls waited to pull you into the cracks and crush your bones, *crik-crak*. Since arriving in Norway, Shrimp lived in special terror of the Snow Queen kidnapping Robert and leaving her all alone to fend in an adult world where nobody seemed to like anybody very much.

'I asked Sholto once during one of those marital moments (you know), what he'd fought the war for. "The freedom not to

change," he said. He'd risked his life for the world to be exactly
as it had been before the war; sufficient but not gaudy. I found
that fixity of outlook depressing. Freedom for the munchkin to
be the sixth generation of Fortescues to go to the same school
and play cricket on the same field for the same team. Fat
chance with the little genius up there.' She jerked her thumb
towards the bedrooms upstairs. 'And, of course, they blame me
for producing an idiot. Fortescue blood couldn't possibly turn
out such a sub-standard product. Well, it's hardly *my* fault.'

In the shadows the Shrimp turned on Robert a face of
adoring love and consolation. Her thin hand, frail as bird-bone,
flittered towards her brother. He must know how much she
loved him. Her love for him might be his loving armour
against the Snow Queen, as Gerda's love had won her brother
back and melted the icicle the Snow Queen had put in Gerda's
brother's heart. So Shrimp's love might win her own brother
when the beautiful woman came for Robert on her ice-
sparkling enchanted sleigh to take him away from the world
that blamed him so for being fat and unable to read, and
transported him to her snowland of pure blue-silver flickering
beauty.

But up here on this dark landing Robert's face was higher
than hers, even sitting down, so all she could see was the
rounded underside of his chin with its downy fuzz of dark
adolescence that lately gave Katya the opportunity to tease
him about girls and safety razors. To the Shrimp it was
annoying that she, so well-used to understanding words,
couldn't understand the meaning behind these teases. She
could tell they brought a sharp edge of glee to her mother,
were meant to make her brother proud but instead plunged
him into a resentful pall of humiliated gloom that sooner or
later led to one of two things. Either he took to his bed for the
rest of the day with the tantrums and the Meccano set, or he
went to the radiogram and lay with his mouth against the
fabric-covered circle that emitted the sound as though he
wished to eat the soundwaves, or himself be absorbed into
their stream. Either way it would be a long time, days
sometimes, before the Shrimp's little food-offerings and shyly
presented consolations didn't meet with an irritable 'Don't
fidget' or 'Don't follow me' or 'Can't you leave me alone?'

The little girl's sparrow-like hand, unmet, flitted back through the mothy dark, withdrawn from her brother as quietly and unnoticeably as it had been offered, leaving the small space between them empty, ambiguous and cold.

'Nostalgia?' Katya was saying. 'Necrophilia might be more accurate. A nation of necrophiliacs. They dote on the dead. As long as it's dead it's okay. Chippendale. He's dead. All those kings. The national pastime is castle-creeping, ruin-worship. They get a kind of religious kick from staring for hours at old furniture and crumbling walls, inhaling the smell of wood-worm and dry rot and dust. Personally I prefer Chanel Number Five. And I'm not really that interested in what Henry the Eighth did here or there. What Sholto and Daphne really look forward to about the future is it being just one long rerun of the past, one eternally drawn-out exercise in nostalgia. What they don't realise is that one day we'll be history too. I tried telling Daphne once. "People will look back on us and we'll be dead and history," I told the old coot. "And then we'll be okay. Even me. Norwegian me. Just look on me as history in the making," I told her, "then you'll see the point of me." '

Gustav laughed. So far he'd found his daughter's dubious logic unusually repellent but the thought of her as history in the making amused him.

Pleased by his laugh, she leaned forward to pick up a shell that had once been home to a hermit crab. It was pretty, a khaki spiral ribbed and rough, flushed rosy pink within. As she spoke she stroked the chalky ridges, put the shell on her finger like a hat and felt the cool pink porcelain interior.

'What I can't understand is this, Father. Why won't they realise that life rushing past today is also history? Someone else will write about today – all today's new things – and make today into history too. Whatever I'm feeling and doing today won't matter to them till tomorrow when someone's written about it and converted it via this crazy fictitious nostalgia into history. But till that's done today won't count in their eyes. I can't wait that long. Besides, there might not be that long to wait with everyone dropping bombs all over the place. Last year it was the USSR. This year Britain. What have the poor Montebello islands done to deserve such a thing? Russia might drop the H-bomb on

America tomorrow. Or America on Russia and then we'll all be just one mushroom-shaped cloud and if my last meal on this earth turned out to be steak and muddy kidney under a yellow hat of suet I just couldn't bear it. I'd die. I want the world new today – and newer still tomorrow! Is it so difficult to see that going forward might be a blast, an adventure, a good thing, an improvement on the sacred past, even?

'The truth is, Father, I can't make any more impression on them than I can on the wallpaper. They'll go on running backwards, kowtowing to their ancestors in their world of cracked teapots, brutish food, half-dead trees and half-dead minds, and my inferiority complex will get huger and huger and make me feel wrong and guilty and extravagant and selfish and Norwegian, which is possibly the worst crime of all – for wanting things different.

'But what I don't get is this. When he married me, what was I doing for Lulu but transforming things? Making them new and beautiful. It's not as if he didn't know. What can I do against this – this link thing that cancels out the possibility of choice? How can any living person have any effect? Drive things forward. Be?'

Katya had long ago forgotten that she'd joined her own fate to the formaldehyde house on the firm if fey misunderstanding that union to Sholto was destined to accomplish the reunion with her own past in the shape of her mother.

'If they won't put a foot on an untrodden path then there's no way to a future. For them or for me. I've come to the end. The duration of hostilities. I'm at the end, Father, the end of my marriage. I'm walking.'

Upstairs in the thick darkness the Shrimp, who could never help but focus on words and sounds of words and the meaning of words, and who would in later life become a translator for the UN, shivered. The veil of the future had been torn. Quite without thought, forgetting Robert's recent rejection, both her small hands quested towards her brother, blind tentacles directionless in a dark undersea. This time Shrimp's fingers were so afraid they didn't flounder in the air but found an elbow, and grasped.

At difficult times, when life became disagreeable for Robert and the obstacles thrown up by his dyslexia became insuperable, the boy simply retired, silent, separate, remote from fact. He listened to music in his head, busied himself with working out the notes in piano-accordion fingering, his tongue often lolling, forgotten, till the inevitable reprimand to put it away. He'd not heard his mother make the terrifying announcement that she was walking. Since the talk about him being too fat and moronic to achieve the great school, he had been busy and happy inside his head (so far as he ever was happy) converting the Pastoral symphony for performance on this most unsuited instrument. Entirely unaware of his sister's existence, chubby arms folded across his striped winceyette pyjamas, the boy's upturned eyes were seeing nothing but the pattern of notes dancing up and down on their lines, and his ears were full from the inside of sounds those notes would make when he played them on the push-me-pull-you.

He shook off Shrimp's hand in irritation. He gave her a look. Shrimp was always interrupting.

Downstairs Katya asked, in her sweetest pleading voice, 'You'd do the same, wouldn't you, Papa?'

Determined as ever to stick to his floozy-chair principles, Gustav grasped the fly-spotted armrests and kept his counsel tight as a crab's trapdoor. He sneaked a look at the aquavit decanter lurking seductively in the shadows of the new-fangled prototype lobster pot.

No.

This conversation was not altogether coming as a surprise to him. Charlotta, the dutiful Charlotta, had seen fit to fill him in on the progress of the marriage as she received reports of it. Not that he wanted to know. The last thing he wanted. But that was Charlotta for you with her insinuating ways. She'd never changed. To this day his sister-in-law had the capacity to make him sit up with a straight spine, glance down at his footwear in a worry that his shoes weren't shiny, and run his fingers nervously through his hair. And that was merely speaking on the telephone.

From under shaggy eyebrows Gustav gave a covert look towards his elegant daughter so artistically composed against the tattered padding of the dirty chair. His withers were unwrung. War among the menus; interior design woe; claustrophobia among the pickled ancestors. Well, he could, if pressed, sympathise with her panic at squandering time in what she called the formaldehyde house but he couldn't condone the fundamental dishonesty of her position. Now, had she chosen, for example, the essential spitefulness of the English hell-bent on stealing Norway's post-war shipping trade, or taken as her subject the dullness of the prim-and-proper British spirit that stifled life and drowned its excellent gin in that revolting tonic, Gustav couldn't have helped but sympathise. But all this household guff. Well, frankly. And so Katya Olovanova's daughter was walking out on her husband too – just like her mother – ¡viva heredity!

He even started to feel sorry for poor old Sholto-non-grata. Poor bugger. Back from a distinguished war and wanting a quiet life. Flying missions completed, Norway liberated. Home from a hard day's aero-engineering, a day in the factory lathe-turning, flogging his brains out at the drawing board. Poor old Sholto-non-grata. Home of an evening, and was the adoring little woman crouched by the fire ready to receive orders, to massage with fragrant oils, to pour the whisky into the crystal tumbler? Not actually.

Who was it said history repeats itself, and absolute history repeats absolutely? Well, not absolutely. These clatches all had their slight variations. The intellectual baubles that had caught the eye of Katya Olovanova had been superseded by a second generation: son of Expressionism. Where was Salome now, where Rilke? Ghosts haunting the tamer shores of shockability. But there existed, even among this fevered lot, evergreens that overarched the fashions of generations: Freud, eternal Freud, he was one, along with the Tarot and the other paralysing systems of prediction; any system that held the seductive promise of removing free will, personal responsi-bility and – above all, this – removing individual personal culpability. These evergreens lived on, eternal cushions supporting succeeding generations.

Gustav's nostrils flared as they filled with the remembered smell that he in his time used to come home to: Katya's coterie, her clatch of pretty, febrile women. Ah, the peculiar scent of the intelligentsia! A cocktail of Turkish tobacco, joss sticks, ponderous significance and bite-size canapés. For years he'd forgotten the mingled smell, forgotten the fordømmet brown bottle.

The women Sholto came home to would look and smell different, of course; while boiling and heaving to the same overheated cauldron their rising steam would have an English flavour. Gaunt, long-boned English countrywomen strewn languorously over the unbeautiful English *stue* giving off a doggy wet-tweed smell and spouting. He'd wager they'd be spouting exactly the same manias that Gustav's own floozies had been spouting at him one by one over the same years. Whether in England or Norway, whether singly or in clatch-battalions, the underemployed women of civilised nations had some collective magic about them that responded simul-taneously to some invisible power (call it *zeitgeist*?), their pretty flower heads turned towards the same sun all at once. Subliminal psychology turned their flower heads, or the atom, monkey glands, Mensendict exercises, Zen; William Reich, that cunning orgasm fellow (now there was a scam!), margarine, the bottomless sayings of that pseudo Tibetan mystic with verbal diarrhoea; health drinks, eternal life through chewing those *fordømmet* sun-dried Hunza apricots that always had gritty little sun-dried ants in them. Who wanted to live to a hundred? It'd seem twice that long if you were going to spend it looking like those shrunk-up old Hunzas and crunching on sun-dried ants. What, he wondered, was his daughter filling the formaldehyde house with? She said what she didn't like but not what she did. What specifically had brought this furniture quarrel to a head? Had she started moving in the samovars he remembered? Turning the spirit of Olde Englande into a *souk*? Cramming it full of mirrors, incense sticks and those *bloody stupid* cushions all over the place.

'D'you have cushions?' he growled abruptly.

These crisp words interrupting her important set-piece were so unexpected she didn't answer them. Later, years later, dwelling on them obsessively and at length, she decided it was his way of showing a concern for her prime interest: furnishings.

Rather touching.

Well, he couldn't be expected to get into the finer points of bullion fringing and so on. Katya melted in tenderness on this sweet, touching question concerning the cushions in her house. At last, she decided in retrospect, at last she had really made the connection. Papa Gustav was prepared to be interested in her on her own terms. Cushions! Too sweet!

Gustav, who had heard the other side of this heritage argument from Charlotta, was dwelling on the conversation he had held earlier this very morning. Charlotta speaking on the radio telephone in advance to prepare him for Katya's arrival and reporting on Katya being put to bed in the wake of the funeral in nostalgic mood casting herself as perpetual little girl demanding hot milk with sugar and cinnamon, and lack of change. This anti-formaldehyde daughter of his was herself a nostalgia merchant who obviously felt particularly strongly about menus and decorations. Her own childhood room at home, the linden tree in the garden and the nursery hot sweet milk she craved were her own equivalent of this old wallpaper put up by the old trout she obviously hated called Jane Austen and this foul muck called steak and kidney which, pray God, he'd never meet. So why the hell had she married into it? His withers were unwrung.

Gustav's experience of life did not necessarily incline him to sympathy and pity yet, whatever his verdict, he knew exactly what was going on. Katya's plaints were not about nostalgia, or even the more interesting thought that she'd joined a nation prone to necrophilia. Maybe she wasn't even going on about sex (despite her own). The marriage was proving difficult and she had no sticking power; that was the long and the short of it.

Most of all, Gustav suspected, it was about the fat boy, the son and heir.

So what if the boy couldn't make his letters?

Brother Oscar had had exactly the same problem. Solved it too, in the woodshed. Chucked school, chopped off the writing finger, proved himself at sea. If Katya was fool enough not to add two and two, if she wanted to blame the furniture, let her.

'If you didn't like the club,' he growled, 'you shouldn't have joined. These things are voluntary, you know.'

Gustav turned his wrist to consult the Radiolite dial on his strap watch. He put down his burning pipe carefully in the ashtray at a certain particular angle. Then he got up. 'I think I'll do a little night fishing. I may have set the net too high, in the circumstances.'

He walked over to the wireless set and turned it off, collected his lion-hunter's hat, and went out of the door.

He hopped into *Hel*. Her motor coughed, caught. Turning his nose out to sea in a minute he was slapping across the waves, leaving a glittering trail arcing the length behind him as *Hel*'s motor churned up the black waters. Galaxies of star-glint phosphorescent *morild* sparkled in his wake, fireworks in the sea. Catherine-wheel vortexes, rocket parabolas spluttering and shining, marked the path of Gustav's deliberate exit from the island and from his daughter's life.

Katya, still in her chair, did not yet connect the growl of the motor-boat with all those previous birthday exits but spent an hour or so deeply contented, smoking sometimes, keeping the fire alive, engrossed in speculation: thoughts ranging about this newly discovered father; such an understanding man, so comforting to be with. Obviously he understood women. She had always got on best with men. Her toe tapped to the invisible dance tune in her head. She pottered a little in the rudimentary kitchen. Hot milk to greet the returning fisher-man? No, hot toddy, surely. And even when at last so tired she went up to bed, still she didn't understand. All night her lips tipped upwards in a little smile while her head on the muffling pillow was living the ghost of breakfast together with her father in the morning.

This time he did not go as far as Marliac-sur-Lot. He went to Oslo, his target to open up his deserted town-house and resume occupation.

'My turn now,' he growled, the pinpoint lights and light-houses of the coast left behind him in the dark as he moved up the fjord.

'Things have changed,' he muttered at the moon, mulling over these things as *Hel* hurtled through the scudding shadows of the night. 'No other Oscarsson in Oslo now. Only me.' Back at the shipping office, at the Oscarsson a/s offices where (he must be prepared for the scorching sight) the damaged black-bubbled Munch frieze would stare and mock, there was tonnage lying idle, waiting for decisions. Shipping hanging on the hooks at the quay, losing money with every moment it was not in the water. Shipping didn't hop off the hook by itself and embark on profitable voyages, not even in this new-fangled day and age. He wasn't going to let some *fordømmet* manager, some salaried man, get his feet under Oscar's desk. Gustav's lean long weatherbeaten cheeks, always red, empurpled with irritation as his spleen rose, anticipating imaginary slights and insults from a paid man.

Arrived in Oslo, he turned the hurricane lantern down low, tied up the savage goddess *Hel*, smack bang in the middle of the Oscarsson *brygge*, which was a good joke, took the bedroll and rucksack from *Hel*'s front locker where they lived permanently, ducked under the beaks of the praying mantis cranes, hopped over their iron rail tracks, and strode out of the dockyard gate. Gustav Oscarsson's journey back up from the quay to resume Oslo-life was in its way as bizarre as his brother's last journey on earth had been. Oscar Oscarsson had trodden the way from the centre of town down to the shipping office at the docks wearing a pair of Russo's scarecrow overalls topped by immaculately barbered locks and shod like an English prince, the incongruous blowtorch and the ladder, one in each arm. Oscar had looked exactly what he was: insulted citizen hell-bent on a clever revenge. Gustav, enacting the journey in reverse, looked more primeval and more of a piece; no cleverness here, no masquerade. Sincerity trod the street. Gaunt as Father Time; chaotically, apostolically grizzled, hump-backed by the snail-house burden on his silhouette back formed by his rucksack and bedroll, he ploughed his grim furrow straight and fast up the streets of Oslo, seeming not to notice that bright streetlights made the swinging hurricane lantern unnecessary on the road he strode.

Oslo once more was gap-toothed to either side. A different gappiness this time. When he and Oscar – tear trembling – spilling – quick, wipe eye on sleeve – had been fooling around putting up their houses the gaps had been virgin, gaps in milk teeth. Now the bomb-damaged town lay like a shipwreck, various bits stove in between the ribs. Gaps in wreckage. The framework was there to be read, to be reconstructed in some fashion. Gustav croaked harshly, bitterly. Was that a laugh? Now Oslo-town could have the fun of that age-old architectural quarrel to the knife: resurrection of pickled-ancestor façade, versus flight into Katya-modern. Ho ho.

His forlorn appearance up at the white balustraded balcony on the second floor of his splendid, if cobwebbed, townhouse was seen by no one. People had long stopped looking for vital signs at that house. He was like a puppet popping up at a dusty forgotten seaside theatre with the audience gone home long ago. Chin out, surveying Oslo, defying heaven, at his back obscurity: the cavern of the marital bedroom yawned, utterly impenetrable to eye and brain, brownish-dark. The hurricane lamp had burned out at last. He had tossed his snail-house bedroll on the cobwebby dust-sheeted hulk of the once-marital bed.

He'd damn' well sleep in it tonight.

For the first time since she'd left.

About time.

The great obstinate head looked down from the balcony, conducting its truculent survey of a shadowed Arcadian Oslo bathed in a greenish pre-dawn light. To the right the sea was crisp and awake, though the harbour traffic was still sleeping. Straight ahead over the shadowed porticoes, roofs, cupolas, window embrasures, flagpoles, pale colonnades and buildings (more buildings now than there had been) a mean vertical slice of his brother's house was still visible. He could see less of it than he'd used to. The Germans had done a bad job; blitzed the wrong houses. A damnfool smiling advertising hoarding between him and Oscar's flagpole. Idiotic grinning brunette enjoining him to chew Fox's lemon for sweet breath. Good God they'd have to do better than that to get him as a customer. The brunette wasn't even pretty.

He turned on his heel to go back into the dark bedroom. That way he could pretend there weren't tears in his eyes. A dark room didn't go blurry the way Oslo had gone blurry. No sparks at his brother's windows. His eyes prickled. He grubbed about in various pockets. Found a grubby linen handkerchief. Rubbed his eyes with the scrumpled thing. No messages in flags. No more. Never more.

Fordømmet Katya. If she hadn't left him he'd still have been here in Oslo. He and Oscar would've climbed the ladder together, burned the whole blasted valuable artwork clean and had a laugh on the tax man.

'No time to waste, Oscarsson,' he creaked. 'Time is well advanced.'

Clearing the fug of ages from Katya Olovanova's triple mirror with his sleeve, he sat down purposefully at her dressing-table. Opened a tin of pickled herring, a packet of flatbread and a tin of condensed milk that he'd chosen as breakfast from his iron rations. But before he'd even put fork to mouth he was getting up again and foraging for his first-aid kit. Kit located, he picked out the razor and the scissors. Contemplated the blades. Sharp enough. Gave himself a long hard look. Gave another long hard look to the rucksack on the floor where the bottle of aquavit was beckoning.

No, he wasn't going on the toot. Not now, nor ever again.

'Work to do, Gustav Oscarsson, and it starts now.'

He picked up the razor, and began to make some sort of respectability of his hair and beard. It was more difficult than he thought, this respectability. Eventually, grey-stubbled, he got up from the dressing-table, unrolled the bedroll, changed his mind, picked up the hurricane lantern. Might as well get down to the office, look over the books. The hired manager would come in the morning to a good surprise: Oscarsson with his feet under the desk. Oscarsson back at the helm.

The death's head grinned. The big jaw dropped and round him in the room the cobwebs quivered in the chilly air, set trembling by the vibrations of deep, harsh laughter.

At eleven o'clock precisely he would be strolling, just like all the other fellows would be strolling, down the docks to Dronningen for a little coffee and maybe a shrimp or two, a little agreeable *middagsmat* and a lot of gossip in the sunny restaurant of the exclusive Yacht Klub. He would be genial, chatty, he would be just like all the other cheerful noisy fellows.

Oscarsson was back.

The next day there was a lot of telephoning. This involved Katya getting from the Fødselsøy to the nearest mainland shore in the dinghy, tying it up with all the anxiety of the amateur in knots, and walking miles and miles of hot beige dust-road between hot grey granite rocks and deceptive inlets choked up with masses of brown spaghetti eel grass and fringed with the fingered popping seaweed called *tang* that at low tide (which was now) swarmed with innumerable little flies that stung like fire. The children got hot and thirsty. The slow-moving greasy inlet waters proved very salty indeed. The children got thirstier. A little cooling was provided when, for a mile or so, a sparse forest crowded the road, giving shade and the damp reek of mushrooms and firs. Eventually the road reached the cream-painted clapboard Kolonial Landhandler that fulfilled the central functions of the invisible community scattered over the stark mainland rocks and islands round about. Not a great deal was bought or sold here. The store-goods were an eclectic mixture of whatever could not be made or made up at home by ingenious and provident coast-folk. Sugar in wooden barrels to be scooped into blue paper bags. Paper of every sort, and nails, tins of paint. Oil in many guises from axle grease to salad oil. Sardines in tins. Bunches of yellow sou'westers hanging from ceiling rafters on hooks alongside hayrakes, Evinrude outboard motors and *blåklær* on hangers with their arms stretched out like scarecrows (this place was Gustav's answer to Savile Row). A telephone.

'Operator? Can you get me Oslo three nine?'

Ting.

'I have the connection.'

'Charlotta? Father's disappeared. We're all alone down here. I'm frightened he might have – he was so quiet ... Oh, I see ... Yes. No. Oh.'

The children listened, not much enlightened.

'Operator. Can you get me the Hotel Bristol in Oslo, please?' Katya put down the receiver, waiting to be rung back.

'Look, kids.' She pointed at a sun-faded cardboard notice advertising the unappetising grey-looking swirls of the very first archetypal ice-cream in all the world. '*Har de is?*' she asked the plain-faced shop woman in the beige dress with a piqué collar that the Shrimp much admired. '*Virkelig?*'

The nicely dressed lady nodded.

'Ice-creams, my darling droolers! Why don't you buy an ice-cream and just mosey on out to the rocks to eat it?'

'I have the connection.'

'Hey, Reggie! Yes, it's me! Katya in living colour. How're the cocktails? Goody ... No. It's a man-free zone down here. Entirely man-free.' She glanced round at her large son. Shrimp felt Robert flinch. 'Why not?' she gurgled. 'A White Lady? In more ways than one ... Oh... Don't be brutish, sweetie, or I shan't be nice. Beat it, kids. Shoo!' She flapped her free hand at her children. 'No. Not you, the droolettes. They're hanging about.

'I said on the rocks. No, not you, the tiny treasures again. They're still hanging. Though now you come to mention it you might have one on the rocks for me. Plenty of rocks. Ice is rare as hen's teeth around here. Tell me about the hotel band. What're they playing in Oslo? What's everybody dancing?'

Out went the obedient children to sit side by side on the rock as recommended. Decorously they sat, well brought-up, button-shoed, knees-together representatives of their tribe and nation, self-effacing on the edge of heated stones where bumble-bees tumbled in the tall sparse violet spires of knapweed, and flycatchers rushed about feeding their young on whatever winged insects were zooming by in that insect-fat season.

Hot and congested, the line of his grey-flannel prep-school shorts cutting a sore red line into the fat pink-mottled marzipan thighs, Robert guzzled his ice-cream and told the Shrimp knowledgeably, pedantically, pompously and at dreary length about the key and pitch in which the crossbills were twittering while foraging for seeds among the crop of cones on the spruce firs.

It was a habit. Robert would launch into these great unstoppable gushes of meandering abstruse discourse, information often spurious, often downright wrong, always badly conveyed. The patent misinformation and mystification of his younger sister was his way of demonstrating the upper hand.

During the monologue neither child was looking at the other. Both of them were looking hard (like stranded shipwreckeds searching the horizon for salvation) back through the window of the general store. The telephone was out of angle. They couldn't see if she was still talking or not. Nevertheless they stared at the point connecting them to Katya and the outer world as if concentration might turn normal vision into X-ray.

When the boy had finished his ice-cream to the last crumb of sweet crunchy cone, the girl automatically put hers into his hand. He hadn't even needed to stretch it out and ask. Greedily he demolished the second thick yellow cream ice, rescuing the spills that dropped on his thigh and finger-slicking the creamy drops from the rocks. Both children's eyes remained strained towards the little window. It would have taken a thunderstorm to distract their concentration.

'Do you think she was speaking to Daddy?' Shrimp asked in English.

'Don't be spastic, Shrimp. Haven't you got the sense you're born with?' People often asked him this, at home, at school. *Haven't you got the sense you're born with, boy?*

'You heard what she said to the operator, didn't you, Shrimp? She said the Hotel Bristol. It's the uncle from the air-liner.'

'Oh.'

Inside, Katya was now at last asking for an English number, but then she called the operator back. 'Scrub it, will you? Second thoughts.'

'Very well, madam.'

CHAPTER SEVENTEEN

'Children are the miners' canaries of society. They show the first signs of the damaging effects of social change.'
  Joe Rogaly, Financial Times, discussing Effective Government Structures for Children by Rachel Hodgkin and Peter Newell

The uncle arrived in the gleaming sort of boat that husbands and other sensible men behold with sorrow and alarm.

'Hiya, kids!' His virility was plain in the ulotrichous hair that the yachting cap was failing to subdue, his vanity in the very white teeth that he was flashing to show off in a dishonest smile, the sort of smile a hairdresser gives a client in the mirror.

'Catch!'

The painter snaked through the air. It was Katya, not the children, who caught it and bent to make the half-hitch.

'Hop ashore and rest your sex appeal a while.' She took the cigarette from between his lips and puffed a couple of times before handing it back. 'So. You came.'

He was mahogany-brown and his sideburns were long, much too long.

'Nice place you got here.'

At the maroon-painted door that was the way into the house, Robert stood his ground, scowling theatrically, pugnaciously, unsuccessfully: impotence thunder-browed. The uncle gave him a look, the sort of look one gives a fly in one's soup. Then he leaned forward, bending down a little to whisper something into Katya's ear. Katya gave her special laugh, twinkling, cocking her head slightly; said some deft words, brushed a shiny wind-caught curl out of her eyes. She

was all movement, light, vivid and adorable, sparkling up at
the uncle.

'You've no idea what a grimbo time I'm having here.' Her
lips moved in a charmingly wry pout. 'It's brutish dull.'

'You're breaking my heart.'

'No music. No dancing. Reggie dear, believe me, I'm having
about as much fun as a stiff in a morgue.'

'We'll have to see what we can do about that.'

Her eyes lit. The uncle's eyes roamed about the place. He
wasn't a man whose eyes ever stayed still for long. They hit the
jealous eyes of the boy, the fat boy who'd been on the plane; the
son who'd been so defensive and so ineffective at Fornebu
airport. No competition here. The uncle's tongue slicked
quickly over the crocodile teeth and he put out his hand to
massage the back of Katya's neck. Robert's throat swelled
convulsively. His eyes dropped. His palms became clammy all
at once. His lips started to move, he turned and stomped
indoors, talking to himself importantly, as though he was off to
perform an urgent task with inordinate energy and efficiency.
Robert gestured with his hands in accompaniment to his
inaudible words, as though there really was this vital task
indoors that required his immediate attention. Under the tight
shorts the pink-and-white thighs wobbled with every step
taken through the shadowed doorway. Soon Shrimp heard the
familiar and – to her loving ear – pretty sounds floating out of
the bedroom window where Robert was murdering 'La Donna
è Mobile' on the nacre-plated piano accordion. Oompah, oompah,
went the heartily pedestrian rendition in gemütlich tones.

Katya and the uncle had already turned back and become
absorbed in each other's gay chit-chat. He was pointing out the
glories of his hired boat and she was giving responsive little
shrieks and cries. 'No! Reggie! Not real sharkskin? You don't say
– and a cooler for the gin, bottle-sized. Tailor-made for
Gordon's! Glam or what? I just don't believe this boat!'

Shrimp had stayed guardedly on the wooden jetty throughout, observing, being invisible, lying flat on her tummy on the
planking so she didn't show. Soon, in the manner of the very
young, she became absorbed by what she could see below in
the water through the slits in between the planking. Down
there in quavering shadowland two metres below her nose

clumsy hermit crabs in their borrowed houses were mountaineering doggedly up the freckled rock. Schools of perfectly synchronised tiny codling with beautifully luminous eyes were darting cleverly and fluently through the wavering branches of eel grass. If she put herself here on the sandy bottom, then the boat and the uncle might be gone by the time she came back above water. If he was gone then maybe he had never been.

'Ankle-nippers,' Katya called merrily, a little later, going into the house, 'the boat's getting restive. Uncle Reggie says it needs to stretch its legs. We'll go for a little run and may get lucky and catch some fish. We'll only be gone for a blink. Shrimp, if I get you a bowl you can spend our brief absence in making a world-beating mayonnaise to accompany our fish catch. Will you do that for Mama, darling?'

Shrimp nodded, swivelled round from prone to sit on the wooden jetty. By mistake her eyes met the uncle's head on. He passed an uneasy finger over his moustache, his eyes sliding away out to sea.

'Fine day for it,' he said, to no one in particular.

No one answered, though indeed he did have a point. It was a blue and gold day with a glimmering sea. The fresh breeze, enough to ruffle the wavelets, was setting rippling white frills against the violet-shadowed rocks. Seagulls swooped and cried their permanent nostalgic heartbreak over water that glinted like diamonds disturbed.

Katya emerged from the house into the sunshine tucking a red cardigan round her shoulders against the breeze. Happy with all the world she stooped to kiss the head-top of the little Shrimp, whose body was entirely lost in somebody's enormously large jumper that reached down below the little girl's thin knees and smelt musty and about a hundred years old. Katya, so far as she was concentrating, didn't recognise the garment. It must have been a remnant left behind by a floozy. Hastily the mother cracked three egg yolks into a stoneware bowl and threw the half-eggshells still containing raw gluey albumen into the air, setting up a hooligan gull-squabble of some proportions. Beak snatched from yellow beak.

'Now,' Katya raised her voice above the fighting birds, 'add the oil drop by drop, stirring like mad with this wooden spoon between drops, and whatever you do don't stop stirring for a second or it'll turn to gloop and brutish scramble and we'll have to give it to the gulls. No more than one drop a minute on pain of death. *Capito?* Count to sixty in elephants before you add the next. And when you've added this whole half-litre of oil you can slowly add this eggcupful of vinegar. Savvy?'

'Savvy,' came the echo, quiet as a shadow.

Shrimp propped herself up against the house wall in the cool angle of shade. Her legs were outstretched in the sun and between her pale thin straight thighs she gripped the thick beige stoneware bowl containing the three yellow juddery hemispheres. Earnestly the child grasped the wooden spoon, added the first solitary drop from the bottle of greenish oil and began to count, in her thin determined voice, 'One elephant, two elephants ...'

Robert, who had been watching everything out of a window, with his stomach in emotional knots and his hands cramming smuggled biscuits into his mouth one after another after another, was drawn downstairs and outside despite himself. An invisible compulsion pulled him to watch the boat's departure. The boy found himself blackmailed even into unknotting the painter from the iron ring and throwing it out to the uncle's waiting hands.

Blackmailed? She was a damned seductive white-painted Palazzo del Gin. She blinded in the sunlight. Cashmere rugs were casually flung over the white sharkskin leather seats. Rolltop chrome ashtrays glinted in the armrests. She'd a polished walnut dashboard to die for, and all the extras a dealer could think of: a giant radio aerial tall enough to receive programmes from Mars, a natty fold-out cocktail cabinet, two big curving red and white fog lights that went round a full circle; a hooter, a carpeted floor and a wind-up gramophone on gimbals.

'I'll give you a ride later, big boy,' the uncle shouted, at Robert's transparent longing. He pressed the red start button and humiliated the landfast Robert further by flashing him a very white grin. The big dolled-up boat idled in the silky water.

'Back in a frog's croak,' Katya yelled, too absorbed to wave.

She was sorting through half a dozen seventy-eight records and taking the brown paper cover off her first choice as the boat gentled through the silky water putting soft black shadow between its stern and the children. 'Never Say Bulbous to a Lady.' She read the title aloud. 'Cab Calloway. Hot stuff!' She checked the sharpness of the needle against the ball of her thumb. The red and white bandanna fluttered, mixed in with her dark hair. The glitter-framed glasses didn't sparkle half so brilliantly as the eyes behind them. The boat was well out from the wooden jetty before she turned to yell gaily on the wind, but her last words were lost as the big white boat reared up on its hind end sudden as a horse but noisier, roared full throttle, leaving the children behind, and the island washed by a huge stern wave breaking high on the rocks, a wave that bred gradually diminishing children, tailing off into the tiniest baby.

'... thirteen elephants, fourteen elephants ...'

Sitting alone, the Shrimp lost count of how many times round she'd counted to sixty. The mixture in the bowl was oily and heavy to stir now. It was getting so thick and the sun in the sky was so high and strong her legs were getting hot and pink but she'd promised Mama not to move, not to stop stirring for a cat's whisker of a second. The mayonnaise must not turn into a brutish gloop. She frowned in concentration.

Robert had gone back indoors after the departure of the white boat. He had been indoors a long time. The sun had moved. The shade had left her feet and the sun was creeping up her ankles, they were getting hot. She tried to pull them up without disturbing the making of the mayonnaise but it didn't work so she slid them back down again. She'd like to go to sit with them dangling in the cool sea but she'd better not stop, not even for the length of a frog's croak.

He was still indoors probably, but she could no longer hear his piano accordion.

She supposed he was still indoors.

He might have gone out. He might be as far away as the high-up freshwater lake with the sparkling waterlilies whose petals were as white and as beautiful as the Snow Queen and whose glistening circle of anthers were as golden as her crown.

'Robert?'

She could not go up there to look for him. Her task would be spoiled. Besides, she dared not scale those grey humpbacked rocks alone. Getting to the waterlily lake meant hopping over three or four of those deep bottomless fissures that split the rock right down to darkness, and that was where the denizens of the dark lurked, the brutal broad-faced trolls who made their home in the whispering underworld and waited, sharp-toothed with hunger, to devour any hapless creature that missed its footing and fell into the void.

It was so quiet, so quiet. Nothing but the gulls. Now and then far-off boat engines. She wished she was old enough to have been given a strap watch. She had been able for ages to tell the time. How long was a frog's croak? It wasn't long. It couldn't be long and it must be over soon.

Shrimp looked up at all the windows of the house, hoping. She looked to see if the barrel eye of Grandfather's telescope had changed angle: Robert might be raking the sea for a view of the approaching Palazzo del Gin. But that hadn't happened. The big barrel still pointed up to the stars at exactly the same angle. Now she would look carefully round outside, sweeping the rocks as far as she could in both directions, which was hurty in the glare of the sun on the bright granite and the wavery haze above the water. She twisted her neck both ways so it cracked, and hurt, hurt, but still she didn't move her body except her stirring hand:

'... fifty-nine elephants, sixty elephants.' Drop. 'One elephant ...'

Nobody. Wind, sunshine, many gulls wheeling. She wanted to call him but he would know she was frightened of being alone and he would say. 'Don't be so babyish,' or 'Don't be spastic.' He might have gone out in a boat like Mama. He might have taken the rowing boat out silently and then she would be the only person on the island; nobody else here at all.

The big gulls had stopped being frightened of her. She would very much like to go indoors to the cool stue, shut the door between her and the gulls and continue her job sitting on a chair with cushions. Her bottom bones were hurting against the hard rock and the gulls, each one so big close-to, were closing in, pecking peevishly within a whisker of her naked unprotected legs. When one of the smaller gulls found a morsel of food the big arctic skuas kept chasing it with harsh screams in hunch-shouldered rushes until the little one had dropped its food and then they would strut about with the food in their beaks like a boast. And when they had gulped it down they would pace about with chests puffed like sergeant majors, like the success-ful bullies they were, looking for the next. They kept coming closer, their heads thrust forward at her, saying things to each other, cocking their heads to one side and glaring as though she was their enemy. One big bully stretched out his big strong wings and hopped very jauntily, grazing her leg. He was interested in the mayonnaise. He had nostrils in his beak. The smell of it seemed to hold a strong attraction for him.

'One elephant, two elephants ...'

Tentatively she cried, 'Shoo,' once or twice, but her voice was never very strong and besides, she was frightened of angering the gulls by shouting. She tried to cry shoo without interfering with the numbers in the counting, but it did interfere. She lost her place. She cried a little then. The horizon was very empty, and so many big birds on the rocks about her. She daren't take the wooden spoon out of the bowl and wave it at them for even the merest instant in case the mayonnaise turned into a failure, a brutish gloop. Mama would know when she came back. She would say, 'Shrimp, you stopped for a nano-second and now it's a washout. Bin it.'

The razor-thin little girl shrank into her right-angle of wall. The sun had crept all the way up to her legs now and the whole area was a three-sided oven flooded in blazing sun. There was no air. The big gull carried on strutting and pecking closer and closer about her legs and talking cockily as if she wasn't there. Her hand was not steady pouring the next drop of oil. She poured too much; some spilled, it ran down from the grey rock between her burning pink legs. The cheeky gull hopped up fast, pecking at the drop even while it moved. His feathers grazed her hot leg-flesh and he looked at her with a malevolent yellow eye above the arrogant beak. She sat still as a mouse. The gull knew she was a child and would be no good at hurting or punishing him. The gull wouldn't be doing this to a grown-up.

'Robert?' she called tentatively, too quietly for her brother inside the house to hear, '... seventeen elephants, eighteen elephants. Robert?'

Small tears splashed into the stoneware bowl alongside the drops of oil, each tear made a round white watery drop marking the glossy yellow surface. She stirred harder. The tears would spoil it and she'd lost the numbers, too. She stopped for a bit then. There was no point. She raised her eyes from the bowl to scan an empty, desolate sea so bright that she could fool herself into thinking the sun's gleam on a far breaker was a white boat coming back. Some white boats did pass by, far out, and with each one her heart lifted, but one by one they passed across the water on their way, never turning in.

A squall cloud far out dropped grey rain and was carried in. She watched the cloud travel across the bright sea towards her. Beneath its heavy shadow the raindrops brought the sea alive as the fish beneath sought food at the interesting rain-plopped surface. The gulls saw, too. Out they flew, a hundred flickering wings, a screaming crowd; she cowered into the rock against the wind of their lifting bodies. They followed the cloud in towards the shore, fishing at the shadowed pool dim in the brightness. '... forty-nine elephants, fifty ...'

'Shrimp.' He emerged from the darkness of the house on to the clean beautiful rock in his green regulation school swimming trunks and she had never been so pleased.

'The gulls ... Oh, Robert! Your eyes are all pink. You look like Georgina the rabbit when she was ill, all sleepy and glum.'

'Don't be spastic. Read this for me.'

It wasn't a book he was holding out, not more revision for school, but a letter. This was odd because no post came here to the island. Post was collected from the store where Mama had used the telephone.

'Where did you get it?'

'Mama's drawer where she hides things under the knickers and things.'

'Oh.'

The words were in English. Katya must have had it before they came here because the envelope was to England. 'Dear Mr and Mrs Fortescue.' He'd got that far by himself indoors. He held out the white paper in front of her pale, pinched face so that Shrimp could read the typewritten rest without stopping her stirring, pain of death, *capito*. But she soon did stop. Her arm was aching and, besides, the words she was reading sent a chill through her strong enough to drive out any other thought. '... despite his apparent lack of aptitude we are convinced that at the heart of your son's problem lies an over-indulgent regime unwilling to face up to the unpleasant task of making the boy realise he must work. We are confident a cure can be effected with little difficulty. You may be certain that a rigorous discipline' (Shrimp stumbled over the words with their horrid resonances) 'will be maintained ...' The children looked at each other.

'It means you will go to boarding school in September.'

Mama had known all along, and not told.

Shrimp looked hard down at the bowl so he should not see her piteous tears.

How would he manage the reading and the writing without her?

The tears must not splash. He would get cross.

How would he manage the ball games that were so important? The numbers? The grown-up teachers at school would behave like all grown-ups did. Like Mama they would enjoy embarrassing her brother and making him squirm. Or like the uncles they would scorn him; mock and laugh. Or they would be like Sholto, shouting at him to make him a man; shouting at him not to fumble the word, fumble the fountain pen, the book, the cricket catch, the football; and their shouting would make Robert's fumbling worse.

And she would not be there to help him. She put out a hand. The day had come. She forgot she mustn't look up and show him her tears, tears of a different hopelessness from the mayonnaise. Indescribably terrified of the future, she forgot, looked up. Eye met eye. Strangely there were no tears in his eyes. His hand did not creep out to meet hers in mutual reassurance as it always had at moments of crisis, all their lives.

'You look different,' she said.

He was looking not directly at her but a little above her. But that was not the strangeness, there was something else. The vein in his forehead was swelled and tensely pumping and his eyes were glittering with some suppressed excitement, almost glee. His big hands were opening and closing with a regular pumping, squeezing motion. He frightened her. She shuddered, feeling death at her back. She felt it breathing down her neck.

'Budge up, Shrimp.'

She let him sit beside her on the rock in the heat under the wall of the house though for once she didn't want him close because he was terribly strange. He smelt queer and he was breathing in a thickly noisy way that was frightening and making her uneasy. He had been breathing like this before in England earlier in the year when she had come up to his bedroom. She had been bringing up smuggled Smarties and he had been so absorbed in looking at coloured pictures in a magazine that she'd crept right up to him before he saw. They were horrid pictures of a boxing match with blood. One man's face was all bashed in, he was a black man, in sweat, in pain. There was a picture right close to his face of the sweat, like glass on the blue-black face and bright blood, and one eye was not an eye at all but only a hole full of blood and bleeding from it shiny and like tears. Shrimp had felt sick. He had shoved the magazine under the bedclothes when he saw she was there, and his face had gone very red and he had shouted very loud in the small room. He had called her a sneak and given her penances.

He might hit her now. Or get in one of his shouting paddies. She didn't move, thinking it might be over more quickly, whatever it was, if she sat still and quiet and pretended herself away invisible.

'Your legs are sunburned.' He put his big pink hands on her thighs near her knickers and started rubbing.

'Don't, Robert.'

Roughly he shoved away the mayonnaise and the wooden spoon, cracking the grey stoneware bowl against the rock in his haste and strength and, as Shrimp reached out to save it, he rolled his big heavy body on top of hers, breathing hard and scrabbling with one hand to pull down his green school swimming trunks.

Later in the lustreless evening the yellow mayonnaise leaked slowly out of the cracked stoneware bowl drop by drop ... one elephant, two elephants ... drip, drip, on to the rock, to the delight of the gulls who had come back to the deserted place, attracted by the tangy salty smell. Their strong sharp beaks pecked up every rich savoury drop, though they delicately avoided the little pool of brown diarrhoea nearby, and the clotted rusty mess of blood and hymenal membrane.

Later still a bluish-green chasm opened up in the bruised brown sky and there came the storm. A glossy black sea rose and swelled under a sky rolling with muted thunder. Narrow cream spume raced towards the shore in lines of heavy lacework, broke sharply against the rock and was tossed high in the saturated air, fell, spattering the next wave with white flecks like white seagull droppings, was gathered up, crashed again; climbed to even greater heights caught up on the violent vortexes, whirlwind gusts. Wave followed wave followed wave. The gulls rose steeply, hanging on quivering wings in air that throbbed in continuous deafening rolling crescendo. Chaos, tumult. All round the island from every direction, water and air were plunging, gliding and flashing, hurling destruction against Oscarsson's cursed grey rock. The wind, desirous of victims, howled. Odin was angry, and he was a powerful and a vengeful god.

This great storm was the ripening of the little rainsquall cloud the Shrimp had followed in with her eyes; harbinger and prelude to a downpour that grew in fierceness and continued mercilessly to attack the island over the next six hours. Gustav's precision instruments had correctly foretold the storm with its waves of water pushing against the air, against the sea, the house and its windows that the children, alone, hadn't the common sense to shut. Nor had they the slightest idea they needed to turn the wheel on the gas bottle to release the propane gas for the cooker. Robert had held match after match to the rings as he'd seen his mother do, without anything happening. The two of them had got a small unsuccessful fire going in the hearth and Shrimp was holding a frying pan out to the flames. Bits of unwashed potato cut up in fat were not cooking properly but Robert scorched his fingers picking them half-raw out of the pan every now and then and putting them into his mouth 'to see if they're done yet'. He had had a tantrum at the gas not working and had gone up to his bedroom shouting and throwing things but now he was down again. He was sitting formally upright in the chair Katya had sat in to air her grievances, the floozy chair,

and when he was upstairs he had taken the opportunity to put
on his uniform of authority, his grey flannel prep-school short-
trousered suit, and he had combed his hair into lines, and in
this tyrannical outfit he was chit-chatting stiffly and
spuriously on formal topics. He informed his little sister at
length, and entirely erroneously, about the degrees marked on
his grandfather Gustav's onion-bellied English-made eighteenth-
century barometer, an instrument of great elegance, sensitivity
and precision hanging from a rusty nail. He concocted a
theory, and delivered it didactically, with a patronising
joviality, in a loud voice against the crashing storm all about
them, as to how the degrees and pressures related to the
rainfall even now clawing at the walls and driving in at the
windows, illustrating each of his made-up points by references
and busy gestures with his clumsy tightly-sleeved sausage-
stuffed arm. At illogical intervals in this long monomaniacal
lecture he stopped abruptly, mid-point, poked at the frying
pan, swallowed some half-dozen pieces of half-raw potato
greedily, before resuming.

'Do get a move on Shrimp. Your cooking is spastic. Everyone
says you're so clever and you can't even cook potatoes. They're
disgusting. I think I'll give you a hundred lines.'

'If there was something that I ... Please forgive.' She stirred
meekly and hastily.

He watched hungrily. Without reason, suddenly, he
switched his tedious and tendentious tale to a different and
completely unrelated topic as the dining table caught his eye,
with its tangle of cane and string looking peculiarly
threatening and sinister in its abandonment. Shrimp kept her
eyes away so he should not catch a whiff of the fearful notion
that came into her mind. There was something of torture about
the tangle of cane and leather thongs that reminded her of that
picture in the Grimms' fairy tale. It was a very dark and
horrible picture and if Robert had seen it he might want to tie
her up to punish her. She started to weep. Meekly she drooped
over the pan to hide the weeping, trying to make no noise at
all, to make herself as transparent as her shrimp namesakes
while he propounded a new elaborate theory inspired by the
cane tangle. 'Lobsters can be hypnotised, you know. Their
catching is a matter of strength and stealth.'

During the two days that the children had been here alone with Katya, after Gustav had left, Katya had not used the dining table but had taken her food and the children's out on the rocks to eat so that Gustav shouldn't find his obsessive handiwork disturbed when he came back, as a part of Katya fervently believed he would. He'd be back any minute. In a frog's croak. Beneath this belief of hers yawned the old terror, the memory of the comet trail disappearing and herself prevented from following it by the iron in the Tëtka's blank, steely eyes and the implacable iron restraint in the imprisonment of the Tëtka's arms.

Gustav had walked out 'in case the net was set too deep'. Katya couldn't possibly permit herself to believe the glimmers of truth stabbing at her mind that her second parent had also walked out, abandoning her a second time all these years later. The writhing cane had been a token of her father's return. It meant a lot to her. Just as it meant a lot to Gustav. To him it was the latest in the line of continuing symbols of his own ingenuity in the face of a world he had rejected but that he thought had rejected him. To the children it was now at this minute a symbol and talisman, a reassurance that their mother and their grandfather would both come back to do their duty, to finish things. Nobody could leave such an important thing and not come back to it. Humbly the children nurtured this faith. What was unimaginable to everybody was that it would never now be finished, but spend the next years decomposing on the abandoned island being eaten away by ants, woodlice and the damp salty atmosphere, so that eventually, at the end of a comparatively short period, it suddenly juddered, collapsing into an ashy corrupted echo of itself and of Gustav's mind process.

Robert dared not actually disturb the symbol of faith, touch the sacred tangle.

'Assuming the lobster to be approaching from a northerly angle ...' he was saying. Dottles of spittle were forming in each corner of his mouth, very white against the pink shiny lips. Shrimp concentrated, she listened hard. There might be test questions later. He might give her lines, like the teachers gave him at school to make him write, and then torment him worse when the lines came out as tangled as the lobster pot. She took the pan away from the fire because her small thin arm, tired

from the long afternoon's stirring, was scorching in the fire's
heat. The fire was too small and badly laid for the flames to
cook the potatoes or for the smoke to go up the chimney. It
filled the room and played tricks with his shadow, which
became big, then enormous and jaggedy, and spread all over,
until everything was taken over. Robert's shadow ruled over
the walls and the ceiling and the floor.

Murderers were hanged.

She had never before hated all that repellent lardy flesh of
her brother's, nor found it disgusting like everybody else did
but now she hated him and was shouting inside her pale meek
exterior that she loathed him, despised him furiously, that she
could not bear to be with him. Maybe Robert could murder
somebody and be hanged. It was the only degree of punishment she could imagine. She hated that bloated pink finger
that came and poked in the frying pan. She hated the way the
shiny oil-pearled lips closed about the half-raw potatoes so
greedily consumed, the way he juggled the searing-hot potato
flesh about his mouth, chewing with his mouth open to let the
steam escape and spitting it out into his hand, then shoving the
half-chewed mess in again to finish it off.

With tears in her eyes because she had loved him so, and
now she so hated him, she asked with the age-old eternal
dependency of the younger child: 'When do you think Mama
will be back?'

He swallowed and in that moment she learned to hate the
solid fleshiness of the chin, the snake-bulge of the swallowing
throat. She couldn't look at the mouth that had slobbered over
hers. She felt sick at the potato-smell of the yellow teeth that
had cut her inside the lip so that she had tasted her own blood
with the bile in her mouth.

The room was very smoky with the fire. She was only crying
because of the smoke. He had an unbearable look in his
unintelligent eyes. Really, it was only the smoke, just that.

There was a certain insidious shift of focus, a smell, an
atmosphere to him, a feel to the moment. 'Come on, Shrimp,' he
said, in that thick voice. 'Come on. You know you want to.'

'I must finish ... the potatoes.' But he grabbed the pan and
the potatoes, too, were spilled, like the mayonnaise, this time
over the floor, a dark oily pool on the floorboards.

*

At almost the exact same time that evening Katya was telephoning Charlotta in Drammensveien, pretending to be broken down and stranded by the storm in Kristiansand and unable to get back to the Fødselsøy. In fact, she was speaking from the Marconi Lounge in the Hotel Bristol not a hundred metres away from Charlotta receiving the call.

'So convenient, telephones!' Katya sparkled, holding a hand over the mouthpiece.

The uncle lifted one perfectly-shaped black comma eyebrow. Squeezed up against his new girlfriend in the hotel's padded telephone booth, he murmured, 'Gorgeous,' and nibbled her ear.

'Couldn't you just send Russo to fetch the kids, Charlotta? They could spend a few days with you. Keep you company now you're all alone.'

'But I don't understand.' Charlotta felt particularly slow, her mind still numbed. It had been only two days since the funeral and here was Katya wanting, as always, other people to do unreasonable things for her. 'Why don't you go back to the children? It will be far quicker for you to hire a boat there in Kristiansand, Katya. For Russo or somebody to come down from Oslo would take twice the time. The children could get into all sorts of dangers there alone.'

'Dangers? No need to chuck a mental, Charlotta. Heavens! The boy's almost thirteen.'

'I'm sorry, Katya darling. I'm feeling particularly dim. So tired, the funeral must have taken more out of me than I ... When will the boat be mended? It must be very bad to take so much time. Are you all right, darling? Which boat was it?'

Katya raised her eyebrows. What a bore all this was. The uncle turned his wrist, flashed his Rolex, mimed time's tedious passing.

Katya said, 'It'll just be a lot simpler if you take charge, Charlotta. That's all I'm saying.'

'Your three minutes are up,' said the hotel operator.

Katya disconnected. She hung up the receiver with a wicked little giggle. 'That's it! My pink ticket. Charlotta will step in and save the situation. It's what she loves. Now, we're free as air. What shall we do first?'

'I've one or two ideas.'

'I bet you have.'

Katya and the uncle had arrived in Oslo ahead of the storm, and before the shops closed too. She'd just had time to nip in to Molstad for absolute essentials and had picked up a terrific cocktail dress in the *Moderne Moter* department. They'd stormed into the Bristol's elegant restaurant dying for delicious things (the provisions on her father's island had left a little to be desired, frankly) and had spent an hour or so unpicking the flesh from dozens of enchanting crayfish cooked in dill, dipping the succulent pink and white tailflesh into a most beautiful mayonnaise. Afterwards, they'd dabbled their fingers clean in glass fingerbowls with a slice of lemon and pale pink rose-petals floating on the surface and taken their time over excellent coffee. The Bristol had always done things beautifully. Sholto had remarked on it even when he was over here to take the capitulation, and that was in the middle of the Germans and the shortages. How had they managed, Katya wondered, as she trailed languorously up the wide staircase to their room to change: uncle into white tux, Katya into the terrific and amusing cocktail dress; ballerina-length scarlet silk taffeta embroidered with all sorts of beaded insects scattering the skirt. There was something delicious and unsettling about the jewelled bodies, the cloud of jet-clustered bluebottle flies, shiny raisin-brown ants, steel-winged beetles and glaucous dragonflies scattering the opulent blood-red. She did her face carefully in the triple mirror over the cut-glass perfume bottles on the dressing-table. The swansdown powder-puff flew over her face with *pointilliste* artistry; full face, left profile, right profile, the three mirrors showed her how much powder she needed to take away the shine without spoiling the fashionable sun-tan. She took a pull at the cigarette in the glass ashtray, spat into her mascara and, while the uncle was in his bath, used the mascara brush to touch up the one or two grey hairs just starting at the temples before wielding the same little brush at her eyelashes, the work it was designed for. Tucking her mascara compact into her evening purse, Katya hesitated, looking thoughtful for the first time since she'd left the island.

At the end of the delicious crayfish meal, after coffee, the bill had been brought and he had patted his pockets and raised his eyebrows. A little awkward silence had hatched, still as a pool into which she'd flung the words, 'Just put the meal on the bill, will you, waiter?' They'd got up from the table and he hadn't left a cash tip on the saucer. She'd better put some traveller's cheques in the evening purse alongside the lipstick, compact, change purse, cigarettes, book matches. They might go on to one of those amusing nightclubs down by the docks and it wasn't quite clear who was paying.

In the elevator on the way down he ribbed her. 'You women! The amount of stuff you carry in your purses!'

She didn't like 'you women'. It was a cheap shot to refer so directly to the fact that she wasn't the first-and-only. It lacked manners. Even though they both knew. Nobody was pretending at first-and-only everlasting love, but there were manners, and there was comfort in pretence.

The elevator reached the ground floor and opened.

There is no smile like the smile of a woman who knows she's beautiful and wearing a new dress. Old Georg, the stuffed-shirt uniformed hall porter who'd been behind the Bristol's solid mahogany desk since all Oslo was young, a grey-haired man whose gravedigger reverence went with the job, was dazzled. When she'd made her scarlet-taffeta rustling way through the lobby he turned to the bellhop with a very lewd remark indeed. The Bristol's clientele would never have imagined good old Georg to have such words in his repertoire, let alone such urges. Both green-uniformed men cast envious looks at the uncle's retreating back-view.

Katya and the uncle closed the Bristol that night. From there, they went (on old Georg's recommendation) to the Black Cat, the red-hottest night spot in town. Here, they drank martinis and they danced all the latest dances to the good-looking white-tuxed boys of the Big Swing Band who were delicious to a man: matching chocolate-melt eyes and oil-slicked hair and bright golden saxophones that knew all the very reddest and hottest because they were fresh from a two-week engagement at Quaglino's in London. Walking back to the Bristol from the nightclub it was windy and storming but who cared? The wind tore at her hair and she took off her shoes, and the wet pavement made her want to dance some more and she danced on up Karl Johan. Remembering Lulu she put out her tongue to see if the rain tasted of champagne in Oslo too, and she found herself sticking her tongue out at the royal palace on the hill, which was very funny, and why had she never thought of doing this before? So she thumbed her nose as well, and they sang 'Riding Down to Dixie' and 'Cheek to Cheek' and the rain made huge wet blobs on her new scarlet skirt.

'The insects have peed,' said Reggie, pointing to the spots, and they discovered how difficult it was to say, 'The insects are incontinent,' without all the words going ishy and wobbly and she made up a little song.

Old Georg shepherded the dripping couple across the Bristol's marble hall and saw them into the lift, pressed the button for them and wished Miss Katya a ceremonious and entirely obsequious good night. When the gold wrought-iron door had closed behind them with a snap and the cage was ascending with a light him-hum, the old employee turned back towards his desk with a heavy face and a sigh. This would give Fru Charlotta Oscarsson no pleasure at all.

He rounded furiously on the only other witness, a junior bellboy. 'A word of this and you are out,' he said, in the voice of Thor the thunderer. 'Out, out!'

By the next morning Katya didn't give a toss who was paying the brutish bill.

'What was that you said about extending the hire of the boat and spending next week cruising down the Swedish coast to Malmö? Sounds bliss.'

Charlotta did not send Russo to collect the children as Katya had suggested. Berndt had now arrived in Drammensveien. He was oddly little comfort to his mother. Maybe because of her ambiguous feelings. Her conventional *hoffdame* side minded that he had arrived too late for his father's funeral; hardly *comme il faut* behaviour. Her instinctive side knew he had been right not to come. Saints had no place at pomp-and-circumstance parades. But it was hard to bear. He was at any rate, she thought in the wake of Katya's telephone call, here at the moment to be of use to his mother. In time to bail out Katya as always, she might have thought, had she ever for a moment permitted a chink of cynicism to disturb her well-regulated feelings for her niece.

When the telephone call came, she had been sitting with her once-golden son; embroidering, not talking much, comfortable; companionable in mutual silence and their separate thoughts. She had been thinking odd things, the way you did when your hands were virtuously occupied at just enough work to exercise the very top surface of your mind. Then the rest of your mind could roam untrammelled and you could blamelessly give in to peculiar things: you could analyse family likenesses and dissimilarities without the nag of disloyalty. It was your mind doing it, not you. Berndt's tough core of absolute certainty was very like his father's. She smiled. Neither had ever seen the similarity to each other. Oscar never would now. Oscar had gone to the grave firm in the belief that Berndt, unworldly, Christian, missionary Berndt, was an odd chip off a diametrically different and most peculiar block. Berndt, too, felt this, echoed and in reverse. Despite Berndt's remarkable depths and his perceptions on the wider canvases of human nature, when it came to his father he was still at the stage of deliberately seeing only the surfaces and the differences. Oscar's solid world versus Berndt's ephemeral Utopia. Jermyn Street versus hempen homespun. So silly. Charlotta gave a small shake to her head, looked up, gave her son a piercing glance and wished devoutly, with all her heart, that whatever his doom might be, it would allow him to live long enough to understand these things properly; to forgive his father and in so doing to forgive himself. As her eyes rested on his long, spare figure she regarded her son with deep pride not unmixed with exasperation.

Mother and son were in the warm, elegant, flowerless *stue*. In the wake of the funeral tributes she never wanted to see a flower again. Berndt was standing, frowning, looking down at the floor while his mother explored his face with her eyes. Unworldliness could be just as aloof and imperious as shipowning, she thought, but the shyness was different, the not belonging, the moving through life unconnected, at first a deliberate choice now hardened and evolved into the inescapable so that his dealings with the everyday world were thin and cautious and not, she thought, ostensibly a great advertisement for Christian brotherly love. She could have wished he'd taken an easier way in the world. Not only for her own sake and Oscar's but for Berndt's as well. It had been agony to see son and father so tortured by shyness of each other, and Berndt's shyness seemed to extend to the whole world.

He was feeling it now. For him, too, it was a sort of personality failure. But, then, his place in this world was always full of complications. Perceived in Oslo as a stylite, an ascetic, disapproving pillar-monk, he wanted to say he wasn't really like that at all. He wasn't standing like some parched Old Testament prophet in judgement on Oslo's vanities and drawing rooms; nor, at this particular moment, on the room in which they both sat. To be sure Oscar's great house expressed egotism, and vanity to a certain extent, but it was neither vulgar nor bragging. It expressed love, too, optimism, and faith in beauty, in man's striving towards perfectibility and in the continuity of God's created world. No, Berndt did not disapprove, but he didn't belong, either; and that was simply because he didn't know how to belong any longer. He could only move through this established hierarchical world he had been born to, alone and unconnected as a stranger, while, paradoxically, elsewhere in his mission field he was perceived as playing the part of unifying communicator and significant to hundreds of strangers every week. He raised an ironic eyebrow, straightened up, lifted his chin, met Charlotta's eyes, his fair cheeks blushed. His mother's eyes dropped to the embroidery in her lap, and he wished he could find the right word, the social polished word to tell her that he loved her and it was only because the chairs in here were so *fordømmet* elegant that he never could find it in his heart to sit down in this room. The chairs had ankles like gazelles. He'd worry about cruelty to furniture. He'd like to tell Charlotta it really wasn't that he disliked the whole idea of his father's Oslo house, merely that since he had grown up he'd an idea he was altogether too unsubtle in the context. *Qua* rooms, this was the most exact room he knew. His mother's creation entirely, it reflected Charlotta like a mirror on her mind: one more touch of gold leaf would have turned prettiness into vulgarity but, then, Charlotta had always been a woman of great tact, a woman of nuances, hair's breadths and scruples.

How ironical then that Katya, the scarlet hot-blooded impulsive streak, should have been doomed to this context and to Charlotta. Berndt's hand went to the rough wooden cross he carried hidden in his pocket. He always touched the cross when his mind went to the vow taken so early in response to the nightly storm of tears from Katya's side of the wall.

The vow had, of course, played a formative part in his early Christian life. His early dealings with the complicated heart-broken Katya had been a prelude and an instruction for what had come later. His loyalty to that boyhood vow had (he saw in retrospect) been the most wonderful stiffener of sinews and affirmer of resolutions for the Nazi gaol to come. During those long weeks that turned amorphously into months and years when, partly sleeping, partly living out the long succession of lightless days of his solitary confinement, he'd hear other prisoners sobbing and keening through the wall and in the half-mad world that passed for his consciousness in those days, it was Katya's sustained, unexplained, deep wounded anguish he heard, and Katya, his poor betrayed little sister-cousin, whom in the more active sessions in the gaol he was defending.

In the pool of warm light cast by the silk-shaded lamp his mother's hands moved unhurriedly at her embroidery. She was embroidering an O, the eternal symbol in this house. Oscarsson, of course, the everlasting family circle; eternity unbroken too. She always had worked the initialled pillowcases herself; a funeral was not reason enough to stop now.

The well-lit white fabric stood out hard against the lap of Charlotta's pearl-grey dress. (She had ordered several, in identical grey. Black was surely too ostentatious. It smacked of the theatre of grief rather than the real thing.) But now was not a time to be thinking of herself. Berndt was home, rare occasion. He'd blushed, and she had wanted to enfold this strange son. He was more faded than his father had ever been in life, or his rumbustious uncle. Berndt's face was as open, vulnerable, as a new-carved Gothic saint, seamed with suffering but not experience. She dared not ask the bird of passage how long he was staying; the question itself was capable of precipitating flight. How she would like time with him, normality, trivia. Enough time and small incidents shared to enable her to be in the same room as him and forget he had ever been imprisoned. She had asked him once if he could ever forgive his torturers.

'Mother,' he said, 'even as I was suffering I saw those men not as they were then, but as they had been, as little children, and as they were capable of becoming again redeemed, as they probably are already, penitent and redeemed by the love of Christ. Now in the context of peace their suffering must be so much greater than mine. You cannot hate little children. Even when they are pulling the wings off a sparrow. I knew it was only common sense to bear the transient pain and to say, "Forgive."'

Charlotta shook the remembered conversation from her head, got up, smiled at her son and drew the long silk curtains early against the storm. The rain, which was lashing its strongest at the island with the abandoned children, tearing violently at the air around them, and driving hard raindrops in through the windows that Shrimp and Robert still had not thought to shut, was behaving in a more circumspect fashion here, rustling more politely against the window panes, as if the weather, too, respected Charlotta's civilised orderly world and understood that here one whispered. Here pertained a different set of rules.

When Charlotta sat down, pale from Katya's telephone call, Berndt said, 'We can't send Russo. It would be very wrong. It must be family.'

'You'll go?'

'Of course. But not until the morning. I will go at first light. I do not want to alarm the children by arriving in the middle of the night. They will be frightened enough without their mother.'

Katya's name, heavy on the air, was not further mentioned between them.

Wherever they looked they were haunted by scraps of Katya-memories. She couldn't be cut out from the spaces shared by mother and son. Berndt looked down at his plastic sandals but there was no getting away even here, even here. The sandals brought to mind a conversation he'd no idea

Charlotta had overheard: since his detention he had been strictly vegetarian, a man who would not willingly harm any created creature or add, even in the smallest way, to the world's burden of pain.

'Earth-friendly,' Katya condemned his ugly plastic sandals.

'Sister mine, one day you will learn. There are worse things than ugliness and comicality.'

Later in the evening Berndt took special care supporting his mother up the staircase, so elegant, so eloquently empty it chilled them both, though neither said.

'Would you like a hot drink, Mother?' Berndt made certain her bedroom curtains were tight shut, holding the two against each other to block out the stormy night. Immediately he turned his back on them the two curtains sprang apart disobediently. She smiled gently at his dear incompetence. He'd never got the knack of curtain cords or any such practical things. 'Thank you, darling, no.'

'Can I get you a glass of water?'

'I shall be all right.' Charlotta stood on tiptoe for her cheek to be kissed, arms to her side so they shouldn't embrace him or she would never be able to let go.

Next morning Berndt left Oslo in darkness, navigating by memory and a gleam of stars. He approached the island by boat in a moment of great beauty. It was as though the weather today was ashamed of its violent convulsive behaviour yesterday. Today it was a good child; good as gold, innocent as butter.

Half-way down the Oslofjord he blew out the hurricane lamp to savour the ravishing scenery. Before the sun was in the sky its pale nasturtium gleams were transforming a smooth sea into a pale nacreous disc ruffled gently here and there by shuddering fish-scale shadows.

Berndt had no special love of the Fødselsøy. He was a man who saw ghosts as readily as presences, who perceived under-currents as readily as the seen and spoken. He shuddered as the familiar huddle of rocks grew larger in the smooth iridescent sea. The fingernail-rim of fiery sun ascended above the horizon. Past unhappinesses wreathed this place. He clasped the long wooden rudder harder and spoke aloud to himself. 'It is so very beautiful.'

Since his two years' enforced enjoyment of German hospitality in the lightless bowels of Akershus castle he had developed this habit of holding quite long and well-constructed conversations with himself; they could go on for days. 'Uncle Gustav always said he chose it because it looked like a family of bathing elephants half-submerged. "In logic," he said, "I had to give it a howdah." The house is the howdah. Playful in form but tragic in spirit. The elephants here have forgotten how to play.'

He turned the bow of the small wooden motor-boat into the lagoon, pointing it at the planked wooden jetty and cutting the engine. The island was oddly light and quiet, floating hazy in air washed clean by the rainstorm, but he did not trust this place for all its deceptive beauty, and today it was putting on its most beautiful face. He jumped ashore and tied up his old-fashioned boat neatly and quietly, for he was habitually a man of quietness and of unhurried actions, having seen and been subjected to enough noise and violence to treasure calm. He straightened up to look around, a tall lean scarecrow of a man.

The gulls, sated with breakfast eaten on the rocks, had been sitting, grey on grey. They took off at his landfall and wheeled resentfully before settling on the pretty pearly sea where they bobbed like so many boats in a miniature flotilla calling out to each other provocatively and raucously as was their nature.

CHAPTER EIGHTEEN

It was all he could hear on the air; the gulls' calls, and a child crying quietly.

Berndt crossed himself, muttered some words to his constant companion Jesus, squared his shoulders and prepared to tread the hunched rocks on this, 'The next chapter of its sadness,' he muttered the words. 'Lord, dear Lord, will there be no end to the grief and abandonment in this family?'

He walked straight towards the sound of crying.

In a grey hollow in the rocks a skinny little girl was sitting stark naked, hunched, her head in her hands. The crying came from her. The thin shoulders were shaking and she was wet. From dew? From bathing? He stopped dead a moment, gathering himself. This was Katya's daughter. These tears, this sadness, were part of the invisible chain running through the years binding and shackling the family in the cumulative disaster. This sobbing girl hadn't just landed all alone out of a clear blue sky. It was not an isolated incident like an apple falling out of a tree.

This was no easy task, he frowned. The key might be found back in those days long ago when he was a child lying listening to Katya at the same age her daughter the Shrimp was now, crying herself to sleep so bitterly night after night those years long ago when the Tëtka was alive and he lay in his attic cot overhearing. He could feel again the hard, helpless fury he had experienced as a little boy gazing fiercely at the wall separating his own tenebrous bedroom from his sister-cousin's, willing that the terrible Tëtka *this* night might not make her cry. 'Please Lord not *this* night too.' Despite the promises and bribes he nightly offered the Lord, the voice would creak on until unfailingly, inevitably, it was overlaid by Katya's rising climacteric sobbing. Then the Tëtka's long black shadow, spreading in the doorway, marking the creaking woman's retreat down the candle-shadowed passage to her own room. Quite helpless, he would lie rigid in the gloom as the sobs went on long, long after the footfalls had receded and died.

Well, now he was a grown-up. Now he could help. He had failed Katya. Never been virtuous enough to deflect the sorrow to himself. Akershus had been some reparation, a stage along the road.

Standing a certain respectful distance from the sobbing girl, gathering himself up, his attention was caught as a further noise joined the seagulls' morning murmurings and was carried towards him on the pale dawn air. From somewhere high up on the far side of the rocks floated the sound of a piano accordion such as sailors play jolly shanties on, but this was an oddly heavy, sagging dirge. It took him some time to recognise the grotesque distortion as some kind of brutal squonking interpretation of the Pastoral symphony.

The girl bowed her head further into herself at the sound; the sobs increased.

'I am your uncle Berndt,' he said quietly but firmly, 'your mother's brother. And you, I know, are Anita, the little Shrimp. Your mother said you were alone here with your brother. She could not come back because the boat had broken down. But she is quite safe. Your mother is not hurt. There is no need to worry. Is there anything I can do for you, I wonder? You look a little cold. The dawn is often chilly. Maybe you would like my coat.'

He was taking off his beige boating windcheater even as he spoke, and wrapping it about her shoulders. Being a man who knew about injury and the invasion of the privacy of flesh, Berndt was very careful not to touch her.

'I am your uncle Berndt,' he said again, giving her time to hear. The jacket covered Katya's daughter entirely from shoulders to tented knees. Such a scrap of a thing. So unlike in spirit to the mother he had sworn always to protect. The seven-year-old Katya would not be sitting huddled in her own misery. She'd be scratching, biting, kicking hard and screaming like a hellcat if he'd any memory worth the name. 'And your mama ...'

The child looked up dully.

'Your mama asked me to come and look after you. To take you away from here – if you want – to the house in Oslo. I am Berndt.'

She looked at him with her pale lips half open, scared as stone, and then her expression changed. A spark of life kindled in the dull eyes.

'You are wearing a hat.'

'I usually do. Against the sun, or the cold. Either way. My eyes are a little weak, too.'

'R-Rob– my brother says you always wear a hat because the Germans made a hole in your head and your brains will fall out if you take it off. Is it true?' She looked at him with apprehension and huge curiosity.

He put his head back and roared with laughter. 'Take it off.' He chuckled. 'Tug as hard as you like. I promise you your brother is talking nonsense. Go on!' he encouraged her.

Life crept into her eyes. Oh, how she longed to tug and see the result. Saucily she flipped the brim. Off came the hat and tumbled onto the rocks.

Brains didn't pour out from a hole in his head.

'You're not dead.'

'No.'

'But you have no nails. That was true.'

'I'd rather have a brain.'

'What did you do?'

'When they were torturing my body? Little Shrimplet, let me tell you. It is not so bad. May I sit down?' Sitting down beside her, he felt her body stiffen. He was careful, fastidious to maintain a space of air between all parts of his body and hers.

'People always want to know but they daren't ask. I'm glad you asked, because that means that I can tell you. I can tell you and you will never be afraid of anything anyone can ever do to you.

'When my body was tortured,' he began, 'I was ashamed in my body and in my soul. I thought I was alone in all the world, that I had been deserted, that there was nobody to help me in all the world. My body was hurt and humiliated but worse was the hurt and humiliation inflicted on my spirit. I felt deeply ashamed. Which was wrong, if you think about it. There is nothing wrong in being hurt. The wrong may come in how you bear that hurt, if you bear it well or badly. But when you are very hurt and there is nothing worse that anyone can do to you, that is the time you realise that there is nothing you need be afraid of, nothing. You are liberated from the shackles of the body, free to enter the endlessly free pure realms of the mind. Nothing is beyond the realms of the mind, nothing. And so, my little Shrimp, I tell you that if pain has been inflicted upon you, now is the time you can start to build, making a strength within yourself, a strength that will be with you all your life.

'When you know you are going to die, you feel more intensely alive. When they tortured me I put myself out of the window in the trees and the hills. Not that there was a window, except in my mind. But I put my mind in this other place and then I could stand what they did to my body.'

'Under the sea there are places.' The thin small voice took him by surprise. So she knew this already.

'Yes,' he said. 'There, too, under the sea. There are places everywhere. Whenever you need them. Wherever you are.

'People think they do not want pain to happen to them, or bad things. They think they would feel happier if all life were innocuous, bearable, and never touched upon a real feeling or a real idea.

'But, my little niece, grief and pain and woe and inadequacy are good. They form the basis of human sympathy and communication. Jesus tells us in the Gospel to take no note of what people do to your body. The body is voided and flushed away. It makes no difference. You may be flogged, crowned with a crown of thorns, abused in your flesh. The body passes, the spirit lives on. That is what I remembered when they were hurting my body.

'At first when the war started I was a young Christian, what they call a pacifist. A pacifist is someone who cannot see how, in any circumstances, it is right to hurt another, or how it could ever be right to fight back in any way, even if his own body is badly hurt. Jesus said we should turn the other cheek, and this was my belief. At first, at the beginnings of the war, I found that I could live like this. I could make compromises with the loss of happiness, even the loss of liberty in my country. Yes, the dictatorship was mad, but one could laugh. Yes, there was random cruelty, but one could excuse individual aberration. Then they started shooting even little children. I thought, I will have to change my mind on this. There is a greater struggle outside my own personal little struggle with my conscience. I had no choice but to become one of the many fighting back.

'One day I was captured.

'One of the others captured with me was a young girl, Kari we will call her. Kari was fifteen and she had the prettiest bubbliest curls that sprang out all round her head and she had pink cheeks and she was very brave and funny and sporty, in fact she was the cross-country champion of her school, brilliant at skiing! We in the resistance used her as a very successful message-taker in the snowy season when the Germans were hunting down the people who were resisting them.

'Let me tell you what it was like when the Germans were here. We Norwegians are few. For standing up against the cruelty, more than a quarter of the population was sent away to prison camps, here or in Germany. A quarter of the population: one person in four. This meant that everybody had an aunt or a mother or a father or a brother who had been sent away. And when I say prison camps I mean those labour camps where people were forced to work until they died. The Germans tried to mobilise Norwegian youth to work voluntarily under the name of "national labour service". Well, our young were not that stupid, I can tell you. When neither young nor old could be tricked into volunteering, they were rounded up by the police. Boys no older than your brother hid in the woods to avoid being sent to these labour camps here and in Germany, knowing it meant inevitable death, and they were shot if they were found. Their mothers smuggled out food to them, unknowingly betraying their sons by their loving trail. Then the mothers were dragged into the streets, made an example of. The mothers, too, were taken into the labour camps. Many of them suffered torture here in Oslo where I was. Several hundred they didn't even bother to torture but shot them dead on the streets of Oslo or up at the official place, Akershus castle. It was a bad time.

'Now, Kari's father was a very clever professor at the university. He was not Jewish but he had dark hair and brown eyes and a very big nose, and he was troublesome. He used to make fun of the Germans in class with his students, clever fun that the Germans hated, and that was enough for them to decide he was Jewish. Now of all the terrible things the Germans did here, the worst they did to the Jews. Not that the Jews were guilty of anything but of being what they could not help – Jewish. Among those deported were seven hundred and sixty Jews, over half the Jewish population of Norway, men, women and children. After the war only twenty-two came back, the rest had practically all been killed in the gas chambers, but that was later.

'Kari had no idea that her work getting the Jews out on the rat run made the Germans think her father was a Jew. Her father's unjust arrest and deportation made her even more brave. Day and night she worked, flying along on her skis taking messages, guiding parties on the run over the frontier to Sweden. Sometimes her pigtails got quite stiff with ice and we would laugh as we melted them carefully by the fire so they didn't just snap off like icicles. All the time after her father was arrested and deported she was brave and pretty and cheerful because she knew she was quite innocent, whatever the consequences. She was strong in her mind because she had right on her side. One day, as I say, she was arrested. Kari was brave under torture. They questioned her and questioned her. They wanted to know the rat run, you see, the route we used to smuggle the Jews out to safety in Sweden.

'When Kari would not tell them they caught her mother and promised to free Kari if she told. Her mother could not bear to see such things happening to her Kari. It was not long before she told what she knew. Kari was freed, and that was cruel. They knew it was a worse punishment to send Kari back to the mother who, out of love, had betrayed her. A few months later Kari killed herself. She was ashamed to have escaped at such a price, you see, ashamed in her soul at the compromise that had achieved her freedom.

'We were all very sad when Kari killed herself. We knew she had not done wrong in keeping silent, nor had her mother done wrong in telling to save her child. We, Kari's comrades, understood that some physical things are very hard to bear, but nothing is too hard if your soul is innocent, like Kari and her mother. They were both innocent, both did right.

'And when people are cruel, when they hurt your body,' he paused, 'or your mind, you must remember, dear little girl, that there is a part of you more important than either of these. And that is your soul.

'Nobody, nobody except yourself, can hurt your soul. And there are only two ways to hurt your soul. One is to do wrong. But the other more complicated way is to hurt your soul by doing what Kari did: by blaming yourself for things you are innocent of, things other people have done to you.

'So I say to you, bear the hurts that other people put on you without shame. It is not your shame but theirs, the shame of those who hurt you.'

Berndt fell into silence beside the little girl. Neither moved or spoke. Had these been the right words to act as shield and defence against the shame and misery he so clearly perceived in her without understanding? He had leaped in with the guess that Katya, the Katya he knew so well, who threw people into ant-heaps to prove some sort of love the only way she knew how, through pain, must be both the root and the immediate cause. How could Katya, motherless deserted Katya of all people, desert her children? But, then, how could she not? Inevitability in this matter was as round and as closed as the Oscarsson O. But to leave them here of all places with the fearsome sound of the last trump from Oscar's fearful theatrical Judgement Day funeral still echoing.

Well, Berndt was right, and wrong. Guilty for once in his life of over-simplification. Katya was certainly the root. Had he known the immediate cause he would have gone chasing over the rocks towards the torturer of the sublime Beethoven hell-bent on curing a very complicated situation indeed. But even Berndt, with his experience of man's inhumanity to man, had no glimmer that he'd stepped only on square one of the complexities of this generational game of Consequences.

A sermon on cruelty was strong meat first thing in the

morning. Looking outwards he raised his chin, contemplated
the world in his inclusive glance, took note of details. Warmth
had entered the sun. Several oystercatchers, excited about the
appearance of some dawn food, were hopping about the rocks
and pointing their long red bills downwards into dark-
shadowed crevasses to extract some helpless form of breakfast.
Their gourmet success was raising strong jealousy and resentment among the local gull population. Pavement hooligans!
Berndt had never warmed to gulls with their strong-arm
tactics. His far-sighted grey-blue eyes strayed out to sea. The
quiet dawntide fleet of gentle fishing *joller* had dwindled
imperceptibly, by some loss of magic giving way to a swarm of
loud over-designed holiday outboards zigzagging gnat-like
over the smooth water, their buzz-saw engines drilling away
the enigmatic enchantment of the place.

All this activity and he had not even thought to give the
little girl some breakfast!

'Oh, how remiss of me.' Berndt clapped a hand to his hatless
head and looked directly at the Shrimp at last. Two swollen
seas of grief met, subsided, tides receded.

'Food! Your grandmother Charlotta packed a hamper. Shall
we go and see what's inside?'

'I am hungry,' she said, in a matter-of-fact voice, getting up
and taking some paces to retrieve the hat she had flipped off
his head earlier.

'I think we should get some clothes on you first and then we
will eat.'

But when she had dressed and he had packed the rest of her
things she showed an unaccountable stubbornness in refusing
to wait in the *stue* as he suggested but, as if deaf, went politely
but defiantly to sit in his boat while he did what he had to do
next: follow the music up the rocks and along to the beautiful
waterlily lake. Here, the fat, white-skinned boy was standing
in his formal clothes, so English in his jacket, shirt and neat
tight tie, so jarring standing calf-deep stockstill in the flower-
studded freshwater shallows where the fragrant lazy blooms
were late-waking from their sleep, slowly furling open their
pale petals again towards another new day. The big piano
accordion's straps were over the boy's shoulders and he was
pulling and squeezing at the fairground-hideous red plastic

mother-of-pearl instrument, making frantic nightmare sagging wheezy music with its exhaling and inhaling breaths.

'Good morning, Robert.' Berndt waved cheerfully, as if all were normal. 'How about some breakfast?'

Odd formality prevailed during the packing up of the brother, the sort of formality he would normally have put down to a lunatic: stilted conversation, with the boy talking loudly, insistently and expressionlessly in illogical and inconsequent slabs of speech, brooking no reply. Unfamiliar with the boy, Berndt put the disconnected inconsecutive irrelevant harangues down to Katya-shock. Such things took different people different ways. Tall Uncle Berndt was infinitely kind, infinitely patient and uncritical listening to the strange slabs of rubbish that came out of the boy's full mouth between him shovelling in great greedy mouthfuls of the *spekeskinke* and *leverpostei* Charlotta had provided in a hamper. At last, at last, it was done. Time to get the children off the island and back to Oslo.

Berndt's unglamorous wooden varnished motorboat nosed its way out into the open seas, heading north, Oslowards. The craft travelled at a slow wallow, nestling deep in the water with the children and the burden of the luggage. The children's luggage was hardly so great in itself but Katya's cases must be included, if for no other reason than to sustain the illusion of a reunion. *Dunk dunk dunk*: the motor knocked steadily, unexcitingly. Berndt sat on his habitual seat to the left of the long wooden rudder, which he grasped firmly with his right hand, to steer. At his feet the Shrimp, who had not protested against the life-jacket, leaned her back against her uncle Berndt's legs, featherlight, supporting herself on him and catching the warmth from the housing of the motor. He looked down at his little niece with loving eyes. 'You've the best spot in the boat.'

'Yes.' Her eyes were tentative. He enjoyed their glance. For once he was being seen as himself. Not as a man once beautiful, now monstrously powdered and cracked by this Job's-trial psoriasis; nor as a living moral beacon and righteous reproach. Just old Uncle Berndt, provider of breakfast, steerer of boat.

'I don't feel sick,' she said abruptly, out of the blue, with the detached evaluation and objective conclusion of the chronic patient.

Since Berndt had been away missioning most of the Shrimp's life he was not equipped to know what a monumental statement this was.

'I should hope not,' he said, matter-of-factly. 'Talk about millponds.'

The overweight boy had taken up position at the very extreme end of the boat. He sat astride the pointed prow, one leg hanging down either side. The boy had not been parted for a moment from his piano accordion. He had worn it even at breakfast, spooning the food in over it like a paunch; he wore it even now at the prow, though the salt spray wouldn't be doing it any good. The instrument's leatherette straps bit two verticals into his plump back but he did not play. What Berndt and Shrimp in the stern could not see was that with his eyes closed he was talking and talking incessantly. Robert was flinging an endless stream of shouted words into the wind without cease the whole two hours' journey up to Oslo.

'They say you read and write for him as well as yourself.' Berndt bent, speaking quietly to his new friend. He loved the odd, brave girl already. Was frightened of the pain around his heart tugging at him. 'That you have a great and unusual talent for words and for language, extraordinary for your age. And that his talent is music. Is that right?'

She nodded, without meeting his eyes.

'I have often thought how strange and mysterious a thing is language. Have you ever thought, Shrimp? About how language is constructed? Constantly I marvel at the miracle that all humankind throughout all ages and countries can communicate whatever they want by the thirty-odd letters of the alphabet. I make the sounds p-t-n, the consonants, the vowels. I put them together; you put them together; Christ put them together two thousand years ago and Plato before that; a Hottentot puts them together in the bush today, tomorrow; and we all make words. With just those few sounds. The words spring an idea – any idea in the whole world – from one mind to another, conveying all human understanding throughout all the world, transcending time and place. Wonderful! Wonderful!

'Poor Robert. To have such difficulty with words. We must

work hard to let him know that his talent is wonderful too. Your brother can put pitch to it, frequency. Music, if you think about it, is even cleverer than words. It can convey simultaneity, weave strands against each other at the same time, happiness against sadness, military precision against lament. It is the only art that can convey two ideas at the same time.

'It can be written down as precisely as words – more so, as precisely as a physics diagram. And it's even more clever than words. It can pierce the heartstrings, touch God. Why should one piece of music make me so sad and another make me cheerful for the rest of the day? Answer me that, little Shrimp. It is a very particular talent your brother has. You must value him.'

Her back had stiffened and broken contact, stopped leaning against his leg.

'I feel sick,' she said, struggled up, grey-faced, and vomited copiously and violently over the side of the boat.

Behind them the Fødselsøy becalmed in an opaline sea, gleamed its impersonal beauty. On the margins of the people-less island the gull mother, who usually fished further out, gathered the easy meat from under the abandoned wooden jetty, and called to her children to come and get it in that harsh croaking Tëtka voice of hers. The quilly awkward grey-coloured teenage children tottered in clumsily to land by their mother and be fed from her beak, greeting the food with shouts of joy, snatching voraciously from the maternal jaws, gulping and immediately demanding more. Off she flew again without repose, to forage under the wooden jetty, entirely intent on her job to find more nourishment for her children.

When Berndt had left the place he had experienced a sudden revulsion, a tightening of the throat.

'Fordømmet place,' he'd muttered, 'I'm allergic to it,' and telling the children he wouldn't be a minute, he'd gone round every room both upstairs and downstairs in Katya's wretched birth house opening all the windows wide and fastening back all the doors for the sea and the wind and the salt and the rain and the strong summer sun and the fierce winter snow-blizzards and ice storms to get to work on destroying it as quickly as possible.

Somewhere in the house a door slammed with a pistol crack. The ugly teenage gulls screamed and scattered over the rock but it didn't want many minutes before curiosity proved stronger than fear. The first gully claw ventured over the threshold. In minutes they were swarming all over the *stue*, perching on the barrel of the telescope, pecking at the shiny face of the good Thomas Campion barometer, feasting on morsels of squashed spilled potato-in-fat, shitting wherever they happened to be. The efficient mother came back from her latest fishing trip and traced her offspring by the noise inside the house.

The mother gull took up position in the rococo-framed doorway, glaring to left and right, resembling in appearance nothing so much as an angry cavalry officer with her staring eye and commanding yellow beak from which the linear codling spawn hung down either side in a magnificent moustache. *Hoopsa!* Now she was over the threshold, the children crowding about her and tugging at the good breakfast she had brought. Huh, things smelt interesting in here. Hey, what was this? Fastidious as a dowager she hopped on to the high back of the floozy chair to evaluate the situation.

'So the brother is to be sent straight back to boarding school immediately.' Charlotta had subsided into relying on Berndt. 'Shall Russo take him to Fornebu with the car? Or will you?'

'Russo. The boy doesn't like me.'

'Oh! You imagine. You have always been over-sensitive since ...' She got up from the breakfast table, picking up the folded newspaper. She still couldn't bring herself to say the word Akershus by name.

Through the window Shrimp was in the resurrected hammock. No, not resurrected, strictly speaking, but a new one and in a new tree, too. The lilac had grown hollow and unreliable. Now there were children in the house again Russo had done a most surprising and unprecedented thing. He had decided, quite independently, to purchase the hammock down at the chandler's. Uninstructed, he had put it, unauthorised, on the Oscarsson account and fixed it between two stout branches in the white cherry that had been a mere sapling, a mere twig in the ground when Russo had first come. And now it was

hammock-bearing. Charlotta had heard him whistling in the
garden for the first time since Oscar's death; and he had
changed clothes. When Charlotta looked out of the window to
spy on the whistle she had seen him wearing his festive
braided red tunic that she hadn't seen for many a month. He
seemed to have filled out, too. His great beaked head no longer
nodded, pointless as a puppet, at the end of a scrawny vulture
neck.

The little Shrimp made a pretty picture in a blue cotton
dress under the ripening yellow fruit of the mop-headed
cherry tree.

'She's always got a book to her nose. Just as you had as a boy,
remember? Katya was always jealous and making all sorts of
little dramas and diversions to come between you and the
page. I wonder,' she glanced down at the day's paper in her
hand, 'if we ought to stop taking *Aftenposten?*'

'Not a bad idea. The girl seems to read precociously in every
language.'

There had been a gossip-piece masquerading as a fashion
note, 'our own Norwegian beauty, *hoffdame* Charlotta
Oscarsson's daughter Katya Fortescue arriving at La Négresse
station, Biarritz, where she will summer accompanied by ...'
and so on.

'It's not Uncle Reggie's face,' Shrimp had observed uncon-
demningly at breakfast, after carefully studying the face
staring out with the air of one well-practised at seducing the
camera. 'Mama looks pretty. It must be a different uncle,' she
concluded, with a gravity that twisted like a knife in
Charlotta's heart.

'And will Shrimp go back to England?' Berndt had been
trained to keep his voice most neutral at times when he felt
most deeply. 'Will she have to go too?'

Charlotta knew her son's vocal tricks and -isms far too well
to be taken in by this pretended calm.

'I feel more inclined,' she said, 'to follow my inclinations than
my duty. They don't seem in a great hurry to get her back. In all
this fuss about getting the boy back in time to attend his new
school they have never once mentioned the little Shrimp. I get
the feeling the English are like those Greek Spartans about girls.
Exposed on a hillside the first night while the parents stay

indoors devoutly praying for rain and wolves. I believe it's even worse and less humane in India – which, after all, is only England in the sun. I wonder if the English caught it from Empire or Empire from them? I don't feel inclined to send them Shrimp. It would be different if they had asked for her.' Charlotta sailed serenely out of the room to talk about domestic arrangements in the house after the boy had left for England.

Berndt was breathtaken.

He shook his head, like a dog shaking out of sleep, gave a little laugh, put his two lips together and whistled. 'Well done, Charlotta, oh, well done.' But he still couldn't get over his incredulity, so he shook his head some more and before he knew where he was he had plumped himself down on one of the gazelle-like thin-ankled chairs. It did not flinch at his weight. Not that he noticed. The corporeal was the last thing on his mind as he thought this thing through, unconsciously reaching for a further cup of good coffee and drinking it in the veiled sympathetic light filtered by the long summer curtains of spotted muslin that muted the glare of the sun-drenched lace-clothed table, the sparkling silver coffee-pot, the clean glaze of the Nymphenburg breakfast service, the speckling of toast crumbs and the two neatly beheaded empty home-laid eggs in their monogrammed silver cups. Left alone among these things in the room with the view of the Shrimp lying blissful in the hammock, Berndt knew himself more than usually aware that he was large and clumsy, and that his mother might easily have been outmanoeuvring him and everybody else all his life. The subtlety so materially evident in Charlotta's hyper-civilised elegant context was but a pale echo of the subtlety of her mind.

What was she up to? Was she really kidnapping the granddaughter-cum-great-niece? Was she really hijacking the girl? Yes. Yes, against all convention, she was.

Great spare-fleshed giant Berndt flung his head back so it overflowed the deliciously carved thing that was the backrest of the gilded chair and laughed and laughed and laughed. 'Wonderful,' he gasped, 'wonderful.'

These last weeks since the funeral, certain things, certain fundamental things, had been very different in this house.

Charlotta had, quite unexceptionally, taken the time of mourning to withdraw a little from her duties in the world. The palace understood and came to visit from time to decorous time. She had written her charities each a holding letter, enclosing a cheque. Her charities felt themselves genuinely the poorer for lack of Charlotta's presence. The cheque was very generous and thank you very much but it was no substitute for her presence. Useful as money was, it could not of itself reassure them that there was no doubt but things were worth striving for. Money fell far short of a justification for existence.

Charlotta stayed firmly at home, showing good grace and gratitude, receiving the guests of distinction. Church, bench, state and Bess paid courtly visits. There remained the air of ranking, of life conducted according to a very specific perceived social correctness. The closed visitors' book was an icon twinned with the hollow emptiness of the silver bowl. There would be no more signatures appended after the day of Oscar's departure from this life. With no host there were no visitors to mark, just as the bowl would remain unoccupied by flowers.

Berndt's continuing presence was not questioned one way or the other; he was made to feel that it was very welcome, very welcome indeed.

'No, little Shrimp, Uncle Berndt is not leaving us yet,' she said, in the evening of the terrible Judas day.

Charlotta would always think of it in that way: the day of the Judas-journey, the day she presided over the loading of Robert into the cattle truck.

The poor, pale, fat, desperately unhappy boy had been allowed as a treat – a treat – to sit in the front seat beside Russo and watch the instruments on the dazzling walnut dashboard during the journey to Fornebu airport, a journey the horror of which Charlotta would never forget for the rest of her life. All the long dusty journey in the car her mind was gnawing, gnawing. What was she to do? Her duty. She could not step between the boy and his one interested parent; the English boy and his English destiny. Berndt had not changed his mind, he had not come with her on the ghastly journey accompanying the boy to Fornebu. He had persisted in the notion that the boy disliked him, that it would not add materially to the boy's comfort – the opposite – if his uncle Berndt made up part of the send-off party. Shrimp had said she would come but the girl had already vomited once that morning and she looked so ill and wretched that Charlotta was really worried she was sickening and forbade her the journey. She left her in Berndt's care, imploring him to telephone dear old Magnus Lund, retired from his distinguished medical practice now, but not too idle still to keep an eye on favourite patients of yore. Berndt might just ask him to come up and cast an eye over the little girl.

The parting with the boy had been unimaginably painful.

During the drive the fat unattractive boy had droned on at Russo, the two of them segregated in their twin front seats, while Charlotta, like a presiding deity, listened. By now she understood a fair amount of both their languages, while not necessarily being prepared to speak a great deal in either. Shocked by the boy's monomaniacal, magisterial diktats she nevertheless simulated interest when consulted and felt all the worse for the dishonesty of this dissimulation.

By the time the poor boy was making the long walk across the dull flat grey tarmac as if in a predestined dream, Charlotta was running back and forth between the vendors of things and the boy, buying things – any things – in expiation: bars of Firkløver chocolate, Fox's square chewy creamy lemony squares wrapped in bright indigo paper, seigemen, those flat rudimentary men made of jelly in naïve colours, dusted with a coating of crunchy sugar whose limbs could be pulled out to grotesque lengths before being popped into the mouth. Frantic with her own ineffectuality within the larger context of the boy's destiny, she at last gave up, turned round before the air-liner had left the ground, was not there waving, when he looked down from the air. She could not.

All her journey home was haunted. Against her eyelids floated the boy's large white flat moon face pressed to the oval porthole, scouring the receding tarmac and seeing no face he knew. When she got home she immediately picked up the telephone to the retired Herr Professor Doktor Lund imploring as urgently and hysterically as she had implored during the telephone call in the wake of Oscar's death to write to Robert's father explaining exactly the latest scientific conclusions that had been reached regarding word-blindness, and to send a copy of the letter to the school principal as well.

Lund was sufficiently concerned at Charlotta's state during this telephone call to fabricate a reason to pay a call on her straight away, though he had not left her house thirty minutes ago after a detailed but gentle examination of the Shrimp during which the old man's eyebrows had lifted infinitesimally, but he had merely scrawled on his pad 'watch and wait', which was his code for noting such unpalatable suspicions.

Replacing the trumpet-shaped receiver in its cradle Charlotta was astonished to see the blood at her fingers' ends; no feelings had told her she had been tearing at her own flesh.

The cattle-truck afternoon left an appalling gash of guilt on their souls. The smell of bad conscience about the house was thick as the smell of cooking. Equilibrium must be restored, normality. They could not sneak about like Judases. The duty must fall on her.

Menial tasks were good for such things. 'Come, darling,' she said, later that same evening down in the cosiness of the lamplit *stue*. She opened her worktable, though God knew it seemed irrelevant enough. 'We must start knitting you a good thick sweater. You will need it soon to keep you warm when the autumn comes.'

The Shrimp was already drawn by the coloured silks, whalebone bobbins, rainbow cottons and scraps in the workbox. Now Charlotta cast on and started to teach the little girl to knit the reindeer- and snowflake-patterns that Norwegian women from time immemorial observed in nature and knitted into their garments. Tongue-tip grasped in concentration between such sweet determined lips, the Shrimp paid rapt attention.

Only a little session this evening. Enough to drive out the emotion of the day; too much would tire the girl. When she judged the Shrimp's focus had been altered, Charlotta asked Berndt, who had been sitting quiet watching – 'Useless as always' as he put it – to put another birch log on the fire, just a little one.

'The fire is more for show than for warmth,' she had taken the girl on her knee, 'though soon it will be needed. The late summer signs are here. That was what made me think of knitting you a sweater.'

She hugged the child. Several stitches dropped out of the piece of knitting and were picked up by the two of them together.

Indeed, the late summer signs were there for all to read in the garden: tall abundant stands of pale yellow evening primrose flowers glowing through the twilight. The prickly teasel cones, that Katya each year had used as hairbrushes for her dolls, were misted with rings of starry pale violet florets. Ageing bumble-bees, youthful judgement gone, were blundering tubbily about, knocking into things. Soon, the summer would be over. They would be into the new season. Soon brisk night frosts would sharpen the colours in the morning. Charlotta's nostrils flared in anticipation of the smell of the birch-forest carpet when the leaves above had turned again to golden pennies and the *kantareller* mushrooms pushed up their matching yellow umbrellas through the green brightness of starfrond moss.

'We shall not live here in Drammensveien. What would we do in this huge great museum of a house, just you and me, hey?'

Shrimp didn't know so she didn't say anything. She looked at her kind grandmother, expecting, trusting.

Charlotta's eyes were closed but she wasn't asleep. She was happy but weary. Could she really begin again? She was sixty. Begin on all that again? Well, there was nobody else. She had Berndt and Russo to help her, and sixty was not so old. The Shrimp touched the beautiful lace of Charlotta's collar with a finger as light as a butterfly. Charlotta opened her eyes. Yes, she could manage this future and make a better fist of it than that first time. But it needed a very big thinking; it needed a thorough through-thinking, if she was to do it right this time.

'My darling,' she squeezed the child, 'we will have some fun! Come on. Bedtime.' Purposely she had not re-created the story-time as it used to be in the old days with Katya and Berndt down in the *stue*. Climbing the baroque sweep of the staircase she found the words coming to her from God knew where. She made a story for the Shrimp about the fun they would have in the little house they would find in the woods with Russo and Mrs Russo. (Though, truth to tell, they were both pretty old and useless now, except for companionship. That strapping, slant-eyed daughter of theirs would be the one to do the hewing of wood and drawing of water when she wasn't in the family way, which Charlotta rather suspected she was. Hmn. She must talk to Russo about offering a handsome dowry – the things she had neglected lately! A dowry would find the girl a husband double-quick.) Charlotta took the steps at a lick. Shrimp had to trot to keep up. Sixty didn't seem so old. No, it was not so old at all.

'You and me, darling.' She looked down at the little girl's cold thin hand. 'Are you always cold?'

'Yes.'

'In the new house together we will put a Jotul stove in your room and if that doesn't work we'll sew you into skins like the peasants in the place where I grew up used to do at the start of the winter. They only unpicked them on St John the Baptist's Day when summer has come.'

'How smelly.'

'Yes, it was. When we go out tomorrow we'll have to make sure we find a snug little house that will keep us warm. I was thinking along the lines of a little doll's-house house up in the hills where the Holmenkollen ski jump is. A *dukkestue* in the fir woods with a high view looking down over Oslo and its fjord. You will go to school just like all the other local little girls and boys, with a satchel on your back. You shall walk to school with the other girls in summer and ski with them to school and back in winter.'

Ski. Like Kari, Shrimp thought. I shall try to be a *langrenn* champion like her.

'I wondered if at school you might like to have special lessons in the Russian language, and in English literature because, you know, my darling, you have a very special family heritage and a very special gift for languages and I thought you might like it if you were the first of all the long line of Fortescues and Oscarssons to speak Russian and Norwegian and English, too. Nobody has done that in the family before you. Not even Katya, your Russian grandmother. She could never get her tongue around the Norwegian language so we had to speak in a sort of mosaic of French and English that made it difficult for us to understand each other's meaning,

and so ... misunderstandings arose. Too many ... misunderstandings ...'

'Don't stop, Bestemama.'

Charlotta roused herself. 'You have your grandmother's very
beautiful eyes that look violet in a certain light and – much
more important – you have her very clever brain, and if you
spoke all the languages you could understand everything so
much better than she ever did, better than any of us have
understood so far. Would you like that, darling?'

Shrimp's eyes shone. She forgot not to clutch because it was
annoying. She clutched in ecstasy, and Charlotta clutched
back.

'May I put the knitting under my pillow?'

'Funny girl. Good night.'

'Till tomorrow?'

'Yes, of course till tomorrow. We shall have an early breakfast
together and a big one. Home-hunting is a hungry business.'

When Charlotta was in bed she sat up hugging her knees
like a girl herself, excited about feeling afraid. The child did
not sleep in Katya's old room but in Berndt's, so as not
deliberately to court perpetuation, and Charlotta had moved
herself into Katya's old bedroom, so as to be reassuringly near
the girl. How odd it was, after twenty-five years in the same
bedroom, now to be high up here in the house where the same
sea sounded different, and the traffic coming at a different angle,
and the moon in the linden leaves made hearts on the curtains.

Charlotta had lost the habit of good sleep since Oscar's death
but her abiding horror of narcotics allowed her nothing
stronger than an infusion of lemon verbena leaves to take to
bed. If she was to sleep many nights in this little room she
must import a larger bedside table. At least, for the short time
before moving to the new house. She couldn't have brought the
girl up in this house with the closed visitors' book and the
stultifying apotheoses of this and that hanging in the air, and
all the burdens of the past that Charlotta had built up as her
own structure and her support and that would not help the
Shrimp one little bit.

Vanity, ashes and dust. One generation's life was another
generation's death. The props and stays of her own life had
nothing to do with the Shrimp's needs.

'The formaldehyde house'. Katya's phrase had seldom left her. No, she could not in all conscience bring this child up in another formaldehyde house. It would have been a good place for her old age alone, but not for this new development of the child. A breeze stirred the curtain at the window. Quickly she made the sign of the Cross over Katya in Biarritz or wherever she might be, but barely paused to think of the mother because she must concentrate on this gleam of inspiration casting light on the future of the daughter. Quickly, before the door closed.

The girl, then, would not be squeezed into the pattern of any formaldehyde house as Katya had been squeezed into the Drammensveien pattern of rank, power, emblems, accepted structures, and rebelled. The childhood-long rebellion had become transformed into the permanent craving for novelty for its own sake.

'The unpalatable part of this,' Charlotta said to herself, 'is that my imposed structure of inflexible routine, even-handed justice and discipline has led directly in a straight line to the string of uncles.'

Charlotta, who had dearly hoped Katya would find peace in a second marriage, realised for the very first time here and now, tonight, that this was impossible. There would never be a final 'uncle', the Shrimp would never be recalled into some happy second marriage.

'Poor child,' she said, though which child was less clear. 'So it's for life.

'I had the fun of making my own way as a young girl in a strange world. We'll give the girl the same, eh, Oscar? And I am sorry that I'm selling your house, our house, but I don't think there's a choice, do you? If so, please tell me.'

She had done her thinking for tonight.

Now it remained to put the day to bed. She lay down, closed her eyes against the moonlit room, curled up as she always curled, with her hands tented, as every night she tented them to say her prayers. Against the navy blue of her eyelids she was closing the day as she always closed her every day, only this time she prayed first for herself: 'Loving Father, you have at last given me the second child I longed for, a second chance for which I bless your merciful compassion and give you hearty thanks. Loving Father, give me strength enough and years enough to see this job out to the end.' Next she prayed for Shrimp. Then, rather desperately and guiltily, for the poor fat unlovable boy, condemned to she knew not what and bundled, frightened and blustering, into his cattle-truck aeroplane. She prayed for Katya and for darling Berndt, before lastly offering the customary prayers for the everlasting repose of her husband's soul.

This was a great change in Charlotta's order of things. Up till now Oscar had always come first of all.

CHAPTER NINETEEN

Wagering It All On An Abstract Harvest

Dukkestue, the doll's house, was further away in space and time, high above Oslo. Below it, through the high folds and crevasses of woods of gilded birch, black fir and tall damp fern, threaded the steep velvety-mossed paths connecting Charlotta and town; paths in summer inhabited by an endless disjointed coloured caterpillar of town hikers, walking up hill and down dale in humped lines with rolled-down red socks and rucksacks. In winter, the same paths were drawn in flaming lines by the bituminous pine torches strung through the trees like gold-coloured flickering tinsel across violet-shadowed snow. Beneath them in the sheen of torchlight, the ant-column of the same townspeople soared and slid on whispering skis with turn-up tips, their busy figures topped off, like so many fly-agaric mushrooms, with red-bobbled *nisselue* hats.

Beyond Oslo; always Oslo.

In the early sun, glimmering soft and rosy and still; in the evening, bouncing and bubbling and wavering and glittering with all the lights from the traffic and the houses and the people and the planes circling like fireflies above Fornebu airport.

High in the hills of Voksenlia, connected but no longer glued, Charlotta had allowed one modernism to intrude on the mossy log-built cottage: she succumbed to fashion and installed what was then called a 'picture window'. For hours on end she took pleasure in gazing down from the Dukkestue through a piece of plate glass the size of a small garden pond upon these things below.

Russo had been awestruck by this glass, disbelieving and

entranced. She had caught him throwing leaves against it to
see if it was air or window.

'Doubting Thomas.' She had wagged her finger and smiled;
but not much later she had cause to administer a serious
reproof, without a smile, when she caught him taking potshots
at the splendid pane with his legacy keepsake, Oscar's old
revolver. Shrimp, the little language scholar, had just mastered
the Russian for 'bullet-proof'.

'It's funny, you know,' Charlotta told Berndt, who was
so much happier up here, 'the one thing I miss is the noise
of *trikken*, the clanking trams with their pretty little bells.
It is a noise that has been in my ears all my married life
and it had nothing to do with my marriage at all. And yet
that is the thing that when I go down to town and hear it,'
she went down once a week to tend the grave, and such,
'I have to close my eyes from missing your dear father.
Funny, isn't it? Oscar never took *trikken*. Of all the inappropriate reminders ... but one cannot choose. These things are
their own masters. You would think – I would think, had I
been given a guess – that it would be the docks and the
wharves and the moonlight on the swaying waves. They
make me nostalgic in a sentimental way, of course, but it's
trikken that makes me cry. So stupid to be old.' She gave a
light squeeze to the hand that was offered her. 'Never become
an old woman.'

'Not much chance of that.' Berndt put a long arm down to
ruffle the head thrown back in the watching chair.

That there was not much to be missed about Oslo, these
days, had, she thought, everything to do with the building of
the huge city hall, Rådhuset, a monster of a thing in red brick
erected in 1950 to celebrate the nine-hundredth anniversary of
Oslo. Was it deliberate that the celebratory building should so
completely change the character of what it was celebrating?
Rådhuset had altered the entire city. You would not think one
building ... But this was something out of the ordinary, more
propaganda than building. Hitlerian in scale and ugliness and
conceit, it had ousted the tall tumble-jumble of Hanseatic
houses she had been used to seeing from her windows at
Drammensveien, and had been used to threading through on
the way to the shipping offices. Her feet might have traced that

familiar path in the darkest night without light, its pattern was
so deeply etched into her sum of being and doing. And now
there was this great monstrous civic erection in the way. It
forced both Charlotta and the wind to take different routes
through the town. It made the seagulls fly in different lines
and configurations. Never in all history had the gulls flown
thus, or the wind blown thus through Oslo. Maybe it didn't
matter that, soon, nobody would remember how these two
things used to happen before the Rådhus giant's great self-
satisfied twin towers frowned down. As she walked in its
vulturine shadow it told her she was out of tune with the
times: an old anachronistic woman who had no part in this
new age. Oslo had moved on since her day. 'Move over, Fru
Oscarsson. Make way for the modern,' said this gargantuan
civic vanity. 'The wild goats of yesteryear have gone from Oslo
now. King Håkon is dead. Bess is dead. The plaster dust that
flies up, these days, is flying at the "genuine historic and
authentic restoration" of such dinosaurs as you put up. You
were here at the start of an age in our town, an age that has
gone. Oh, and by the way, Fru Oscarsson, how does it feel to be
history?'

Is that what it came to in the end? She drowsed in her
chair before the picture window. Just another formaldehyde
house? My darling husband's youthful spit-in-your-eye construction, Oscar's nose-thumb at a disapproving society. Is
that what it became in the end? A heritage relic? A restoration
opportunity?

She was remembering her own dread that last morning,
leaving the house behind her. The topic of the world's vanities
had been much on her mind as she stood at the *stue* window.
She had been feeling like a madwoman that last morning; a
gambler, out of character entirely, staking it all on the Shrimp.

Churning with anxiety, with memories, with lack of conviction and regret; already regret, even before the deed was
done, she had never felt so abandoned. And then Providence
had sent Fru Snadö, genteel Fru Snadö, organiser *par excellence*
of every expensive society do in the name of charity, sailing
down the road outside the house, proceeding on the back seat
of her English Rolls towards lunch at the Dronningen Yacht
Klub, lunch-time hat sitting just so upon the perm, day-time

diamonds not flashing gaudily but glittering discreetly at about the same twinkle-level as the burnished British coach-work on the side panels of the limousine.

The sight had acted like an injection of Dr Pauling's vitamins on Charlotta. She had summoned Berndt, and Russo too, for an impromptu burning in the garden. No poetic Viking pyre this, no nostalgic long drawn-out ceremony but a practical immolation of all the wooden spoons in the house, all the old elk heads from the trophy room, shoes that still had wear in them but hadn't seen use for a hundred years, all combustible domestic paraphernalia not wanted by the Russian legation (God or, indeed, Lenin help them) who had bought the house, which now would be that country's embassy.

Russo had balked, jutted his grizzled beard, put out his great square Russian jaw at pulling down the beautiful white silk curtains, the snowfall curtains that had been the silent background to so many words in the stue, custodian to so many secrets.

The further jutted Russo's jaw, the further Charlotta insisted.

There was no place for such things, she pointed out, in the modest vernacular Dukkestue they were all moving to, any more than there was a place for them in the canon of Communist propaganda masquerading as People's taste.

Curtains or no curtains, Russo's sulks couldn't long with-stand the excitement of a bonfire. The dancing flames, almost transparent in the strong sunlight, spoke directly to his childish nature, they entered his soul. Soon he was darting about finding things, lobbing them on and laughing. The new hammock she'd been planning to take with them to the new garden and string up for the Shrimp – why it had hardly been used! – but dear old Russo lobbed it from afar. And even she got excited as it flew through the air, untangling from a flying cat's-cradle into a most beautiful parabola that enmeshed the flames in its net as it fell, imprinting on the flames for a second ashy white; as ashy white as, thirty miles down the coast on the Fødselsøy, Gustav's decayed prototype lobster pot lay collapsing and mummifying in dusty echo of itself.

Since the morning Berndt had left the island taking the two children with him, the morning after the storm, not a person had set foot on it, from that day to this. The place had been left to the birds with their wide audacious wings. They had taken full possession of the island; it was their cruel kingdom now. They loved it in their predatory way, sailed over it on wings outflung in lustrous folds, patrolled its rock-toothed marches ready to defend to the death with claw, curved beak, battle scream and full wingbeating grandeur.

Just for that one tiny second that the cosy hammock imprinted its ash-net pattern on the flames, Berndt thought, It's exactly like a lobster pot I've seen somewhere, his memory vaguely stirring but failing to find the connection before the white pattern was consumed in the transparent flames; gone.

Russo whooped, took a great flying leap over the pyre like a wild Cossack in his prime, something Charlotta had to remind him sternly he wasn't any more, but whether he really understood as little Norwegian as he pretended (there had been that one spine-chilling word thunderously uttered at the end of the war, Hevn: revenge), or whether his misunderstanding was as selective as she suspected, he continued to leap high over the blazing white silk curtains, blithe as Nijinsky and irresponsible as a romantic poet, grinning his steel grin and crinkling his eyes in utter rapturous happiness the while. In the end Charlotta had no option but to give in, laugh and clap in time to his leaps, infected by his cabaret performance despite herself.

How Charlotta's eyes would have widened could she have seen the replacement curtains hung by Russo's co-nationals in the legation. Her plain white was, in fact, replaced in the new USSR order of things by infinitely grander, knock-your-eye-out red silk brocade produced by fat State Farm silkworms gorged on the mulberry trees of Samarkand, dyed the closest shade that red could get to the Tyrian purple of the Roman emperors, and woven into a florid stylised neo-Baroque interpretation of the hammer and sickle motif repeated ad infinitum and enriched by lively scrolling interpolations of the letters CCCP. Enough meterage of this silk was woven to make the magnificent stage curtains of the Bolshoi Theatre where they are today the subject of ping-pong political ideological debate and may not hang much longer, and to have leftovers to clothe the windows of embassies such as Drammensveien.

She was a stupid old woman to be thinking about these things in the past.

Drammensveien had been left in 1956; today was 1970. She was remembering a bonfire of fourteen years ago. What a waste of time when there was the little Shrimp's aeroplane to watch out for.

She opened her eyes to find she was alone in the room. Berndt must have tiptoed out. Maybe he had left to collect the little one already. Charlotta's eyes resumed their watching of the sky for the aeroplane coming in from London. Not that there was much sky to see, nor earth neither. Oslo had disappeared, even had her eyes been younger. Beyond her window all the world was snow; not the sparkling snow of a sun day, but the brown-submersed shadow-world of snowfall. The sun was a pale disc, more like the moon, just a staring circle in the grey misty sky stretching down to the grey misty garden just outside her window. The view had gone, melted out by the thickness of mist and the slow vertical drift of snowflake behind snowflake. Charlotta started to worry about Shrimp's journey up here from Fornebu airport.

Shrimp, in her turn, was worrying about the urn. She was buckling her seat-belt in the sky, refusing airline food (old habits died hard) and wondering about the nature of deception: what in the end she would tell Charlotta that would be least upsetting. Up above her, in the aeroplane's locker, the urn of reconstituted stone, with a practical screw-top lid precluding spillage, was empty as air when it ought to have been full of funerary ashes.

Shrimp had not been altogether surprised when the telephone had rung in her student digs in London.

'Shrimp? Babe, are you keeping young and beautiful? I'm taking molasses. There's this special sort. You can only get it in Harrods. It costs heaps.'

Shrimp heard the faint tintinnabulation of her mother's charm bracelet down the phone. 'Where are you living, Mama? The university doesn't allow students to put up guests, I'm afraid.'

'That one slipped out with indecent haste, darling. Charlotta obviously failed you in lessons in tact. Actually,' inhale, 'I'm with Lulu. Deepest Battersea. How are the mighty fallen. A slum, darling. Low-life by the dogs' home. Wuff wuff wuff all night and the lowest ceilings in the world. We're in deep danger from curvature of the spine, bent as coat-hangers from crouching. So we take these glamorous little cod-liver oil bombs that lubricate the joints and when we get out of the front door miraculously we can stand again. *Homo erectus* in all our glory. Not that Lulu's glory is much to speak of, these days. She's not on the pill like me. Marvellous for the skin. It makes sense if you think about it. Keep having your monthlies and you simply never grow old. Peter Pan. Are you on the pill, darling? I know you're only sixteen.'

'Twenty.'

'Jeepers. That ages your old ma. Shall we call it eighteen and split the difference? It's never too soon to start lying about your age, believe me. I can easily get you the pill. Charlotta would disapprove like mad, of course. Dear old Dr Viridian sends it to me wherever I am in the world from Switzerland in batches. Under plain cover.'

'But, Mama, you're too old. It's terribly dangerous, isn't it? Blood clots.'

'Never mention the O word. Brutish age. As for blood clots, you don't want to believe all the popular medicine you read in the health pages of the newspapers. Dr Viridian explained it all beautifully over the telephone. I can't tell you what a success it is. Are you pretty these days? Last time I saw you I reckoned it could go either way. Two years ago.'

'Three.'

'Why don't we all meet for lunch at the Causerie?'

'All?'

'Me and you and Lulu. Then you can judge the skin. I've given you a tremendous inheritance if you think about it. The best. The Olovanova skin, and the bones. You'll never be old and ugly.'

'... and of course I said I would be there.' Shrimp took Charlotta's dear soft-skinned hand. Charlotta was seventy-four now, and getting sleepy. There was a blue tinge about her nose and mouth that spoke of a heart not entirely right. But Shrimp refused to see it; everyone had a blue nose in winter and the sleepiness was only winter-sleepiness like a dormouse hibernating. Shrimp could not bear to face that her darling

Bestemama had started the last journey, was growing gently towards her grave. The very possibility made the Shrimp feel sick with unhappiness.

'That was the last I heard from Mama.'

'But you went along to the Causerie?'

'I took a bunch of flowers.'

'Good girl.'

'And waited and waited, sitting at the table, which is always embarrassing.'

'Yes, it is embarrassing when you are young. And such an expensive place, too.'

'But the waiter was kind. And the next thing was Lulu and the police.'

'Katya was dead of a *thrombose* you say?'

'The pill. She was mad to take it at her age. It is well known.'

'Ah.' Charlotta gave a gentle ironic smile. 'Dr Viridian was always killing people through giving them their dreams. His medical theories raised the hairs on my head. He never did your mother's health any favours but he made her happy. Happier than I ever imagined through the conventional and cautious channels. Eternal youth! Freia's golden apples, he promised her.'

'She died walking down the King's Road, which is a sort of perpetual fashion and beauty parade like Karl Johan but more frantic. She just fell down dead but the nice thing she would have liked is that the person who telephoned told the police a young girl had fallen down dead in the street. "A young girl", she would have liked that.'

'Best of all.' Katya always engendered a nagging ache in Charlotta's head. 'And apart from you and Lulu, there was just one other, only a funny little man at the crematorium, you said?'

'Such a funny one. He didn't look at all like one of her ... you know. He was small and thin and wispy. Uncles were never wispy. A grey little man, quite bald and undistinguished and, well, he was more like Russo, like an old family servant. But one I didn't know. And when we were going out after the horrid bit in the crematorium he went out first and he was outside taking a pull at a bottle of beer in the garden place that is round about the awful depressing little chapel place. He had half concealed himself behind one of the unhealthy bald rose-bushes. And he stuck the brown-glass bottle back in the pocket of his suit, a rather old and shiny and not expensive suit, but carefully preserved and mended. He was ashamed of the bottle when he saw us, and I went over to shake hands and to thank him for coming.'

'And he was the night porter at Harrods, you say?'

'Yes. Ever since she had first come to London as Lulu's paying guest just before the war they had been telephone friends. It started because when Katya first came to London she had no idea Harrods ever closed and so she used to ring up in the night when she had finished a book to order a new one. And that way they became detective-story friends. She told him about the American ones she read and he started to read them, too, because he had all the long night on his hands and it would be rude not to read her favourites. But in reality he thought they were not a patch on the more serious and intellectual exponents of the form (that was his phrase, "serious and intellectual exponents of the form"), Agatha Christie and Sir Arthur Conan Doyle.

'That was at the start what they talked about, and later, too, mostly, he said. But other things came into it later, though he never knew she had a daughter. He was interested when I said I was her daughter and looked at me rather too nosily, I thought, to be polite. But that was before I learned that they had never met. He asked me what she looked like and when I said she was beautiful, far more beautiful than me, it made him happy. He nodded and dropped his eyes to look within himself and smiled quietly.

'For long, long periods over the years, weeks would go by without her telephoning, months even, he said. But there were patches when she telephoned every night, once or twice, or more. Often she would be in an exotic place. She seldom said where she was but he could tell sometimes by the telephone line that she was abroad: "It sounds different when it's coming along the cables under the sea. I fancy you can hear the waves." Once she had told him she was in the stinking armpit of the world where hairdressers came to die and she was surrounded by the pavement classes, and she was very low and fed up. But then she soon brightened on hearing his news.

' "Your news?" I asked him, expecting something personal
and momentous, a grandchild perhaps or a new car.

' "Oh, yes, Miss, I always kept the news for her. 'Bobbie!' Her
voice would come so bright, so quick. She never said hello, just
'Bobbie!' and I knew straight away! She'd always start in that
way that brightened my night like ... like seeing a brightness
suddenly in a dark night sky. She was that unexpected. You
never knew. You'd be thinking it was a long dull night
stretching ahead, counting the hours till morning, frankly,
Miss, eking out the Woodbines. And then it'd be 'Bobbie!' on
the telephone and her voice lit up the whole world. It was like
... like ... Well, when I was at school there was a picture of
Halley's Comet and the teacher told us we could all be like
that, each one of us. Nothing was impossible. If we wanted we
could blaze across the sky. Not me, Miss, not me. But she did."
He shook his head; a little man, but I did not get the
impression he was sad about being little. "You'll forgive me,
Miss. I meant nothing personal or disrespectful. Talk about
unexpected! Your late mother was certainly that, if I may say
so. What a card. You never knew when she'd pop up next with
her 'What's new, Bobs? Tell me what's hip in SW7.' "

'He would save cuttings to give her the news of the things
that interested her: the season's colours, the season's hemlines,
what people were dancing and where they were dancing it. He
made notes in a notebook that he took into work every evening
in case she should ring. Notes from the gossip columns in the
Daily Express and the *Daily Mail*. It gave him a wide range of
interests keeping up with such things. "Your mother, if I may
say so," he told me, "opened my eyes to new worlds. It was a
privilege to know her. She was a real lady, of the old school.
And," he added, rather bravely, "if you turn out to be half as
great a lady, Miss, you will be doing very well, if I may say so."

'We were having this conversation sitting on a miserably
hard wooden bench in the memorial garden. The next cre-
mation party had gone in, more numerous than ours, and I was
wondering if we could get away before the smoke from this
one came out of the chimney but Lulu, who was still with us
on the bench and smoking very desperately because she hated
that place more than anywhere she had ever been, had by
then finished the bottle of beer belonging to the Harrods

porter as well as her own hip flask of cherry brandy for the cold and she was the one who came up with the idea... it was her plan ... I'm so sorry, Charlotta.'

'What is it, my dear?'

'Well, the thing is, I wasn't going to tell you. I was going to pretend the ashes were in there.' Shrimp indicated the depressing urn of reconstituted stone with the screw lid that had sat up above her on the aeroplane. 'But, in fact, they're in Harrods' book department. Lulu jumped up from the bench in the crematorium, you see, and made a great fuss to collect them there and then, which was unconventional and strong objections were made. But Lulu determined and rather drunk is a force not to be balked. It was not without its funny side, I can tell you, Bestemama.'

'Graveyard scenes seldom are.'

'He let us into Harrods at night, through the staff entrance. It was quite empty except for the three of us. He knew when the cleaners went home, you see. Lulu had changed. She came in pomp, faded state. She had dressed up in long fox furs like a vamp in an old black-and-white film and a rather moth-eaten lace mantilla that smelled of camphor and she carried a round box of chocolates with a violet silk bow. Violet crèmes from Charbonnel et Walker that she kept munching because there was nothing like chocolate for sadness and she kept offering them to me, very insistently, but I hate violet crèmes so I had to pretend to eat them but smuggle them in my pocket not to seem rude. We went up to the second floor by the stairs because the lifts were switched off at night and we scattered her among the vintage crime section, among Dashiell Hammett and Raymond Chandler and Mickey Spillane. Lulu also at the last minute kept back a pinch and put it in the air while we were going back through the perfumery and cosmetics department. I do hope you don't mind? In the end I had to tell you. I could not ... I knew your plan to take her back to the F-F-F-Fødsel-el-l ...' Shrimp could not say the island's name. That and her brother Robert's name were the only two words that she, star trilingual interpreter, stumbled on and stuttered around and could never manage to get out '... to the island where she was born. I'm so sorry, Bestemama.'

'And I,' Charlotta said, 'am so relieved. There was no reason to take Katya there except a neatness of idea and geography: an idea of completing the full Oscarsson circle. But it was certainly never a place where your mother belonged or, indeed, was particularly happy.'

Remembering the disastrous birthday outings, Charlotta knew this was one of the great understatements of her life. The day, the shocking day, that Gustav's hollow voice had flung with such brutality his father's curse across the grey boiling waters at his daughter was a day she now almost wondered if she had dreamed, so deep had she buried it in the pile of the unwanted. Only at night when Charlotta was not responsible for her mind did it wander of its own accord along the track of speculation, the parallel track of invisible lines drawn in some other dimension along their own lives. If, her mind told her, she had not been strong enough to deflect Gustav's curse from his daughter Katya or the fruit of her womb in the shape of her son Robert, she had at least been strong enough to deflect it from the daughter, the little Shrimp, but only (wryly realised) on the terms that myths and legends required. Hard terms: the screeching of brakes and burning of tyres, the headlong turnabout of her own life, the turning topsy-turvy of the virtues she so far had followed: duty, precedent, conventionality, society's edifice turned upside down. The throwing into confusion and turning on its head of the edifice of her own life; that was the blood-price of saving the Shrimp.

'And now, my dear, I think we must get ready. We don't want to be late today of all days. I hope you have a thick coat. It will be cold either end when we are not in the car.'

Upstairs getting ready, dealing with white hair and hairpins, making her own image in the mirror, Charlotta could not shake the boy out of her head: Robert.

Maybe she ought to be thinking of Katya rather than the boy. Maybe she should be dwelling on the final details of Katya's end as related by the Shrimp, and lamenting. Harrods' book department! Her chief mourner a telephone stranger! Not so much cause for lamentation. At least her mourner was a man, a faithful man. Faithfulness was something Katya never achieved in the succession of uncles; never achieved in giving or, Charlotta was pretty certain, receiving. The beautiful smug male faces that smiled out beside Katya's in time's procession of photographs got older and older until a certain moment when a switch was pulled (Katya's fortieth birthday?) and the companions' faces got progressively younger and, according to *sekretaer* Fulman, who was a trustee, commensurately more costly to keep.

All in all the little Shrimp's account of Katya's end was, in fact, happier than Charlotta had anticipated: sudden, quick, not undignified. Unlike the poor boy. Robert, poor Robert.

The day Charlotta consigned Robert to follow the diktats of his particular heritage was second in horror in Charlotta's mind only to the day Gustav had flung his father's curse at his mortal line. The cattle-truck day: her stomach still churned with deep disquiet at the recollection, just as her stomach had churned with a deep disquiet as she had sat, passive instrument of fate, in the back seat of the car behind Russo and the boy, taking him to Fornebu on his way back to the boarding school in England. Time had not softened the journey in her mind; still it was labelled the day of knowing betrayal, source of great shame. Shame that grew with the unfolding of subsequent events.

But in truth what would she have done that day had she known she was delivering him up to a vindictive, punitive future: the boy lobbed between a succession of schools and the formaldehyde house where poor Sholto and the ageing Daphne did their unsuitable well-intentioned best to mould the much-expelled disgraceful boy into something they could recognise, some imprint of Fortescue.

Sholto, in his mounting incomprehension and frustration, hardly knew whether it was worse to have the blinking, blundering, violent boy at home or to send him to the ever more bizarre and, eventually, uncouth *soi-distant* schools that, quite soon, were the only establishments that would take him in. Even from these Robert was thrown out with indecent haste. Time and time again Sholto was overwhelmed with horror at leaving his son, his flesh and blood, in the transparently sub-standard care and custody of some appalling headmaster grinning obsequiously while clawing at the seat of his trousers, his shoulders a snowfall of dandruff. This could not be right. Never had Sholto felt so ineffectual, but what other road was there? Wearied, he was far from surprised when the downhill succession of dubious schools slipped into

borstal. Almost it was a relief. Here at last was the end of the
road. There was no more he could do. What could he have
done?

Charlotta, on the other hand, blamed herself fair and square
for these dim depths. 'I was the only one in a position to take a
stand on the boy's word-blindness, the one most aware of the
real problem. From good manners I did not. It was very wrong
of me to put manners before human necessity.'

Charlotta was never one to shirk issues. As Nazis were
uncovered in the aftermath of the war and as they were
brought to trial and pleaded, with stunning lack of originality
and imagination, that they were 'only obeying orders', she
thought of herself in the back of that car 'only obeying
society's orders'.

Is there anything sadder than retrospect? Than lamenting
your own lack of courage in taking a course of action that you
knew was wrong at the time? Thus Charlotta wrung her hands
and found herself guilty of subsequent events. She might have
felt quite differently about things had she known that by the
time she was shipping the brother off to his undistinguished
fate in England he had, by his own actions against his sister, set
himself, that storm night, upon the criminal road that
unwound before him.

But Charlotta could not know. Shrimp had never told.

'Good girl.' Downstairs, Charlotta approved the warmth of
the Shrimp's coat.

Today, unlike that terrible cattle-truck day, Charlotta had
the Shrimp for company in the back seat of the car. The
minute they were seated, the Shrimp's smooth young unused
oval hand moved towards the liver-spotted vein-knotted hand
of age. The two of them held hands entirely naturally and
openly above the car rug, as they sped easily down the hairpin
road from the high hill of Voksenlia. Gorges and cliffs and
pinnacles and great black pine-clad clefts loomed suddenly
here and there, diaphanous and fluid shapes coming and going
through the ghostly snowfall, but when they came down to
the coast and the city they blinked and screwed up their eyes
at the blinding radiance.

Down here in the city, the big disc of the sun was shiny-
yellow as straw against bright azure sky. The sea was

twinkling and sparkling. An uproar of seagulls wheeled over quick choppy white-topped waves. Flags danced red and white and blue, bending and folding and stretching in the frosted clarity of the air above snow-buried gardens. The snow-ploughs' work framed the roads in winged drifts. Thick snow blankets, toothpaste-white, muffled roofs. Glitter-dust drifted from filigree pavement trees, frosting the shoulders of bundled-up people pushing paths through their gardens with long-handled iron-bladed *snemåker*. Children played their way home from school early before it got too cold, chattering in twos and threes, long flaxen pigtails flying out from under knitted hats, innocent excited breath rising in little bursts on the air.

Berndt was at the wheel of the car. These days, Russo's role was more ceremonial than strictly useful. He was a presence on the front seat, an upright, proud and entirely contented presence. Life held no doubts. It had been good. He did not slide his narrow Uzbek eyes towards the Russian embassy as they drove down past the Drammensveien house and on through the dream-pretty cream and white suburb the house had inspired. The whole area had now been designated a heritage district with all the tiresome building constraints that imposed. Not a window-catch could be changed without official say-so. More work for the builders: scrupulous historic restoration.

Had Russo forgotten his dignity for a moment, had he deigned to look, he might have seen the ambassador, a thickset Muscovite townee, pale from a youth overshadowed by a diet of too much Party indoctrination and too little actual proper food, emerge on to the old familiar semicircular steps and wait for his Zil car to be brought round. The ambassador was also to be part of this party at Gustav's house that Charlotta's car was heading for. In fact, the ambassador had done a very odd thing in a quixotic moment. Spurred by a meeting with Charlotta, who for all her age had lost none of her capacity to make people behave in ways that astonished them, the ambassador had offered to host the party at the embassy because of it being Oscar Oscarsson's old home. Immediately after the offer was made he regretted it. Sweat started out on his thick squat white-skinned *petit fonctionnaire's* body at the thought of what he had got himself into. But luckily the Norwegian minister of culture quashed the idea immediately. For this party to be hosted by the official presence of the Soviet Union would send very odd messages to the world. The party, accordingly, was to take place at Gustav's house and this was where they were all heading through the snow-bright streets.

The occasion was the handover of the Munch frieze to the state. The destruction of the frieze had been, as well as Oscar Oscarsson's last act, one of his few (very few) failures. The blast of wrath that killed him up the ladder had come in the first initial surge of blowtorch fury. Only one small oval patch had bubbled up under fire, liquesced and run down the wall, weeping black oily tears at Oscar's fall. This small patch was ruined, part of a maiden, part of a moon. A great deal was left. And this great deal continued to be coveted hungrily by a yearning state.

The last thirteen years, the years since Oscar's death, Gustav had spent enjoying a spirited, prolonged and subtle battle withholding the tax that the state insisted was due on the frieze. 'And where the hell was their sense of decency in the circumstances? They might as well tax brother Oscar's dead body while they were about it.'

Gustav tore into the legal battle with a will. Legions of lawyers were instructed at great cost. Cunning loopholes and jurisprudential vagaries were discovered beyond the lawyers' wildest hopes. Gustav won. And now he'd won, what the bugger was he to do with it?

Gustav sank his head on his chest, deep in thought. For a moment he looked exactly like his brother.

'Sometimes principles have to be sacrificed,' he said.

Remarkable words in an Oscarsson mouth of all mouths, showing how time mellows even the most resistant material, eventually.

The plain truth was that Oscarsson Shipping a/s had so out-grown its original dockside offices that it was only keeping them on to spite the state. Now he was handing the whole thing over, lock, stock and artistic barrel. Far more than the state expected. Good joke. Oscarsson Shipping was moving offices. The new offices were twenty minutes nearer, as it happened, to Charlotta and the little Shrimp, his grandchild.

Charlotta, subtle woman, took the hint, managed things so as to release Gustav from his self-imposed isolation down in his splendid house all alone. At first when Gustav had moved back into town from the Fødselsøy Charlotta made certain to give him plenty of excuses 'just to run up the hill'. Time passed and nobody seemed to be noticing whether he needed an excuse or not. These days, Gustav's life devolved along the most orderly domestic lines. On Tuesdays and Thursdays he took the midday meal at Charlotta's, and on Mondays, Wednesdays and Saturdays by way of a change he took his evening meal up there. In the tiny cosy house, his sister-in-law kept a good, unpretentious Norwegian table; and if the little Shrimp his granddaughter happened to be home, or that nephew of his, Oscar's boy, well, that was no hardship either.

The meal today, the civic meal marking the handing over of the frieze to the State of Norway (today embodied in the pale, puddingy, over-earnest minister for culture), was taking place in Gustav's house.

Gustav looked down his long table in his dining room.

The groaning board. He raised an eyebrow at his invisible brother. Oscar, if thou couldst see us at this hour! A civic dinner! Earnest young ministers on best behaviour. In this house of all houses, after all these years. Gustav's years as a self-imposed recluse on Fødselsøy were a world away. He could hardly remember the daily detail of them now. At the time he had thought they were his life for ever.

Gustav crumbled his bread and kept a straight face in the presence of all this properness and dignification. Jolly pleasant it was too. The groaning board a great credit to all concerned. Unmistakable similarities to a UNO bunfight. He'd seen a few of those in his time. Little bunches of flags down the table. Alternating with the Oscarsson silver – a bit grander than the UNO plated rubbish – the old Georg Jensen, collector's pieces now, worth a small mint, sell 'em and you'd get yourself a pretty sizeable yacht these days. No flowers. Charlotta vetoed flowers. She had a thing about them. Taken him a bit of time to notice. To twig to the fact that since brother Oscar's death she wouldn't have them in the house. Only the little bunches the

Shrimp brought indoors, the little bits and pieces picked from the woods and fields, *skogblomster*, *markblomster*, wild flowers in jam jars, a rose or two from the garden.

Katya, his itinerant daughter, sent a bunch every year without fail, winging from wherever she was in the world towards Charlotta's birthday. Always an opulent bunch. Typical tactic. Rubbing it in. Woman to woman. Message being, 'You're one year older today.' Ho ho.

Gustav had been up at the Dukkestue paying his birthday respects on more than one occasion when the overwrought birthday bunch from Katya had arrived in the florist's van. Charlotta had received the crackling Cellophane triangle, bestowed on it the faintest smile required by protocol, and the smile had hardly touched the ground so to speak before Russo was sent for to fairly wing down with the buggery bunch to the children's home.

And that had started him off thinking about his sister-in-law's allergy to flowers. It dawned on him that the whole thing had started at that *fordømmet* floral waterfall the day they buried Oscar. Those buggery funerary tributes cascading down the steps of Drammensveien. Yes, yes, he knew he had been drunk as a lord that day, the whole world knew that, but he wasn't so drunk he hadn't registered Charlotta's look of horror, and heard her quiet word, 'Enough.'

She'd meant it too; and for the rest of her life.

The question of flowers had come up on the agenda when the two of them had been planning today's official meal (and fun they'd had about it!).

Charlotta had taken the wind out of his sails. He ought to be used to that by now but still he was amazed when she said, 'Flowers? Munch and flowers had nothing to do with each other. He never painted them,' she stated accurately. '*Blodblomst*,' the word meaning flower of blood, more specifically the blood-flower of virginity, 'was Munch's only flower piece, so far as I am aware.'

Case closed. You couldn't argue with that.

Gustav cast a look containing a lifetime's respect and a rather shorter period of love and understanding down the table to where Charlotta sat, straight-backed as always, quiet and beautiful with a different beauty now that she was tired of this world and longing for the next. He had been able to see this for some time in her and it sent coruscating flashes of terror through his soul. He doubted his ability to sustain this new-found equability, this humorous benevolent sanity if she was not there every day to anchor him firmly in the worth-whileness of the everyday. Without her, he would be drift-ice again, blundering around in the howling terror of polar darkness.

Charlotta knew there was not so long now but she would have been amazed that Gustav had the insight to realise. She thought she had hidden these things so well. Here she sat, eating enough for politeness' sake, obeying all the rules of the outward game while intent on the parallel introspection.

Herr Professor Doktor Lund's successor, sweet boy, had pussyfooted around, in the mistaken idea of saving her feelings.

'I only want to know roughly how long I have so that I can organise things in a realistic way, and spare those about me any trouble and shock,' she had said, but the young doctor had blustered and blundered, embarrassed, muttering palliatives, provisos, evasions. In the end she had wanted to comfort the young doctor: the mere fact of mortality seemed to upset him so much. It was not such a great thing to die, she wanted to say, and if it was such a problem to him maybe he had chosen the wrong profession?

There sat the little Shrimp, battling valiantly with the Russian ambassador. Little no longer; a woman of twenty-one. Charlotta must remember that she herself, at the same age, was already married and a mother. To have this little Shrimp mitigated all sorts of things: the invisible germ of the future she herself would not be here to see.

Shrimp's hand had found hers in the back of the car just at the moment on that misty journey down to Oslo when Charlotta was thinking that it was like driving through one of those Chinese scroll paintings with odd bits of landscape floating in nothing. She was wondering, as one nonsensically did, if she minded that life had not ever taken her to China, nor ever would now. The sort of things you thought about when you knew doors were closed to you for ever. Above them the veiled sun in the snow-shrouded sky could be glimpsed as through a glass darkly. And then the little hand had found her fingers and the thought had come into her mind that the little Shrimp was the spark glimpsed in the dark glass. She was the pale constant disc waiting to shine, her full glory at present veiled; spiritual presence already in place, promising to shine when its time came and its context allowed; promising to illuminate the obscurity of the future. Yes, Shrimp mitigated the terror of death and the guilt. She mitigated the guilt of being an iconoclast, of the decision to break the rules at the last possible moment, to turn her back on the house Oscar had built, reneging on all the rules of materiality written by the society that she had spent all her life building up and supporting, her decision to wager it all on an abstract harvest.

And there she was, that harvest. Was it vanity, Charlotta wondered, to see so much more of herself in Shrimp than of Katya? Well, at least it had been the night porter of Harrods who had turned up, not some lover. Shrimp had been spared that horror. And Lulu, of course. The Shrimp must never know how Lulu had resisted surrendering Katya's effects. Well, what was a pearl necklace or two, an emerald ring? But the cheques. That was another matter altogether. The cheques – so badly forged! – and cashed on Katya's bank account weeks after her death, they could not be tolerated. *Sekretaer* Fulman had (even in retirement) moved with the efficiency of a demon. He had galvanised the Metropolitan Police. Their materialisation on her doorstep had prompted Lulu to shriek loud top-A shrieks before returning the twenty-five thousand pounds she had written to herself in Katya's name. With luck, the Shrimp need never know that her mother hadn't made even one honest friend through life.

How upset had the little Shrimp been at this legendary mother caught up with only through improbable reports in the cold morning light of society journalism? They had never spoken of it. What was there to say? How pretty the dear girl looked, chattering so capably to the awkward Russian, taking the trouble, and succeeding. How odd it was that one might only enter Oscar's house, these days, if invited by this little man, this ill-educated blood-soaked fellow who was the Russian ambassador, a man who had risen like boiling scum to the surface of the cauldron of a society of terror: torture received, torture imposed, mental, physical, social, intellectual, it was all the same. This little man with hairs like a bracelet of black wires about his brutally thick white wrists that stuck so raw and inelegant from the base funnels of his immalleable cardboard suit (and was there not some facet of truth in Oscar's equation of physical elegance with refinement of mind?). This small dough-dense pasty bullet-shaped ambassador had undoubtedly climbed to his present heights on the slipperiness of blood shed, betrayals made.

But who was she to condemn? Charlotta was all too perpetually aware of her own guilt. Whenever she saw Berndt's face she knew herself far from innocent of the very same crimes. The real regret was that she had spoken, had uttered words during that time of questioning with Berndt imprisoned in Akershus. She had been wrong. She ought to have remained wordless, borne imprisonment and whatever else imprisonment had brought, for Berndt's sake. At the time she had been naïve in inexperience. Now, today, she condemned her former self for expecting justice – justice of all absurdities! – for being stupid enough to offer innocent words in the expectation that her blameless version of truth would shine like a pure beacon, dazzling the eyes of Berndt's oppressors. She, product of generations of history, had been guilty of simplification and optimism in the face of a known historical phenomenon she ought to have been able to recognise. Hitler was no different from Attila, from Eric Bloodaxe. The tyrant was nothing new. In the light of historical knowledge, an educated past, she ought to have known that ignorance was no justification.

Two places down the table on the opposite side sat her dear son, greyhound-thin, razor-profiled. He had never left since that day he had brought back the Shrimp. Every morning, every moment, she had expected him to resume his faraway missioning. He had found things to do at home instead. Deep immersion in the reconstruction of Norway. Increasingly, Norway had stood outside the growing European coherence. The country determined to stand outside what it saw as the morally questionable character of the large political bloc; to cling to its own brand of fresh-faced naïvety, often mocked, as Katya had mocked Berndt's plastic sandals. But, like the plastic sandals, it did a job, did nobody any harm, and was founded on the principles of kindness and of blameless respect for the individual, and consideration for the world. See with what earnestness Berndt was talking to the sleepy overfed minister of culture. Her son would end up in Parliament if he wasn't careful; a civic aspect to her son, well, well.

The Russian ambassador, already a little drunk, was thoroughly over-excited. He had come here with one aim and one aim only: to eat all those delicious things his regime seemed to think unnecessary. And here he sat, tummy unfilled and food forgotten, counting the world well lost for talk. Here beside him was this most beautiful young woman, slender as a willow-wand in the graceful national costume, the pale blue and grey Oslo *bunad* embroidered round the hem and on the breast with wildflowers of the country, a young woman with quiet eyes the colour of blackberries and pale delicate lashes; an enchantress whose greatest wish was to converse in his own language about whatever topic he cared to raise. For a middle-aged *fonctionnaire* with all the charm, looks and polish of a toad recently emerged from twilight this was an unlooked-for bonus.

The ambassador wondered if he had read enough forbidden Imperialist literature to risk the sort of compliment gallants used to pay, with such success, to beauties in the old Imperialist Romanov days. His diplomatic training had taught him it was rude to stare. But it was impossible not to! His eyes ate the small blue line traced under her skin at the white throat. He longed to put his lips to that soft fluttering hollow whose vein put him irresistibly in mind of the great blue-black stain on the marble floor of his embassy.

They said the stain was Oscarsson blood spilled, and the ambassador believed it. That Oscar Oscarsson. Hadn't he killed himself by his own temper? And earlier, it was whispered among the dough-faced, terror-nourished Russians, who skulked about the grandeur of Oscar's house, terrified of themselves and each other, of microphones and shadows, earlier the man Oscarsson had killed his sister-in-law, a Russian woman: her blood stained that very spot. It could never be scrubbed out. Oscarsson had dashed her to pieces on the marble floor for committing adultery, for being unfaithful to his brother, the very man who was hosting this lunch today. The stain on the floor was blue. Blue blood. The indelible stain of blue blood that spread over Russia. He, who had only thick red peasant stuff flowing through the river of his veins, gazed with venal longing at the delicate aquamarine pulse shivering and trembling at Shrimp's throat.

Thus Katya's furious hurled inkwell of long ago lived on to fuel the fires of at least one man's erotic imagination.

Shrimp, too, was elsewhere in her imagination, but she was inhabiting a far from erotic land. She was back in England a week or so before Katya's phone call about if she was keeping young and beautiful. Shrimp was in her student digs, so tiny the RSPCA would complain loudly about cruelty were she a hen. Not that Shrimp minded. It was possible to be happy in the smallest of spaces so long as there was room for her dictionaries, tapes, brain and pencil, the small paraphernalia required for the higher echelons of translation.

She had a tiny radio, too. It had been a great shock to hear her brother's voice in the interview on the radio. The timbre of Robert's voice had hit her guts and bowels like a blow. She had run along the corridor to the shared loo and not made it in time, watery diarrhoea in her pants and on the carpet, but even as she ran she clutched the small radio to her ear.

Long after the interview was over the import of the words rang round her head and through her soul: that the justification of an acknowledged malefactor can become a cause.

Robert had become a cause for the professional discussing with Robert the fascinating case of his repeated offences against young girls. She was struck by the great blinkered vanity of the professional, appointed society's doctor and spokesman on such cases; the man who, thrown up by the politics of the time, in a hushed reverential voice, relished her brother as a 'case', an innocent 'case', the complex product of a broken home. Who spun a one-dimensional argument that glamorised her brother, that freed him from the possibility of choice. His words gave Robert limitless dispensation. Robert's behaviour was sending 'important messages to society', his actions were not his own responsibility but an inevitable out-come of a certain equation:

mother x, plus father y = inevitable rapist of young girls

But if this was so then why, the Shrimp was capable of wondering even in her extreme distress, why did not she, product of the same equation, behave in the same way as her brother? Why did not she maraud about, sending important messages to society by doing her own share of violating and destroying? This neat predestination equation could surely not be so?

Gustav, had he heard the radio broadcast, would have thrown back his great leonine head in roaring appalled recognition of clatch-speak. The arguments holding up Robert as helpless victim of conniving circumstance were directly descended from the pseudo-mystic-scientific cauldron cooked up in Katya's clatch; half-digested this-and-that, bits and pieces picked out of here and there. Gustav's broad brain would have had no difficulty in tracing the radio broadcaster's theories back to the books Katya Olovanova's elbow rested lightly upon in that yellow circle of light from the beaded lamp: the first edition of Mann's *Holy Sinners* as well as Freud's *Psychoanalysis*, common root among others of all clatch-speak. Had she not rejoiced, before her flight, in reading out its tortured psycho-sexual familial complications in her hoarse, fascinating, Russian-accented German to the pretty little coterie, whose nice family pearls shivered in their ears at the frisson of Herr Doktor Freud's guillotine-edged concoctions: infantile sexuality, castration complexes, incestuous complications.

This psycho-something making these excuses for Robert, saying on the radio with great authority that life had dealt Robert a hand that rendered it impossible for him to exercise virtue through his own free will, was only the latest spokes-man for the long line of evaders of responsibility, those who chose to sit comfortably in the armchair of fatalism: the Romanovs, the Olovanovas, the clatches, the two Katyas, with all their preferences for laying responsibility at the doors of the occult and preordained, of heredity, cod-liver oil bombs, horoscopes, anything, anything at all but personal respon-sibility. How wonderfully these things freed them from conse-quences, and from blame!

Shrimp had no idea of the two generations of clatches preceding her. If only Grandfather Gustav had thought it a suitable thing to discuss with his granddaughter. But he had not. Absolutely not. And so she sat on the lavatory all alone with her bowels turned to water and the radio clutched to her ear with all the desperate tenacious clutch of rigor mortis while the words, the endless words, presented as a crusade for under-standing such offenders as Robert in the name of compassion were entirely without tolerance or compassion for his victims; they were not even mentioned, they had no names, they might not have existed but in one dimension, as tools-with-a-purpose, as vehicles for mending this poor broken 'case history', this 'product of a broken home and of a fragmenting society'.

Robert himself, when his voice came on – and how the Shrimp shuddered in fear and doubled in pain on hearing her brother's voice – took up this moronic pragmatic interpretation of his life: himself as victim. When his voice – that voice, that flat-textured monotone that ran terrible through her dream – spoke of himself and his own life she did not recognise the patterns he was putting on his boyhood experiences. He was squeezing his own life into the label psycho-science was offering, an arrangement that suited both Robert and his therapist admirably. To be labelled was to be absolved entirely from culpability, to be a syndrome rather than a person. And with this borrowed perception of himself, this label, out had flown any possibility of empathy for his own victims. The warm sympathetic blanket of understanding con-veyed by the label shut the doors of perception, excluded any sense that he had inflicted hurt. Penitence was no longer possible if you were hero of the play.

Robert's and society's healer, the mimic man who called himself society's sticking plaster while beating his breast and lamenting the evils of society that gave rise to such things, was unable to prevent an edge of relish creeping into his voice that Robert's particular case presented his religion with as neat a case history as could be made to prove his one-dimensional theory. Mr Sticking Plaster seemed entirely happy that his glamorous pink elastic strips were designed to ornament the wounds of the guilty, the perpetrator, disregarding entirely the slashing consequences among the innocent. In fact, Mr Sticking Plaster seemed very content indeed with his own all-conquering liberalism, his secular religion that was so happy to replace a tormented conscience with self-justification.

Robert 'talked this through' with his 'counsellor' at some length, though a miraculously short period given Robert's capacity for loquaciousness. The programme lasted half an hour. Exhausted, tear-streaked, empty, Shrimp dragged along the cold corridor to lie down on her narrow bed. The jaws of a cosmic monster had closed around the scruff of the world and shaken it till the old order rattled. It was too horrible that it had to be seen like this. She could not, would not, believe Robert's fate was sent as this sticking-plaster man suggested.

She might have believed this version and believed herself inevitable victim had it not been for the native armour supplied, curiously enough, by Dr Viridian. The great Dr Viridian, dream-giver, killer of her mother, and producer of the eight-month Shrimp, whose engineered arrival into the world a month earlier than God planned had left her in a permanent state of dubiety concerning such things as an inevitable fate written in by star sign and circumstance; he had planted this very firm belief that fate was there to be controlled rather than to do the controlling.

That night after the radio interview the recurrent dream changed. The birds, constant harbingers of horror in the night with their outsize wings that grazed and tormented her, no longer wheeled above her, avid for victims. They were no longer alive. She lost the intolerable feeling of terror and powerlessness. The birds were disintegrated on the rock: feathers, claws and wings, dried-up objects blowing about in a dry creaking little wind that shuffled them about in rasps and whispers. She was walking the same grey rock she always walked, but now that they were dead the birds' blowing remains neither touched nor tormented her, and for once the motion and glitter of the sea was not something to be frightened of.

And now.

She came back to a very physical present.

What was this?

The distinct pressure of a plump, courageous ambassadorial knee speaking to hers under the table.

The Russian was raising his glass, proposing a toast, making what she hoped was a stock compliment comparing the *champanski* bubbles hopping right out of the glass into the air with the joy that bubbled in the oxygen round his heart, so far as she understood, but that couldn't be right because even *he* couldn't think he had oxygen around his heart.

'Will you forgive me please?' She turned her prettiest, shyest smile on the hopeful Soviet and started to get up from the table. 'I saw my grandmother leave the room some minutes ago and she has not come back. I think I should see to her, just slip out for a minute to make certain she is comfortable.'

He sprang up, pulled back her chair gallantly, bent over her hand with very unCommunist lips, and watched her quick progress towards the door with a pure nostalgic regret he had not felt since he was a lad of fourteen; a sweet, soft emotion he had altogether forgotten existed.

Shrimp moved quietly, opening with silent care the door she had seen Charlotta take. She pulled it to behind her, shutting away the festivity and noise and warmth and merriment. She had made certain to leave just before the civic speeches; once they began it was stay and be counted.

Even as she was slipping through the door, Gustav was pinging the glass with his knife. The high note trembled on the air, hushing the babble of speech, making way for the heavy, well-weighed words to be launched on waves of richly smelling air, a state procession of words, a benison to be poured out on the occasion by the appropriate mouths in the proper order of precedence and wafted through the marmoreal splendours of the room's stupefying air, already so richly laden with food and perfume, with universal benevolence and social content.

Shrimp waited, leaning back on the door between the two rooms, accustoming her eyes, changing the nuances of her mind.

Before her, the hall of Grandfather Gustav's house was tall and cool, a primrose-coloured cave of sun-saturated stone. Through the stained-glass panel in the window the sapphire blue and emerald green of the Oscarsson flag flowed with coloured undulations across the marble arch of Constantine, rising splendid with its three openings. The two stairways on their way to heaven floated horizontal-barred up into a chiaroscuro haze. The twin lamp spheres, restored, electric now, glowed steady as moons in either minor side-arch. The light they gave was entirely without narcotising properties these days, though you would not think so, to see the two old people asleep in the circles of their soft-hued light. Against the left-hand moon great Russo leaned, asleep on his feet like a horse, grey beard sunk on the festively braided Sunday tunic, chest shaken at regular intervals by earthquake rumbles that blew through his beard like the sharp-edged wind finding its way through grey reindeer moss on the faraway steppe.

When Charlotta had left the party Berndt, whose long eyes never missed any slightest thing, seeing her slip out shadowily, had also taken his leave unobtrusively in her wake, anxious to keep an eye without putting a corset on the general rejoicing. Against the right-hand moon he had settled his sleepy mother, tucking a rug over Charlotta's knee before running down to the kitchen to dig Russo out from the jolly below-stairs party and sending the old warrior upstairs to keep an eye on his mistress. Russo, much honoured to be called to this official duty, had marched to his watching post ramrod-straight, quiet felt boots militarily precise, as he took up his position to stand steady as an obelisk in the astonishing aura cast by the garlic cloves he chewed these days for his heart.

Taking pity on an old man's varicose veins Berndt had indicated a hall chair.

'Nyet.' Scowls and fierce pride.

But it had not been many minutes before the large meal taken in the middle of the day, accompanied by a certain number of toasts in wine at an age when he should have known better, exercised its inevitable effect and sent Russo into this deep, noisy, standing-up horse-sleep.

Shrimp, at the door, met Berndt's eyes as he stood in the curve of a slender blue shadow, contemplating the old. His affectionate, regretful, musing eyes changed in an instant from private to public: they lit and danced almost effortlessly with the humour necessary to encourage the young on their way through this old, tired world. He signed in pantomime that he must get back. Speech to be made. Civic pudding to be eaten. Indigestion to be courted in the line of duty.

Passing by the Shrimp on his way back through the doorway he stooped, dropping a hasty kiss on her hair. Her kiss on tiptoe found his passing shirtfront.

Charlotta was so small in the huge frame of the quiet stone

arch. Her figure curved so feather-softly against the tall enclosing arc of the nightwatchman's chair of dark buttoned leather. Her stillness touched Shrimp with a finger of ice. In the yellow vapour of the lamp's circle Charlotta's grey silk dress shone iridescent as the rainbow soap bubble bearing her away on this ever-moving sea of time, this dancing consequence of waves: past, present, never, now. Charlotta sat so still. Was there breath? Impossible to hear if she was breathing above the volcanic rumbling snores of the old bodyguard and the hubbub coming through the door. Speeches now in full swing: clapping, songs, toasts, hurrahs!

Charlotta was dead. Charlotta was dead without saying goodbye. Grief filled Shrimp's world. The details of the past, the little memories, the nevermore, the terror of existing without Charlotta rushed through her head, burned and prickled behind her eyes. Impelled by the need to know the one thing she did not want to know at all, Shrimp crossed the gold-misty hall and felt so odd and unreal, it was as if she was stepping across a dream. Time, evanescent time, vanishing even as one thought about it, was solid here, and claiming them both equally, marching no less inexorably for herself than for Charlotta. But no corner of her mind could find comfort in the logical nature of this; nor in the conclusion that lay at the end of time's inevitable equation. Tenderly, lovingly she bent over to touch Charlotta's soft hair.

The faded eyes continued their dream, not yet ready to give up the trailing clouds of glory. She had started her journey to the bright place. Now she was being called back.

It is a place, she was convinced, there is a definite difference, something more than chemical. Even here, at this half-way house, she was, in her deliberately practical way, analysing. Death was no reason to change the habits of a lifetime and go vague and soft, though dear old Magnus Lund – rapscallion scientist! – would have us believe it is all down to some cocktail of natural opiates and morphines exuded by the body to lend a kindly narcotic exaltation to the brief, physical process of death. When I am dust, she thought, as I was well on my way to becoming before this dear girl called me back, what then?

The reckoning was floating up to the surface of her conscience.

She could see it all quite clear, if small and distant as though through the other end of Gustav's magnificent Zeiss telescope. How harsh he had been. Those curses flung over poor little Katya across the water. Gustav, these days so soft, so gentle, so loving. How harsh they had all been, each one caring so much for his own tiny segment of present as if it was detached from the rest; as if it was so much more important than the future. When you were young you were full of trifles that bothered you and seemed to cover all the world. It was unkind that people should die young, as the two Katyas had died, well before their time, taken in the flood-tide of all their selfish passion.

'Charlotta.'

The eye of the telescope was entirely filled by the near-to image of Shrimp, dear girl, obliterating the rest. She was the olive branch in the beak of the dove brought into Noah's Ark from over the broad sea, the Oscarsson sea.

Words floated by. Berndt's words in the long-ago lamplight, pessimistically tracing 'this generational game of Consequences', meaning the chain set off by that dreadful massacre long ago in the Russian forest. Katya's parents. Yes, well, nothing inevitable about tragedy. You could dodge it if you kept on your toes. You could evade fate with its outflung curses, and if you were lucky you could end up with something as altogether miraculous as this little Shrimp here. Everything would pass. Meanwhile, 'Shh.' A dreamy smile. The eyelids fluttered, opened.

Oh, the relief! Shrimp's senses returned. She heard real things. Through the door of the dining room faint applause was rising and falling on the air.

Even before they focused Charlotta's eyes started to dance with the curiosity and the vivacity of her favourite grey wagtail, the bird that all her life had darted so blithely in the long grass of the green garden and skittered in and out of the glass surfaces of pools on sun-flecked, sea-beaten rock. Charlotta's darting eyes did not miss the swaying giant in the corner, shaking the world with his garlic-freighted snores.

'Hush, darling,' her hand came out, 'we must be quiet. See, old Russo is asleep.'

AUTHOR'S NOTE

During this century the Norwegian language has under-
gone various spelling upheavals. I have tried consistently
to use spelling that would be appropriate at the time of
the action of the novel.

Oslo was the name of the Norwegian capital until 1624
when it became Christiania (after the Danish King
Christian IV). In 1877 the spelling was changed to
Kristiania and it was not until 1 January 1925 that it again
became Oslo. *Magnetic North* opens in 1917 when,
obviously, Oslo would correctly be referred to as
Kristiania. In the interests of clarity and simplicity, I
have called it Oslo throughout.